THE ANUBIS SLAYINGS

THE ANUBIS SLAYINGS

Paul Doherty

HEADLINE

First published in 2000 by
HEADLINE BOOK PUBLISHING

10 9 8 7 6 5 4 3 2 1

British Library Cataloguing in Publication Data

Doherty, Paul
   The Anubis slayings
   1. Detective and mystery stories
   I. Title
   823.9'14 [F]

ISBN 0 7472 6269 1 (hardback)
ISBN 0 7472 7595 5 (trade paperback)

Typeset by Palimpsest Book Production Limited,
Polmont, Stirlingshire

Printed and bound in Great Britain by
Clays Ltd, St Ives plc

HEADLINE BOOK PUBLISHING
A division of Hodder Headline
338 Euston Road
London NW1 3BH

www.headline.co.uk
www.hodderheadline.com

To Pamela Broughton
Head teacher of Benyon Primary School, South Ockendon,
reader, embroiderer, lover of quiet pastimes,
good company and cats

List of Characters

THE HOUSE OF PHARAOH

Tuthmosis I:	Pharaoh of Egypt, father of Tuthmosis II and Hatshepsut or Hatusu
Tuthmosis II:	half-brother and husband to Hatusu
Hatusu:	Pharaoh-Queen of Egypt
Senenmut:	her Grand Vizier, lover and confidant, nicknamed the 'Stonemason' by his enemies
Ineni:	master-builder under Tuthmosis I

THE HALL OF TWO TRUTHS

Amerotke:	principal judge of Egypt
Norfret:	his wife
Ahmose and Curfay:	their sons
Shufoy:	Amerotke's servant
Prenhoe:	scribe and kinsman
Asural:	Chief of Police in the Hall of Two Truths

THE HOUSE OF ENVOYS

Weni, Mareb, Hordeth:	heralds and envoys of Egypt

THE MITANNI

Tushratta:	King of the Mitanni
Wanef:	kinswoman and Mitanni princess
Benia:	Tushratta's sister, married to Tuthmosis I
Hunro, Mensu, Snefru:	Mitanni lords

THE TEMPLE OF ANUBIS

Khety:	priest
Ita:	priestess
Tetiky:	captain of the temple guard
The Dog Master:	official in charge of the Sacred Park
Nemrath:	vigil priest

LOCKSMITHS

Lakhet:	master locksmith of Thebes
Belet:	his son
Seli:	Belet's wife

HISTORICAL NOTE

The first dynasty of ancient Egypt was established about 3100 BC. Between that date and the rise of the New Kingdom (1550 BC) Egypt went through a number of radical transformations which witnessed the building of the pyramids, the creations of cities along the Nile, the union of Upper and Lower Egypt and the development of their religion around Ra, the Sun God, and the cult of Osiris and Isis. Egypt had to resist foreign invasion, particularly the Hyksos, Asiatic raiders, who cruelly devastated the kingdom. By 1479–8 BC, when this novel begins, Egypt, pacified and united under Pharaoh Tuthmosis II, was on the verge of a new and glorious ascendancy. The Pharaohs had moved their capital to Thebes; burial in the pyramids was replaced by the development of the Necropolis on the west bank of the Nile as well as the exploitation of the Valley of the Kings as a royal mausoleum.

I have, to clarify matters, used Greek names for cities, etc., e.g. Thebes and Memphis, rather than their archaic Egyptian names. The place name, Sakkara, has been used to describe the entire pyramid complex around Memphis and Giza. I have also employed the shorter version for the Queen-Pharaoh: i.e. Hatusu rather than Hatshepsut. Tuthmosis II died in 1479 BC and, after a period of confusion, Hatusu held power for the next twenty-two years. During this period Egypt became an imperial power and the richest state in the world.

Egyptian religion was also being developed, principally the cult of Osiris, killed by his brother Seth, but resurrected by his loving wife Isis who gave birth to their son Horus. These rites must be placed against the background of Egyptian worship of the Sun God and their desire to create a unity in their religious practices. The Egyptians had a deep sense of awe for all living things: animals and plants, streams and rivers were all regarded as holy while Pharaoh, their ruler, was worshipped as the incarnation of the divine will.

By 1479 BC the Egyptian civilisation expressed its richness in religion, ritual, architecture, dress, education and the pursuit of the good life. Soldiers, priests and scribes dominated this civilisation and their sophistication is expressed in the terms they used to describe both themselves and their culture. For example, Pharaoh was the 'Golden Hawk'; the treasury was the 'House of Silver'; a time of war was the 'Season of the Hyena'; a royal palace was the 'House of a Million Years'. Despite its breathtaking, dazzling civilisation, however, Egyptian politics, both at home and abroad, could be violent and bloody. The royal throne was always the centre of intrigue, jealousy and bitter rivalry. It was on to this political platform, in 1479 BC, that the young Hatusu emerged.

By 1478 BC Hatusu had confounded her critics and opponents both at home and abroad. She had won a great victory in the north against the Mitanni and purged the royal circle of any opposition led by the Grand Vizier Rahimere. A remarkable young woman, Hatusu was supported by her wily and cunning lover Senenmut, also her First Minister. Hatusu was determined that all sections of Egyptian society accept her as Pharaoh-Queen of Egypt. Hatusu, like all great Pharaohs, had to 'bare her arm' and 'deal out judgement' to Egypt's enemies. She proved to be equal to the task. She spread Egypt's glory well beyond its frontiers. Egypt saw itself as the centre of the world and all other kings as vassal princes. The events of this novel are a fictitious interpretation of Hatusu's work to win glory abroad.

Paul Doherty

EGYPT C. 1479 B.C.

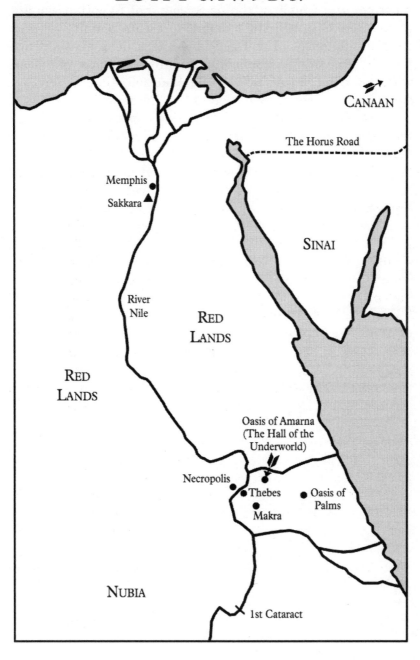

CANAAN

The Horus Road

Memphis

Sakkara

SINAI

River
Nile

RED
LANDS

RED
LANDS

Oasis of Amarna
(The Hall of the
Underworld)

Necropolis

Thebes

Oasis of
Palms

Makra

NUBIA

1st Cataract

Anubis: based on a very ancient Egyptian god,
'Imy-wt' – 'He-who-is-in-his-wrappings'.

PROLOGUE

Silence shattered the Temple of Anubis which lay to the north of Thebes within bowshot of the shimmering, snaking Nile. The evening sacrifice was finished. The god had been put to bed, the naos doors closed. The flagstaffs which surmounted the soaring pylons on each side of the principal gateways were stripped of their coloured pennants. The conch horn wailed: night was fast approaching. The great sanctuary with its black and gold statue of the jackal-headed god was now empty except for a young novice priest. He sat cross-legged, half asleep, savouring the fragrant incense which curled like a forgotten prayer through the temple.

He started and stared fearfully across at the throne of Anubis. Wasn't that the howling of dogs? He relaxed with a sigh. He was new to the temple. He had forgotten about the great pit where the pack of wild dogs sacred to Anubis were kept. A fanciful notion of the high priests: the dogs were savage, a gift sent by a tribe south of Nubia. The young priest had visited the pit once: a great rocky cavern where the dogs prowled in the caves and were fed morning and night by the Dog Master. The novice priest remembered himself. He dipped his hand into a nearby stoup of holy water and rubbed his lips with the tips of his fingers, as an act of purification before bowing his head in silent prayer. It was his task to keep vigil. He must pray for the temple, its high priest and hierarchy of scholars, librarians and priests. Nor must he forget the Lord Senenmut, vizier, some people even whispered lover, of the Pharaoh-Queen Hatusu. The

3

Temple of Anubis had been chosen as a meeting ground where Senenmut could negotiate with the envoys of the Mitanni king Tushratta. A great peace treaty was planned. Tushratta would give his daughter to one of Hatusu's kinsmen in marriage. The Mitanni king's armies had been decisively defeated by Hatusu and, despite his arrogance, Tushratta desperately needed the peace. Egyptian armies now controlled the Horus road across the Sinai desert. Chariot squadrons, Egypt's best, massed along Mitanni's borders. Tushratta could fight but common sense dictated peace.

The novice priest had listened very carefully to the temple gossip. The Pharaoh-Queen was now accepted at home. She had usurped the throne after her half-brother and husband's mysterious death. Once Tushratta signed the treaty, Egypt's most powerful enemy was publicly accepting her, so in time the Nubians, the Hittites, the Libyans and the rest would bow the knee and kiss her sandalled foot. The novice priest dreamed on.

The Anubis temple settled for the night. The great hypostyle hall with its blue ceiling and gold star-bursts was clear of pilgrims: its sacred walls, covered with inscriptions to Anubis, were no longer studied. The repellent, evil animals and reptiles, hacked by daggers to keep them immobile, stood in silent watch. The columns, decorated at base and top in green and red and garlanded with banners, stood in shadowy rows. Elsewhere in the temple, all was locked and bolted with clasps made from the finest Asiatic copper. Only soldiers, wearing the insignia of Anubis, stood on guard, spears and shields in hand. The scholars of the House of Life had doused the lights. The works they were copying or reading, the books and great parchments sheathed in pure leather listing spells for the overthrow of the Evil One or the repelling of crocodiles, had been stowed away: they would not be reopened until the following morning. Tetiky, the captain of the guard, in bare feet because he was on sacred ground, patrolled the mysterious portals, the small side chapels, the House of Delectation where banquets were held; the House of the Heart's Desire where, during the day, the handmaids of the gods waited; the raiment room where the sacred cloths were held. Satisfied, the captain passed on. The sanctuary and libraries were secure, as were the granaries stocked with barley and oil, wine, incense and precious cedar wood from Lebanon.

Tetiky went into the heart of the temple, the warren of corridors around the Holy Chapel where the sacred amethyst, the Glory of Anubis, was held. He passed a priestess, a handmaid of the god, and turned to admire her sinuous walk, hips swaying, long hair swinging. The priestess carried a jug. Tetiky frowned, angry at not being able to recall her name. Ah yes! Ita, she was responsible for bringing refreshments to Khety, the priest who guarded the door to the Sacred Chapel. Tetiky walked to the end of the gallery. Khety squatted there, leaning against the cedarwood door. Inside, the vigil priest, Nemrath, guarded the sacred amethyst. Nemrath kept the key; he would allow no one in until he was relieved just before the dawn sacrifice. A long night, Tetiky reflected, without food and drink. The captain shivered. His men talked of the god Anubis, jackal-masked, being seen walking his temple. Did he visit the Sacred Chapel and gaze on that gorgeous sacred amethyst winking from its statue? A sombre place the Sacred Chapel, with its pool guarding the door, its recessed walls and soaring roof. Tetiky remembered himself and coughed. Khety heard this, turned and raised his hand as a sign that all was well.

Satisfied, Tetiky went out into the gardens. He paused to savour the scent of resin and sandalwood. The temple grounds were a veritable paradise with their shimmering lakes, well-watered lawns, flowerbeds and shady trees dark against the night sky. Tetiky heard the sound of singing and grinned. A dancing girl, a heset, was probably entertaining a client. He walked on past the cattle-byres, the beasts within lowing vainly against the morning and the waiting slaughterer's knife. He paused and bowed as a group of priests, in their linen kilts and panther shawls, passed by on their way into the city.

Tetiky returned to his post. He did not know it but heinous murder was to visit the Temple of Anubis that evening. Seth, the red-haired slayer, would make his presence felt yet the victim, the dancing girl in one of the small garden pavilions, was full of life. She was naked except for a loincloth. Her hair,

5

drenched in oil and fringed with beads, moved like a black veil from side to side as she swayed, shaking the sacred sistra. She glanced quickly at her customer. Was he one of the Mitanni? Male or female? All she could glimpse were arms; the rest of her customer's body was hidden in a white gauffered linen robe, head and face hidden by that terrifying black jackal mask.

The heset had been approached earlier in the day whilst walking along one of the temple's dark-shaded porticoes. She would have refused except for the silver bracelet the masked customer had offered. He, or she, now sat in the shadows but the bracelet lay shimmering in the pool of light from an oil lamp the girl had brought. The heset was a professional dancer, a singer in one of the temple choirs. She was also a courtesan, skilled in the art of love with both male and female, of enticing the most jaded customer to excitement. She danced and swayed, moving her oil-drenched body alluringly, turning her back, glancing coquettishly over her shoulder. She would earn the silver bracelet, boast about it then sell it in the marketplace. All she had to do was please this customer. She moved closer and began to sing a love song, one of the hymns the priests chanted to Anubis.

'Thou art crowned with the majesty of thy beauty.
The light of your eye warms my face.
I will come to you and be one with you.'

The dancer paused.

'Are you happy?' she whispered into the darkness. 'Am I not comely? Do I not please you?'

She felt a trickle of sweat run down from her neck as well as a pang of annoyance. She had danced and sung for some time. All she had heard was a grunt of approval but no clapping, no invitation for her to go out and lie in the darkness.

'I am tired.' She tried to keep the petulance out of her voice. 'The day is finished. Shall we stay here? Or go out beneath a sycamore tree? The evening is cool.'

'Then you should sleep,' the voice whispered.

The dancing girl stepped back. There was something in the

tone she did not like. She heard a long sigh and felt the quick prick of pain. What was that? She stood shocked; her hand went to her belly. Had she been poisoned? She turned towards the door but she was already dying. Her chest felt so heavy, a strange froth soured the back of her throat. She could hear a voice counting and then she collapsed. For a short while her body shuddered. Only when she lay quiet did her killer stop counting, get up and walk towards the corpse.

Sinuhe the traveller paused and glanced across the Nile. The inundation was now complete. The Nile had risen, flooding the fields around. Now it lay like some great ringed serpent basking in the sun. Sinuhe's crinkled face broke into a smile. He clutched his leather bag more tightly. The papyrus book it contained was the treasure house of his journeys. He stared at the war galley, with its billowing white-and-green-chequered sail, its snarling prow cutting the water, the captain on the raised platform in the stern. Around it clustered barges, punts, small fishing boats. Sinuhe closed his eyes and sniffed the morning breeze. It was tinged with the lush corruption of the Nile: the tang of mullet and catfish which the fishermen were now piling into a boat; the faint odour of oil and human sweat. Sinuhe prided himself on his sense of smell and sharp eyesight. He glanced down. Today he was dressed in his best red-capped sandals and thick linen robe. He'd even shaved his face, burnt dark brown by the sun, whilst his hair had been cut the previous evening. Sinuhe had sat, allowing the barber to gossip whilst the barber's wife crumbled a bread loaf to make a mash to ferment beer. They'd been pleased with his custom. Everyone liked Sinuhe, or at least his tales. After all, Sinuhe had seen the world. Under the old Pharaoh, he had travelled beyond the fourth cataract, through Nubia, Kush and into the dark, impenetrable jungles of the south. Sinuhe had battled wild tribes who ate the flesh of their captives or made bloody sacrifice to grimacing wooden idols. He had been east to Punt and brought back precious herbs as well as tales about spices and gold jewels.

Sinuhe had also crossed the Red Lands to the west of Thebes, fought the sand-wanderers and desert-dwellers, the fierce Lybian tribes. He had even sailed across the Great Green, the huge sea into which the Nile debouched. And, of course, he had listened to other travellers. Men who described frozen lands to the north. Well, of course, they would be freezing, wouldn't they under the cool breath of Amun? On the coasts of Canaan he had talked to other seafarers about wild oceans to the west, exotic civilisations to the east, places where dragons and monsters lived.

Eventually Sinuhe had come home. At first his tales had been listened to with wonderment followed by derision and laughter. He smiled and stared dreamily across at the sunburnt houses of the Necropolis, the City of the Dead. Sinuhe's ambition was to buy a tomb there so that when he travelled west on that final journey to the eternal fields over the Far Horizon, he could sleep in peace. Perhaps he would take another woman to replace the concubine who had died three seasons ago. When was it? Ah yes, the Season of the Planting.

After she had died, Sinuhe had bought papyrus, a cake of black ink and a quiver of leaf pens and he had begun to write. Word had spread about his great work, people began to take an interest. Temple priests, merchants and now even the Vizier Senenmut, the Pharaoh-Queen's chief minister, had visited his little house. Sinuhe had simply smiled and kept his manuscript secret. He knew what they were after: not so much his stories but the maps he described. What was it like beyond the fourth cataract? What paths existed? What dangers? And, in the Red Lands, the great deserts which sprawled on either side of the Nile? Oh yes, they might know about this oasis or that but Sinuhe knew more. He could describe the desert tracks, how to map their way according to the heavens, where water might be found. The same was true of the Great Green: Hatusu's galley captains would love to know what he knew. When was the best time for sailing? Which seasons should be avoided? What dangers? What islands? Did they have safe harbourage? And now, oh yes, Sinuhe hugged his leather bag like a mother would a child, even foreigners were interested. All of Thebes knew how Tushratta and his court were out at the Oasis of Palms whilst his envoys treated for peace in the city. Tushratta's envoys had also sought out Sinuhe and offered him a fortune to see his book. The bartering had continued. Now Sinuhe was ready to hand it over. The person he was doing business with had told him to come to the derelict Temple of Bes the Dwarf God, further down the Nile.

'It's the best place to meet,' the Mitanni envoy had declared. 'Away from prying eyes.'

The envoy had come at dusk, staying in the shadows so her face remained hidden, though her perfume had been sweet and cloying.

At first Sinuhe had objected. It was all too dangerous, too lonely, but then he reflected. Of course, if anyone had seen him with the Mitanni, tongues would wag. Moreover, the Mitanni had left him a small ingot of pure gold which Sinuhe now carried in his wallet. How could he resist the lure of even more?

Sinuhe hurried on. Thebes lay behind him. He was now out in the countryside. Palm trees soared against the blue sky. The chatter of the fishermen carried on the breeze. Across the fields the peasants were out hacking the earth, preparing it for the planting. The sun was high, growing stronger, but the heat didn't trouble a man like Sinuhe. He had known the torrid blast of the desert where the sand stretched as far as the eye could see! Sinuhe raised his head and glimpsed the ruins of the Temple of Bes. He had come here as a boy and it brought back memories. All his playmates were now dead. Most of them had become soldiers. Two had fallen into disgrace: they had been in the slave gangs, marched out to the Valley of Kings to excavate the old Pharaoh's tomb. They had never come back. Sinuhe shivered. Dead men didn't tell tales! Pharaoh Tuthmosis I had been such a harsh and cruel man.

Sinuhe slipped into the ruins. Fallen columns lay about; every year the place grew more derelict. The copper clasps and any moveables had long been stolen by the peasants. He looked at the tidal marks on the walls showing where the Nile had flooded. The ground was still damp. Sinuhe went over and sat in a shady corner. The Nile gave life but it also brought death . . .

'Have you brought the book?'

Sinuhe looked up. All his courage deserted him. At first he thought he was seeing a vision. Anubis, God of the Dead, who weighed souls with the feather of truth. Then the vision moved. Sinuhe noticed the fine sandals, the leather war-kilt; it was the jackal-headed mask which frightened him.

'Have you brought the book?' The voice sounded hollow.

'Yes, yes, of course I have.'

Sinuhe pulled himself on to his knees and opened the leather sack. He felt a small prick at the side of his neck. A fly? Some insect? He raised his hand. His killer stood silently watching him. Sinuhe knew there was something wrong when the terrible pains began. He had never experienced the like in all his journeys. His fingers lost their feeling, the leather sack fell to the ground. Sinuhe tried to rise. His killer approached. Sinuhe closed his eyes. He opened his mouth to beg. He could feel a terrible drumming in his ears; the pain felt like barbs of fire. He was in the jungle again and the warriors, black as night, were streaming across the clearing, faces daubed with paint, shields up. Death was coming!

The killer waited until Sinuhe's body stopped convulsing. He took the leather sack and hid it in a crevice: dragging Sinuhe's corpse by the ankles, he pulled it out of the ruins, down to the river bank and tossed it in. He then stood and watched the eddies of the river ripple and break against the thrusting snouts of the approaching crocodiles.

Anubis: the principal Egyptian God of the Dead.

CHAPTER 1

In the Hall of Two Truths at the Temple of Ma'at, the Goddess of Divine Speech, sentence of death was about to be passed. Amerotke, chief judge of Thebes, sat on a low cushioned chair carved out of acacia wood. Its light green and gold cushions were of sacred fabric and embroidered with hieroglyphics extolling the exploits of the goddess Ma'at. On the walls around the hall, interspersed by soaring columns, were brilliant pictures and carvings of the Forty-Two Daemons of the Duat, the Underworld: 'Breaker of Bones', 'Eater of Souls', 'Blood Gobbler'. These beings dwelt in the mansions of the gods, ready to devour souls who, on being weighed by Anubis on the scales of divine justice, were found wanting.

Before the chief judge were cedarwood tables bearing the laws of Egypt and the 'words of Pharaoh's mouth'. The holy documents were not there to be consulted but to remind Amerotke that he delivered sentence on behalf of Pharaoh. The clerks, scribes, temple police and spectators all stood hushed, staring at Amerotke. Some of the scribes, seated down one side, found the tension difficult. They plucked at their white robes or bent shaven heads over the small desks. Prenhoe, the youngest scribe and Amerotke's kinsman, became so agitated that he moved around the palettes of red and black ink, the water pots, the sharp knives for cutting the papyrus. One knife fell on to the marble floor, clashing like a cymbal. Prenhoe picked it up and stared guiltily at his kinsman. Amerotke was a cunning man, a courtier born and bred, but one noted for his justice and his severity. Now his thin, dark face had turned thunderously angry. He was staring down at the closed doors of the hall, lips moving slightly. Now and again his hand would touch the lock of gleaming black hair plaited with silver and green which hung down over his right ear. Amerotke breathed out and rearranged the blue-bordered robe which fitted him so elegantly. He moved on the cushion and the sunlight, streaming in from the gardens on either side, sparkled in the gold chain round the judge's neck. The pectoral of Ma'at which lay on his chest shimmered as if the goddess herself had come down to dispense justice. Amerotke played with the ring depicting the insignia of the goddess and, stretching out his hands, touched the sacred manuscripts before him.

'The prisoner known as Bakhun. Do you have anything to say before sentence is passed?'

The young man chained between two guards shook his head. At the urging of the guards, Bakhun bent down so his forehead touched the floor.

'I have sinned!' he wailed. 'And my sin will be always with me!'

'You sinned,' Amerotke replied, 'and intended to escape the justice of Pharaoh.'

Amerotke gazed round the court. At the back near the door stood Asural, chief of the temple police. He had already taken a step forward as if eager to pluck this malefactor from the sacred precincts. Amerotke was silent, not for effect but to control both his anger and his fear. Anger at the terrible crime Bakhun had committed: the heinous deaths of his victims. Fear because the crime stirred dark phantasms in his own soul, chilling nightmares from his childhood: of running along a street, pursued by a rabid dog. It had caught him and, had it not been for the intervention of a passer-by . . . Amerotke closed his eyes. His wife Norfret told him to put such thoughts out of his mind. At night, however, the dreams came creeping back like serpents beneath the door, ready to coil themselves around his soul: the mad eyes, the slavering jaws, the lips curled back, the jagged teeth, the sharp claws scraping his knees. Amerotke had

14

always had a love for dogs but, since that day . . . He blinked. The court were waiting.

'Bakhun,' he declared, 'you had no kin except your aged uncle and aunt. They had made you their heir. They had even reserved a place for you in their tomb in the Necropolis so you could journey into the west together. They were old and infirm. What you did was an abomination!'

'I didn't mean to,' Bakhun protested.

'You plotted maliciously,' Amerotke retorted. 'You took a rabid dog, mad and frothing at the mouth. You trapped it in a cage and brought that cage down to your uncle's lonely farm outside Thebes. Under the cover of darkness you opened the door and let the dog in. Your uncle and aunt were too weak to resist. They could not even climb the stairs or defend themselves. The dog attacked and killed both. Their bodies were grotesquely mutilated; even the embalmers found it difficult to prepare them for their final journey. You would have escaped if it had not been for the vigilance of witnesses who saw you leave Thebes in a covered cart, early on the day your relatives were so horribly murdered. I see no grounds for mercy. Pharaoh's justice will be done. Your uncle and aunt's property will be sold to cover their funeral expenses. The rest will go to the House of Silver for distribution to the poor.'

Bakhun sat back on his heels. Amerotke was glaring at him. It was the custom in Egypt to make the sentence fit the crime. Out of the corner of his eye Bakhun glimpsed the Dog Master, the keeper of the sacred pack in the Temple of Anubis. Amerotke had summoned him as an expert witness.

'Asural!' Amerotke called. 'And you, Dog Master, approach!'

Both men came before the court. The Dog Master was lean and sinewy, dressed in leather, marching boots on his feet; in one hand he carried a whip, in the other a small spear. Asural, in contrast, was dressed in the full ceremonial uniform of the temple police. He marched up, his bronze helmet under his arm, as if he was about to ride out and charge all of Pharaoh's enemies. Asural's bald head and fat face gleamed with sweat; he had caught the mood of his master. The news of this abominable crime was all over Thebes. Bakhun had not only murdered his kinspeople but, because their corpses had been torn and wrenched, he had hindered the souls of his uncle and aunt in their journey through the underworld.

'Asural, Dog Master!' Amerotke ordered. 'Bakhun has been found guilty of murder and sacrilege. He is nothing but a stench in the nostrils of Pharaoh, so Pharaoh's justice will be done.' Amerotke touched the medallion on his chest. 'Pharaoh's word leaps down from her lips. It will run its course through the entire earth so all may see her justice. Dog Master, you are to take this prisoner back to his uncle's house. He is to be placed inside and the doors and windows bricked up and sealed.'

Amerotke paused. 'Before he is immured, you are to take two rabid dogs from the streets of Thebes. They were his associates in murder; let them be his companions in death. Sentence is to be carried out before dusk. Take him away!'

Bakhun threw himself forward in a rattle of chains. The guards seized him. Bakhun jumped to his feet, his face a mask of fear, but the silence in the court, the murmurs of the scribes, showed he'd find no sympathy here. Cursing and screaming, the prisoner was dragged away.

Amerotke relaxed. The court took time to compose itself. Prenhoe got up and went and checked the great water clock, a huge jar with a carving of a baboon on the front. It stood in the corner of a portico leading out to the gardens. Amerotke watched him go. He wished he could follow, go into the temple gardens or paradises and sit beneath a tamarind tree. Would there be a breeze? Would it be cool? He glanced at his chief scribe and nodded, a sign for the court to continue. Asural had now returned, having handed Bakhun over to a cohort of temple guards. Amerotke wondered how Asural could stay cool in his heavy leather corselet and skirt, not to mention the greaves on his legs. Asural, also a distant kinsman, was a stickler for discipline and proper dress. As Amerotke had remarked to Norfret: 'He'd rather die of sunstroke than break regulations!'

Amerotke recalled the next case and muttered a prayer for patience. The chief scribe got to his feet.

'Let those who desire Pharaoh's justice approach!'

The cedarwood doors at the far end opened. In waddled the dwarf Shufoy, carrying parasol and walking-cane. He was attired in his best robe, a garment of pure wool which covered his little body from neck to ankle; new sandals on his feet, a dark blue coat strapped elegantly about his neck. Amerotke had insisted that he did not turn up in court unshaven and dressed in his usual collection of motley rags. Shufoy liked nothing better than to appear poor. A sharp contrast to Amerotke, whose friend, servant, adviser and herald Shufoy was. He walked pompously forward, ignoring the muffled laughter. Amerotke kept his face severe but his heart went out to the little man. He was small and squat, his hair, despite the oil, a tousled mess, whilst nothing could be done about the hideous disfigurement to his face. Shufoy had once been a leather worker. He had been falsely accused of a crime; his nose was cut off and he was banished to live with the other rhinoceri in their walled compound to the south of Thebes. Amerotke had investigated the case. He'd established Shufoy's innocence and, as compensation, taken him into his own household. The judge found him fascinating. Shufoy was a true chameleon. He could change from the self-proclaimed herald of the chief judge to a confidence trickster, selling false potions and amulets to the incredulous of Thebes.

Shufoy paused, went down on his knees and prostrated himself before the judge's chair. Oh Ma'at be my witness, Amerotke thought, please, Shufoy, do not start. The little man raised his head and winked at Amerotke. A wicked grin transformed his disfigured face. Amerotke glared back.

'What is your business?'

'Oh great judge of Thebes. Incarnation of the Wisdom of Ma'at. Beloved of Pharaoh.' Shufoy's deep voice rose round the court. 'He who has looked on Pharaoh's face and felt the warmth and strength of her friendship. Chief Judge in the Hall of Two Truths, High Priest of Ma'at . . .'

'Enough of that!' Amerotke snapped. 'State your business!'

Shufoy, his face a mask of servility, scrambled to his knees. The parasol and walking-cane lay alongside him. He threw his hands out in a dramatic gesture.

17

'State your business,' Amerotke repeated. He glared at one of the scribes, who'd giggled. 'The plea will be heard in silence.'

'I am Shufoy, page and wretched servant of the great lord . . .'

'I am going to count,' Amerotke interrupted. 'If you have not stated your business by the time I reach thirty . . .'

Shufoy caught the warning glance.

'My name is Shufoy,' he gabbled. 'I represent Belet and Seli. Belet is a very good locksmith,' Shufoy continued. 'Seli comes of good family; her father cuts papyrus.'

'Twenty-three . . .' Amerotke declared warningly.

'They wish to marry.'

Shufoy's lower lip came jutting up, a sign that he was losing his temper. He had been looking forward to this for weeks. Shufoy loved the drama, the solemn majesty of this court. Above all, he couldn't resist the opportunity to tease this most solemn of masters. Amerotke knew what Shufoy was going to ask; he just wished he would get on with it.

'What is the problem with this marriage?'

'Can I bring them forward?' Shufoy asked.

Amerotke raised his hand.

The young woman who entered the hall was comely enough: slender and sweet-faced. She was wearing her best oil-drenched wig and a simple white linen robe. The young man was dressed in a woollen tunic which hung just below his knees, but his face was covered by a leather mask. One of the guards came forward and whispered in his ear; the man removed the mask. Amerotke closed his eyes. Once, the young man must have been handsome, broad-faced, but, like Shufoy, his nose had been removed.

'You have been convicted?' Amerotke asked, ignoring the muted outcry from the court.

'I am a locksmith.'

Amerotke glimpsed the pain in Belet's eyes.

'I asked when you were convicted.'

'Four years ago, my lord.'

One of the guards came forward to press the man to his knees, as was the custom when anyone addressed Pharaoh's judge. Amerotke raised his hand and shook his head.

'Continue!'

'I committed a number of crimes,' Belet continued. 'I entered the shops and houses of those I sold locks to.'

'Why?' Amerotke demanded.

'My parents became poor. My father drank too much. They had no tomb.'

Amerotke nodded. One of the causes of so much crime was the overwhelming desire by the prosperous tradesmen of Thebes to secure an appropriate tomb in the Necropolis across the Nile.

'And you paid for your crimes?'

'Yes, my lord.'

'And now?'

'I cannot live in Thebes. I cannot marry. I cannot carry on my trade. My lord,' Belet fell to his knees: no drama intended, just a pleading honesty, 'I have come to beg for Pharaoh's clemency. I have my wound.' He gestured at the scar which disfigured his face. 'I have endured my exile. I am prepared to take the most solemn oaths. I have the testimony of others,' he continued in a rush, 'that my life for the last four years has been blameless.'

Amerotke raised his hand. Asural and Prenhoe had investigated the case. The young man was speaking the truth: he'd been involved in no crime.

'This is my sentence,' Amerotke declared. He glanced at Seli and smiled. 'You love Belet?'

'Yes, my lord.'

Amerotke could see the young woman was agitated; sweat coursed down her face.

'This is my verdict,' Amerotke repeated. 'Belet will take the most solemn oaths. Here, in the Temple of Ma'at, he will swear to do no wrongdoing. The scribes will write out a revocation of the previous sentence. This will be done before dusk. You know what will happen,' he glanced warningly at Belet, 'if these oaths are broken? Perpetual banishment from Thebes, the confiscation of all property.'

Shufoy, alarmed that he was going to be ignored, now jumped to his feet.

'Witness the wisdom of Pharaoh!' he shouted. 'Praise and thanks to the great lord Amerotke who walks in the truth, who has looked upon the face of . . .'

19

'Clear the court!' Amerotke bellowed.

He rose from his seat as a sign that the session was ended, walked to his left and entered the mysterious portals, his own private side chapel. He loved to rest here, in this long, high chamber of white basalt stone, its concave ceiling painted a light green. On the walls were paintings of the goddess Ma'at ministering to her father Ra. There was a stoup of holy water, mingled with natron, on an offertory table; stools and cushions. In the centre, on the altar, stood the barque in which the goddess was carried. Behind it the naos, the sacred cupboard or tabernacle, which contained the gold and silver statue of Ma'at. Amerotke took the incense boat from the table. He went and knelt before the naos, sprinkling some of the incense on the slow-burning charcoal in its copper dish. He watched the smoke curl up.

'May my prayer,' he murmured, leaning back on the cushions, 'rise as sweet incense in your sight!'

He stared at this beautiful depiction of the Goddess of Truth garbed in her cloth of gold. He admired the shiny black hair, the beautiful long face, the full lips and the slanting kohl-edged eyes, the bracelets, anklets and elegant sandals with which the priests had adorned the statue. Amerotke smiled. Every time he prayed, the statue always reminded him of his wife Norfret. He half expected those lips to move, that beautiful head to turn and those dark eyes to look at him so coquettishly. He laughed softly. Do I worship the goddess, he thought, or my wife, or both?

Amerotke tried to live in the truth. He loved his wife and his two sons Ahmose and Curfay. He strove to do his best without being pompous or proud. He wiped his lips with his middle finger, which he'd dipped into the holy water stoup. He tried to speak the truth but sometimes it was difficult. He thought of the case he had just dealt with: that obscene murder, those old people trapped in their house with those slavering, rabid mongrel jaws closing in. Amerotke took off his pectoral and ring and placed them on the floor beside him. He recalled his own terrifying experience. Where had he been? Oh yes, running home to his old nurse, a half-mad old woman who told him stories about a mysterious king who lived in a beautiful oasis somewhere in the eastern Red Lands. Amerotke closed his eyes. He'd been nearly home when the conch horn brayed in alarm. Gates were slammed shut; the awful patter of that rabid dog hurtling like a shadow down the narrow alleyway towards him. Amerotke heard a knock on the door but ignored it. He was back in the house of Bakhun's victims, its silence being rent and torn by the horror of that sharp-toothed killer. He began to tremble. He opened his eyes and concentrated on the statue. He should pray; Ahmose was ill with a slight fever. Shufoy had promised to bring him an amulet soaked in sacred crocodile blood. Again the loud knock on the chapel door.

'Come in!'

Asural, Prenhoe and Shufoy entered. They took one look at Amerotke's face, and quietly sat down, their backs to the wall.

'Is it done?' Amerotke demanded.

'It is being done,' his chief of police replied.

'You will be criticised,' Shufoy added warningly.

'Why, what else would you recommend?'

Shufoy clambered to his feet.

'You haven't eaten. I have fruit, some charou wine! I know a cookshop . . .'

Amerotke laughed and turned to face them.

'You are pleased by the other decision, Shufoy? Your friends will be happy.'

'I will get drunk at their marriage and dance.'

Amerotke studied the painting behind Shufoy: Nubians bringing gifts to the old Pharaoh Tuthmosis, perched on his throne protected by the feathered wings of Ma'at.

'And what is the chatter in the city?'

'The Lord Senenmut is at the Temple of Anubis. He meets with the Mitanni envoys,' Shufoy replied. 'Tushratta and his court stay out at the Oasis of Palms.'

'And?'

'There are rumours.'

'About what?'

'Murder, at the Temple of Anubis.'

Amerotke stirred restlessly. Pharaoh Hatusu had placed much emphasis on these negotiations. She had smashed the

Mitanni army. Amerotke had been at her great victory. Sometimes, in his dreams, he went back to that battle: the crash and rattle of the chariots as they broke the Mitanni flank; the Maryannou, 'the braves of the king', savagely finishing off the wounded; the rocky ground turned slippery with blood which gushed like wine from cracked jars.

A loud rapping on the door broke his reverie. Shufoy scrambled to his feet, threw it open and stepped back in surprise. Two men entered, both dressed in the robes of courtiers, hair cropped and bound by filets. Amerotke recognised the insignia of the Shadows of Pharaoh: members of the imperial corps of heralds and envoys with their white wands, red-edged robes and large wrist guards displaying the emblems of Horus the Hawk and the Eye of Osiris. Amerotke rose to greet them: the first was rather plump, small black eyes hidden in rolls of fat. He waddled rather than walked. The second was younger, thin-faced, of slender build; he had a slightly crooked nose but his eyes were laughing and his mouth widened into a smile as he bowed first towards the naos and then to Amerotke. The first herald was more concerned about the heat and busily wafted a fan to cool himself. The younger one stood rather pompously, one foot slightly forward as if he was about to recite a poem.

'You are?'

'Weni,' the small fat one replied gruffly.

'He has a sickness of the nose,' the younger one declared, 'and it should be treated.'

'I have marvellous remedies,' Shufoy offered, edging forward.

'Are you a physician?' Weni asked.

'Oh, greater than that. I know the secrets of the anus, the nose and all the other orifices. You take scorpion dust, mix it with viper blood, then . . .'

'And you'd be dead within a week,' Prenhoe added.

Shufoy made to protest but Amerotke held his hand up.

'And you are?'

'Mareb,' the younger herald declared. 'Personal herald to the Divine Hatusu.'

He lifted his arm and opened his hand. In his palm lay the scarab beetle which bore the small cartouche of the imperial

Pharaoh-Queen. Amerotke bowed and kissed it. Weni hastened to add how they were both the personal envoys of the Divine Hatusu to the Mitanni camp at the Oasis of Palms.

'We come from the Temple of Anubis.' Mareb smiled.

'Ah yes, the negotiations? They go well?'

'They were,' Weni declared pompously, still glaring at Shufoy.

'Hush now,' Mareb soothed. 'The Lord Senenmut is the incarnation of the will of Pharaoh. He will . . .'

'I know who he is,' Amerotke replied. 'I want to know why you are here.'

'The negotiations are going well,' Mareb replied. 'King Tushratta, or rather his envoys, is prepared to concede everything. He has certain demands but the betrothal will go ahead, the peace will be signed.'

'But there have been murders?' Amerotke asked. 'I've heard rumours.'

'You have sharp ears, my lord.'

'I am also impatient.' Amerotke gestured at them to sit. 'Tell me about the murders.'

The two heralds made themselves comfortable. Shufoy rearranged the cushions. Amerotke sat opposite them, his retinue around him.

'You have heard of the Glory of Anubis?' Mareb began.

'Everybody has: it's a beautiful jewel, a sacred amethyst, the size of a man's fist. It hangs on a gold chain round the statue of Anubis in one of the side chapels of the temple. It is as ancient as Thebes,' Amerotke continued. 'Some people claim it was left by the god himself . . .'

'Well, it seems to have been taken by the god himself,' Mareb broke in cheekily. 'You are correct, my lord,' he added hastily. 'I mean no offence. The statue is kept in one of the mysterious portals; its chapel is very similar to this. Except,' he pointed to the entrance, 'there is a sacred pool, very deep, along the doorway.'

'Yes, I've heard of it,' Amerotke agreed. 'And one priest keeps a nightly vigil before the shrine. The door is secured with the best copper lock?'

'Correct, my lord. Another priest stays on guard outside.

23

The corridors and galleries are patrolled by the captain of the guard. One of the priestesses, a handmaid of the god, brings refreshment to the priest outside.'

'But not the one within?'

Mareb shook his head.

'Oh no, the vigil priest is locked inside from dusk till dawn. He turns the key and keeps it on his person.'

'And what happened?' Amerotke asked.

'Well, in the morning the vigil priest is supposed to let himself out, to allow his colleagues in to celebrate the dawn service, but Nemrath couldn't be roused. The captain of the guard was called, the chief priests, even Lord Senenmut. The door was forced. Inside, the sacred pool had not been disturbed. No footmark, no imprint of any kind, but the vigil priest Nemrath was dead, a knife straight through his heart.'

'And the Glory of Anubis was gone?'

'Yes, my lord.'

'Who was the priest outside?'

'Khety: he claims to have heard nothing amiss. He dozed, said his prayers but he was disturbed by no commotion.'

'And the priestess?'

'Her name is Ita. She served Khety food and drink during the night. She, too, heard nothing.'

Amerotke sat in puzzlement.

'So, we have a chamber like this, with a sacred pool before the door . . .'

'Yes, my lord, and that door was locked from the inside by Nemrath, who held the key.'

Amerotke raised a hand for silence.

'But the following morning the pool had not been disturbed. Nemrath has been killed and the Glory of Anubis has disappeared. The galleries and corridors were patrolled, the soldiers noticed nothing amiss?'

Mareb agreed.

'And the key was found on Nemrath's corpse?'

'Oh yes, hidden in the folds of his robe.'

'And the door was securely locked?'

'Yes, my lord.'

'Who forced it?'

'The temple guard at the command of the High Priest.'

'And there are no secret entrances or passageways?'

Again a shake of the head. Asural whistled softly under his breath.

'The Divine Hatusu,' Amerotke remarked, 'will be furious. The Glory of Anubis is a sacred relic.'

'There's more,' Mareb continued. 'Naturally, the finger of suspicion has been pointed at the Mitanni. You can understand why, my lord: they, too, pay devotion to a dog god; they also regard the jackal as sacred.'

'Of course!' Amerotke breathed. 'And if Tushratta gets the sacred amethyst, or even if people think he has it, the Divine Hatusu becomes a laughing stock.'

'There are also rumours,' Mareb added, 'of the temple being haunted, of Anubis the jackal god being seen there.'

Amerotke had to bite his tongue. He would have dismissed that as nonsense. Deep in his heart Amerotke did not believe in jackal-headed gods, or those in the shape of a falcon. He only believed in Ma'at, the Truth, but considered it best to keep such beliefs to himself.

'So,' he declared, 'theft, murder, sacrilege. What more?'

'The same evening the Glory of Anubis was stolen,' Weni moved his fat rump on the cushions, 'one of the temple hesets, a dancing girl, was found dead in a paradise pavilion. She had been poisoned but there's no trace of her killer.'

'They *think* it's poison,' Mareb declared.

'She'd been frothing at the mouth,' Weni snapped. 'And she's not the only mysterious death. Two sheep from the temple flock have also been found poisoned, as have certain fish.'

Amerotke closed his eyes. Two weeks ago he had attended a banquet in the royal palace, the House of a Million Years. Hatusu had acted very much the imperial Pharaoh-Queen, loudly declaring how she would bring the Mitanni to book and bind them to her as allies. Now someone was making a mockery of these negotiations.

'But it can't be the Mitanni,' Amerotke declared. 'They have so much to lose.'

'They won't own up to it, will they?' Asural spoke up.

'No, they won't,' Amerotke agreed. 'So, what are your instructions?'

'By the time another hour has passed,' Mareb replied, 'you are commanded to join Lord Senenmut in the Temple of Anubis: he has matters to discuss.'

'I am sure he has,' Amerotke declared drily.

He got up, picked up the pectoral and the ring and gave them to Prenhoe, who put them in a casket in the far corner of the chapel.

'Tell me,' Amerotke knelt down to tie the thong of his sandals, 'has the guardian priest Khety been questioned?'

'Oh yes, my lord. He knows nothing.'

Amerotke stood, staring at the statue of Ma'at. How could the criminal have carried out such an act? he wondered.

'There are no windows?'

He glimpsed Mareb's face.

'No, of course, there wouldn't be.' Amerotke answered his own question.

Weni gestured towards the door. 'The one at Anubis,' he explained, 'is even thicker. Panels of the best cedarwood, fastened on either side.'

'So, no panels can be removed? And the lock?'

'So securely turned,' Mareb declared, 'it had to be forced.' His cheerful face became grave. 'No one can explain how it happened. Some claim Anubis walked his own temple, killed Nemrath and took the Glory of Anubis. The handle of the dagger which killed the priest . . .'

'Oh yes?' Amerotke asked.

'No one has seen its like before: black and shaped in the form of a jackal's head. What do you think, my lord Amerotke?'

The judge stared at the statue of the Goddess of Truth. He did not believe Anubis walked his temple, but Seth, the god of murder, certainly haunted its precincts.

Anubis: 'Lord of the Necropolis'.

CHAPTER 2

'I have been to Akharit. I have travelled beyond the known limits of the world. I have encountered hunger, thirst and enemies. I have confronted the sharp-tailed hyenas. I have travelled through unknown deserts, the first man to tread their burning sands.' The story-teller beneath the sycamore tree in the great courtyard before the Temple of Ma'at was attracting custom. 'I have seen griffins with human heads on their back, winged panthers, cheetahs with necks longer than a giraffe, hyaenas with square ears and tails as thick as arrows. I have climbed the Mountain of Ivory . . .'

Amerotke paused in admiration at this story-teller.

'Another Sinuhe!' Herald Weni scoffed.

Amerotke would have loved to have stayed. He liked to hear such tales and later relate them to his sons. Shufoy was jumping up and down, banging his parasol on the black obsidian stone of the courtyard.

'Do you want to stay and listen?' Amerotke demanded.

'I want you to stay and listen, Master.'

Amerotke gestured at the heralds.

'But I have business . . .'

'Master, this is pressing. Belet,' Shufoy referred to the exiled locksmith whom Amerotke had agreed could return to Thebes, 'he wishes to speak with you.'

Amerotke sighed and stared round the huge courtyard, a great square with colonnaded walks on either side and a broad, shimmering pool in the centre. The builders had cleverly left a wide range of trees standing: sycamore, acacia, terebinth, date and palm. These now provided natural shade and shelter for those who set up stalls to serve the many visitors and pilgrims to the temple. All the conjurors and scorpion men of Thebes were there, as well as barbers, herbalists and wandering priests. A group of dancers circled one tree and, to the reedy tune of a flute, joined hands and danced round it. They were not good dancers, being rather overweight and sweaty. They wore short sleeveless gowns and braided loincloths, whilst bangles and necklaces circled wrists and necks. One of these broke, scattering the heavy beads, much to the delight of a group of urchins who scrambled greedily for them and so brought the dance to an abrupt end.

'I can't see your friends,' Amerotke replied. 'If they wish to give thanks, let them do it in the temple.'

The others, led by Asural, were looking expectantly back at him. Shufoy stood on tiptoe.

'It's very urgent, Master. Belet has important information. Tonight is his wedding night. After which he must return to the village and collect his possessions.'

Amerotke pursed his lips. He felt hot and dry. Shufoy's eyes were bright with excitement. Amerotke often teased him but he never underestimated this little rapscallion's genius for collecting useful scraps of information.

'He has to speak to you now,' Shufoy urged. 'He and Seli.'

'Very well,' Amerotke sighed. 'Prenhoe, Asural!' he called, pointing to a beer stall beneath a palm tree. 'Take our visitors and refresh yourselves there.'

Shufoy slid his hand into his.

'Why didn't you tell me about this when we were in the temple?' Amerotke demanded.

Shufoy pulled him closer. 'Master, the walls have ears.'

'You mean you didn't want Asural and Prenhoe to find out?'

Shufoy grinned wickedly. Amerotke let him lead him across the temple precinct, past a wild-eyed wandering priest, hands raised, intoning a garbled prayer to some unknown Kushite god. They went down a narrow, shady alleyway which ran off from the square. Amerotke realised they were going to one of Shufoy's favourite eating-houses: a square, white-stoned building with kitchens, eating-rooms and a pleasant garden beyond.

'I told them to wait here,' Shufoy explained, slipping through the entrance.

They crossed the small, fragrant-filled room used as a store place. Geese, chickens and ducks, freshly slaughtered, hung from poles, bowls placed beneath their half-open beaks to catch the blood. Outside the garden was a small paradise, dissected by a canal which brought in water from the Nile: this was a mere rivulet to keep the grass, shrubs and flowers fresh and sweet-smelling. Behind a terraced fence, covered by creeping plants, stood a range of earthenware stoves, packed with wood and charcoal and topped with a grill, on which pieces of quail, antelope, duck and partridge were roasting. A little boy, completely naked, ran up and down with a ladle basting the meat with a variety of herbal sauces. Clouds of smoke carried the fragrant aroma across the garden. Belet and Seli were waiting on a small wooden bench beneath a palm tree. They sat, hands clasped together; despite his disfigurement, Belet looked radiantly happy. If Amerotke hadn't stopped him, he would have fallen to his knees.

'A stool for my lord Amerotke!' Shufoy bawled at a group of servants standing in the shade of another tree. 'Lift your hands and thank the gods that your humble abode has been graced by his august . . .'

'Shut up, Shufoy,' Belet whispered hoarsely.

The mannikin recalled himself and positively danced with embarrassment. The servants brought stools and placed a square, four-legged table between them. Amerotke thought of the others waiting yet he had no choice but to accept the jug of cool beer and strips of roast meat served on a bed of lettuce and sprinkled with chopped onion. Seli demanded copper knives. Once these were brought and the servants withdrew, Belet leaned closer, beads of sweat coursing down his face.

'My lord Amerotke, you have my thanks. I shall pray for you every day.' He grasped Seli's hand. 'If our first child is a son, with your permission, we'll name him after you. I shall offer

31

incense in your temple. Your generosity and kindness have sealed me as your worthy servant.'

Amerotke waved his hand.

'You are a free man,' he replied quietly. 'You've purged yourself on oath.' He smiled. 'You'll become a famous carpenter and have many children. I don't wish to be rude but I am busy. The day is wearing on . . .'

'Very well.' Belet sipped his beer, then touched his forehead in salute. 'My lord judge, I come from the village of the Rhinoceri which, as you know, lies just to the south of Thebes. Shufoy was innocent of any crime and kept his soul. Many have turned bitter. They have been disfigured and stripped of their freedom. They sacrifice to no god except Seth the Great Slayer, or Meretseger the serpent goddess who strikes without warning.'

'I know,' Amerotke agreed. 'Such communities breed outlaws. I have heard tales of men, their faces swathed in rags, who plunder lonely travellers, wage war against Pharaoh's subjects. There are those in the royal circle who would have your village, and other such places, razed to the ground.'

'Now and again we are approached by outsiders,' Belet continued. 'Our kind regard anyone with the face the gods made them as a foreigner. Such foreigners hire the likes of me to do this or that. Others come to enjoy our women, taking great pleasure in coupling with one who is disfigured. About ten days ago, just after the Nile began to subside, I was approached.'

'By whom?' Amerotke interrupted.

'My lord, I cannot tell you. This was not the marketplace of Thebes where people meet and talk eye to eye, exchange the kiss of friendship, spit on the palms of their hands and seal a contract. It was dusk. The two masked men, who knocked on my door, sat outside and refused to come in. Their message was simple: I was to go to the Place of the Hyaenas shortly after dusk.'

'Why should they approach you?' Amerotke asked. 'And more importantly, you could have refused to go.'

Belet's eyes fell away.

'He regretted it, my lord,' Seli whispered, grasping Belet's arm. 'He was desperate and needed money.'

'Not everything we do is illegal,' Belet added, fingering the new necklace of polished stone around his throat. 'I needed silver to buy my way to Thebes.'

'How did you meet Seli?' Amerotke asked curiously.

'That's what I mean.' Belet sighed in relief. 'Seli's father brought down furniture to be repaired, locks to be mended. He knew I came of a very good family. Over the years I became his friend.'

'And his daughter's,' Shufoy added wickedly.

'So, the Place of Hyaenas?' Amerotke demanded.

'About a mile from the village: a great outcrop of rock where we bury our dead. My two guides met me there. The place is riddled with caves. I was taken into one. They put a rag around my eyes and led me in deeper. I then recognised that whatever was planned was against the law. I was made to sit. The evening had turned chill and a fire had been lit. The place stank of camel dung. I was given good wine to drink. I remember the cup was cracked but, once I drank it, I realised my visitors were not from the village. I waited in silence for some time. The wind outside rose. One of my guides muttered something, footsteps sounded and a third man joined us. The newcomer was certainly not from the village of the Rhinoceri. We have our own smell, customs, way of talking. He did not give me a name but began to praise my family, my work, particularly the intricate locks I could make, as well as those I could open.'

'And what did this man want?' Amerotke asked.

'He first asked if I still had my father's tools, chisels and mallets. "Sir," I replied, "similar can be bought in Thebes." "Ah yes," came the reply, "but those who use them can't. Would you like to be rich?" the man continued.'

'Did you recognise his voice?'

'No, my lord. It was like the desert wind, hard and menacing. I asked why they would want my expertise. "That is not for you to know," he replied. "Where would I have to go?" I asked. "Beyond Egypt's borders?" The man just laughed. "You will go to a place few people have been. However, when you are finished, you will be richer than many a man has been." I asked if it was dangerous. "Life is dangerous," came the reply.' Belet sipped from his jug. 'I didn't know what to do. Since my punishment and exile I have been law-abiding. I have kept well away from the troublemakers. After I met Seli, my only dream was to obtain a pardon.'

'What happened that night?' Amerotke demanded.

'I asked how many other men would be going? Again he refused to tell me. He promised I would become wealthy, be able to leave Egypt and live like some prosperous merchant beyond its borders.'

Belet lifted his face and glanced to where the servants still thronged beneath the tree. They immediately looked away. It was considered unlucky to stare at anyone disfigured. Belet gestured with his hand.

'You can see why I was tempted, my lord.'

Amerotke held the cold beer jug against his hot cheek. Now he'd met Belet, a faint suspicion stirred. The man undoubtedly meant well but he had agreed to meet this mysterious stranger. He glanced quickly at the locksmith and caught a calculating look in his eyes. Have I done right? Amerotke wondered. Is this man committed to the path of light? Amerotke turned to his manservant.

'Shufoy, tell me, why should strangers approach the village of the Rhinoceri and ask your friend for assistance?'

Shufoy, who had been studying a bee-keeper working on the far side of the garden, grimaced and blinked his eyes.

'A robbery, Master?'

'Did that occur to you?' Amerotke asked Belet.

'Of course.'

Amerotke swilled the beer round the jug. Robberies did occur in Thebes: rich merchants with their coffers and treasure chests, their warehouses and casks stuffed full of precious cloth, stones and spices.

'Come, Belet,' he urged. 'You must have questioned them?'

'I asked them that,' he replied falteringly. 'I pointed out how the merchants and the wealthy ones had their houses closely guarded.'

'And?'

'The man laughed. He said there would be no guards.'

34

'No guards!'

Amerotke immediately thought of the Necropolis, the City of the Dead across the Nile, with its honeycomb of tombs full of precious objects. It was not unknown for bands of outlaws to break in and plunder them.

'Grave-robbers?' he asked.

Belet looked shamefaced. 'I also mentioned that. Again he laughed. This time it was mocking. "Do you really think," he taunted, "that we'd rob the good people of Thebes?" "Where then?" I asked. "A place few people know. So, are you with us or not?" I replied I would have to think about it. The man gave me two days and said he would return.'

They were distracted by a babble of chatter from the servants. Amerotke glanced round. The story-teller from the forecourt of the temple had now arrived. He'd placed a linen robe round his sun-darkened skin and his black hair was bound up by a gold filet.

'I have spoken enough,' the story-teller boasted. 'And my throat is as dry as a desert wadi.'

The man was apparently popular, as the servants flocked to serve him. Shufoy gazed enviously over.

'I wish I could tell stories like that.'

'You do,' Amerotke replied coolly. 'It's just that no one believes them. Belet, continue with your tale.'

'Two days later I was taken back to the Place of Hyaenas after dark. I was led blindfold into the cave. The man was waiting for me. I told him I was nervous, that my skill was not what it should be. I pressed him for details. He scoffed at me so I refused. I thought he had finished till I felt a snake coil over my leg. "Do you feel that?" the voice asked. "Why, yes, Master," I replied. "And you will keep silent about what you have been asked?" "Master, how can I tell people what I don't know?" "You're a fool," the visitor replied. "You may have lost your nose but your ears and tongue can still be taken." I swore great oaths that my lips would remain sealed. I was taken from the cave and brought back into the village.'

'Did they approach anyone else?' Amerotke demanded.

Belet shook his head. 'I don't think so.'

35

'Why are you telling me now?'

'Because I got to know,' Seli replied. She'd sat shoulders hunched, her pretty face pulled into a frown during her husband's confession. 'I nagged him.' She smiled. 'Yes, even before our marriage!'

'They came to me,' Shufoy spoke up, 'and asked for my advice.'

'And you said to speak to me?'

Amerotke closed his eyes and rocked backwards and forwards on the stool. He was tempted to dismiss this as some foolish escapade, a planned robbery which might never take place. He opened his eyes and stared at the groom and his bride.

'You think this is serious, don't you? Some sacrilege planned? The robbery of a temple, perhaps?'

'The Glory of Anubis,' Shufoy intervened. 'The sacred amethyst has been taken.'

Amerotke shook his head. 'No, they wouldn't enter a temple like Anubis. It's not only closely guarded by temple soldiers but, because of the Mitanni, members of the royal bodyguard are also close by. Brigands would be cut down as soon as they entered the temple grounds.'

Amerotke watched a bee move from flower to flower.

'I told you,' Belet spoke up, 'because I want my conscience clear, my lips and heart pure. Pharaoh has shown me great mercy. If a heinous robbery took place, I would never know peace . . .' His voice faltered.

'It will certainly be a mysterious robbery,' Amerotke agreed. 'Along the waterfront and in the slums, you can hire cutthroats and murderers for a deben of copper. So, why should this robber chieftain go out to the village of the Rhinoceri to look for help? Something is planned which, when it is finished, the fewer people who know the better. If the robbery is not here in Thebes . . .' Amerotke scratched his brow. 'Perhaps elsewhere? The silver mines . . . ?'

'My lord!'

Amerotke glanced round. Asural had found where they were and was glaring across at them. Amerotke thanked Belet and got to his feet.

'If you learn any more . . .' He stretched his hand out and clasped those of the groom and his bride. 'I wish you peace.'

He walked over and joined Asural. They re-entered the alley-way and Shufoy caught up with them.

'Great lord,' he trumpeted, 'your mercy and wisdom are to be praised. Belet is, once again, in Pharaoh's favour, like his father. He . . .'

'Thank you, Shufoy.'

Amerotke paused, hand on Asural's shoulder.

'If I was planning a robbery, to steal something precious, to become rich beyond my wildest dreams, where would I go?'

Asural shrugged. 'The houses of Thebes?'

Amerotke thought of his own house: a mansion standing alone, surrounded by extensive gardens. Time and again Norfret had advised him to hire more guards and sentries. Was it a place like his? Distant from Thebes, easy plunder for a desperate group of cutthroats and brigands? But would such thieves need a locksmith?

'The heralds are waiting,' Asural insisted.

Amerotke patted Shufoy on the shoulder.

'I have heard what your friend said. At the moment I can make little sense of it. But come, other matters wait.'

In the garden the story-teller, laughing and talking to the servants, chewed on roast goose and gulped greedily from a jug of beer. He laughed and flirted with the maidservants. Every so often he'd glance across to where Belet and his bride sat, hands clasped, heads together, planning their future. The story-teller watched them intently. For the moment, they did not concern him. They were nothing but crumbs. No, the story-teller slurped from the beer and winked at one of the maidservants, they did not concern him. However, they had spoken to Amerotke, judge in the Hall of Two Truths, and that was a story he must tell his master.

Later that day, out at the Oasis of Palms, in the Red Lands east of Thebes, Tushratta, king of the Mitanni, bathed in a pool shrouded by palm trees. He stood lapping the water with his hands. Slaves and servants standing around its rim watched his every movement. The King allowed his body to float, so his servants could gaze on the battle wounds their warrior king had suffered in the defence and expansion of his empire.

Tushratta turned on his back and stared up through the palms at the brilliant blue sky, empty now except for a vulture, hovering on the breeze, feathery wings expanded. Was that a sign? Tushratta wondered. An augury for the future?

He addressed the scribe sitting on a stool, a roll of papyrus across his lap, ink horn strapped to his belt, quill in his hand, ever ready to take down his master's words. 'What do the Egyptians call the vulture?'

'Pharaoh's hens,' the scribe replied.

Tushratta closed his eyes. He recalled that great battlefield to the north: the vultures gathering thick and black as flies on a corpse.

'Will you hunt this evening, my lord?' his chief groom asked. 'Game is getting scarce.'

Tushratta raised his hand as a sign for silence. He drifted to the edge of the pool. He sat on a rocky outcrop just beneath the water, allowing his body to feel the sway and lap of the gushing spring.

If I went hunting, Tushratta considered, it would not be gazelle or antelope. He clawed at his thick black beard: his quarry would be that young Pharaoh-Queen. How he'd love to march through Thebes and, like the Hyksos before him, turn it into a sea of flame. He'd sack the temples, level its palaces and mansions, leave not one stone upon another. He would plunder the tomb of Tuthmosis I. He would take Senenmut, Grand Vizier of Egypt. Yes! Tushratta looked up at the skies: he'd crucify Senenmut or stake him out in the desert, fodder for the lions or hyaenas. As for Hatusu, the Pharaoh-Queen . . . Tushratta narrowed his eyes. He sank deeper into the water, allowing its coolness to lap between his legs. He'd take her into his harem, he would teach her who was the master!

Tushratta, to the surprise of his surrounding courtiers, angrily splashed the water. All because of that battle, the King fumed, his world had been turned on its head. Every clan and tribe of the Mitanni, each household in his great city, had lost men. The number of wounded and disabled seemed without measure. Mitanni armour and chariots now littered the northern desert or were paraded as keepsakes, mementoes of victory, in the temples and mansions of Egypt. Before he'd left for the Oasis of Palms, Tushratta had gone down into the deep vaults beneath his own palace and stared at the empty treasure chests, their contents long gone, on armour, supplies, accounts and hordes of mercenaries. It had all been in vain! The news of Egypt's victory seemed to have spread even across the Great Green, as well as to the savage tribes north of Caanan. Oh, Tushratta had plotted revenge. He had gathered with his generals and they had taken careful stock of chariots, carts, horses, javelins, bows and arrows. Which troops could march, who could be trusted. At the end of the tally, Tushratta had gloomily concluded that revenge, like the sky above him, was beautiful but unattainable.

'We cannot muster a proper army,' one of his generals had confided. 'And if we strip the kingdom . . . ?' He'd let his words hang: it was always prudent to allow Tushratta to draw his own conclusions.

'If we march,' the King had declared, 'then we leave our own borders defenceless. The tribes will swarm in. Our own towns and villages will be sacked.'

'Then there's the harvest,' another general had said.

Oh yes, there had been the harvest, and if the granaries and storehouses were empty . . . Tushratta looked down at the water. He had clawed his way to the throne: intrigued, plotted, murdered and betrayed. He had even had three of his own half-brothers strangled so they would pose no threat. Tushratta had sprawled on the great bed in his palace, tossing and turning. He wanted revenge but a new war was futile. The Pharaoh-Queen Hatusu had proved as cunning and as dangerous as a cobra. She was a goddess to her troops and flushed with her triumph. If Tushratta took the path of war and was unsuccessful a second time . . . The water on his back turned cold. He had to watch the clan leaders. The Mitanni court was little more than a wolf pack. After his defeat at the hands of Hatusu, Tushratta had used one pretext after another to execute wavering courtiers, generals and captains. The blood-letting may have purged any thought of revolt or treason but he knew the rest were waiting.

'Calm down and plot,' his half-sister Wanef had advised. 'Let Egypt grow fat, prosperous and lazy. Let Hatusu's body become more full and rounded. Gather your strength and wait. One day Egypt could be yours and I'll watch you play with their Pharaoh-Queen in your harem.'

Wanef was his chief councillor, lover, adviser. When the hotheads demanded war, she counselled peace.

'Lie, bow, kiss the ground with your forehead. Promise anything, for the time being!' she urged.

Tushratta had reluctantly agreed. His country needed peace; his merchants demanded safe passage here and there. He had accepted Hatusu's ultimatum. Her peace proposals proved humiliating and demeaning. Tushratta would come to Egypt; he would seek audience with Pharaoh, listen to her terms and seal whatever she asked. Tushratta had heard them out. Once the envoys had withdrawn, he'd indulged in a paroxysm of rage. Once again the Princess soothed his temper.

'Think,' she urged. 'Think of the future . . .'

'My lord?'

One of the scribes, concerned at his master's black looks, had decided to intervene.

'My lord, what is it?'

'The peace treaty!' Tushratta demanded.

The scribe opened the small coffer beside him. Still balancing the roll of papyrus on his knee, he undid the scroll. Tushratta closed his eyes.

'Read me the terms.'

The scribe did so. Tushratta congratulated himself that he felt no spurt of anger.

'Enough!' He held a hand up.

Wanef and the others, Tushratta grinned to himself, oh yes, they were now busy in Thebes. Like foxes scampering around through the rocks, they would hide and turn, object and protest. They'd seek for time but, in the end, they would seal the treaty.

'Let Hatusu think she has her way,' Wanef had whispered to him in the dead of night, her lips almost kissing Tushratta's ear. 'Let her strut with Senenmut her stonemason. Our time will come.'

'But it will take years!' Tushratta protested.

'Revenge tastes better when it's cold,' Wanef retorted. 'Now listen, my lord.'

She had spun him a marvellous story: about Sinuhe the traveller and his detailed maps showing trade routes across the Red Lands to Kush and Punt, where precious spices could be collected in huge chests; of secret waterways, of what might even be beyond the Great Green. Tushratta had heard her out but the marvels hadn't stopped there. She also described the Temple of Anubis and its sacred, precious amethyst.

'What would you give,' she whispered, 'to hold the pride of Egypt in your hands?'

'But they would know!' he'd protested. 'Hatusu would demand vengeance.'

'Not if she can't prove it,' Wanef replied.

Tushratta had been pleased. For the first time since he'd fled that hideous battlefield, leaving the Mitanni dead heaped in piles as tall as a man, Tushratta had felt his heart glow and the laughter bubble within him.

'And how can you do this?' he'd asked.

Wanef had slipped from the bed, wrapping the sheet around her shoulders. She was not the most beautiful of women but her lovemaking, like her plans, was cunning, subtle and original. Tushratta trusted her completely. She had led him from the royal bedchamber and out across the palace yard to show him something in a dungeon dug deep beneath the walls. Tushratta had clapped his hands and embraced her tenderly.

'If you can do this for me,' he had whispered fiercely, 'you may have whatever you wish.'

'No, no, listen and listen well!'

She had then spun one of her intricate plots. Tushratta heard her out, admiring the skill and delicacy of her argument. She drew a picture of an arrogant Hatusu, of spies and traitors, of people whose souls could be bought. Tushratta had envied the

41

way she had collected scraps of information, drawing others into her web. He deeply regretted not listening to her advice before he launched that invasion across the Horus road into Egypt.

'Are you sure this can be done?' he had asked.

'Yes. Let's go to Egypt, my brother and, if necessary, bend the neck, kiss the strumpet's painted toes, but we'll heap one villainy upon another. Take away her sheen of glory. The Egyptian bitch will have no proof but the months will pass into years.' She waved her hand. 'And the stories will become public. People will laugh behind their hands and say, "The gods are not with Hatusu of Egypt." She will become an object of ridicule to her enemies. Oh, she can stamp her little foot and demand this or that.' Wanef clapped her hands. 'But that's the beauty of it, my brother-king, if we have sealed the peace treaty, so has she! If we are bound by its clauses, so is Egypt. If she protests, we'll cry injury, that Hatusu of Egypt does not keep her word and that she is only looking for a fresh pretext for war.' Wanef, using her hands, described how the arguments could rage backwards and forwards. 'In the meantime,' she continued, 'the Mitanni will grow stronger. We'll raise new war horses, build more chariots, expand our trade, fill your treasure houses with wealth.'

'And if we fail?' Tushratta, more cautious, questioned. 'What happens, dearest sister, if your fine plans turn to dust?'

The pleasure drained from Wanef's face. Tushratta knew why. He never forgave those who failed him.

'If we fail,' she'd replied offhandedly, 'then what have we to lose? How can Egypt prove that we were involved? They may suspect, they may point the finger.' She laughed nervously. 'We'll dismiss it as lies, claim Egypt is still desirous of war.'

'It will be sweet wine,' Tushratta had murmured, 'to wash the defeat from my mouth. But what about the others? Hunro, Snefru, Mensu? The royal council are determined that they accompany you to Egypt. They may relish the plan, but can they be trusted?'

Wanef drew closer, flinging her arms round Tushratta's neck.

'Now, my prince, let's discuss my lords Hunro, Snefru and Mensu . . .'

Now Tushratta smiled in pleasure, spread out his hands and lowered his body deeper into the water of the oasis.

'My lord!' He glanced up; one of his captains was standing on the edge of the pool.

'What is it?' Tushratta demanded.

'Envoys from Thebes.'

Tushratta made a sign to dismiss the rest. He thrust the linen cloth at the captain and, once the others had departed, got out of the pool and wrapped it around him.

'They wait on the outskirts of the camp,' the captain continued.

'Describe them!' Tushratta demanded.

'They have come on dromedaries, well armed. They won't show their faces, only their eyes. They claim to come from the Princess Wanef and will speak only to you.'

'How many?' Tushratta asked.

'Three in all.'

'Bring the leader to my tent,' Tushratta ordered. 'Have some of the mutes on guard!'

The captain hurried off. Tushratta picked up a brocaded robe and draped it over his shoulder. He walked quickly to his pavilion. His eye was caught by a group of dwarfs, black-skinned people, crouched in a circle chattering like children. They were naked except for their loincloths, through which small cylinders had been pushed. Tushratta paused and smiled. He thought of Wanef, Thebes and the mischief she would inflict there. He snapped his fingers; the chamberlain opened the flap of the pavilion and Tushratta entered its perfumed coolness. He dressed and made himself ready, sitting on a pile of cushions. On the table before him stood a cup of charou wine, cool and fragrant; beside it, a dish of ripe plums. Tushratta waited until a servant had tasted and investigated both before eating and drinking himself. The tent flap was pulled back and Lady Wanef's envoy slipped in like a ghost. He went down on his knees, his forehead touching the ground. Tushratta made him stay there a while.

'Come no further,' the King ordered. 'You may sit up.'

The man began to remove his face cloth but Tushratta made a cutting movement with his hand.

'I watch your eyes,' he warned, 'and that's enough. Just speak, do not move and you will be safe!'

The messenger was aware of the tent flap opening behind him. He glanced quickly over his shoulder. Two Kushites, dressed in white kilts and leather armour, stepped in, arrows to their bows.

'You bring messages from Thebes?'

The man bowed again.

'I bring great news, my lord. That which is precious to Egypt will soon be precious to us.'

Tushratta hid his excitement. 'And the maps?'

'What is precious to Egypt will, my lord, soon be ours.'

'Soon?' Tushratta queried.

'The Lady Wanef advises caution. It's better to wait and be safe.'

'And the other matter?' Tushratta demanded.

'Everything goes according to plan, my lord.'

'And Benia's sarcophagus?'

'Lady Wanef is rightfully demanding that it be returned to the care of the Mitanni.'

Tushratta closed his eyes. He thought of his sweet sister's face, her mummified corpse lying beside that of the great bully Tuthmosis I. Tushratta ground his teeth. His hatred for Hatusu was only equalled by that for her father. Had not Tuthmosis also sent his chariot squadrons across Sinai, raiding the soft valleys and unprotected villages of Cannan? Had not Tushratta vowed to ransack his tomb and seize his mummified heart? Tushratta sighed. He had tried and lost, but Wanef was right. The gods had given him a fresh opportunity.

'You know what to do?' Tushratta opened his eyes.

'Yes, my lord.'

'And the locksmith?'

This time the messenger's eyes flickered.

'You have failed, haven't you?' Tushratta snapped.

'My lord, I have informed the Lady Wanef how the creature

44

called Belet has sued for pardon before Lord Amerotke, Chief Judge in the Hall of Two Truths.'

'Amerotke!'

Tushratta glanced at the Kushites behind the messenger. Time and again Princess Wanef had mentioned that man's name! Of all the councillors in Hatusu's royal circle, she had warned, two must be watched: her lover, the stonemason Senenmut, and Amerotke, her principal judge.

'When we start this mischief,' she'd warned, 'Hatusu will go to Senenmut for advice and Amerotke will start picking like a vulture: he must be watched.'

'It is essential,' Tushratta snapped, 'that this locksmith bend his neck to the yoke.' He breathed in noisily, broad nostrils flaring. 'We send our greetings to Princess Wanef. You have your orders. You may go.'

The messenger withdrew. Tushratta sat for a while, popping one plum after another into his mouth, chewing noisily. Amerotke, he thought. How could he deal with him? Tushratta, lost in his thoughts, stared down at the cup.

'So far so good,' he whispered.

He lifted his head and clapped his hands. A chamberlain stepped into the pavilion.

'Tonight, I make sacrifice. Tell my priests to be ready at sunset.'

The chamberlain bowed and withdrew. Tushratta would go out into the desert that night. He would take a captive with him and make the blood sacrifice, calling on his own dark gods to help him confound those of Egypt.

Anubis was considered to be the son
of Osiris and Nephthys.

CHAPTER 3

Amerotke stepped into the gloomy embalmers chamber under the Temple of Anubis. Lamps glowed, high, narrow windows allowed in shafts of sunlight, though these did little to lift the dark, oppressive atmosphere. Against the far wall a huge granite statue of Anubis loomed through the billowing smoke. The air smelt of salt and natron, as well as the spices which the embalmers used to fill the corpses. Above the statue Amerotke made out the inscription: 'BEWARE! RESPECT THIS GOD! HE LOVES THE TRUTH AND DETESTS LIES AS AN ABOM-INATION!'

The sombre chamber was in marked contrast to the lavishly decorated Halls of Waiting and Appearance Amerotke had just passed through, where brilliant paintings glowed like rich jewels on snow-white walls. Or the pleasant gardens, the paradises of the temple, where cool ornamental pools and lakes shimmered under the shade of acacia and sycamore trees.

At any other time Amerotke would have found his visit a delightful experience, except for the howling of those dogs, the so-called sacred pack, in their deep pit at the far end of the temple. The place was busy. Priests passed in incense-shrouded processions; querulous petitioners queued; scholars scurried about, hunchbacked from poring over their books in the House of Life. This death chamber was a totally different world. The judge peered through the murk. He could make out the figures of the embalmers bending over the corpses sprawled on their stone slabs. One of these was a woman's; the embalmers were busy over a second, tutting and complaining at the mangled, torn flesh.

A figure emerged from the darkness. Amerotke recognised the burly outline, shaven head and strong, broad face of Senenmut: a man of infinite talent, the power behind the throne. The soft-skinned, carefully painted courtiers sniggered behind their hands at Lord Senenmut; they regarded him as an upstart, and that was what he was. A builder, turned soldier, turned politician; the court wits lisped the jibe 'Stonemason' – at least behind their fingers. On this occasion, despite his status, Senenmut looked like one, in his simple linen robe, devoid of any pendants, rings or insignia, the sweat glistening on his muscular shoulders. Amerotke strode forward. He was about to bow but Senenmut stretched out his hand for him to clasp. The judge did so.

'Follow me!' Senenmut ordered.

They walked across the embalming room and into a bare stone chamber. A few stools around a table, earthenware jars on shelves against the wall. It reeked of salt and putrefaction. Crude graffiti on the walls depicted a number of lewd sexual scenes. The cowled figure studying these turned. On recognising Hatusu, Amerotke should have genuflected but she shook her head. A simple robe covered her from neck to ankle, a linen shawl hiding her hair. She was the Imperial Pharaoh-Queen, the Lord of the Two Lands, the Wearer of the Double Crown, the Atef and the Nenes, the imperial cloak. However, apart from bracelets and anklets, Hatusu wore no royal insignia. She gestured at the graffiti as they sat down.

'The human heart,' she grinned, 'well, at least the male, very rarely changes. My lord Senenmut, any lover who adopted such postures would be left with a sore neck or back. Wouldn't you agree?'

Senenmut coughed and glanced away. Hatusu laughed behind her green-tinged fingernails.

'We will dispense with ceremony,' she said, sitting down. 'I like it here. No one can hear us.' She glanced at Amerotke. 'And how is my Chief Judge of Thebes?'

'To look on your face is pleasure enough.'

50

'I am sure it is, but let's be blunt! I am not supposed to be here.'

'And neither am I,' replied Amerotke. 'So, we are all not supposed to be here. Anyway, what are we not supposed to be here to talk about?'

'That's my Amerotke: blunt but still a trifle stuffy!'

Hatusu waved away a buzzing fly. She waited for Senenmut to serve wine and join them.

'There are three corpses outside,' she began. 'The priest Nemrath, the singing girl and what's left of Sinuhe the traveller. The heralds may have told you some of what's happened. By the way, where are they?'

'They left me in the antechamber but, yes, they told me what had happened.'

'Right!' Hatusu made herself comfortable and sipped at the chilled white wine. 'I won't bore you with repetition. Somewhere in this temple are the four envoys from Tushratta. Their names are Wanef, Hunro, Mensu and Snefru. Well, that's the Egyptian version of their names. Now, all four are powerful Mitanni. The three men represent some of the most prominent warrior clans in Tushratta's kingdom. They do not like me, they do not like Egypt but they are forced to make a peace treaty.'

'And the woman?' Amerotke asked.

'Yes, she's raised a few eyebrows.' Hatusu laughed. 'In fact, that's the problem. Tushratta has to bend the knee before a Pharaoh-Queen; he doesn't like it. Wanef is his half-sister. It takes a woman to know a woman. I suspect that's the thinking behind her presence here.'

'And more?' Senenmut broke in.

'My lord Senenmut,' Hatusu purred, 'as always, is correct. Wanef is Tushratta's principal adviser. She's cunning, quick and ruthless. She wants peace. She wants the borders opened, trade resumed, a military alliance and the betrothal of Tushratta's daughter to my kinsman. She's a good-looking girl so our boy can't object.'

'And what else do they want?' Amerotke asked.

'Well.' She tapped the table. 'Officially, they want the return of the corpse of Benia. My father had more concubines than

51

a bird has feathers. Benia was Tushratta's kinswoman, much loved and respected.'

'But she's dead and buried?'

'Oh yes, but they want her mummified corpse brought from my father's tomb so they can take it back to their royal mausoleums in the Mitanni capital.'

'But no one knows where your father's tomb is.'

'I do.' She smiled.

'Then there's no problem?'

The smile disappeared from Hatusu's face.

'I don't know,' she murmured. 'I won't say much except I heard rumours about Benia's death.' She gestured with her hand. 'Enough for now: the Mitanni also want Sinuhe the traveller's manuscript.'

'I've heard of him.'

'So has all Thebes. A navigator, a wanderer. Sinuhe's memory was a treasure house of knowledge: sea routes, trade routes, paths across the desert, the whereabouts of water wells and oases.'

'And?'

'Sinuhe's corpse, or what was left of it, was fished out of the Nile. According to neighbours, Sinuhe left his house yesterday morning clutching a leather bag. A fisherman saw him going down to the ruined Temple of Bes. Later in the day Sinuhe was found dead, his manuscript gone.'

'Could the Mitanni be responsible?'

'Perhaps. Then there's the Glory of Anubis, stolen from its shrine.'

Hatusu got to her feet and stretched elegantly. She smiled and winked at Senenmut.

'Finally, there's what's happening here at Anubis. A dancing girl was found dead in one of the pavilions. Two of the temple flock, and some of the fish in the sacred ponds, have also been poisoned.'

'If these deaths didn't begin,' Amerotke replied, 'until the Mitanni arrived, then it must be them. Until the peace treaty is sealed, Egypt and the Mitanni are still at war.'

'I know. I know.' Hatusu sat down. 'Tushratta's out with his chariot squadrons at the Oasis of Palms. He will not come to us, we will not go to him, not until the peace is sealed.'

'But why should the Mitanni do all this?' Senenmut wondered.

'As you say, Divine One,' Amerotke declared, 'Tushratta does not want to bend the knee and kiss the feet of a woman.'

'I am Pharaoh.'

'In my eyes, yes,' Amerotke replied. 'But Tushratta might like to cause a little chaos. A few deaths, the theft of the Glory of Anubis; whilst the Mitanni would love to lay their hands on Sinuhe's document. They, too, have merchants eager to learn the quickest and safest routes to the land of Punt or further down the gulf. Perhaps they even dream of sending a fleet across the Great Green.'

He caught Senenmut's puzzlement.

'But you don't believe that, my lord, do you? Why should they commit murder in Thebes? And what's the use of sealing a peace treaty with Egypt, if we discover that the Glory of Anubis is in their possession? And would the Mitanni stoop to blasphemy and sacrilege? They worship the dog god: their priests might draw the line at such a sacrilege.'

'Yes, but the Mitanni would love to make us a laughing-stock,' Senenmut replied. 'Both the assassin and the thief could be someone in the temple wishing to humiliate us in the eyes of the Mitanni and everyone else. Or it could be someone in the pay of Tushratta with the same purpose in mind.'

'Traitors?' Amerotke queried.

'Politics is like the Nile.' Hatusu spoke up. 'It hides many things. You've met our two heralds, Weni and Mareb. Weni is our official envoy, our mediator with Tushratta. We know that he has been bribed and bought by Tushratta and Wanef. Oh no.' She raised her eyebrows. 'Don't look so surprised. Weni's treason is at our request. He is faithful and loyal enough but the Mitanni think they have a spy in our midst and that's the way we want it. Now Princess Wanef reports back to Tushratta. To put it bluntly, one of her messengers met with a slight accident and our escorting chariot corps was ready to help.'

'You had a glimpse of the correspondence he carried?'

Hatusu just smiled.

'We thought we were being clever,' Senenmut declared drily. 'Now it seems there is another traitor in Thebes. A person they call the Hyaena: that's the only reference Wanef's letter made.'

'So.' Amerotke cradled the earthenware cup between his hands. 'The Mitanni are here to negotiate. They want peace. They think they've bribed Weni to be their traitor when, in fact, he's nothing of the sort. However, the Mitanni have a real spy, a man they call the Hyaena, a scavenger. Could Weni and the Hyaena be one and the same?'

'It's possible,' Senenmut replied.

'Or someone else, here in the temple. What we don't know,' Hatusu continued, 'is what Tushratta is plotting. A tangle of mysteries, eh, my lord Amerotke? Now, I want Sinuhe's manuscript and the Glory of Anubis back in our possession. I also want to know who the assassin is here at Anubis. You will join Lord Senenmut in the negotiations. Keep an eye on everyone.'

Amerotke gestured round the dark, gloomy chamber.

'Have I been told the full truth? Divine One, your mind can curl like a serpent . . .'

'You are not a toy,' Hatusu soothed. She lowered her head and looked at him coquettishly. 'Don't you trust me, my lord Amerotke?' She shook her head. 'This is no game. It is as I've described it. All I want is the Glory of Anubis, Sinuhe's manuscript back in my hands and Tushratta's envoys kissing my sandalled foot. I must not be made to look a fool in the eyes of Thebes and all of Egypt. I don't want Tushratta raising his head and grinning at me slyly. And, above all . . .' She paused.

'What?' Amerotke asked bluntly.

'Those who accompany Wanef do not want peace. I don't want some heinous murders to cause them to clutch their robes and scuttle away, proclaiming Mitanni envoys are not sacred or respected in Thebes.'

'Could it come to that?' Amerotke asked.

'If given a chance, Wanef's companions might seize it.' Hatusu got to her feet. 'But the envoys are waiting and, as I said, I'm not here.' She pointed to the far door. 'The Maryannou,' she referred to the royal bodyguard, 'are waiting.'

Hatusu stretched out her hand. Amerotke had no choice but to kneel and kiss the green-tinged fingernails. She stroked him gently on the face.

'You are not a toy or a dog, Amerotke: in this matter you are the Eyes and Ears of Pharaoh.'

Then she was gone.

Amerotke got to his feet. Senenmut grinned and clapped him on the shoulder.

'We have another hour yet. Do you wish to view the dead?'

Amerotke agreed and followed the Vizier out of the chamber. They first inspected the corpse of the dancing girl. The embalmers had already been busy, removing her internal organs and placing them in sealed canopic jars, though they had yet to draw the brains out through the nose. The table looked like a flesher's stall. Amerotke, so used to death, found it difficult not to flinch.

'She'll be buried by the temple,' Senenmut whispered. 'She died in the service of the god.'

The young woman had undoubtedly been very comely. She had a pretty face and a full, ripe body, narrow-waisted with the long, muscular legs of a dancer. Now the embalmers had reduced her beauty to nothing. Amerotke felt a pang of sadness. Such loveliness and youth snuffed out like an oil lamp.

'What was the cause of death?' Amerotke asked.

The bald-headed, long-nosed physician shook his head.

'The eyeballs were slightly protruding.' He pulled back one eyelid then tapped the chin. 'The mouth and throat were very dry as if she had drunk some fiery liquid. She'd undoubtedly frothed at the lips.' He picked up an arm and let it fall. 'The muscles are rigid as if she died in shock or was bitten by a snake, a truly venomous one.'

'Did you find any wound?'

The physician shook his head.

'Nothing at all. Spots and cuts but I could find the same on your body, mine or Lord Senenmut's.'

'But a young woman like this wouldn't die of a seizure?'

'She may have done. Her belly,' the physician continued in a bored tone of voice, 'contained nothing strange: bread, roast meat and a cup of wine she drank some time before she was killed. The food was already digested.'

'What makes you think it was poison?' Amerotke demanded.

'Because I can think of nothing else,' the physician snapped. 'The liver and spleen were slightly enlarged and there was discoloration of the internal organs. I understand the young woman's corpse lay there all night. It is sometimes difficult to distinguish between the effects of death and its cause.'

'If it *was* a poison,' Amerotke insisted.

The physician pursed his lips and spread his hands.

'My lord, there are poisons so powerful they can strike like fire.'

'Is that possible here?' Amerotke asked.

'All things are possible, my lord.'

Senenmut led them over to the second slab, on which the priest Nemrath had been laid. A short, plump man, body slightly pale, glistening fat, a bull-like neck. The embalmers had yet to begin on him. The cause of death was obvious from the deep, dark purple stain under his left breast.

'Did you find anything else?' Amerotke asked. 'I mean, you know the circumstances.' He gestured with his fingers. 'Nemrath was young, powerful?'

'There is no sign of violence,' the physician replied. 'No scratches.' He picked up the dead man's hand and let it fall. 'The fingernails are not broken nor do they contain anything. No cuts or marks on the body.'

He paused as one of the embalming priests went up to the statue of Anubis and, hands extended, began to chant a ritual hymn to the dead.

Amerotke turned. His foot slipped on some oil, his hand grazed the ice-cold flesh of the dead priest. Senenmut grasped Amerotke by the arm.

'Careful, my lord!'

The physician, once the priest had finished the hymn, sniffed and picked up a sharp, hard-boned knife.

'Nemrath was killed with one blow from this to the heart.' The old eyes of the physician creased into a smile. 'I know about the theft but there is little mystery about Nemrath's death.'

Amerotke took the knife and studied its black handle, carved in the shape of a snarling jackal. The blade was long, its edges serrated.

'How could someone get close enough to use this?'

The physician shrugged.

'Was Nemrath drugged?'

'Impossible. True, we have yet to remove the stomach. But, according to the evidence, he ate and drank nothing before he was killed.'

'Sexual activity?'

The physician chuckled.

'Nemrath was well endowed. According to the rite, he had to abstain from sexual contact for at least three days before he began his ritual.'

'And did he?' Amerotke asked.

'Please accept my word.' The physician smiled. 'Nemrath was celibate, certainly on the day and night before he died.' The physician scratched his balding head and looked at Amerotke shamefacedly. 'I know you to be the Lord of the Hall of Two Truths but even this murder will tax your wit.'

He came round the table and plucked Amerotke by the gown, leading him away as if Senenmut was an eavesdropper.

'It is all over Thebes,' he whispered. 'I've been to the chapel: no secret passages, no forced door, the sacred pool was not disturbed. Yet Nemrath is dead and the Glory of Anubis gone.'

Amerotke stared at the billowing smoke. Throughout the physicians' chatter, Senenmut had remained passive, a dark, brooding presence. Amerotke wondered what was really happening in the Temple of Anubis. He stared at the far wall. Some painter had depicted the paths into the Duat, the Underworld: different galleries, some leading nowhere, the rest twisting and turning, like a child's puzzle, or a snake in a maze which has to find its way out. He was now in a maze, but who was leading whom? Had the Mitanni stolen the Glory of Anubis, so as to provoke Hatusu? Had someone in the temple stolen it for profit? Or to embarrass the Divine Hatusu? After all, the

Pharaoh-Queen was barely tolerated by the priests of Thebes. Or was it more sophisticated? True, Egypt wanted peace with the Mitanni but Hatusu was also a spider, an actress who wore many masks. The same was true of Senenmut. Had they stolen the Glory of Anubis? Were they looking for a pretext for war?

'You are puzzled, my lord Amerotke.'

Senenmut was watching him, sly-eyed. Was he smiling? Amerotke recalled Hatusu. Were these two princes, the Pharaoh and her lover, engaged in some devious game?

'I am confused,' the judge replied. 'However, I am only beginning. One thing I assure you, my lord Senenmut: I will find the Glory of Anubis; its thief, and his villainy, will be proclaimed to all of Egypt.'

He was disappointed. Senenmut's face did not betray any emotion.

'The third victim,' Amerotke demanded.

This time the physician handed each of them a piece of cloth to cover their noses and mouths. Amerotke soon found the reason why. Sinuhe the traveller's corpse was mangled and torn. Chunks of flesh had been plucked from the face and torso. A hand was missing, the fingers of one hand reduced to lumps of flesh.

'May Osiris, foremost of the Westerners, show him compassion!' the physician intoned as he took away the corpse's veil.

'Those who found him,' Senenmut explained, 'noticed the crocodiles thrashing in the Nile and had to drive them off. They did their best.'

'Was he dead before he entered the water?' Amerotke asked.

'I think so,' the physician replied. 'Though I can find no bruise or blow.'

'He must have been,' Senenmut added. 'Sinuhe was clever. He knew the danger from crocodiles.'

Amerotke stared at the remains. Despite the perfumed cloth, he caught the stench of putrefaction. The embalmers would do their best but they could do little to remedy the damage done by the beasts of the Nile. Amerotke lowered the cloth. He was about to leave, go back into the small chamber, when he glimpsed what must have been the remains of Sinuhe's clothing, piled beneath the table. He crouched down and inspected these carefully. He rubbed the torn and bloodstained linen between his fingers and inspected the expensive reed sandals.

'Now, why is that?' he murmured.

'Why is what?' Senenmut asked, crouching down beside him.

'Was Sinuhe a rich man?' Amerotke asked.

'No, like all travellers, his wealth came from his stories.'

'You have made enquiries?' Amerotke asked. 'Did anyone see him leave this morning?'

'He lived by himself, down by the waterfront. We do know he left early for the Temple of Bes.'

'So, we know he was going to meet somebody,' Amerotke declared. 'Now, Sinuhe was a man who cared little for status; that's the mark of these travellers. They claim to have seen everything and are impressed by nothing. Now look at this, Lord Senenmut.'

Amerotke dragged the remains of the sandals and clothing towards them.

'Sinuhe was not a rich man, but this morning, he decided to dress in his gauffered robe and best sandals. I'm sure when his possessions were searched . . .'

'His house is sealed and guarded,' Senenmut interrupted.

'I will search it,' Amerotke declared. 'We'll find he had other, less fitting robes and sandals.'

Amerotke pushed the bundle away and got to his feet. He thanked the physician and his helpers and left the chamber.

'What are you implying?' Senenmut asked, closing the door behind them.

Amerotke tapped a finger against his teeth, looking up at the light streaming through the windows.

'Sinuhe cared for no one. So, why did he dress in his best robe and sandals to go to a ruined temple?'

'To meet someone powerful?' Senenmut asked.

'But Sinuhe didn't want to impress anyone,' Amerotke continued. 'So, why should he care? Now, his papyrus book has gone. Yes?'

Senenmut nodded.

'So.' Amerotke sat on a stool and put his face in his hands. 'We have this famous traveller, dressing up, leaving his house early in the morning. He took his precious manuscript to the temple, a place he would know. He must have met his murderer but we don't know who. Sinuhe was killed, his body fed to the crocodiles and the murderer escaped with his manuscript.' Amerotke took his hands away from his face. 'Now, if Sinuhe was meeting a Theban, he wouldn't have dressed the way he did. So he was meeting a foreigner, someone he had to impress. Someone he didn't want to be seen near his house.'

'The Mitanni?' Senenmut asked.

'Possibly. It makes sense. They wanted Sinuhe's manuscript. They'd also love the opportunity to mock Hatusu.'

'And the other deaths?'

'A mystery,' Amerotke confessed. 'The dancing girl was certainly poisoned, but how and why?' He shrugged.

'And Nemrath?'

'Yes.' Amerotke sighed. 'That is a real mystery. Someone got into that chamber, crossed the sacred pool, stabbed him, took the sacred amethyst and left without opening the door. The temple guards report nothing untoward. No sign of resistance from Nemrath, a powerful young priest.' Amerotke raised his hands in mock supplication. 'Are the Mitanni waiting for us?'

'In a little while,' Senenmut replied, 'they will gather in the Hall of Words.'

'Then let us see where Nemrath died.'

Snefru the Mitanni envoy finished his wine and lay down on the bed. He loosened his clothing, pulling the white gauze sheets over to protect himself against the buzzing flies. He shivered: for some strange reason he felt as if he was shrouding his own body. Was it a premonition? Snefru stared up at the ceiling. The beer had worked its effect; his body felt slightly flushed. He would sleep for a while, calm his mind. He thought of the negotiations and tried to control his anger.

'We shouldn't be here,' he whispered, his voice low and guttural.

If he had his way, Snefru would ride out to the Oasis of

Palms and demand an audience with King Tushratta. Snefru was a warrior, a royal commander. True, the bitch Hatusu had smashed their army but had they to bend the knee so quickly? Bow so low? How old was the wench? Not yet twenty summers, proclaiming herself to be the Pharaoh god. He recalled the violent arguments in Tushratta's council. The King's saturnine face, those deep-set eyes, that slightly twisted nose, the mean mouth which could issue vile insults and berate them. And, of course, always Wanef. Was she Tushratta's lover? Had he adopted the Egyptian custom and lain with her in his inner chamber? Snefru resented her commitment to peace with Egypt. Like many others, Snefru belonged to the Mitanni war party. They argued how they should close their borders with Egypt, lick their wounds, raise a new army and attack. Tushratta had shaken his head.

'It would take years,' he declared. 'Our treasury is empty, the army is demoralised. Not a family, not a clan amongst the Mitanni but have lost two or three of their menfolk. We need to make peace, restore trade, get our prisoners returned.'

Tushratta, supported by Wanef, had argued eloquently: at last he'd got his way. The King, surrounded by his council, had sealed a pact. They had gone into their temple before the jackal god, a much fiercer, more warlike figure than the one worshipped by the Egyptians. Their priests, clothed in the skins of dogs, faces and bodies daubed with blood, had the victims prepared: two maidens and a young man. Each had been stretched out on the stone. Snefru had watched the high priest slash their throats, fill the sacred bowls with blood.

Perhaps the sacrifice had worked. Egypt would be discomfited. Here, in the Temple of Anubis, hadn't the sacred amethyst been stolen? Weren't there rumours that the manuscript of the famous Sinuhe the traveller, who had visited Mitanni territory, had also gone missing? Snefru closed his eyes and dozed. He dreamt again of the Hall of Sacrifice; its flickering torch lamps. He heard a sound and opened his eyes and stared in terror. Was he seeing a vision? He glimpsed the jackal mask, the black corselet which hid the top part of his vision's body. Snefru rubbed his eyes. Was the god visiting him? He tried to rise but somehow the sheets were tangled round his legs. The jackal head was bending over him; a knife pricked his throat.

'Lie back!' The voice sounded hollow.

Snefru did so, and death came quickly.

Anubis embalmed the murdered Osiris' body.

CHAPTER 4

The Temple of Anubis was busy, packed with worshippers. Priests were filling the flower bowls with hyacinths and lotus blossoms. Others were preparing for the late afternoon rituals: censers poured out incense smoke which curled along the galleries and corridors. Senenmut walked through in his nondescript clothes, the cowl of his robe pulled up to hide his features; Amerotke no longer wore the insignia of office. They left the temple by a side door and entered the well-watered gardens. Amerotke paused at the ominous baying from the sacred dog pack.

'I could not live with that for long,' he remarked.

Senenmut shaded his eyes against the sun.

'I know what you mean, but they were a gift for the god from some tribes south of the cataracts. Every so often,' he grinned, 'some strange creature appears out of the jungle, the forest lands to the south.' He patted Amerotke on the shoulder. 'And brings gifts for our temples.'

'Do you believe in any gods?' Amerotke asked, following him along the path.

'Like you, my lord judge,' Senenmut called back, 'I believe in the Power of Egypt and the Glory of Pharaoh!'

'And the advancement of my lord Senenmut,' Amerotke added.

Hatusu's first minister just grinned over his shoulder.

They continued on, bypassing the inner and outer halls, and reached the centre of the temple around the sanctuary. The light was dimmed along its dark corridors and galleries. Very few people were allowed to wander here, even more so after the sacrilegious theft of the sacred amethyst. Temple guards in full armour stood at corners and in doorways. Amerotke and Senenmut crossed an open courtyard into the mysterious portals and the Glory of Anubis Chapel. It lay to the side of the temple, along a gallery which could be viewed from either end. The chapel's heavy Lebanese cedar door had been repaired, but one look at its close-set timber planking, copper hinges and bronze lock and Amerotke realised that it had been forced.

'To prise open a door like this,' he murmured, 'would rouse the entire temple.'

The captain of the guard, Tetiky, came up; he stood a little way off, one hand grasping the hilt of his sword. He looked suspiciously at them and would have intervened if Senenmut had not curtly informed him to mind his own business.

Amerotke examined the door and the side walls as well as those at the front and back of the side chapel. He could see no crack, no opening, nothing to resolve the mystery.

'The smallest mouse couldn't get in!' he exclaimed.

He crouched down and tried to stare under the door but it fitted snugly into its surrounding lintel at both bottom and top.

At Senenmut's insistence, Tetiky unlocked the door and swung it back. Immediately inside was a long glistening pool about three yards long and the same across. Senenmut snapped his fingers and Tetiky brought a cedarwood plank which served as a bridge. He positioned this carefully so they could gingerly cross. Amerotke stared around: the chamber had dark recesses; there were no windows or ceiling vents. The chapel was gloomy and smelt thickly of incense and wild flowers. Amerotke stood whilst the lamps were lit. He looked back at the sacred pool. He'd heard of similar obstacles or traps in other temples: no one could enter or leave without help. It would prevent someone from blundering in. The vigil priest, or anyone else entering, would need the assistance of that makeshift bridge.

In the light of the flickering lamps, Amerotke could now distinguish the dark shapes in the chamber: the naos, its doors open; the black and gold statue of Anubis staring out. Around it the sacred plates, cups, incense boats, holy water stoups, cushions and prayer mats. The walls were painted cunningly in red and gold, depicting the jackal god Anubis weighing the souls of the dead against the feather of truth. Amerotke walked towards the statue of Anubis. It was painted black and gold; the eyes were green emeralds. On its chest was a small enclave where the amethyst had been placed. Amerotke examined this carefully.

'The statue has been kept out,' the captain of the guard declared. 'The high priest says it cannot be enclosed in its tabernacle until the jewel is returned!'

Amerotke ignored him and walked back to the cushions. He glimpsed the bloodstains. The chamber was still polluted and would be until this mystery was resolved. Amerotke studied the high walls, marble floor, the unbroken ceiling and heavy door. This is a mystery, he thought; how could any man enter such a place, kill a priest and steal such a treasure? He glanced at Senenmut.

'There is no secret gallery?'

'None,' Senenmut replied. 'However, my lord, this mystery will wait; the Mitanni will not!'

Amerotke washed his hands and face, rubbing in some perfumed oil, in one of the side-chambers. Senenmut did the same, garbing himself in more ostentatious robes.

'I still look like a stonemason,' Senenmut joked. 'But at least I won't smell like one!'

He then led Amerotke up the stairs into the splendid Hall of Words set aside for the negotiations. Hatusu had undoubtedly chosen it. The hall was elegant, pillars along each side. Large open windows allowed in the light and sweet scents from the garden. however, the eye-catching wall paintings were its main attraction. On the left, the great victories of Tuthmosis II, Hatusu's late half-brother and husband, painted in a brilliant array of colours: Pharaoh leading his armies in his war chariot, the double crowns of Egypt on his head, over his back his shield, the royal bow pulled taut ready to mete out death. On the other wall Hatusu had ordered a series of equally vivid paintings, celebrating her great victory the previous year against Tushratta. Amerotke glanced quickly at them. They had nothing in common with his experiences of battle: the thunder of the chariots, the screams and crash of arms, blood spilling, men hacking and clawing at each other; dust clouds billowing; the vultures, wings extended, floating down like black ghosts to gobble on the blood and gore.

Amerotke felt Senenmut's slight nudge and broke from his reverie. Three people were waiting at the head of the long, polished acacia-wood table; the two heralds, Weni and Mareb, stood slightly to one side. Senenmut and Amerotke walked up the hall. The Mitanni waited just a few seconds before going down to meet them. They were dressed in the Egyptian style, though their linen robes were coloured and embroidered. The two men, Hunro and Mensu, had their hair closely cropped; large, thickset faces; the small jewels fixed in their ear lobes contrasted strangely with the peculiar tattoos along each arm. Apart from the copper bracelets, the type used by bowmen, they carried no arms. They clasped Amerotke's hand and spoke in the tongue common to all nations, the lingua franca of the marketplace.

The woman approached last: she was different. In many ways she was an older version of Hatusu, smaller, more plump, high cheekbones, cat-like, heavy-lidded eyes. Amerotke didn't know if her lips were twisted into a smile or a smirk. Once beautiful, he reflected, Princess Wanef looked as if she had the cunning of a reptile. She was dressed elegantly in a long white robe, a necklace of precious stones round her sinuous throat with jewelled earrings to match. She wore black leather wrist guards and Amerotke recalled how, according to Senenmut, this princess loved to drive chariots. A strong face, devoid of any paint or cosmetics: her hair was shaved and the wig she wore was oiled and braided with red and gold twine. She didn't stand on ceremony but, once Senenmut had made the introductions, grasped Amerotke's hand.

'Who has not heard of the Lord Amerotke?'

She raised her eyebrows. Amerotke didn't know whether it was an invitation to laugh at himself or with her.

68

'You are surprised at my knowledge of your tongue?'

Amerotke shook his head. He could see that she wasn't finished.

'Nevertheless, I am surprised that you are here! Why should the Divine Hatusu's Chief Judge in the Hall of Two Truths be involved in drawing up a treaty? You are not a scribe from the House of Peace? You command no regiment?'

'You know why he is here,' Senenmut answered. 'Princess Wanef, we cannot stand here for the rest of the day exchanging pleasantries. My lord Amerotke is to help me with certain matters.'

'You mean the deaths?' Wanef retorted. 'The dancing girl, the priest Nemrath and, I understand from your embalmers, the mangled remains of Sinuhe the traveller. A perplexing time,' she continued, her hard black eyes never leaving Amerotke's face. She paused, putting her head to one side at the distant howling of a dog. 'I know they are sacred,' she murmured. 'But I do wish I could sleep elsewhere.'

Hunro, standing on her left, his coarsened face twisted into a scowl, spoke quickly in the harsh Mitanni tongue. He jabbed his fingers at the floor. Mensu would have joined in but Wanef brought her hands together as if in prayer and glared at each of them. She closed her eyes and breathed in deeply.

'My companions wish the negotiations to continue.' She sighed. 'They cannot understand the delay. They are also concerned at these deaths; the theft of the jewel. We understand too,' she opened her eyes and glanced at Senenmut, 'that some of the fish pools have been poisoned whilst sheep from the flocks of Anubis have been mysteriously killed.'

'Animal fatalities,' Senenmut replied. 'We have the matter in hand.'

'But are we safe?' Hunro broke in.

'You are safer here than you are in your own cities.' Senenmut's voice was almost a drawl. 'And, if you agree to Divine Hatusu's terms, you and your cities will be safer yet.'

Senenmut gestured at the table. They took their seats. Clerks and scribes appeared with manuscripts, maps, ink horns, pallets and pens. One map in particular was laid before Senenmut, detailing the Horus road across the Sinai desert. The negotiations proceeded. Wanef was obviously the diplomat, the skilled envoy, whilst Hunro and Mensu were deeply opposed to any peace. Amerotke studied both men carefully. He noticed the recently healed scars along their necks and shoulders, the usual place for soldiers to be wounded when defending their lines against Hatusu's charioteers. Amerotke recalled the bloody massacre following the battle. These warriors must have lost companions, family, kin in that terrible rout. It must be hard for them to come and beg a peace, especially from a woman. Nevertheless, Wanef's authority was undisputed. She kept both her companions silent as she and Senenmut argued over border posts, patrols, licences to travel, taxes which could be imported and exported, the use of oases and water wells. Senenmut's replies were clear and simple. Hatusu and Egypt laid sovereign claim to Sinai. Mensu became agitated and whispered in Wanef's ear. She made a cutting movement with her hand.

'My lord Snefru has not arrived,' she explained. 'We need his expertise.'

Senenmut snapped his fingers at Mareb.

'You and Weni,' he ordered, 'go to his chamber. Perhaps my lord Snefru took some wine and has fallen asleep? Rouse him, do so gently, and bring him here.'

The two heralds hurried off. Senenmut declared they should pause a while. Servants brought in wine, grapes, bread, different cheeses and dishes of roast goose. Senenmut acted the efficient envoy, filling the silences with chatter and petty gossip.

'You'd best come quickly.'

Amerotke whirled round. Mareb was in the doorway; he'd thrust aside the guard. Amerotke sensed his fear; the young man had lost his foppish pose.

'What is it?' Senenmut snapped.

'Lord Snefru, we cannot rouse him. The servants have not seen him since he retired shortly after noon.'

Hunro and Mensu sprang to their feet, as did Wanef. Senenmut ordered Mareb to rouse the temple guard. They hurried from the chamber along corridors out across the edge of a pool where ibis and flamingo birds stood bright in the afternoon sun. The Mitanni had been given one of the temple mansions: a two-storeyed building with a flat roof, its square windows screened with gaily decorated shutters. The interior was cool as the building was ringed by shady trees, the windows and doors positioned to catch every breeze. Downstairs were kitchens and a dining room. Snefru's chamber was on the second floor, near the stairs leading up to the flat roof; its door was of hardened acacia. Weni stood outside, shuffling from foot to foot. Now and again he'd tap on the door. Wanef pushed her way forward.

'Are you sure he is in there?'

'Yes, my lady.' One of the temple guards came clattering down the steps. 'I was on guard downstairs when Lord Snefru came in. He took a bowl of grapes and a jug of wine. He said he wanted to sleep for a while; he went up the stairs and never came down.'

'Has anyone else entered the house?' Wanef demanded.

The guard, a mercenary from one of the auxiliary corps, shrugged; he cared little for these strangers or their doings in the temple.

'I am paid to guard,' he replied. 'I search the floor for snakes and scorpions. The house is busy. People come and go. I noticed nothing amiss.'

Amerotke pounded on the door.

'Why were you on the roof?' Senenmut asked.

'I went to see if the shutters were open; they are not,' the soldier replied.

Senenmut went back downstairs, gesturing at Amerotke to join him. They brought up a wooden bench, told the Mitanni to stand aside and pounded on the door. It buckled and flew back on its leather hinges. The chamber inside was dark and musty. Amerotke could see the faint outline of a man lying on the bed. Mareb hurried to open the shutters. Amerotke looked at the corpse and groaned. Snefru had been murdered. The body was strangely twisted, tense, the hands up, a frothy trickle seeping out of the corner of the gaping mouth; his eyes were wide open.

'It's as if he's been frightened to death,' Senenmut murmured.

Amerotke felt the corpse. The muscles were hard, rigid.

The rest of the Mitanni delegation entered. Hunro and Mensu stared at the corpse. They showed no compassion or grief but started talking to each other in their guttural dialect. Wanef intervened. Hunro, the more aggressive, snarled back, gesturing at the corpse. Wanef looked quickly at Amerotke; was the glance baleful or cunning? the judge wondered. She opened her wallet, took out a ring, put it on her finger and gestured at her two companions to follow her out.

'She carries Tushratta's personal seal,' Senenmut murmured, once they'd left.

'They show little grief,' Amerotke observed.

Senenmut went and knelt by the corpse, touching the sharp-boned face, the rigid jaw.

'There's no love lost between the Mitanni,' he replied. 'Their kingdom is a federation of powerful tribes. Tushratta is the most cunning and most able, that's why he's king. None of the men like Wanef; she likes none of them. Hunro and Mensu don't like each other. Tushratta is as cunning as a jackal. He knows they won't betray him, they are too busy watching each other. Well, is this murder?'

Weni, standing in the doorway, remained silent, as did Mareb, leaning against the windowsill. Amerotke turned the corpse over.

'It's very similar,' he declared, 'to what we saw in the embalming chamber: the muscles are hard, the body rigid, whilst I can detect no obvious wound.'

He pointed to a small red mark on the neck and others on the side, as well as small cuts to the chest.

'Scratches and flea bites,' he murmured.

He lifted the man's robe and noticed how it had been loosened. On the table on the other side of the chamber the wine cup was empty; only the grape stalks remained.

'Snefru apparently came in here,' Amerotke observed. 'He drank the wine, ate the grapes and closed the shutters. They were closed, Mareb?'

The herald agreed: he pulled one shutter over and tapped its wooden clasp.

'Closed and locked,' he replied.

'He then lay down on the bed, to sleep or rest.'

Amerotke moved to the window and stared at the shutters.

'He loosened his robes to let himself relax. Why should he do that, Mareb?'

'To catch the coolness, my lord.'

'Of course,' Amerotke replied. 'He'd had a busy morning. It's now the heat of the day. He drank wine and lay down on the bed.'

'But he should have kept the shutters open?' Senenmut queried.

'Yes, my lord, he should have done,' Amerotke agreed.

'When we forced the door, the room was sweltering hot. Why should a man escaping the midday heat block out the afternoon breezes?'

'Perhaps he wanted silence,' Senenmut declared.

'But the Temple of Anubis is not a rowdy marketplace!'

'Perhaps he wanted to be alone,' Senenmut replied. 'Or he may have been frightened. After all, the door was locked and bolted.'

'Yes, yes, it was.'

Amerotke walked back to the bed. It was a simple affair fashioned out of reeds with an ornamental headrest and transparent linen sheets to keep the bed free of fleas and insects.

'How did he die?'

Amerotke turned.

Wanef and the other Mitanni now stood in the doorway.

'My companions think he was murdered!'

She walked languidly into the chamber. She still wore the official ring.

'My companions say it's murder,' she repeated, 'and feel they are not safe here.'

'Then you are free to leave,' Senenmut retorted. 'But if you do, you are not only implying that Lord Snefru was murdered but that somehow the Divine Hatusu was responsible. That would be taken as blasphemy as well as a lie!'

Wanef raised her hands in a gesture of peace. The jewel on the ring was carved in the shape of a dog's head.

'My lord Amerotke.' She hardly turned her head, but watched Senenmut. 'Do you think it was murder?'

'It could have been a seizure,' he replied. 'Lord Snefru may have been bitten by a snake.'

He ignored Wanef's snort of derision.

'What do you really think?' she insisted.

Amerotke was about to reply when the physician from the embalming room, followed by his assistant, hurried in. He winked at Amerotke, nodded quickly at the rest and went across to the bed. He took a sharp knife from his assistant and summarily cut Snefru's robes.

'Well, well, well!' He pulled back the clothing and looked down. 'A fine specimen of a man; a warrior. Note the strength in the arms and calves. The face is composed enough but there was some violence.'

Wanef was about to angrily intervene but he waved his hand.

'Peace, peace!' he murmured. 'My lady,' he protested as Wanef approached the bed, 'I would be grateful if you would stand out of the light. And you too, sir.' He gestured at Mareb, who was still leaning against the windowsill. The physician turned the corpse over. 'Slightly clammy,' he continued as if lecturing a group of scholars in the House of Life. 'The muscles are hard. Putrefaction has not set in but it will do so soon. The belly is slightly swollen and distended.'

He examined the buttocks, turned the corpse over and studied the groin.

'He died of a seizure?' Wanef asked.

'He no more died of a seizure than he did flying through the air!' the physician snapped.

'Are you sure?' Amerotke asked.

'My lord judge.' The physician looked at him sternly. 'You know the world of law, I know medicine. There is no mark of violence: he was found lying on the bed?'

Amerotke nodded.

'So, very like the ones we've got below.' The physician pulled the linen sheets back.

'Poison?' Amerotke asked, glancing fearfully at Senenmut.

'I am afraid so, my lord.'

74

The physician bent over the corpse, opened its mouth and ran his finger along the dead man's teeth. He sniffed at the parted lips.

'He'd drunk and eaten.' He wiped his fingers on the damp cloth the assistant carried. 'But I can smell nothing untoward. Poison, taken by the mouth, usually stains the gums and the soft part of the throat. No such stain can be detected. I cannot see how else he died. I've said poison but I would have to study the entire corpse.'

'We don't want an Egyptian cutting Snefru as if he was a piece of offal,' Mensu growled.

'It's necessary,' Wanef disagreed. 'The body won't keep; it will have to be prepared.'

For a while confusion reigned as the physician called in more assistants waiting in the gallery outside. The corpse was taken out on a makeshift bier. Senenmut closed the door behind them and turned to face the rest.

'My lord Amerotke, you are Chief Judge in the Hall of Two Truths in Thebes.' He ignored Hunro's snort of derision. 'What do you think this is?'

'Well, Snefru didn't die of a seizure. There's no visible wound on the body. Therefore it must be poison.' Amerotke pointed to the platter and jug, around which flies now hovered. 'That could be poisoned but I doubt it.'

'How do you know that?' Mensu sneered.

'Because this is Thebes in Egypt. Snefru was a foreigner whose country, only a short time ago, was at war with Egypt. I wager he would be very careful what he ate or drank.'

Wanef, seated on a stool just inside the doorway, looked discomfited.

'It's true,' Amerotke insisted. 'You don't trust us, we don't trust you. If you attend an official banquet you watch what people eat or drink. You have tasters. Yes?'

Wanef nodded.

'And if you want refreshment like Lord Snefru did, you'd go down to the temple kitchens and personally organise your food. Correct?'

Again Wanef nodded.

'So.'

Amerotke got to his feet, walked to the window and stared down at the gardens bathed in glorious sunlight. Butterflies and bees were busy. The air was heavy with the fragrance from the exotic plants the temple had imported from Lebanon and Canaan. He listened to the sound of a chariot from a distant courtyard. On the breeze came the chanting from one of the small chapels and that dreadful baying from the dog pit. He recalled the man he had sentenced to death early that morning. He must go out and meet the Dog Master; at least look at this sacred pack.

Senenmut coughed as a sign he was getting impatient.

'I think it's murder,' Amerotke began. 'Before Snefru came up here he went to the temple kitchens to collect wine and food. He ate and drank. Now, for a man wanting to rest in the cool of the day, he should have left the shutters open but he didn't. However, that may not be too extraordinary.'

Amerotke walked over and gestured at the flies buzzing above the wine cup.

'Perhaps he found these an irritation. Anyway, Snefru finished his small meal and lay down on the bed. Weni and Mareb come up with a summons to join our meeting. He does not respond.' Amerotke went across and stared at the door. 'This was locked on the inside.' He gestured at the key twisted in the lock. 'No one came up here. Snefru allowed no one in. Yet he was murdered.'

'The assassin could have come through the window,' Mensu insisted.

Amerotke went across and studied the windowsill but could see no trace of any entry. He closed the shutters and brought down the wooden clasps into their sockets.

'When we came into the room,' Mareb spoke up quickly, 'it was definitely closed. You saw, I had to open it.'

Amerotke agreed. He rubbed his thumbnail round his teeth and shrugged.

'Even if we established how the assassin entered,' Wanef declared, 'how could he poison Snefru without the alarm being raised? Snefru was a warrior; he'd resist.'

'We must await the physician's report,' Amerotke replied. 'But somehow, and it is a mystery, Snefru was poisoned in this chamber.' He picked up the wine cup and bowl and thrust them into Weni's hand.

'Take these down to the physician. Ask him to study them carefully. He is to report back to me.'

'So.' Wanef got to her feet. 'We don't really know how Lord Snefru died. We don't know who's responsible . . .'

'And, above all, we don't know why,' Amerotke added.

He studied the Mitanni princess' sly face. Amerotke believed he had the truth of her two companions. He could find similar men amongst the leading officers of the Egyptian army; brave warriors, strenuous in battle, unaccustomed to negotiating, especially with a Pharaoh-Queen who had so ruthlessly smashed their military might. Snefru had probably been no different, but this one, with her sly, narrow face and those strange mocking eyes . . .

'Are you upset?' he asked abruptly.

'Upset?' Wanef grimaced. 'Lord Snefru was no kin of mine but he was a warrior, one of Tushratta's favourites. Along,' she hastened to add, 'with my two companions here.'

'Did he want peace with us?' Amerotke insisted.

'That is none of your business. He was an envoy . . .'

Amerotke took a step forward.

'My lady, I regret his death, but this is Egypt. You were quick to point the finger though we don't truly know who the murderer is.'

Mareb the herald coughed. 'My lord,' he interrupted.

'This is not the council chamber,' Wanef retorted; she smiled at Amerotke. 'Let my lord judge speak. Are you implying that one of us could be responsible for Lord Snefru's death?'

'That's a lie,' Mensu shouted, his hand falling to where his sword should have been.

'Don't be so impetuous,' Amerotke warned. 'We may all be as innocent of this man's death as anyone, but if you want the truth, I must ask questions.'

'Then ask them.' Wanef sat back on the stool, gesturing with her hand for the two nobles to be silent.

'Were there any differences between you?' Amerotke asked.

Wanef looked at Mensu and Hunro and shook her head.

'So he was your friend,' Amerotke insisted.

'He was a Mitanni,' Hunro declared. 'A leader of a clan.'

'Was there any blood feud between you?'

Again the shake of the head.

'If you must look for differences,' Wanef said quietly, 'not all Mitanni want peace with Egypt.'

'Did Snefru?'

'I have answered your question, Lord Amerotke.'

Again the judge caught the slyness in her eyes and voice.

'Snefru will be mourned by me, his kinsmen and members of his clan.'

Amerotke had his answer: there was apparently no love lost between these three and the dead man.

'I suggest,' Senenmut came forward, 'that we adjourn the meeting for today. My lord Amerotke will take up residence here in the Temple of Anubis. Chambers will be prepared for you and your servants.' He opened the door. 'My lady . . .'

Wanef bowed courteously to Amerotke and, followed by her two companions, left the chamber.

Senenmut glanced across at Mareb.

'What you hear today is not for discussion.'

'Of course, my lord, I am a herald.'

Senenmut breathed out; his heavy face was lined with concern. He leaned against the door, beating his fingers against his side.

'Are the Mitanni killing each other?' he asked.

'Impossible,' Mareb interrupted. 'My lord, no one has been up here. Nobody except Egyptians.'

'Then who?'

Senenmut opened the door; he used it to shield his face from Mareb.

'My lord Amerotke, you have walked this path before. The shadow of Seth the killer lies over this temple!'

'Aye,' Amerotke said, finishing his sentence. 'And undoubtedly he will kill again!'

Senenmut closed the door. Amerotke stared at its latch.

Strange, he reflected, how all the mysteries which had confronted him, or at least a greater part, involved doors and locks. The theft of the amethyst; Snefru's murder; that strange conversation with Belet in the cookshop. Was there a common thread? he wondered. Nothing which had happened was due to chance. Was this all part of one great strategy to confuse and confound Egypt? And would he make the mistake of separating one incident from another and so fail to penetrate the mind of the person responsible for it all?

Anubis is supposed to have devised the method
of wrapping the body in bandages and shown
what embalming oils were to be used.

CHAPTER 5

The physician pulled the veils of gauze over Snefru's corpse. Amerotke had waited hours to speak to him. Outside in the gardens, the sun was beginning to dip, the heat of the day was dying and the priests of Anubis were preparing for their evening's sacrifice. The song of the hesets, as they danced in front of the procession, echoed through the temple.

> 'Oh, Anubis, we petition you.
> Hail to you, Lord of Death!
> Lord Anubis, the great!
> Lord to the very limits!
> Foremost in the Barque of Millions!
> Master of the dead.
> The Weigher of Souls!
> Your glory . . .'

'His glory is missing,' the physician remarked sourly. He waved away the assistant waiting to continue the embalming process. 'The god is displeased with us,' the physician continued.

He plucked Amerotke by the elbow and led him into a small recess packed high with pots and jars. He offered Amerotke the only stool whilst he sat on a corner of the table.

'What do you think?' Amerotke asked. 'I mean,' he added hastily, 'about the Glory of Anubis?'

The physician's wrinkled face turned more sour.

'I have worked here, my lord, since I was a boy, in the House of Light then the House of Scribes. The Glory was a great asset to this temple. No one knows where it came from. They say it was part of a great rock which fell from the sky.'

'Well, it certainly hasn't gone back there!'

The physician shrugged. He leaned down and tightened a thong on his sandal.

'Some people,' he murmured, 'claim the god has taken it himself.'

'I doubt that, and so do you.'

'Yes, my lord Amerotke, I do. It has been stolen and the gossips blame the Mitanni. Snefru's death will only make it worse.'

'Why is that?' Amerotke asked.

'The gossips will allege the Mitanni stole the Glory and are being punished for it.'

'And how was Snefru punished?' Amerotke asked.

'I just don't know: the wine and grapes were not poisoned. There are small scratches and cuts all over Snefru's corpse, but that's the same for any of us: flea bites, scratches, old wounds.'

'He was poisoned?'

'Yes, my lord Amerotke, I think he was, but what the potion was, and how it was administered, remains a mystery.'

The physician went over and closed the small wooden door, then came back.

'In my youth I studied many things. Poison was one of them. Some poisons can kill by being smeared on the skin, or inflict death if breathed in. Some can be administered through the ear. Some are slow-acting: days, weeks, even months. Others can kill,' he snapped his fingers, 'like an oil lamp being doused. No one has fully classified the poisons which are available: the asp, the snake, plants, even certain fruits of the earth . . .'

'And that's only half the problem, isn't it?' Amerotke interrupted. 'Snefru was powerfully built, a warrior. He wouldn't just lie and allow someone to kill him. He'd protest, struggle, scream, lash out. Yet none of these happened.'

Amerotke got to his feet. He clasped the physician's bony shoulder and squeezed it gently.

'Divine Father, I am grateful for what you have done. I'd be even more grateful if you'd tell me anything you discover.'

'Where are you going?' the physician asked.

Amerotke smiled over his shoulder.

'I don't think the lord Anubis came in and took his own amethyst from the mysterious portal. You don't believe that, neither do I! I am going to catch that thief.'

Amerotke opened the door, walked through the embalming room and up the steps. The shadows were now lengthening. The air was thick with the scent of roasting flesh and incense. Priests and scholars strolled in the small paradises, enjoying the cool of the evening. Amerotke paused at the baying of the dogs.

'Master?'

Amerotke started. Shufoy appeared from behind a bush, parasol in one hand, a small leather bag in the other. He grinned like the dwarf god Bes.

'I've been waiting,' he declared mournfully. 'Master, my heart has been pining for the sight of your face.'

Amerotke crouched down and wiped the crumbs from either side of Shufoy's mouth.

'And you've also been eating sweet cake and dates and drunk more charou wine than is good for you.'

Shufoy swayed slightly on his feet and blinked.

'I've been waiting, Master.'

'Of course you have.' Amerotke got up.

'Are we going home tonight?' Shufoy asked. 'I am lonely, Master.'

A dancing girl abruptly appeared, a thin robe round her bare shoulders. She came from behind the same bush Shufoy had. Her oil-drenched wig was slightly askew, the dark kohl-rings round her eyes runny and her carmine-painted lips slightly smudged.

'I've lost it!' She ignored Amerotke. She tapped her wrist. 'I've lost my bracelet!'

Shufoy tried to move her away.

'It probably fell off behind the bush!' he slurred.

Amerotke, laughing to himself, walked off in the direction of the dog pit. Behind him rose the dancing girl's exclamations and Shufoy's protestations. Eventually the little man caught up with him.

'I was just very lonely, Master, and she was so agreeable. I gave her a small cube of copper to make another bracelet.'

Amerotke looked down at him.

'And you watched her dance?'

'That's right, Master. As the poet says: "The heart becomes lonely, especially in the evening when the soul takes wing . . ."'

'Thank you, Shufoy,' Amerotke interrupted.

'Where are we going?'

'To see some dogs.'

They crossed the temple gardens, past granaries, oil and wine presses, the air sweet with their crushed fragrance. Priests, acolytes, hesets and servants sat in the shade of sycamore, acacia and acanthus trees. The sun was slipping fast. A cool breeze had sprung up. Amerotke glimpsed the Mitanni delegation in one of the garden pavilions; they were having an outside meal, probably discussing the events of the day.

'My lord Amerotke.'

He turned. Mareb the herald appeared as if out of nowhere.

'What do you want with my master?' Shufoy, chest out, strutted forward.

'My lord Senenmut,' Mareb ignored the dwarf, who stamped his foot in anger, 'has now left the temple for the House of a Million Years. Your rooms are ready in the Mansion of Stillness.'

'I will go home this evening,' Amerotke replied. 'I must see my wife and children, then I shall return.'

The herald bowed, giving Shufoy a sneering look. The dwarf responded with the most obscene gesture, learnt in the quay-side taverns.

'I can't stand heralds,' Shufoy growled. 'They are so pompous.' He ran ahead of his master. 'Make way for the lord Amerotke!' he bellowed. 'Chief Judge in the Hall of Two Truths; friend of Pharaoh, member of the royal circle! He who has received the smile of the Beatific One!'

Amerotke groaned but let Shufoy have his way, ignoring the

commotion caused. They left the parkland, crossed sun-parched common ground, through some trees and over a bridge which spanned one of the irrigation canals from the Nile. The great wall of the dog pit soared before them. The breeze carried its fetid, feral stench as well as the occasional yip or howl. The huge wooden copper-reinforced doors to the compound were firmly locked. The guards on either side lowered their spears as Amerotke approached but Shufoy waved them aside. The men relaxed.

'Where is the Dog Master?' Amerotke demanded.

'I am here,' a voice called out from behind the gate.

One of the guards hastened to pull up the bar. The Dog Master emerged dressed in leather skins. In one hand he carried a sharp pointed trident; across his shoulder a coiled leather whip. His hands were bloodied and, for risk of pollution, he kept his distance. He smiled and bowed.

'My lord judge, you do us great honour.'

Amerotke hid his own unease and fear. The stench was almost unbearable, whilst a heart-chilling howling broke out from the darkness beyond the gate: like a chorus of demons threatening to rise up from the underworld. Amerotke felt he was no longer a judge but a little boy, fleeing for his life down the alleyways of Thebes.

'Do you want to see them?' the Dog Master asked.

He went across and cleansed his hands and arms in a barrel of water. He told the guards to check the gates, then led Amerotke around the curtain wall, up some steps and into a watchtower. Shufoy followed. Amerotke stared down. The pit was formed from the cavernous side of a hill. Some trees, a little grass, a few bushes. Amerotke was attracted by the pits and caves in the side of the hill.

'You are safe,' the Dog Master assured him. 'The dogs could never climb the wall so they are allowed to roam as free as they wish.' He gestured with his hand. 'Six to eight acres of land here, some more behind the hill. Nothing but scrubland.'

'Where are the dogs?' Shufoy murmured.

'They have been fed,' the Dog Master replied. 'They are resting.'

'Do you go in there yourself?' Amerotke asked.

'Only so far.' The Dog Master pointed to the pathway inside the gate. 'What we do is take the meat in and throw it. The dogs come out; there is fighting and yapping but every animal has its share.'

'Where do they come from?' Shufoy stared at the caves, fascinated by what they might contain.

'From the jungles and plains beyond the cataract: a gift to the high priest during the time of Tuthmosis II. They are not hyaenas or jackals but a breed of wild dog. Look now.'

A huge dog emerged from a cave and loped down the hill. Others followed. Amerotke felt a chill of fear. They were black as night; squat, snub faces, broad jaws, long stiff ears and curling tails. They moved with the skill of a hunting pack, bodies rippling with muscle; short, glistening fur. Their leader caught a glimpse of the Dog Master and Amerotke and loped towards them. It sat and stared up.

'They are intelligent,' the Dog Master remarked. 'They rely on each other.'

'Are they tame?'

'They are wild,' the Dog Master explained, 'the descendants of the original pack. The temple priests have tried to train them but it's too dangerous. One slip, one sign of weakness, a whiff of blood and they'll attack.'

Amerotke stared down at the dog. Its dark eyes glared back: huge jaws open, its pink tongue lolling. It threw its head back and gave a yip-yip bark to the others around it.

'They have killed,' the Dog Master continued. 'Never trust them. If you went down they'd attack. They can smell fear like they can blood. I have spoken to travellers who have met them before. They are very loyal to the pack and will hunt their quarry for days, even weeks.'

The dogs were now thronging forward. Amerotke's stomach curdled.

'Have they ever escaped?'

'Not in my time,' the Dog Master replied. 'You've seen the gates and they are guarded. I've heard stories about arrogant, drunken noblemen trying their luck. One was stupid enough to take up a challenge.' He blew out his cheeks. 'Afterwards, they found it difficult even to find a little bone.'

Amerotke felt slightly giddy.

'I've seen enough.'

He turned and went down the steps. Shufoy stuck his tongue out at one of the dogs and followed. At the bottom of the steps Amerotke thanked the Dog Master.

'You carried out the sentence of the court?'

'The man is dead, my lord. The dogs didn't leave him long. It was a just verdict. I also killed the rabid dogs who slaughtered his aged uncle and aunt: they must have died a terrible death.'

'All death is terrible,' Amerotke replied. 'I bid you good night.'

He walked back through the grounds, Shufoy trailing behind him.

'Master, I'm tired. I want to go home.'

'Naturally, little one. You've eaten, you've drunk and you've been pleasured. Now you want to curl up and sleep. Well, we still have business.'

Amerotke entered the precincts of the temple. He stopped near a small fountain and purified his face and hands; followed by a protesting Shufoy, he made his way across the sanctuary into the mysterious portals. He summoned an acolyte and explained who he was.

'I want to see Tetiky, captain of the guard, the priest Khety and the priestess Ita. Bring them here now!'

While he was waiting, Amerotke went into the chapel which had contained the Glory of Anubis. The sacred pool still glistened; the bridge across was marked with footprints. The flowers in the vases were dying and gave off a sweet-sour smell. The black obsidian statue looked haunting in the flickering lamplight. Amerotke examined the door and stared around. This was a holy place where the whispers of the gods could be heard; now it had been desecrated by sacrilege and murder. The chamber itself was unpretentious. Amerotke felt the wall and deduced that this must be an ancient part of the temple, probably a small shrine, which had been built around and developed over the years. A sheer rectangle of stone with its shadowy recesses. Amerotke examined these carefully but there was no crack or crevice, not even a vent-hole for incense. It was, in fact, a secure room, the best place to keep the brilliant amethyst. Amerotke went round smacking at the walls. Sometimes these ancient places had secret passageways or tunnels. Amerotke had seen the same in the Temple of Ma'at. He satisfied himself that the room was secure, and carefully re-examined the door. According to Senenmut this had been broken down. It had now been repaired. Amerotke scrutinised the cedar panels and the copper lock but could detect no sign of trickery. He heard footsteps and walked back across the sacred pool.

The captain of the guard came first, dressed in a leather kilt, marching boots up to his ankles, a sword belt slung across one shoulder. He reminded Amerotke of Asural: squat, formidable, with a harsh, fat face. A man born and bred for the military. He saluted Amerotke, hand up, head slightly down, and formally re-introduced himself as Tetiky, captain of the temple guard in the shrine of Anubis. He then stood aside as his two companions crossed the narrow bridge. Khety was dressed in the simple linen robe of a priest: his face was ascetic, with large, protuberant eyes; his lower lip stuck out slightly, as did his ears, which gave his otherwise pleasant features a rather grotesque cast. Ita the priestess was small and svelte, plump shoulders above her linen gown. She wore her own hair down to her shoulders, kept in place by a filet round her head. Sweet, childish features with butterfly eyes, a snub nose and a rather pretty mouth. The anklets and the bracelets on her wrists jangled as she walked. In her haste she hadn't fastened her sandals: she smiled in apology and crouched down to fasten them. All three were plainly nervous as Amerotke stared at them.

'You asked to see us?' Khety broke the silence, his voice rather squeaky. He coughed to clear his throat and shuffled his feet. He didn't seem to know what to do with his hands, so he folded his arms and glanced sideways down towards the statue.

'Close the door!' Amerotke ordered.

He sat down, his back against the wall, and made the other three squat opposite in a semi-circle.

'Where is the Glory of Anubis?' he began.

'My lord judge, we don't know.' Ita's voice was soft and soothing.

'Then who will bear responsibility?' Amerotke asked Tetiky.

The captain of the guard scratched his bald pate and looked sheepishly at Amerotke.

'The temple suspects us, my lord. But, there again . . .' His voice trailed off.

'There again,' Amerotke finished the sentence for him, 'they can't blame you, can they?' He gazed round the chamber. 'This is what it looks like: a rectangle of stone, no vents, no apertures, no secret passageways?'

'None,' Tetiky confirmed. 'That's why it was used to keep the Glory of Anubis.'

'What did the Glory look like?' Amerotke asked. 'I remember seeing it as a boy, but from a distance, when it was carried in processions round the temple.'

'Brilliant purple, as large as a man's hand. No one has ever seen such an amethyst.'

'And where did it come from?'

'I don't know,' Tetiky answered. 'Its origins lie in the mists of time. Some people say it was part of a huge rock which fell from the skies: a gift from the gods. Others claim it was found in mines hundreds of leagues to the south of the Third Cataract.'

'And some say,' Ita offered, 'the god himself brought it here. A gift to the Divine House.'

'Now it's gone,' Amerotke murmured. 'Tell me, Tetiky, you are a policeman; you've served with the Maijodou, I suppose?' Amerotke referred to the city police.

'Aye, and before that I was a member of the Scorpion brigade in the Isis regiment.'

'So you have been a soldier or a policeman most of your life?'

'Yes, my lord.'

'If I stole a jewel, what could I do with it?'

'Sell it.'

'But to whom?'

'Foreigners like the Mitanni.' Tetiky made a face. 'Perhaps I could try and cut it up but that would take time and energy. Or I could smuggle it down to the merchant quarter in the city. The amethyst is precious: its worth in gold and silver cannot be reckoned.'

'No, of course,' Amerotke agreed. 'But the thief could get a good price. He could live in leisure for the rest of his life. Do any of you,' he continued, 'know how that jewel was stolen?'

A chorus of dissent greeted his words. Amerotke got to his feet, took a bracelet off his wrist and walked down to the statue. He placed the bracelet in the enclave on the breast of the statue of the god and walked back.

'Let us,' he began, 'pretend that bracelet is the Glory of Anubis. I am Nemrath the guardian priest. When would I begin my vigil?'

'At dusk,' Tetiky replied. 'Once the sun dips over the far horizon and the conch horn is blown.'

'And what happens then?'

'I escort the two priests down here,' Tetiky explained. 'I knock on the door. The priest who has completed the day vigil opens it; I swing it back.'

'Excuse me.' Amerotke leaned forward. 'But look at the pool. It must be three yards across. How can the priest open it without the bridge being there?'

Tetiky grinned. 'Come, my lord.'

The captain took him to the edge of the pool. He stepped forward as if walking on water, grasped the handle of the door, then stepped back. Amerotke exclaimed in surprise and crouched down.

'Ingenious,' he murmured.

He hadn't seen this before: a stone plinth near the chapel end of the pool. It was coloured to blend cleverly with the dark green water.

'The priest stands on that,' Tetiky explained. 'It can easily be done. He inserts the key, unlocks the door and steps back. I then place the bridge.' He laughed. 'The plinth is supposed to be a secret, but most of the priests know about it. It's not only for security but to ensure the vigil priest doesn't drink copiously whilst on watch.'

Amerotke nodded.

'So if he did, he would lurch and fall into the pool?'

'It has been known,' Tetiky retorted. 'The remarkable aspect is that the plinth can be stood on by the priests in the chapel but not by someone coming into it. An intruder could try and jump, but the pool's too wide.' He shrugged. 'That's the temple routine. On the night Nemrath died, the day priest opened the door and stepped back. I pushed the bridge across. One priest left and the other entered. I lifted the bridge and swung the door closed, holding it fast whilst Nemrath, on the other side, locked the door, removed the key and began his vigil.'

'And you are sure it was locked?' Amerotke insisted.

'My lord, you have my oath on it. It's part of my duty: I hear the key turn, I try the door. I did the same that night.'

Amerotke led him back to the rest.

'And where would Nemrath keep the key?'

'On a small hook on his girdle,' Tetiky replied.

'And how many keys are there?'

'Just the one.'

Tetiky went across, lifted a cushion and brought the key back to Amerotke. It was a long, thin, intricately carved copper key with the clasps, or teeth, on one end, its handle fashioned in the form of a jackal head.

'The lock is intricately made,' Tetiky explained. 'And its key is finely cut, difficult to replicate.'

'So, Nemrath locked the door,' Amerotke took the key, 'placed the key on his girdle and began his vigil?'

Tetiky agreed.

'And what did you do, Khety?'

'I began *my* vigil.'

'And you?' Amerotke turned to Ita.

Her eyes creased into a smile.

'I am the handmaid of the god, my lord. Once darkness has fallen, Khety's fast is over. In the second watch I brought him some roast goose, grapes and a jug of beer. On the night

Nemrath died, I noticed nothing untoward. I talked for a while with Khety and returned to the kitchen.'

Amerotke glanced at Tetiky.

'I was on duty and did my patrol,' he replied. 'I saw nothing amiss.'

'How many times did you walk past this chapel?' Amerotke asked.

The captain pulled a face.

'Three or four times, in each quarter of the night. It was silent. I glimpsed Ita bringing some food. On one occasion I passed, Khety was awake; on another, he was asleep. Nothing untoward happened. At dawn I brought down the day priests. I followed the ritual and knocked at the door, but there was no answer. I knocked again, shouting Nemrath's name. I thought he may have had a seizure. I called the high priest and members of the guard; the door was forced.'

'How did you force it?'

'We took a bench,' Tetiky explained. 'The lock snapped. We placed the bridge across the pool and entered the chamber.'

'And where was Nemrath?'

'Sprawled against the wall.' Khety pointed to where the cushions lay. 'The dagger was in his chest. I rushed across. He was dead, and the Glory of Anubis,' his voice quavered, 'had gone.'

Amerotke, one hand cupping his mouth, stared down the chapel. He felt tired and confused; he could make no sense of this.

'The door was definitely locked?'

'Of course!' Tetiky snapped.

'And the key?'

'Still on the ring on Nemrath's girdle.'

'You are sure of that?'

'I examined it,' Khety replied. 'And so did Tetiky.'

'And who was present when the door was first forced?'

'The high priest, myself, other guards and priests. Lord Senenmut also came down.'

Amerotke got to his feet. He stared at the black and gold statue of Anubis. His gaze shifted: on the near wall was the famous picture of the god weighing a soul against the feather of truth. Help me, Amerotke prayed. How can a priest be murdered, an amethyst stolen, yet the door was not forced? It remained locked from the inside and the key was still on the dead man's girdle.

Amerotke closed his eyes. He must collect all the evidence. Yet he had done that . . .

'Khety!' he called out, not turning round. 'Did anyone approach that door during your vigil?'

'No, my lord.'

'Did you ever leave the passageway outside for any reason?'

'Just once.'

'And when was that?'

'When Ita brought down the provisions.' He laughed nervously. 'I had to relieve myself.'

Amerotke turned and walked back.

'And you, Tetiky, you noticed nothing out of the ordinary?'

'I tell you, my lord, I came by here. Khety was at his vigil. On one occasion he was asleep. I saw Ita bring the jug of beer and later return to the kitchen.'

'Khety, you were outside, did you hear any commotion within?'

'I should have done but I heard nothing.'

Amerotke nodded.

'Then I've kept you long enough.'

He dismissed them and waited until the captain of the guard crossed the bridge, closing the door behind them. He crouched down against the wall. There was a tap on the door.

'Come in!'

Shufoy pushed it open.

'Be careful!' Amerotke called out.

'Don't worry, Master.' Shufoy stood grinning on the threshold. 'I've heard of this.'

'And what have you heard elsewhere?'

'Nothing, my lord. The night Nemrath was killed there was no disturbance. Khety never left his post. Ita took him provisions from the kitchen and returned with the empty jug.'

'And what else?'

95

'Khety and Nemrath were on good terms. Khety is a scholar. He and Ita are also close.'

'And Nemrath?'

'According to rumour, rather lascivious, liked his food and drink.'

'Show me a priest who doesn't.'

Amerotke got to his feet and carefully crossed the sacred pool. He stood in the corridor and stared back into the chamber.

'Who did it, Master?'

'Oh, I know who did it. Khety, Ita and Tetiky. One, two or all of them are involved, but how it was carried out?' Amerotke shook his head. 'Only the god Anubis knows!'

'And what about Belet?' Shufoy demanded. 'He has invited me and Prenhoe to have supper with himself and Seli. He's still anxious, my lord . . .'

'Have you discovered anything else?'

Shufoy shook his head.

'And neither have I,' Amerotke added drily. 'All I can say, Shufoy, is that a robbery is planned. They needed a locksmith so they chose Belet because he lived with the Rhinoceri. They thought he'd have nothing to lose.'

'A place like Anubis?' Shufoy demanded. 'A robbery has taken place here.'

Amerotke stared across at the door.

'No,' he murmured and lifted a finger. 'Remember what Belet said. How the place chosen had no guards. No, the theft of the Glory of Anubis would need more than a locksmith. It required careful plotting and the cunning of a serpent.'

Anubis is depicted in Egyptian art as either a
jackal or a man with a jackal's head.

CHAPTER 6

Amerotke walked through the marketplace. Shufoy trailed behind, softly singing a love song.

'Flee her my heart and hurry!
I know only too well, this love of hers!
I will not wait for her to catch my tunic.
Or let her cool hands calm the ardour of my soul!'

'A lovely song.' Amerotke swung his cane and glanced back at the woebegone Shufoy. 'Are you singing about the heset?'

'Ladies in general,' Shufoy replied mournfully. 'They are like butterflies in the garden of my heart. I have given them the best years of my life. In the morning,' he continued sonorously, 'a man's hopes are water, but by evening, they have turned to dust and the bowl is cracked.'

Shufoy stopped and wiped a tear from his eye. Amerotke solemnly promised himself not to smile or laugh. There was nothing more lugubrious than Shufoy in love.

'Come on, little man,' he urged kindly. 'A jug of beer on the cool of the roof, some sweet cakes, a bowl of fruit and I'll let you sing one of your songs. Why all this?' He gazed down at the dwarf. 'Why this sudden absorption with love, Shufoy? Is it because your friend has been married?'

'A man without a woman is a body without a soul: Prenhoe warned me about this. He had a dream two nights ago: I was riding on the back of a dancing girl. She took me down to the Nile but then turned into a hippopotamus . . .'

99

Amerotke burst out laughing, so loudly that the traders and vendors, preparing their goods for the night market, looked up in wonder at this judge in his white robes and sacred purple-edged sandals, and his deformed companion. Amerotke moved his cane and grasped Shufoy's hand.

'Come on, my little Bes. The day is done and so are we. Don't be so mournful. We are all for the dark.'

'I'm glad to be free of that temple.' Shufoy fairly skipped at his master's show of friendliness. 'It's a sombre place. I don't like those Mitanni or the guards with their jackal insignia. It truly is a place of ghosts.'

'Ghosts?' Amerotke paused. 'Why ghosts, Shufoy?'

'That's what some of the guards told me. Anubis has been glimpsed walking his temple: his sandals are black, a war kilt of the same colour, his face covered by a huge jackal mask edged with gold.'

'They've drunk too much,' Amerotke snapped.

'Well, that's what they told me,' Shufoy repeated plaintively.

Amerotke walked on. Despite nightfall the market was still busy. Barbers shaved customers under trees. Soldiers, off duty, grew noisy and raucous as they searched for a pleasure house. They kept well away from the police: these carried thick cudgels and patrolled the streets round the temples, eager to crush any sign of disturbance. The fleshers' stalls were empty, the meat being either sold or destroyed as putrid. Beggars ran up offering to fan away flies; Shufoy bellowed back that that was his task. All the denizens of the waterfront had swarmed into the city looking for easy pickings. Beggars and thieves, conjurors and tricksters; a group of drunken musicians, who had spent too much time in the wine shop, played a raucous din to the delight of the passers-by. These refused to throw any gifts but stood jeering at the musicians' frantic efforts. Amerotke kept his head down and clasped Shufoy's hand more tightly. The little man had a tendency to wander off, particularly to watch the travelling physicians, those hucksters who claimed to possess magical skills and offered exotic potions to cure a whole range of ailments.

'You've given up medicine?' Amerotke asked.

100

'Too many traders in the marketplace.' Shufoy retorted. He held out his parasol as if it was Pharaoh's sceptre. 'The gods are calling me to a new trade.'

'And what is that?' Amerotke asked.

'A love poet.'

Amerotke chewed his lip.

'A seller of poems and potions,' Shufoy continued. 'No, Master, don't laugh. I teem like a well: an eternal spring bubbles inside me ready to gush out songs and poems which will enrapture the heart.'

'Norfret is not going to believe this,' Amerotke whispered. 'Come on, Shufoy!'

They hurried down towards the city gates: two huge pillars dominated by soaring towers. The gates themselves had been locked and barred. The watchman on duty recognised Amerotke and let him through a postern door on to the basalt-paved causeway which ran along the Nile. To his right Amerotke glimpsed the river, glinting in the pale light of the moon; fishing smacks, still busy, darted like beetles across its surface. Lanterns winked. The breeze carried the shouts and cries of the fishermen mixed with the splash and gurgle of the water, the constant croaking of the frogs, and the call of birds which, now and again, would rise and soar gracefully along the banks of the Nile.

'Those boats should be careful,' Shufoy muttered. 'The hippopotamus does not like being disturbed. Where there are fishermen, the hippopotamus always appears and the crocodiles are not far behind.'

Amerotke gestured at the mud-packed hovels they were now passing through.

'The people are poor, Shufoy. Their only trade is to provide fresh fish for the morning's market.'

They continued on past night traders streaming into the city. Others were going to meetings, banquets and parties. The highway was packed with the rich and the poor: wealthy merchants on their donkeys or palanquins, the poor clustered together like a gaggle of geese. At last the crowds thinned. They left the jumbled maze of mean, one-storeyed tenements, the air acrid with the smell of cooking fish, cheap beer and sour bread. The Valley of the Unclean, people called it: a maze of slums built by the workers who flocked to the city. Eventually they were out in the open countryside. Across the Nile the lights of the Necropolis winked and fluttered. Sounds faded. Shufoy returned to muttering a love poem. Amerotke let his hands slip, lost in his own reverie about the day's happenings. Only when Shufoy gently tapped him on the wrist did Amerotke become aware of the footsteps behind. He turned quickly, grasping his cane. Five or six figures stood there, grotesque shapes in the darkness.

'What is it, stranger?' Amerotke called out. 'Are you following me or do you wish to pass?'

'We want nothing of the sort, Lord Amerotke.'

The judge breathed in to calm his panic. Time and again Norfret had warned him against these walks home at night, insisting he had a retinue or at least Asural to guard him. Amerotke always refused; now he wished he had a sword. Shufoy had moved away. The little man put down his parasol. He opened his bag and took out a jagged Caananite dagger.

'We mean you no harm.' The voice was soft. 'My lord Amerotke, we are the Children of the Nile.'

The judge relaxed. 'Then come forward.'

They did so. Amerotke stifled his unease. He had heard of the Children of the Nile: a guild responsible for feeding the sacred crocodiles and drawing what they could from the river. They lived in their own small sanctuary a few miles to the south and worshipped Sekhmet the Destroyer, the goddess in the shape of a lioness. The Nile gave these creatures sustenance and profit. Accusations were also levelled that sometimes they lured craft on to the treacherous sandbanks. They deliberately wrecked them, seizing their goods and sacrificing those who survived as offerings to their own dreadful goddess. They always dressed in untreated animal skins and so were classed as uncleans. Each wore upon their head a helmet or hat shaped in the form of an ibis, a crocodile, a hippopotamus, a snake: all those creatures who lived along the banks of the Nile. The leader was small and fat. He took off his makeshift scorpion helmet. One eye was half closed, nothing more than a small, milky pool; a glaring scar cut across his face. He reeked of sweat and that fishy odour so common to the mud of the Nile. His companions stayed further back. The man bowed.

'My lord Amerotke.'

'It is night,' the judge replied. 'You can find me in the Hall of Two Truths.'

'Or the Temple of Anubis,' came the reply.

'What do you know of my doings?' Amerotke snapped.

'My lord, don't be angry.' The man tried to smile, his good eye screwed up.

'Get to the point!' Shufoy growled.

'Hush, little man, we mean no danger. How could people like us threaten the great Amerotke? You know why we are here,' he continued hurriedly. 'We are unclean. We are forbidden to enter holy places. However, we have information to sell, or rather give you free of charge.'

'Tell me what you have. I will make sure gifts are left in your sanctuary.'

'Two things, my lord. Sinuhe the traveller? We took his body out of the Nile. I'd met Sinuhe before. He told us fascinating tales, claimed to have seen where the Nile originates at the centre of the earth. Sinuhe did not care about the way he dressed. Now the crocodiles have turned his corpse to a bloody mess, but did you notice, my lord, that he was wearing his best robe and a fine pair of sandals?'

Amerotke recalled the bloodstained garment he had glimpsed in the embalming room.

'And secondly?'

'The morning Sinuhe was killed, one of my companions glimpsed what he thought was the god Anubis near the old Temple of Bes.'

'Gods don't walk,' Amerotke retorted.

'Perhaps not a god,' the man replied. 'Perhaps a priest of Anubis dressed in a long leather kilt and a black mask?'

He turned to one of his companions and chattered in the high-pitched lingua franca of the waterfront.

'I heard that.' Shufoy spoke up. 'He said it wasn't Anubis.'

The leader stepped closer.

'Little man, you have no nose but ears sharp enough. You are correct. My companion says that he has been out to the Oasis of Palms.' He grinned through the darkness. 'Well, close enough: the Mitanni priests wear such masks.'

'Is there anything else?' Amerotke asked.

The fellow shook his head.

'As I've said,' Amerotke declared, 'you will have your reward by tomorrow evening. May the goddess look favourably on you!'

His strange visitors disappeared into the darkness.

'What do we have here, Shufoy?' Amerotke asked. 'Sinuhe dressing up to meet someone important? A Mitanni nobleman? Or noblewoman?' he added. 'And why the mask?'

'To hide his or her face, Master. It is easy to confuse. Anyone would think it was a priest from the Temple of Anubis.'

Amerotke rubbed his arms as a cold breeze caught his slight sweat. The meeting had startled him: he realised how tired and hungry he had become. He grasped Shufoy by the hand and walked into the darkness.

Lights appeared. They passed the high walls of other stately mansions, their polished, wooden gates locked and barred for the evening. This was a pleasant, lush area, near enough to the Nile, but safely protected against any flooding. At last they reached Amerotke's house. Shufoy hammered on the gates, loudly demanding entrance. A side door swung open and Amerotke stepped into his own private paradise of flower-filled gardens, vineyards, beehives and shady trees.

Shufoy and the porter began taunting each other. Amerotke walked ahead. Everything was in order. Oil lamps lit, the summer house closed. Lights and flowers had been laid before the garden god Khem. He went down the avenue of acacia trees and up into the main house fronted by painted columns. The entrance hallway smelt sweetly of the polish rubbed into the rich cedar beams. Small jugs of myrrh, frankincense and sandalwood were placed in corners. Shufoy, who had caught his master up, now bellowed that Lord Amerotke was at home. Servants brought jugs and basins. Amerotke sat on a stool and washed his face, hands and feet, cleansing his mouth with cool white wine.

The door opened at the far end. Norfret swept in, her sloe eyes sparkling with pleasure. She wore a white gauze robe with an embroidered shawl across her shoulders. She was barefoot and the necklace which she had tied round her neck suddenly came off and clattered to the floor. She scooped this up, and came and bent over her husband. She kissed him on the brow, her eyes dancing with mischief, those lovely lips parting in a smile.

'All hail to Pharoah's judge!' she whispered. 'The wisest man in Thebes!'

He took her face between his hands and kissed her on the lips.

'All hail to Norfret, goddess of perfumed flattery!'

Ahmose and Curfay bounded into the room. They shouted hello then remembered their manners, made their obeisances, grabbed Shufoy and ran out.

For a while confusion reigned. Servants bustled in and out. Norfret tried to tell Amerotke how Ahmose's fever had abruptly subsided, that one of the dogs had got into the fish pond, whilst she couldn't make sense of the honey steward's accounts. At last, however, they were alone on the roof of the house, reclining on couches, a table of food between them. Norfret loved to sit here at night. She was fascinated by the stars and often described to Amerotke how different ones moved. Tonight, however, she was more insistent on learning about the Mitanni at the Temple of Anubis.

'I have heard stories,' she fluttered her eyelids mockingly, 'how Mitanni priestesses are skilled in love. They are taught all the arts from the moment their courses begin. I heard how a visitor to the Mitanni capital died of pleasure . . .'

'Stories,' Amerotke scoffed. 'The Mitanni may well be great lovers but they are also formidable warriors: they like killing and bloodshed.' He leaned across and stroked her cheek with his fingers. 'If they attacked Thebes, sacked it and captured you, it would not be pleasant.'

Norfret shivered and pulled the shawl close about her.

'They wouldn't take me!' she hissed. 'Come, come, my lord judge, you are no longer in court. You are confused? Puzzled? A woman's wit, a wife's wisdom?' she teased.

Amerotke leaned back on the head of the couch.

'The Temple of Anubis,' he began, 'is now a place of death.'

'Explain!' Norfret urged.

'First, we have a series of unexplained, mysterious deaths: some animals and fish have been poisoned, though its cause is unknown. A dancing girl was also found dead in one of the garden pavilions. There's no sign of her drinking or eating poison but the physician, and I think he's an astute man, points to the rigidity of her muscles and believes some noxious potion was administered. But how, why and by whom remains an enigma. Then we have one of the Mitanni delegation, Lord Snefru. He retires to his chamber, the door and windows are locked and shuttered. When the former is forced, Snefru is found dead; same symptoms as the heset, but the source of the poison and how the murder was committed remain a mystery.'

He paused and stared out towards the city. Despite the river mist, its lights twinkled and glinted through the darkness.

'And you have no idea why these deaths have occurred?'

'None. We also have two other incidents. You have heard of Sinuhe the traveller?'

'Of course! A great teller of tales.'

'Apparently he visited the derelict Temple of Bes further down the Nile. He was killed, his body thrown into the river. The corpse was savaged by crocodiles before the Children of the Nile pulled it out. We know Sinuhe had a papyrus book which described his journeys. A veritable source of paths across the desert. That would be very useful to the merchants of Thebes or to our House of Silver. The treasury is always eager to exploit unknown trade routes; to plot caravan paths across the desert or send a fleet across the Great Green and discover new spices, fresh sources of silver, gold and precious jewels.'

'And Divine Pharaoh?'

Amerotke caught the tinge of sarcasm in Norfret's expression. His wife was always deferential but she had her own ideas about the self-proclaimed ruler of Egypt. Norfret was always wary when Amerotke was summoned to her presence.

'She's a woman,' Norfret insisted. 'True, a Pharaoh, a god; the incarnation of Horus; the emanation of the god Ra, but she's still a woman. I suspect the Divine Hatusu uses her charm and looks as much as she does the power of Amun.'

Amerotke smiled across at his wife.

'The Divine Hatusu would love such a manuscript. She has the priests under her heel, the armies eating out of one hand.'

'And she would love to have the merchants eating out of the other,' Norfret laughed. 'Continue.'

'Sinuhe was definitely going to meet someone important. A man who cared little for courtesies, he had donned his best robe and sandals.'

'But it must also have been someone he didn't want others to see,' Norfret added. 'That's why he chose to meet him or her in such a desolate spot.'

'Correct, light of my life.' Amerotke smiled. 'And whoever met Sinuhe killed him. The Children of the Nile claim that someone dressed like Anubis, in a black leather war kilt and mask, was seen near the temple. Sinuhe was a courteous but tough character. He would not have given up his life lightly. Yet he is dead and his manuscript gone.'

'And the Glory of Anubis?' Norfret asked. 'I have heard the rumours.'

'Now, there's a true mystery . . .'

Amerotke picked up the cup of wine and sipped at it.

'. . . which would delight my sons. The Glory of Anubis is a brilliant amethyst, kept in a side chapel of the temple. There are no secret entrances. The door is secure, a pit of water prevents anyone blundering in. A guardian priest locks himself in at night. Another sits on vigil outside; he is served by a handmaid of the god. The temple precincts are patrolled by the captain of the guard. Nothing amiss happens, but the following morning, the door has to be forced. The guardian priest is found stabbed and the Glory of Anubis gone.'

'Are all three crimes connected?' Norfret asked.

'Perhaps, perhaps not.' Amerotke tapped the wine cup against his teeth. 'It's possible,' he continued, 'that the Mitanni were behind it all. They are led by a woman as wily as a mongoose. I am not too sure the Mitanni want peace or war. One of them could be trying to create chaos so their King

Tushratta withdraws and the peace negotiations collapse. Yet how and why that person is committing these murders is a mystery. I mean, the death of Lord Snefru fits into a logical argument. But why a poor dancing girl? What danger can a heset at the Temple of Anubis pose?'

'You could twist it round.'

Norfret turned on her side. She moved an alabaster jar of oil so she could see her husband's face more clearly.

'Perhaps the murders were committed by the Divine Hatusu, or at least on her orders? She could wish to cause chaos. Perhaps she wants Tushratta to withdraw and provide her with a pretext for more war and glory.'

'That's possible,' Amerotke agreed. 'If Wanef is a mongoose, the Divine Hatusu is just as cunning.'

'Senenmut?' Norfret asked.

Amerotke shook his head.

'No, no, the man is honourable. He has the physical strength and stamina to kill; he can be wily, but the peace is a good idea. It was he who persuaded the Divine Hatusu . . .'

'In the council chamber or in bed?'

Amerotke grinned. He was about to answer when he heard one of the boys cry. Shufoy came to the bottom of the steps and said it was only Curfay in his sleep.

'It could be the Divine Hatusu,' Amerotke continued. 'But the Mitanni are more likely candidates. They could be killing to cause chaos as well as to give a pretext for withdrawing. They then add insult to injury by stealing the Glory of Anubis and Sinuhe's manuscript.'

'I would agree with that.' Norfret filled her cup. 'You told me they worship a dog god. The masked man seen near the Nile could be one of them. They'd love to seize Sinuhe's manuscript and have the Glory of Anubis decorate one of their temples, but, if that was the case,' she concluded, 'it would mean that the Mitanni possessed some way to get into that side chapel.'

Amerotke stared up at the sky. He was convinced that he had met the killers of Nemrath, those who had stolen the amethyst: Khety, Ita or Tetiky? Had they been bribed by the Mitanni delegation? Were they given secret help to commit murder and sacrilege? Was that why Sinuhe went out to the Temple of Bes? He wouldn't want a Mitanni near his house: that might explain the masked figure glimpsed near the ruins. Amerotke beat his fist against his thigh.

'There is little logic to any of these events.'

Norfret swung her legs off the couch. She came over and sat beside him.

'The key to the chapel, where was it kept?'

'There is only one key. When the door was forced, it was still on the dead priest's girdle.'

Norfret smiled and edged her way along the couch. She ran her finger down Amerotke's face, tracing its contours.

'You are going to brood, aren't you? You are going to sit here until the sky becomes bright and the Divine Amun's breath ushers in the morning.' She slipped her hand down his robe. 'Or, there again, you could come into my court. We can discuss other things.'

Amerotke kissed her on the lips.

'Are you trying to bribe me?'

'Why, my lord judge.' Norfret fluttered her eyelids. Amerotke drew her closer. He kissed her fragrant-scented cheek.

'There is no need,' he whispered.

'In which case,' Norfret made herself more comfortable, 'court is in session!'

Weni the herald had also enjoyed himself that evening: a young dancing girl had visited his chamber. They had taken food and wine, after which Weni had danced with her. Now she was gone and he had received a summons. Weni put on a cloak, pulling the hood over his head. He looked round the untidy chamber and, once again, splashed water over his hot face. He had drunk too much wine and the heset girl's exertions had exhausted him, but he had to go. He picked up the small sycamore twig pushed under his door, together with the leaf from the tamarind tree, the agreed signs to meet in the usual place. He heard the sound of the horn proclaiming the beginning of the third watch of the night: the temple and its gardens would now be silent.

Weni opened the door and went out along the passageway.

The mansion he shared with Mareb and various scribes sent from the House of Peace lay silent. He paused at Mareb's door and pushed it open. The other herald lay fast asleep in his bed, clothing and sandals tossed on the floor. Weni grinned to himself and slipped out down the stairs. The old porter at the bottom opened his rheumy eyes.

'You are going out late, Master,' he croaked.

'I can't sleep,' Weni replied.

He opened the door. The night air was cold but full of the fragrance of the gardens: the smell of flowers, sandalwood and myrrh from the sacrifices; roasting meats from the kitchens. Weni slipped across the grass. In the far distance echoed the howling of a dog. The moon hung like a silver-white disc. Birds fluttered and chirped in the trees. From the sacred pool came the incessant croaking of the frogs. Now and again Weni stopped to make sure he wasn't being followed. He went deeper into the gardens, past vineyards, orchards, trellises, into a small copse of sycamore and tamarind trees. He squatted down and waited. Time passed. Weni became impatient. He was about to move when a pebble danced in front of him.

'Are you there?' Weni called into the shadows.

'Of course I am here! I was here before you ever came!'

'Then why the wait?'

'I had to make sure you weren't followed. You wouldn't betray me, Weni, would you? These Egyptians are suspicious. The Glory of Anubis is gone, whilst those dreadful deaths . . .'

Weni strained his ears. Whoever was talking was disguising their voice. He couldn't distinguish whether it was male or female, Egyptian or foreign.

'Now.' The voice turned conversational. 'We had a bargain, Weni, remember? Have you put Sinuhe's treasure somewhere safe?'

Weni swallowed hard; his mouth went dry.

'Crafty Weni,' came the purring voice. 'To whom are you going to sell such a treasure? The Egyptians or the Mitanni? Mind you, Nubian and Libyan merchants are also busy in the market-place. They'd pay a good price.'

'Ah, the manuscript!' Weni exclaimed.

'I do admire your family tomb, Weni.'

'What has that got to do with it?' Weni stuttered. 'My wife is buried there.'

'And that's where the manuscript is, isn't it? Who'd ever think of searching a family tomb?'

'Stop taunting me.'

'Weni! Weni! Who really employs you now? You're half Mitanni, aren't you? Do you work for the Divine Hatusu or Tushratta? Oh, I know you are supposed to be a spy. Shall I tell you a secret? I think Weni works for no one but himself.' A soft chuckle followed. 'But don't forget, Weni: I know all your little secrets! About your wife. Her lover's corpse still mouldering under its slab in the Temple of Bes. The other accidental deaths. Your relationship with the Crocodile Man. Your treacheries and betrayals. Nor must we forget the Glory of Anubis. I'll be coming for that soon! You're nothing but a whore, Weni, up for the highest bidder.'

'I can lay my hands on the amethyst,' Weni retorted, 'faster than you think.'

'Oh, we don't want it yet! And how about secrets, Weni? What has the stonemason Senenmut told you? What are the Egyptians' real intentions? War or peace?'

'I don't know. You are confusing me. First the manuscript and now all this . . .'

'Hush now.'

Weni froze.

'Did you hear that?' the voice urged.

'I should leave.' Weni backed away.

'No, no, tonight we will reach an agreement. Look,' the voice continued earnestly. 'We will move from here. I feel uncomfortable.'

'Where to?' Weni asked.

'Near the dog pit. A large holm oak on the edge of some waste ground. It's deserted: I'll introduce myself again, then we'll do business.'

'But the guards?' Weni asked.

'Don't worry,' the voice purred. 'Count to one hundred then follow me, but not before.'

'What happens if I withdraw?'

Weni was now frightened. He felt tired, slightly drunk; a deep unease at what was happening.

'How can you withdraw, Weni? You are involved in Sinuhe's death and the theft of his manuscript, not to mention the Glory of Anubis and the other murders. I can prove it all. If Divine Hatusu realises you're not to be trusted, who can you go to? And if I tell the Mitanni who you really are, what comfort would you find there? No, I'll be waiting for you near the holm oak.'

Weni, shivering with fear, heard a slight movement. He began to count. Now and again he stumbled, but eventually he finished and made his way across the temple grounds. Here and there torches had been lit. The nearer he approached the holm oak, the louder grew the baying of the dogs. Weni shivered. He wanted treasure for his tomb: that was how this game had begun. His secret visitor had approached him just after the Mitanni had arrived. Weni had been terrified by how much his mysterious contact knew about his secret dealings. He had no choice but to agree to his terms, and there again, the bribe had been so attractive.

Weni reached the holm oak, its great branches stretching out like the tentacles of an enormous spider. He jumped at a scurrying in the nearby undergrowth. He looked round: from where he stood, he could see the gate to the dog pit. The animals themselves had gone strangely quiet. Weni also glimpsed the pools glinting in the moonlight. He turned away, then paused in terror. Pools? There had been no rain! He looked again. It seemed as if someone had been slopping water from the gate to where he stood. Weni took a step forward, crouched and touched the dampness. He brought his hand to his nose and sniffed. It wasn't water, it was blood! He heard the sacred pack howl, this time much closer. Weni started to his feet. A dog had appeared. He could see its black shape in the moonlight. Others were grouped round it. Where were the guards? The Dog Master? The animals shouldn't be free! As if in a nightmare, the lead dog charged towards him. Weni broke from his fear and fled into the darkness, pursued by the howling, snarling dogs of Anubis.

Anubis is painted in a symbolic black, which
could, perhaps, represent rebirth.

CHAPTER 7

The carnage at the Temple of Anubis shocked Amerotke. Asural and Prenhoe had woken him just before dawn with terrifying stories about how the sacred pack had broken loose. Amerotke quickly completed his ablutions, dressed and, with a grumbling Shufoy, hastened into the city. The Dog Master was already there, pale-faced with fright. The temple grounds were full of archers, expert bowmen from the Cobra squadron of the Ibis regiment. Senenmut, angry-faced and tight-lipped, was directing affairs. The vizier grasped Amerotke by the elbow and took him into a portico.

'You are going to see something, my lord, which will make you think the Season of the Hyaena has returned.'

He led Amerotke across the gardens and paradises. Under a cedar tree lay blood-soaked bundles, corpses, sheets covering them. Amerotke flinched when he saw a severed hand lying nearby. Corpses of the dogs also littered the gardens. Close up they looked just as fierce, even in death: pierced by arrows, their throats slit for good measure, pools of blood snaked out of their now silent, snarling jaws.

'May the gods bless us all,' Amerotke muttered.

Senenmut waved at the sprawling corpse of a dog.

'You'll find the like all over the temple grounds. Two of the beasts even got out into the city. The archers are still hunting them.'

'What happened?'

Amerotke paused as Mareb came hurrying over, face unshaven,

115

his body wrapped in a robe tied with a piece of cord: he was no longer the elegant herald.

'What news of the Mitanni?' Senenmut asked.

'They are sheltering in their quarters. They are insistent that they return to the Oasis of Palms and consult with King Tushratta. They claim they are not safe here.'

'The dogs didn't attack them, did they?' Amerotke asked.

'No, they were safe enough,' Mareb replied. 'But Wanef pointed out how it is their custom to rise just before dawn and make sacrifice in one of the groves.'

'But that didn't happen, did it?'

Mareb shook his head.

'The incident occurred during the third quarter of the night.' He smiled ruefully. 'But I can see their point. If they had been out, there would have been no survivors. They think the ambush was planned for them.'

'Does this mean the end of negotiations?' Amerotke asked.

Senenmut shook his head.

'No, I suspect they are as mystified as we are. We'll let them go out to the oasis. Well,' Senenmut gestured at the herald to draw closer, 'you've spoken to the Dog Master?'

'According to him everything was secure. The door to the pit was bolted and locked. One guard was left: from what I can gather he, too, was killed, his key taken and the door unlocked.'

'How would the dogs know the gate was open?' Amerotke demanded.

'Oh, it's quite simple. Apparently the guard's corpse was placed in the gateway. Moreover, a bowl of blood, taken from one of the sanctuaries, was used to soak the ground around the gate.'

'Of course,' Senenmut interrupted. 'The dogs smelt the blood and came seeking its source.'

'How many people were killed?' Amerotke asked.

'A number: two dancing girls had fallen asleep in one of the pavilions. They heard the commotion and were unfortunate enough to leave. Some guards in the outer precincts also didn't get away in time.'

Senenmut led them back to the bundle of corpses and quickly pulled back a sheet. Amerotke turned away, hand to his mouth. He could just make out Weni's features but the face and body were hideously mangled. Senenmut threw the sheet back over the body. They waited whilst Mareb retreated to be sick: the herald returned, wiping his mouth on the back of his hand.

'Let's examine the dog pit.'

They found the gate locked and heavily guarded. The captain of the Cobra squadron had his men fanned out around it, arrows notched to their bows. A crestfallen Dog Master sat beneath the holm oak. He got up and came sheepishly forward.

'How many dogs were killed?' Senenmut demanded.

'They were a pack of thirty-four with some cubs. Sixteen have been killed; two were injured and I have cut their throats.'

'They are quiet now,' Amerotke declared.

'I put a potion in their drinking-water.' The Dog Master shrugged. 'They have hunted and they have eaten; they will sleep for the rest of the day. My lord Senenmut, the temple will demand compensation.'

'How did it happen?' Amerotke asked.

'From the little I know,' the Dog Master rubbed red-rimmed eyes, 'someone came down and killed the guard: there's not much left of him either.'

'Was he vigilant? Could he have made a mistake?'

'No, he was a good man, a very good soldier,' the Dog Master replied. 'I can't understand it: there are no arrow wounds in what's left of his body and it would take a good archer to shoot through the night. Whilst, at close quarters . . .' His voice trailed off.

'He could have held his own?' Amerotke finished the sentence.

'Yes, he wasn't some sleepy-eyed recruit. He was well paid for his task.'

'Continue,' Senenmut demanded.

'The assassin then took the key from the guard's belt.' He pointed to the gate. 'He unlocked it and dragged the guard inside.' The Dog Master indicated the russet stains on the pebble-hard ground. 'He then took a wineskin or jug full of blood, and left a trail from the gate to this holm oak.'

'Wouldn't that be highly dangerous for the assassin?'

'No, my lord Amerotke, it would take some time for the dogs to be roused by the smell of blood. They would be curious, cautious. Have you ever seen a pack preparing for the hunt? They go through a dance, a ritual. However, once the leader gave the signal, there was no stopping them. They poured out through the temple grounds. The screams and their barking roused me and others but there was little we could do. An urgent message was dispatched to the nearest garrison commander. The archers came with infantry holding torches; those dogs are only frightened of fire. The rest you know.'

'I can understand,' Amerotke turned to Mareb, 'how the two hesets and the guards were caught out in the open, but what was Weni doing wandering the grounds in the early hours of the morning?'

'I asked the porter,' the herald replied. 'Weni apparently entertained himself last night. Perhaps he drank too much and went for a walk to clear his mind?'

'Did you hear him go?'

'I think I did,' Mareb retorted. 'I was lying on my bed half asleep. The door opened as if Weni was checking on me, then he left.'

'Why should he do that?' Amerotke demanded.

Mareb shook his head. Amerotke thanked both of them; he and Senenmut walked away. The sun was now strengthening. The temple grounds were busy with servants removing the corpses, clearing up the mess. The daily ritual had been disturbed: no singing from the mysterious portals or odour of sacrifice on the morning breeze. Amerotke and Senenmut entered by a side door and sat in a cool corridor.

'Everyone is going to be furious.' Senenmut groaned. 'The Divine Hatusu, Wanef, Tushratta, the temple high priests. The Divine One will demand an explanation.'

'Divine Pharaoh will have to exercise patience, my lord Senenmut.'

'You have made no progress in these matters?'

'None whatsoever. Except to confirm that the priest Khety, the assistant Ita and Tetiky, captain of the guard, are suspects in the theft of the Glory of Anubis. But let's leave that for a while. Why were the dogs released?'

'To cause confusion? To frighten the Mitanni?'

'True,' Amerotke replied. 'But why was Weni down in the gardens? Do you know?'

Amerotke stared across at a red and green painting of Pharaoh in his chariot.

'I suspect Weni was invited down to the garden to meet his killer.'

'Why?' Amerotke asked.

'I can only speculate. Weni was the Divine Hatusu's herald. Yes? Though he persuaded the Mitanni that he was really their man in peace and war: in other words a traitor. Perhaps someone discovered he was not.'

'And so they killed him,' Amerotke declared.

'They?' Senenmut asked.

'I don't know how many killers there might be,' Amerotke replied. 'Whatever, Weni was lured out into the temple grounds: the dogs were released to kill him as well as cause chaos.'

Senenmut was about to reply when the door opened. Wanef, Hunro and Mensu came in. They had taken their time: dressed in exquisite robes, their faces carefully oiled, as if they wished to demonstrate that they had not been disturbed by the previous night's happenings. Senenmut and Amerotke got to their feet.

'My lord Senenmut.' Wanef smiled with her lips but her eyes remained hard. 'I do not wish to discuss what has happened but, you will agree, this state of affairs cannot continue. We wish to return to the Oasis of Palms. We must report to King Tushratta and ask his advice.'

'Are you withdrawing from the negotiations?'

'No, my lord, I do not wish to repeat myself. We must consult, whilst King Tushratta will demand proof of Egypt's continuing good will in this matter.' Her eyes moved to Amerotke.

'And to show our good faith, as well as to guarantee that we tell the truth,' Senenmut touched Amerotke's arm lightly, 'my lord Amerotke and the herald Mareb will go with you.'

Wanef gave the slightest of bows.

119

'Agreed. Do give the Divine Hatusu our deepest condolences on the death of her herald Weni. We mourn the death of a man who shared our blood.' She smiled thinly. 'He was such a busy little man!'

'What are you implying?' Senenmut asked.

'We wonder why a herald,' Mensu spoke up, 'should be wandering the gardens of Anubis in the dead of night.'

Senenmut shrugged.

'An unfortunate accident,' he murmured. 'The dog pit will be closely guarded: it shall not happen again.'

Wanef and the Mitanni left. Amerotke leaned against a pillar.

'I am a judge in the Hall of Two Truths, not an envoy from the House of Peace.'

'You must go to the Oasis of Palms,' Senenmut demanded. 'We need to send a person we trust and someone whom Tushratta knows we trust. You have a quick eye and a sharp mind. Perhaps you can discover something. You will go?'

Amerotke sighed and agreed.

'The Mitanni are nervous,' Senenmut explained. 'They do not want our chariot squadrons near them. They will regard you as a sacred envoy; you will be safe.'

'Weni was half Mitanni?' Amerotke asked.

'Yes, I think so, on his mother's side.'

'He had a chamber here in the temple?'

'Oh yes, and a house in the city.'

'In which case I shall not waste your time any longer.' Amerotke bowed and left.

Shufoy, Prenhoe and Asural were waiting in the shadow of one of the pylons near the main entrance to the temple. He collected them and, taking directions from a servant, they made their way across the gardens to the small mansion where Weni had an upstairs chamber. The door was unlocked. Amerotke went inside. Shufoy opened a window and they began their search.

'What are we looking for, Master?'

'The truth, whatever that is.'

He paused at a knock on the door. Senenmut came in.

'My lord,' Amerotke exclaimed. 'We've talked enough!'

'Yes, but I was thinking of the Glory of Anubis. Should we have the priest Khety and the others arrested?'

'On what charge?' Amerotke retorted. 'Not a shred of evidence links them to the theft. No, my lord, leave them for a while.'

Senenmut left and they continued their searches.

'Weni did drink a lot last night,' Shufoy remarked, pointing to a wine jug. He picked up an armlet. 'And he had company.'

Prenhoe was looking beneath the bed.

'Last night I dreamt that an eagle was carrying me across the Red Lands . . .'

'Thank you, Prenhoe,' Amerotke snapped. 'Never mind your eagle, is there anything there?'

Prenhoe brought out a small sycamore coffer and a mud-encrusted bundle. Amerotke took the coffer, put it on the bed and opened it. It contained seals carried by an envoy: the royal cartouche of Hatusu which would allow a herald to pass or establish his authority. Amerotke picked up another one, oval-shaped, coloured green, with an armed scorpion on one side, a snake on the other.

'This is not Egyptian, is it?'

He passed it to Asural.

'It's Mitanni,' Asural confirmed.

Amerotke emptied the rest of the contents out on to the bed and saw a dagger.

'Quick!' he urged Prenhoe. 'Seek out my lord Senenmut, anyone in authority. I want to see the dagger used to kill the priest Nemrath.'

Prenhoe hurried off. Amerotke sifted through the rest: rings, bracelets, pieces of papyri, but there was nothing remarkable about them. He picked up the dagger and studied its Canaanite blade, the dog-shaped handle. Prenhoe returned with the knife which had killed Nemrath; Amerotke realised they were a pair.

'What's the matter?'

Amerotke weighed the daggers in his hands.

'Shufoy, you know the marketplace. Daggers such as these are often sold in pairs?'

'Oh yes, you can buy a set. Sometimes three or four, even more.'

Amerotke threw the knives back on the bed.

'I'm wrong about Khety and the rest. According to the evidence, the herald Weni was involved in the theft of the Glory of Anubis. This dagger matches the one which killed Nemrath.'

He undid the mud-stained bundle Prenhoe had also drawn from beneath the bed. He took out a pair of sandals. They were the type soldiers used, thick, with an anklet guard and thongs. Amerotke was more fascinated with the mud on the sole along the side. He sniffed and put the sandals on the floor.

'Asural, have a look at those. Where do you think their wearer has been?'

The captain of the temple guard studied them carefully.

'Nile mud,' he declared.

'Very well.' Amerotke sat down. 'Shufoy, go into the marketplace. Take this dagger and see if you can find the merchant selling them. Asural, Prenhoe, go to the keeper of the records. I want you to discover where Weni's house is. If necessary, take the door off its hinges, search it from cellar to roof. Now, later today, herald Mareb will escort me out to the Oasis of Palms. Shufoy, no, don't question me! You can't come! You will inform the lady Norfret where I will be and that I shall be safe. I would be grateful if you would go and return as quickly as possible.'

Once his companions had left, Amerotke breathed a sigh of relief and closed the door. His legs hurt with the tension of what had happened, a dull ache flared in his neck: he felt listless and hoped he hadn't contracted Ahmose's fever.

'Or is it my imagination?' Amerotke murmured to the empty room. Norfret was forever teasing him about the way his mind turned and twisted like a bird falling from the sky.

He should be back in his court, but cases would have to either wait or be referred to a lesser court, or another judge. Amerotke tried to ignore his own aches and pains. What have all these mysteries in common? he reflected. A missing amethyst. The death of a dancing girl. Dead fish and animals in the Temple of Anubis. The murder of Lord Snefru. The destruction of Weni the herald. The discovery of evidence which showed that Weni was, perhaps, not what he claimed, or even what he pretended to be.

If I can only find a connection, Amerotke thought. He lay down on the bed, turning on his back. He tried to make sense of all that was happening. What would he say to Tushratta? Why was Wanef insistent on returning to her king? Was it just a diplomatic gesture? Amerotke's eyes grew heavy and he drifted into a deep sleep. Asural and Prenhoe woke him, both leaning over him anxiously.

'We thought something had happened,' the captain of the temple guard declared.

Amerotke sat up, rubbing his eyes.

'How long have you been gone?'

'At least two hours, and we found what you wanted.'

Asural emptied the contents of a leather bag on the floor. Amerotke started excitedly. A black and gold Anubis mask; a leather war kilt and a small satchel, battered and used. Asural dug inside and handed over a piece of papyrus.

'Read the inscription.'

Amerotke realised the papyrus was old, rather dry, the sort used by scribes for documents. It contained strange hieroglyphics, doodles and marks. Amerotke recognised the word *Sinuhe*.

'Anything else?'

Asural pulled a face. 'Isn't that enough?'

'What would Weni need with an Anubis mask and a black leather war kilt?' Prenhoe asked. 'Wasn't a figure dressed like that seen near the ruins of Bes when Sinuhe was killed?'

'It makes sense,' Amerotke agreed. 'Weni used the mask and the kilt. He could be taken for either an Egyptian or a Mitanni. He must have invited Sinuhe out to that lonely spot and murdered him. This bag belongs to Sinuhe, but his manuscript . . .'

Asural shook his head.

'Nothing: no sign of it whatsoever. A strange one, Weni, his house contained very little.'

'He was a herald,' Amerotke replied. 'Constantly travelling.'

'We asked a neighbour.' Prenhoe spoke up. 'He says a strange-looking woman entered Weni's house yesterday morning. He couldn't give a description but he glimpsed an oil-drenched wig, a coloured shawl. The neighbour called out, "Good day". The visitor replied in a rather strange, guttural tongue, as if . . .'

'Wanef!' Amerotke exclaimed.

'Possibly; the neighbour thought Weni's visitor was foreign.'

'He was a proper chatterbox,' Asural declared. 'I asked about Weni's habits, where he spent his money and time. Apparently Weni's one and only topic of conversation was the fine tomb he'd bought for himself and his dead wife. "Always visiting it," the neighbour declared; constantly buying gifts to adorn it.'

Amerotke got to his feet. He felt more refreshed, clear-minded.

'It would seem,' he said, 'that our Weni definitely worked for himself. Hatusu's herald he may have been, but he was bribed by the Mitanni to steal the Glory of Anubis and Sinuhe's manuscript. At least the evidence points that way.'

Amerotke stood chewing his lip. He had heard of people like Weni who saw the purchase and adornment of a fine tomb as their greatest ambition in life: as well as in death, he thought wryly. The growing wealth of the merchant class, the courtiers, the career soldiers openly manifested itself in the Necropolis, where the embalmers and funeral shops, coffin-makers and casket-carpenters were doing a roaring trade. Such tombs were not only a sign of wealth and status . . . Amerotke paused in his thoughts and smiled.

'What's the matter, Master?'

'Get your cloaks.' Amerotke walked to the door. 'We are going across to the Necropolis. I know where Weni has hidden Sinuhe's manuscript.'

The Nile quayside was busy when Amerotke and his two companions climbed into the small fishing dhow which plied as a ferry up and down the Nile. The three-man crew looked their passengers up and down and chattered amongst themselves in the lingua franca of the waterfront.

'Shut up!' Asural bellowed. 'I understand exactly what you are saying. We are not as stupid as we look. We'll pay one piece of copper, and nothing more!'

The three men pulled faces and sardonically waved Amerotke

and his two companions to seats. They turned their craft, loosening the sail, heading across a narrow part of the Nile to the small landing quay on the edge of the Necropolis. The heat was now oppressive: flies and mosquitoes thronged in black clouds above the marshy river banks. Now and again flocks of birds would burst out in flashes of colour. The river itself was empty and silent, as fishermen, ferrymen, merchants and travellers sheltered from the noonday heat. The smells were as pungent as ever: salted fish, tar and sulphur and, as they passed midstream, that eerie odour of the City of the Dead, cloying spices tinged with natron salt, glue and resin.

'Going to visit your tombs?' the tiller-man asked. 'That's what I'd like, you know: a nice little tomb for myself and my wife, a place we can plan. Go out there on festivals with my relatives and show them what we've got.' He looked at Amerotke sitting on his left. 'Do you have a tomb, Master?'

'A small one,' Amerotke replied. 'For my parents and elder brother.'

Asural looked up in surprise. Amerotke very rarely referred to his elder brother: some mystery or scandal lost in the mists of time. Amerotke turned away as a sign that he did not want to continue the conversation. The question of the family tomb was a constant cause of debate between him and Norfret. Amerotke believed in the rites, the journey to the Under-world, but as he'd confessed to her, he found the religious symbolism, the absorption with caskets and coffins unsavoury. Powerful Theban nobles and merchants even arranged dinner parties and invited guests to come and inspect their latest caskets. Amerotke shook his head and cleared his mind. He stared up at the warren of streets, the shops and booths now clear of the haze as they approached the quayside. Above the Necropolis soared a reddish outcrop of rock, the Peak of the West, dedicated to the serpent goddess Meretseger, the lover of silence.

'Beware of the goddess of the Western Peak.' Asural murmured his favourite prayer. 'She strikes instantly and without warning.'

'Perhaps not today,' Amerotke quipped back.

125

The ferry now slowed down, the sail was lowered and the tiller-man expertly brought his craft along the quayside. Amerotke paid a deben of copper, thanked them and climbed ashore. They took the road which wound up into the Necropolis, pausing before the new shrine to Osiris, foremost of the Westerners, the god of the dead. They followed the ritual, muttered a short prayer then climbed deeper into the City of the Dead. Even on a sunlit day it was an eerie experience, with the close-packed dwellings of the embalmers, coffin-makers, chandlers, painters and fashioners of funeral furniture. Through open doors and windows, Amerotke glimpsed the coffins leaning against the walls: shops where customers could choose the best design. Apprentices stood in the doorways with trays of miniature mummy-cases slung round their necks. The air reeked of natron, palm wine, incense, myrrh and cassia; the embalmers used these to pack the corpses once they had been gutted and cleaned.

They left the market, following a path which wound up to the honeycomb of tombs carved out of limestone granite. They stood aside for a funeral cortège to pass. The mummy-case rested on an ox-drawn sledge; the mourners came behind, their wailing and crying almost drowning the prayer of the funeral priests. At last Amerotke reached the office of the Superintendent of Tombs, a fat, portly man who sat in the doorway fanning himself, acknowledging the salutations of passing traders.

'I need to see the tomb of the herald Weni.'

'Do you now?' the fat man purred, not even bothering to look up. 'And who may you be?'

'Amerotke, Chief Judge in the Hall of Two Truths!' Asural snarled. 'And if you do not move your fat arse, you'll be needing a tomb yourself. We are here on the Divine One's instructions.'

The superintendent moved like a lizard scuttling away from a plunging hawk. He jumped up, ran into his office, knelt on a reed carpet and made the most profound obeisance.

'My lord Amerotke,' he wheezed, his plump face wreathed in smiles, his hands going out. 'I did not know, you bear no badge of office. But of course.'

Amerotke opened the small wallet he carried and showed

Divine Pharaoh's cartouche. The superintendent almost had a fit. He crawled like a dog on all fours and kissed it, and if Amerotke hadn't stopped him, he would have done the same to the judge's sandals.

'For the love of truth,' Amerotke murmured, 'get to your feet and fetch your records.'

A short while later, the superintendent, scurrying in front, took them up the tomb path. The climb was hard in the full heat of the day and they were soon bathed in sweat. The pathways were deserted.

'It's the heat, you see,' the superintendent wheezed. 'Perhaps Your Excellency could have waited only another hour?' He smiled. 'But of course, Your Excellency cannot wait. I understand.'

Weni's tomb was built on the far side, in a rocky enclave; the huge boulder which sealed the entrance was bonded by the superintendent's mortuary seal.

'Are these tombs guarded?' Amerotke asked as the superintendent broke the seal.

The superintendent pulled out a small whistle and blew a shrill blast. Amerotke stared in surprise. Huge Nubians, armed with bows and arrows, clubs and spears, emerged from different caves above and to either side.

'No one approaches here,' the superintendent declared, 'unless they carry a pass and are recognised.'

He finished breaking the seal. Two Nubians came over and moved the rock, allowing them access into the tomb. It was like many others Amerotke had visited: a small house with adjoining chambers. One room contained mummy-cases, another ornaments, caskets, chests, coffers, pieces of furniture. There were drawings on the wall, ledges for vases; some flowers had been placed there but these had now died.

'Is there something wrong?' the superintendent asked. He took a flaming pitch torch one of the Nubians had brought in. 'Isn't Weni coming to visit the tomb himself?'

'Oh, he'll be visiting,' Amerotke replied, 'and staying for good. Weni is dead.'

'Ah well, he'd paid all his dues.'

'I am sure he had.'

Amerotke gazed round and whistled under his breath. The more he looked the more apparent it became how Weni must have been a very wealthy man. The caskets, boxes, furniture and vases were all of precious materials, most of them thickly gilded with gold or silver. Precious stones winked in the strengthening torchlight.

'It's a treasure house,' Asural whispered.

'More like a robbers' den,' Prenhoe added. 'Where would a herald find such wealth?'

Amerotke grasped the superintendent's shoulder.

'How did Weni account for this?'

'I don't know.' The superintendent's fat face creased into a smile. 'Will it stay here?'

'It's Weni's tomb,' Amerotke replied. 'He will have to answer for whatever crimes he committed in the next life, not this.'

'Your Excellency's wisdom is only matched by his generosity,' the superintendent blubbered. 'What is it you are looking for?'

'Weni came here?'

'Oh yes, this was his house of delight.'

'And he brought gifts?'

'Oh yes, look at the vases.'

'Did he ever bring anyone with him?'

The superintendent grinned slyly. 'Now and again a heset. You know how it is, Your Excellency? A jug of wine . . .'

'Did he bring anything here recently?'

The superintendent looked around, fingers to his lips.

'Sometimes he sent things with written instructions.'

'Like what? Something in the last few days?' Amerotke demanded. 'A casket, a box?'

The superintendent scuttled away and came back with a sandalwood coffer about a yard long. The lid had been sealed with the sign of the Ibis, a common practice amongst clerks and scribes. Amerotke broke this and, ignoring the superintendent's gasp of concern, opened the coffer. He took out a roll of papyrus and some other sheaves tied together by a piece of string. He looked through these carefully and smiled at the superintendent.

'You can have the coffer; I'll be keeping these.'

'But Your Excellency, this is a tomb. You know the ritual. Nothing can be removed without the owner's consent.'

'Precisely,' Amerotke snapped. 'And Weni did not own these. He stole them from the Divine Hatusu. He may even have committed murder for them. On second thoughts, I'll take the coffer as well. Lord Senenmut will be pleased. Did Weni bring these himself?'

'No, no, a messenger did, a woman.'

'Can you describe her?'

The superintendent spread his hands.

'Your Excellency, so many visitors . . . I can say no more.'

Amerotke sat down on a stool and stared at the entrance to the tomb. He recalled Belet sitting in the garden of that cookshop talking of a robbery where there would be few guards. Was he referring to the Necropolis? Was Weni's tomb the place the brigands had chosen? Was there some connection between the man who had approached Belet and this mysterious dead herald? Amerotke glanced up at the superintendent.

'Have you noticed anything suspicious?'

The man was truly cowed. It was obvious he wanted Amerotke to leave as quickly as possible.

'Great lord,' he wailed, 'I look after the dead; the living do not concern me!'

Anubis was the patron god of the
17th Nome of Upper Egypt.

CHAPTER 8

The priest Khety and the god's handmaid Ita were making love. She, washed and perfumed, had slipped into the priest's chamber. She'd quickly loosened her robe and crept on to Khety's narrow bed. The priest's joy was complete. Ita was a consummate lover. He had never experienced such pleasure as he did in these secret, furtive meetings. They turned and twisted, confined by the narrow space.

'I will do anything for you,' Khety groaned.

Ita just smiled, rubbing her hands over his body, coaxing him gently. So engrossed were they in their pleasure, they failed to hear the door open. Only the forced cough made Khety push Ita away and stare across the darkened chamber. Only one window, high in the wall, allowed in a sliver of light. This was the old part of the temple. A place of dappled shadows and dark corners. Recesses constantly cold because the sun never penetrated. Ita knelt on the bed, pulling the robe around her. Khety's hand went out to the dagger on the table. He jumped as an arrow smacked into the wall high above him. Ita quietly cursed.

'You should have locked the door!' Khety hissed.

'She was too intent on her pleasure.' The voice was low, muffled, as if the speaker, male or female, wore a sacrificial mask.

'Please don't be anxious. You are only in danger if you leave that bed.'

Khety narrowed his eyes: a sing-song voice; the speaker was deliberately changing his, or her, intonation. Sometimes it was guttural, other times the words slipped smoothly out.

133

'What is it you want?' Khety demanded.

'Well, I could say I'd like to sit and watch you consummate your pleasure. Ita, you are such a pretty little thing. Both of you are certainly bold enough not to be frightened.'

'Why should we be frightened?' Khety retorted. 'I am a priest, unmarried, and Ita is a handmaid of the god.'

'Yes,' came the dry reply. 'But you are not a god, Khety. You may think you are. Anyway, as I was saying . . .'

Khety jumped at the twang of a bowstring: another arrow smashed into the wall.

'Just a reminder,' came the soft voice. 'Aren't you frightened of Lord Amerotke, the judge with the hard face and ever-seeing eye?'

'He's a fool,' Khety grumbled. 'He can swagger around and ask his questions. Why should that concern us?'

'But it does concern you. You've just confessed as much. Where is the Glory of Anubis?'

'We did not take it.'

'Didn't you now? Amerotke thinks you did.'

'How do you know that?'

'Just a matter of logic. Nemrath was killed. You were on guard outside the chapel; its door remained locked and Nemrath had the key. Something very strange must have happened. You can appreciate that it's difficult to believe you were not involved.'

'If I was involved,' Khety replied, 'they'd put me under arrest.'

'No, no, they won't do that. You're a priest, you can't be tortured and there's not a shred of real evidence against you. You apparently did nothing wrong. Moreover, if you did steal the Glory of Anubis and tried to sell it . . .'

'I don't know what you are talking about.'

Khety peered through the darkness. He couldn't recognise that voice: low, high, guttural, smooth, ever-changing in intonation. His mysterious guest had prepared his visit carefully.

'Oh, by the way.' The voice fell to a whisper. 'You've just admitted that the pretty little Ita is also involved.'

Khety closed his eyes. He had made a mistake! Ita had remained silent throughout. If this was any other concubine, she would have exclaimed in surprise.

'Now, as I was saying, you stole the Glory of Anubis. How did you do it?'

Khety remained silent.

'Was it your idea or Weni's?'

'Weni?' Khety asked. 'Who is Weni?'

'Oh, now you *are* lying. He's the Egyptian herald working for us Mitanni.'

Khety stiffened. Why had the speaker made such an admission?

'The Mitanni want the Glory of Anubis. King Tushratta will take it back to his dark temple. He is humiliated and angry at being forced to sign a peace treaty with a Pharaoh-Queen and kiss her painted toes. Every so often, during the years ahead, Tushratta will soothe his temper. He'll calm the raging in his soul by opening that secret casket and bathing in the beauty of the Glory of Anubis. How he'll laugh, whilst Hatusu can only grind her teeth till the sun freezes over.'

Khety felt his leg biting with cramp. He couldn't help moving. Even as he did, another arrow smacked just above his head.

'I have cramp!' he moaned.

'That's not what I saw a short while ago; a stallion and his mare, yes? The Glory of Anubis. How did you steal it?'

'I cannot, I will not answer that.'

'You must be sad,' the voice purred. 'I mean, Weni's dead. Everyone knows that. They are gossiping about it in the market-place. So, don't lie to me about who was Weni and where is Weni. Weni has gone to the Far Horizon. I hope he has his answers ready for the gods. What will you do now? How much did Weni offer you?'

Ita was now coming out of her shock and moving restlessly. Her lower lip began to quiver. Khety grabbed her wrist.

'Look,' the voice continued more urgently, 'you have the sacred amethyst. What can you do? Take it down to the market-place and offer it like a hawker selling a parrot or some pet monkey? Will you take it to the Libyans or the Nubians? You must make a decision.'

'Let us say you are correct.' Khety chose his words carefully. 'Let us say, for sake of argument, that you have been sent by the lord Amerotke to trap me.'

'Pick it up and go back!' the voice ordered. A small seal was thrown into the pool of light.

'Carefully,' the voice insisted.

Khety got up, stretched his legs and picked up the scarab. It wasn't of Egyptian design. Turning it over, Khety recognised the royal seal of Tushratta.

'You could have stolen this.'

'But I didn't. Again.'

This time a clinking leather purse was thrown into the pool of light. Khety picked it up and eagerly undid the twine. He poured the contents into his hand: gleaming miniature ingots of gold, each no bigger than his fingernail. He weighed the cubes in his hand: these were the purest metal.

'There's more,' the voice called out. 'Much more than Weni offered. But not now. Now is unsafe, isn't it, Khety? When it is safe, we'll have a sign: young Ita has a necklace of cornelian with a gold scorpion head in the centre. See how much I watch you? On the day you are prepared to hand it over – and listen carefully, Khety, that day must be when the Mitanni are about to leave Thebes – Ita will appear, wearing her necklace, beside the pool outside the mansion where the Mitanni are staying. You will make sure that the Glory of Anubis is left in this chamber in a small casket. You and Ita will stay away from this chamber for all of that day. When you return, the Glory of Anubis will be gone but both of you will be wealthy beyond your dreams.'

'How do I know that?' Khety snarled.

Another purse was flung into the pool of light.

'More will be left. Think now, Khety. After I disappear, sit with your beloved, sing her a love song. Count your wealth, plan where you are going to flee. Who knows, if you take the Horus road, King Tushratta might welcome you into his kingdom. Please,' the voice urged, 'sit back on the bed.'

Khety hurried to do so. Another arrow smacked into the wall. The door opened and closed, leaving the two lovers sitting on the bed, staring into the darkness.

An hour later Mareb the herald, a slight sheen of sweat glistening on his shoulder, his mind teeming with all he had to do, came hurrying up the stairs. He paused at the top and caught his breath. He was certain that Lord Amerotke had left the temple but he had received the message: an old priest mumbling how Pharaoh's judge wished to see him urgently. Mareb had glimpsed that little mannikin, Shufoy, hurrying across the grounds to the temple. So perhaps the judge had returned? The gallery in front was deserted. The temple servants had swept and polished the wooden floorboards, rubbing in a special perfume, arranging flowers in little copper bowls. Mareb wiped the sweat from his face. He'd be glad when this was all over. Outside he heard a hymn, a mortuary priest declaiming a lament for the dead. Poor Weni, perhaps it was for him. Mareb grinned, went along the gallery and knocked on the door. No answer; again the herald knocked.

'My lord Amerotke!' he called.

He pushed the door open. The room was dark, the shutters closed. His eyes grew accustomed to the gloom. He could make out the bed, its ornate headrest and other items of furniture.

'My lord Amerotke!'

He walked into the chamber. He had gone to open the window when he heard the sound. Something was wrong. The door slammed shut behind him. A pair of powerful hands sent him spinning across the room. He crashed into the bed, knocking the wind out of him. He turned gasping. Mareb had expected this: treachery, treason and intrigue was a herald's lot. Was this a warning? He threw himself towards the dark figure. Still dazed and confused, Mareb didn't realise the man was armed: his assailant's leather war club smacked him in the face, sending arrows of shooting pain through his head. He screamed as the blood spurted out of the cut on the corner of his mouth. Mareb looked around: a dagger, a vase, anything! His shadowy assailant stood silent and menacing.

'Stay where you are, Egyptian herald,' the voice ordered.

'What is it you want?' Mareb gasped. 'Why this?'

'On your knees!' the voice ordered. 'On your knees! Your back towards me.'

Mareb obeyed but panicked. Was his throat going to be cut? 'I am . . .'

He tried to rise, only to be pushed, sent crashing into a corner of the room. Sounds clattered in the corridor outside.

'Silence!' the voice ordered.

Mareb froze. The door was opening. He recognised the small outline of Shufoy. The mannikin was abruptly seized and hurled across the room like a sack of clothes. Shufoy blundered into a piece of overturned furniture: a cry of pain followed by loud curses. The door was then flung open and the attacker disappeared.

For a while all was confusion. Shufoy moaned and groaned. Mareb's legs ached and the side of his mouth was slightly swollen. He pulled the shutters back. Shufoy stood nursing a sore arm. The mannikin gazed round at the chaos.

'It's lucky I came here,' he declared. 'You have no idea . . . ?'

'None whatsoever,' Mareb replied testily. 'I thought the lord Amerotke wanted to see me. I opened the door.' He smiled and stretched out his hand. Shufoy clasped it. 'But I do thank you for coming. Only the gods know what would have happened if you hadn't.'

'Who delivered this message about the lord Amerotke?'

'An old priest,' Mareb replied. 'And I'm sure that if I searched him out, he'd be too blind or confused to describe who it was.'

Shufoy hobbled off. The downstairs of the small mansion was empty. A servant, moony-eyed and munching on his gums as he tended a flowerpot, could only shake his head. He had seen or heard nothing amiss. Despite the heat of the day, Shufoy went and roused the house servants: water, napkins and unguents were brought. Shufoy tended to his bruises, and those of Mareb.

'For a while,' the little man declared, 'the girls won't look at you, but you'll heal soon enough.'

Mareb thanked him. Shufoy went out and brought back some dried meat, fruit and a little bread. He'd also managed to filch a small jug of wine from the kitchens, and they used this to ease the pain as well as dab at their wounds.

'I could have been a physician, you know,' Shufoy declared proudly. 'I would have specialised as a guardian of the anus.' He searched Mareb's face for any sign of mockery. 'I can recognise every potion. I know all the symptoms, from the swelling of veins . . .'

'Yes, yes,' Mareb interrupted hastily. 'But Shufoy, why did you come here?'

'Lord Amerotke has gone to the Necropolis,' Shufoy declared sonorously. 'Apparently he wishes to visit Weni the herald's tomb.'

'I didn't know he had one. What on earth does he want to do that for?' Mareb added quickly.

'Whatever.' Shufoy smiled. 'I have news for him about the knives.'

Mareb looked puzzled.

'I found the seller. An old acquaintance of mine: the Crocodile Man. So, if the lord Amerotke isn't here,' Shufoy, full of self-importance, stuck out his chest, 'then perhaps I had best take care of the matter myself.'

'The Crocodile Man?' Mareb whispered.

'No more questions. Our wounds will heal and the day draws on.'

On the way out of the temple Shufoy described the Crocodile Man.

'He was a sailor once, then a fisherman. He doesn't do much business in Thebes because some people regard the crocodile as a god. In season he goes hunting them, out in a flat-bottomed boat, a fat little pig dangling over the edge. The trick is to bring one crocodile into the shallows. Sometimes, of course, he brings in more than one.' Shufoy laughed. 'And has to flee for his life.'

They left the temple complex and made their way through the market. Their bruises and dishevelled looks attracted strange glances but Shufoy had no difficulty in getting through the crowd, laying to his left and his right with his parasol.

'Make way!' he bawled. 'Make way for the lord Amerotke's servant! Clear a path for the messenger of Divine Pharaoh's justice!'

Surprisingly the people obeyed. They were not accosted by the sellers of gazelle meat or those who traded in potions and elixirs to keep away rats and scorpions. Even the aggressive sellers of song birds proved no obstacle for little Shufoy. Mareb couldn't decide whether people gave way because of who he was, who he represented or in deference to his size and appearance. The little man, with his pugnacious, disfigured face, did look like the incarnation of the dwarf god Bes.

The great palaces and houses gave way to meaner, narrower streets and more tawdry tenements. The scents and perfumes of the marketplace were replaced by the odours of oil, fish and tar, all the spicy smells of the waterfront. The quaysides were busy: fishing craft, war galleys, merchantmen and barges full of produce. Soldiers and sailors swaggered about. The Guild of Prostitutes was busy looking for trade, its members dressed in ornately ostentatious wigs, faces gaudily painted; their coloured robes made them look like a group of squawking parakeets. Shufoy, grasping Mareb's hand, made his way round them, down a narrow lane and into a small, ill-lit beer shop. It reeked of leather and tannin because it adjoined a flesher's yard. A man in the corner rose to greet them. He was grotesquely dressed in crocodile skins; narrow-faced and mean-mouthed, his eyes ever watchful. He wore leather wrist guards and his arms and hands were streaked with old scars and cuts.

Shufoy ushered the herald to a stool. As wine and beer were served, Mareb studied the Crocodile Man whilst Shufoy, perched on his own stool, scrutinised Mareb in return. When they had first met, the herald had appeared to be a court fop, rather languid in his ways. Men who worked in the herald corps were usually of noble families, and Mareb was no different. Shufoy could see how Mareb was badly shaken by the assault but there was something else: an ill-concealed fury which the herald betrayed in the tight line of his mouth. A good fighter, Shufoy considered, who wasn't cowed by the fearsome Crocodile Man, busy with his usual trick of frightening all he met.

'I've heard of you.' Mareb put his beer jug down. 'Shufoy says you are a legend along the river. Very few men survive a crocodile attack.'

'Once you know how to deal with them,' the Crocodile Man grinned back, 'and you're careful, they pose no real danger.'

Shufoy would have disagreed. He had once been on a boat

with Amerotke which had begun to sink after being attacked by a horde of the marauding river beasts. An experience Shufoy vowed he'd never forget.

'Never mind that.' The dwarf pulled his stool closer. 'We've come to talk about Weni and knives.'

'Weni and knives?' the Crocodile Man mimicked. 'A strange one, Weni.'

He scratched the sweat on the back of his neck and waved at a prostitute who had slipped through the doorway.

'Are you wasting our time?' Mareb asked.

'No, sir, but you could be wasting mine,' the Crocodile Man retorted. 'Nothing moves along the Nile that I don't know about.'

'So, you are a boaster as well.'

Mareb pushed back his stool as a strange creature stepped out of an alcove behind the Crocodile Man.

The newcomer was tall, slender, with a strange girlish face, shaven head and goatee beard. He, too, was dressed in animal skins. He reminded Mareb of the skirmishers, mercenaries who served with the imperial army as scouts and foragers. The herald couldn't decide whether he was fearsome or funny. The man tightly grasped the handle of a dagger, pushed in its sheath, and a similar weapon also hung on a rope round his neck. Mareb decided he was fearsome, with his thin, yellowish face, womanly lips, the gaudy earring hanging from one lobe and that straggling beard.

'Who's this?' Mareb challenged.

'He has no name.' The Crocodile Man smiled. 'Except Shadow. Where I go, he goes. Pretty, isn't he, in a strange sort of way?'

He turned and gestured with his fingers. The man opened his mouth. The Crocodile Man grinned.

'Shufoy has no nose and Shadow has no tongue.' He leaned over and jabbed a finger in Mareb's face. 'You should spend more time along the waterfront. Stranger sights are to be seen there than in the land of Kush.'

Mareb just winked at the bodyguard.

'Why aren't you blunt?' Shufoy protested. 'You agreed to see me. You know about Weni and the daggers!'

141

'What I know about Weni is worth more than a cup of beer. He is dead, isn't he? We've all heard about what happened at the Temple of Anubis!'

The Crocodile Man's tongue darted in and out like a lizard's.

'I am truly thirsty, Shufoy.'

'Then drink your beer!' he snapped.

The Crocodile Man looked over his shoulder at Shadow.

'Go and amuse yourself with her.'

He gestured across at the whore who stood just within the doorway. Shadow's face broke into a smile. He gestured at the girl, who accompanied him out through the back door of the beer shop.

'Three debens of silver,' the Crocodile Man declared, 'and I'll tell you everything I know.'

'Two debens,' Shufoy replied. 'I also give you the word of Lord Amerotke, Chief Judge in the Hall of Two Truths, that you will not be arrested for complicity in any crime.'

The Crocodile Man swallowed hard, as if he hadn't thought of that.

'Agreed,' he replied throatily. 'So I won't be visited by the police? Dug out of some brothel at the dead of night?'

Shufoy sighed, opened his purse and put two small silver ingots on the table before him.

'You're safe and they are yours.'

'Right!'

The Crocodile Man went to take the pieces of silver but Shufoy smacked his hand away.

'We'll eat your meal first and then we'll pay.'

Shaking his head at such a lack of trust, the Crocodile Man picked up his sack and emptied the contents on the table. The knives clattered out. Shufoy grabbed one and studied the strangely carved bone handle shaped in the form of a jackal or dog's head.

'I bought . . .' The Crocodile Man coughed.

'You stole,' Shufoy interrupted.

'I borrowed these,' the Crocodile Man grinned, 'from a trader I met in Memphis: the work of some Caananite craftsman. I couldn't sell them there so I brought them to Thebes. I have no licence in the marketplace so I stayed beyond the walls. Weni bought some.'

'You are sure it was Weni?' Mareb interrupted.

'Oh yes, I knew Weni. He wasn't the good little boy you think he was.'

'He was a royal herald.'

'To be perfectly honest, sir,' the Crocodile Man snorted, 'I couldn't care if he was Pharaoh's son and spent his days in the House of a Million Years. No one is ever what they appear to be. Weni bought two knives. He gave me one of those.' He pointed to the silver lying on the table between them. 'And I was very happy.'

'I hope this is good,' Shufoy broke in. 'You've heard of the theft of the Glory of Anubis?'

The smile disappeared from the Crocodile Man's face.

'What are you implying?'

'A knife like this was used to kill Nemrath the guardian priest.'

The Crocodile Man put his hands over his face. When he took them away, all bravado had disappeared. He looked hungrily towards the door, then at the back entrance through which the whore's muffled squeals echoed.

'I wouldn't leave,' Shufoy declared. 'As I said, the meal has only begun.'

'I didn't know that,' the fellow stammered.

'But you've heard it's been stolen?'

'All of Thebes has. You know how priests chatter and gossip?' He snapped his fingers. 'So, that's what Weni meant?'

'Oh, I am sure he did.' Shufoy smiled. 'Keep talking. You know me and I know you. These knives were stolen: that's what you are good at, isn't it, Crocodile Man? You take stolen goods and sell them. I am sure Weni paid you for more than just the knives.'

'Yes, yes, he did. He said he had something to sell, something very precious. No,' the Crocodile Man tapped his forehead, 'he said there were two things. One he wouldn't name; the other was a book, a manuscript.'

'Sinuhe?' Mareb interrupted.

143

'Who?'

'Sinuhe the traveller.'

'Of course!' The Crocodile Man recovered his poise though he slurped quickly from the beer jug. 'He's gone into the west as well, hasn't he? One last journey? Anyway, Weni chattered on, claiming he wished to sell these goods. I asked to whom. After all, the Mitanni are in Thebes and out at the Oasis of Palms. Weni smiled and shook his head. "Who?" I demanded. "Libyans," Weni replied. "Or the Nubians." I, of course, acted coy and confused.'

'Of course,' Shufoy murmured. 'Keeping to character as always.'

The mannikin jumped as a rat scuttled across the floor. He sprang to his feet, knocking the stool over. He grasped the empty beer jug.

'What sort of place do you call this?' he bawled at the sleepy-eyed, dishevelled owner. 'Can't you keep the floor safe?'

'You're safe from the rats,' the fellow jeered. 'That's why we have the snakes.'

Shufoy glared at him and retook his seat.

'I hate rats,' he declared, 'whether they have four legs or two.'

'Weni was a rat,' the Crocodile Man agreed, 'and much more dangerous than you think. Now you know me, Shufoy. I know everyone in the city, all the Libyan and Nubian merchants who come here to collect information or to spy.'

'And the safest people for a thief like Weni to approach?'

The Crocodile Man agreed.

'They always carry gold and silver and they can call up more from their envoys in the city. Whatever they buy is loaded on barges and away it goes.' The Crocodile Man whistled between his teeth. 'But the Glory of Anubis?'

'And what did you do?' Mareb asked.

The Crocodile Man pulled a face.

'I made enquiries. I told Weni that I would see what I could do, but I don't know why he bought the knives. Was Sinuhe killed by a knife? Isn't it a small world?' The Crocodile Man chattered on. 'I steal knives, sell some to Weni and he used one to kill fat Nemrath.'

144

'But you sold them to other people?' Shufoy demanded. 'Do the names Khety and Ita mean anything to you?'

The Crocodile Man shook his head. He paused, listening to the whore's squeals of protests, or joy, from the yard outside.

'Shut up!' he bellowed. 'A man can't think!'

The noise, however, continued unabated.

'I knew Nemrath.' The Crocodile Man jabbed his thumb at the door behind him. 'And so did that whore. Nemrath was as lecherous as a goat on heat. He was well known by the ladies: not a brothel in town which he didn't grace with his presence.'

'Let's go back to Weni,' Shufoy insisted. 'So, he bought the knives and asked if you could dispose of certain property?'

'Agreed.' The Crocodile Man nodded.

'How many of these knives have you sold in Thebes?'

'About a dozen.' The Crocodile Man scooped the knives back into his leather sack.

'To anyone interesting?'

A shake of the head.

'None of the Mitanni delegation?' Shufoy demanded.

'I wouldn't know. Sometimes I'm drunk when I sell them. No one whose face is memorable, except for Weni.'

'But why would Weni do that?' Mareb murmured. 'If the thief used one of those knives to murder Nemrath and steal that amethyst, sooner or later the knife would be traced back to him.'

Shufoy lifted his beer jug and held it up to cool his flushed face.

'I hadn't thought of that,' he remarked crossly. 'But there again, it might take some time before the knife was traced.'

'Of course it would,' the Crocodile Man broke in. 'You don't think I told Weni the truth, do you? I informed him that these knives were on sale all over Thebes. Moreover, just because he bought one doesn't mean he used it.'

Shufoy bellowed across for more beer.

'And you're forgetting one very important thing,' the Crocodile Man added. 'If Weni hadn't died, I wouldn't be sitting here talking to you.'

'The lord Amerotke is not going to be pleased.' Shufoy declared mournfully. 'For if Weni bought the knife then he must have been involved in Nemrath's murder.'

Shufoy paused whilst a fresh jug of beer was brought.

'The rat sends his regards.' The beer shop owner grinned.

Shufoy made an obscene gesture at his retreating back. Shadow appeared in the doorway and went to stand behind his master. The prostitute, all dishevelled, followed sheepishly, her amulets and bracelets jangling noisily. Shufoy grasped her arm as she passed.

'Did you know Nemrath the priest from the Temple of Anubis?'

The prostitute looked pointedly at the beer. Shufoy poured her a cup. She leaned down amidst gusts of perfumed sweat.

'Little man,' she murmured, 'if you can find me a whore in Thebes who *didn't* know Nemrath, then I'll buy you a drink!' She waddled off.

'You didn't believe me.' The Crocodile Man spoke up petulantly.

'You still haven't earned your silver. We were talking about Weni.'

'So we were, and aren't you in for a surprise?' The Crocodile Man preened himself. 'You've heard of the Amemets?'

'Who hasn't?' the dwarf answered. 'They were a Guild of Assassins who followed the Divine Hatusu's army north, then disappeared.'

'How do you know that?' the Crocodile Man asked.

'Oh, get on with your story!'

'Well, as you know, my dear Shufoy, in Thebes you can buy anything: a knife, an amethyst, a dagger. Well, most things,' he added hastily, seeing the warning look in Shufoy's eyes. 'The lord Amerotke's honesty is well known. You can also hire assassins, not just men from the guild or some cutthroat from the quayside, but people . . . how can I put it . . . who carry out a certain task for you. Weni was one of those.'

'He was a herald!' Mareb exclaimed.

'I have answered that,' the Crocodile Man retorted. 'Our very busy Weni carried out a number of murders. Do you know he was married to a Mitanni woman? According to rumour she died of an accident.'

'You're not saying Weni killed her?'

'Oh yes. Weni took her for a boating trip along the Nile. They drank some wine, she went swimming and promptly disappeared. Her corpse was discovered some time later bearing no mark of violence. Weni thought he was safe. However, the very evening he chose for his little boating trip was when I was doing business on the Nile. I'd pulled my craft into the reeds. I saw what really happened. She was asleep and he smothered her with a cushion then tipped her corpse overboard: that's how Weni and I got to know each other.'

'You mean blackmail?' Shufoy interrupted.

'More a business agreement. I pointed out how skilful he was. Weni accepted my proposition. I brought him names, possible victims, and he carried out the task. He liked gardening, did Weni: flowers, trees, plants and, above all, herbs. He was quite an expert on poisons. He wasn't violent.' The Crocodile Man gestured at Shufoy's beer jug. 'How do you know I haven't paid the owner to put poison in that? You wouldn't, till the belly cramps started. I'm only joking,' he smiled. 'As I said, I'd bring the name. Weni would send them a present: food, wine. It's surprising how many people wish to rid themselves of a business rival, their wife's lover or a suitor they've tired of.'

Shufoy sat in disbelief, though he accepted the Crocodile Man was telling the truth. Death took many forms in Thebes: heat stroke, a variety of diseases, accidents on the river, polluted food or drink, a snake bite. How many times had Lord Amerotke wondered, when studying the Roll of the Dead posted outside a temple, which deaths were natural: how many of the victims had been helped over the Far Horizon?

'You could stand trial for murder,' Shufoy accused.

'What murder?' the Crocodile Man replied innocently. 'What name? Where's the corpse? Where's the proof?'

'I have Mareb as a witness.'

'Who'd believe you? I'd say I was joking.'

'So, why are you telling us this?' Shufoy demanded.

147

The Crocodile Man emphasised his points on his stubby, dirty fingers.

'First, I want your word, Shufoy, that I am safe. Only the gods know, now the pool's been stirred, what dirt will rise to the top. Secondly, I want to be paid. Finally, before Asural grasps my neck, I want to be safely out of Thebes.'

'You are frightened, aren't you?' Shufoy accused.

'Yes, I'm frightened. We are not dealing with the small people along the Nile but the lords in their heavenly mansions. Weni's dead and I will be gone. I don't want to be crucified against the walls of Thebes.'

'So, you think Weni stole the Glory of Anubis?'

'Perhaps.'

'He may have also killed Sinuhe?'

'Perhaps.'

'Was Weni working for anyone?' Shufoy demanded.

The Crocodile Man scratched his cheek and looked wistfully at the door.

'I don't know. Weni was as lonely as a jackal. All he was really bothered about was that tomb in the Necropolis; called himself the Gardener, he did.' The Crocodile Man pulled a face. 'He saw himself as someone who cleaned up, weeded out, imposed order.'

'Before he died,' Shufoy insisted, 'did he tell you anything? Had his mood changed?'

The Crocodile Man picked at his jagged teeth. Outside the tavern a man began to sing a love song:

>'My love is unique, without peer,
>Beautiful above all Egypt's lovely girls.
>Sweet are her lips,
>The line of her neck.
>Her young breasts are full and firm,
>In the bouncing light.
>I will give her some figs.
>Malachite leaves.
>Barks of green jasper.
>A sea breeze from the Great Green.'

Shufoy listened intently. He'd remember those words. He glanced quickly at Mareb. The herald sat as if fascinated by the Crocodile Man. Shufoy felt a slight unease. He looked over his shoulder: the beer shop owner stood barring the door. In the sunlight outside, Shufoy glimpsed shapes; men were lurking there.

'You're safe for the time being, Shufoy.'

The Crocodile Man's eyes came up. For a moment he looked like that terrible beast of the river, with his hard, unblinking eyes.

'I hope we *are* safe,' Shufoy whispered.

He drew his small knife from its sheath and pricked the Crocodile Man's knee beneath the table.

'You are safe,' the Crocodile Man murmured. He scooped the pieces of silver towards him. 'To answer bluntly, Weni was worried, anxious, but I don't know why: that's all I can say.' He scraped back the stool and stood up.

'My master will ask for the proof.'

'Then let him find it. Do you know the old Temple of Bes where Sinuhe was murdered? Well,' the Crocodile Man leaned over the table, 'in the entrance to the side chapel lies a flagstone; move that and you'll find a corpse.'

'Whose?'

'After Weni murdered his wife, I watched him. I followed him for days. He killed someone else: his wife's lover. He invited him down to the Temple of Bes and struck him behind the head with an axe.' The Crocodile Man smiled. 'He was busy burying him when I introduced myself.' He lifted a hand. 'Now, hush, Shufoy: I will leave you to pay the bill. Wait for a hundred breaths then you are safe to go. My regards to Lord Amerotke.'

Shufoy watched him go.

'What's the matter?' Mareb asked.

'Nothing.' Shufoy shook his head. 'The Crocodile Man's a rogue, it's in his blood. I've known him for years and I've never known him to be so loquacious or helpful.'

Anubis was the patron of all embalmers.

CHAPTER 9

The buzzard swept in from the Red Lands; the sun was beginning to dip, and the heat of the day ebbed. A cool breeze ruffled the waters of the Nile and sent the thickets around the derelict Temple of Bes swaying like dancers. The bird's sharp eyes watched for movement as it searched for carrion. It swooped, wings slightly back, until it glimpsed the two men walking into the ruins. The buzzard recognised the dangers, the threat of the throwing stick, the arrow or spear. Frustrated in its search for easy pickings, the bird rose higher. It glimpsed further movement in the thicket. Another man stood there, strangely garbed in the black leather kilt of a soldier, a mask over his face. Too much movement for the buzzard, too dangerous a place for it. The bird soared up and across to the mud flats along the Nile.

Impervious to the bird or anything else, the killer in the thicket, face hidden by the jackal mask, watched Lord Amerotke and his servant Shufoy enter the main hall of the ruined temple. In one hand the killer clutched the instruments of swift and sudden death; in the other a short horn bow. The killer realised any shot would be too long, too dangerous. Amerotke and Shufoy did not present a clear target. Perhaps they might draw closer. It was time the judge's sharp eyes were closed in death. The killer stared up at the sky. So far everything had gone according to plan except for one matter. So, should this blow fall now or later? The killer moved, pushing aside the sharp thorn bush, going down on one knee, the eyes behind the mask

153

intently watching the judge and his servant as they surveyed the temple. An arrow could be loosed but would it hit the target? And if it missed? Yes, there would be other times. The killer let the thorn bush go, and leaving the ruins, ran swiftly away, keeping to the shadows.

In the temple Amerotke, oblivious of how close he'd been to an attack, studied the flagstone in the entrance to the side chapel.

'Can we move it?' Shufoy asked.

He stared round. A feeling of danger prickled the hairs on the nape of his neck. Were they alone? The thickets and coarse vegetation which choked the pathways and lanes leading to the temple lay silent. The setting sun shimmered along the Nile. In the grass, crickets whirred, a bird shrieked from the reed beds along the river bank. Shufoy didn't like this threatening, desolate place.

'We should have brought Asural,' he moaned. 'Or at least a couple of guards.'

'We are safe.' Amerotke smiled back, wiping the sweat from his face.

Shufoy and Mareb had been waiting for him on the quayside. Shufoy immediately reported what he'd learnt from the Crocodile Man.

'It fits what I learnt at the tomb,' Amerotke declared. 'Weni was a very wealthy man: claimed he was the Gardener, eh?'

'Have you heard of him?' Prenhoe had asked.

'Once or twice, in different cases,' Amerotke retorted. 'Passing references in police reports.'

He had thanked Mareb for accompanying Shufoy and told Asural and the rest where they would be.

'The Crocodile Man may have been selling a bundle of lies,' he declared. 'There's only one way to find out.'

Amerotke and Shufoy had left the thronging quayside, following the same lonely path Sinuhe must have taken the morning he was killed. Shufoy felt distinctly nervous. He didn't trust the Crocodile Man, the Shadow or, indeed, anyone else. Moreover, he wanted to return to the temple. He had a new love song for that heset. She had been so skilled, so accomplished, but

Amerotke had insisted they come here. Shufoy felt angry, nervous and envious at Mareb and the rest going back to comfort and safety whilst he trudged this desolate place.

'Why?' he demanded.

'Because we are collecting evidence.' Amerotke sighed. 'How do we know the Crocodile Man wasn't paid to tell his story?'

'But you've got the proof,' Shufoy protested. 'Weni was far too rich.'

Amerotke shook his head. 'Evidence is like beads on a string, Shufoy. You take one at a time, a little bit here, a little bit there.'

Shufoy stamped his foot.

'Well, we are here now; can't we get on with it? The lady Norfret will be waiting and didn't you say you had to leave for the Oasis of Palms?'

'They'll both have to wait.'

Amerotke grabbed Shufoy's knife. He knelt down and ran the blade along the mud around the paving stone.

'The lord Amerotke is not a labourer.'

'The lord Amerotke *is* a labourer,' the judge replied. 'I quarry for the truth. Now, Shufoy, are you only going to stand there and lecture me?'

Shufoy grabbed a pointed stick and began to dig, clearing away the packed earth. He found a stout pole cast up by the Nile. The day drew on as they fought to prise it under the flagstone. At last, they did: the stone slab worked loose and they pushed it back. One glance was enough. A skeletal hand thrust through the loose soil beneath. Amerotke cleared this away and stared down at the skeleton. He turned the skull over.

'You are polluting yourself,' Shufoy warned.

'No, I'm not.'

Amerotke tapped the jagged, cruel hole at the back of the skull. He wiped the dirt from his hands and got to his feet.

'The Crocodile Man wasn't lying. Weni killed and killed again.' He walked away and sat on a stone plinth. 'So, what do we have here, Shufoy?'

'I don't know,' Shufoy replied absent-mindedly staring down at the skeleton. 'By the way, Master, where is Sinuhe's manuscript?'

'I gave it to Asural. He will take it back to the palace. Shufoy, what is the matter?'

The dwarf was now digging. He reminded Amerotke of a puppy in the garden.

'Look at this.' Shufoy held up a thick copper bracelet.

'Well I never!'

Amerotke got up, took the bracelet and translated the hieroglyphics along the rim.

'So, the man's name was Hordeth,' Shufoy explained. 'I've heard of him.'

'So have I.' Amerotke turned the bracelet over and over again. 'He was a master herald from the House of Envoys. He disappeared about four years ago.'

Shufoy was digging away and pulled out a piece of papyrus. He blew away the dust, looked at the faded red ink and recognised the curse.

> 'May the demons act against you,
> Enduringly, lastingly for all time and eternity.
> Bad be your sight, bad be your hearing.
> May your soul be smitten.
> In the scales of Anubis,
> May your soul weigh as heavy as a rock.
> May the Devourers rend your spirit,
> May you never see the eternal light of Ra.'

He handed it to Amerotke.

'I suspect that was written by Weni, an act of vengeance . . .'

Amerotke turned at the sound of chariot wheels and the neigh of a horse. Shufoy grabbed his dagger and ran forward.

On the trackway separating the temple from the river bank stood a beautiful chariot of wickerwork and bronze. Its two horses were milk-white steeds from the royal stables. Shufoy exclaimed in surprise as Mareb dismounted and came forward.

The herald had dressed and changed; his hair was oiled, and he wore a fresh white tunic with a gold braid belt around his waist.

'You look the part.' Shufoy smiled.

Mareb stared round the temple.

'Asural told me you would be here. I bring a summons from the Divine Hatusu.'

'What's the matter?'

Amerotke came forward, still holding the bracelet and the piece of parchment.

Mareb thrust forward the royal cartouche for Amerotke to kiss.

'Your presence, my lord, is required at the House of a Million Years. The Divine One, the emanation of the . . .'

'Thank you,' Amerotke broke in. 'We are all alone, Mareb, in a derelict temple.'

Mareb noticed the paving stone pulled away, the disturbed earth.

'My lord, you should not be here. What is the matter?'

'I asked you that,' Amerotke replied.

'The Divine Hatusu requires your presence. The Mitanni envoys are about to leave for the Oasis of Palms. We should be going with them. Now it's too late.'

'We will go at daybreak,' Amerotke retorted. 'There are matters to discuss with the Divine One. I have just discovered the corpse of one of her heralds.'

'A herald?' Mareb exclaimed.

'How long have you served in the House of Envoys?' Amerotke demanded.

The herald grimaced and glanced over his shoulder at the chariot.

'Yes, you'd best hobble the horses,' Amerotke declared. 'I have something to show you.'

When the herald returned, Amerotke led him up into the side chapel. Mareb glanced down into the pit and moved disdainfully away.

'I have washed and bathed,' he explained. 'I have purified my lips and hands.'

Amerotke noticed the bruise high on the herald's face and recalled Shufoy's story of how they had both been attacked.

'You never explained why you were looking for me.'

'I don't have to.' Mareb laughed, staring down at the pit. 'It was apparently a trap. You never sent for me and the assassin was waiting.'

'You were very lucky I arrived,' Shufoy interrupted.

'I know. I'll give eternal thanks.' Mareb moved closer. 'But all that can be explained to the Divine One. You said this was a herald?'

Amerotke showed him the bracelet and the scrawled curse.

'Do you recall the name Hordeth?'

'Of course.' Mareb made the sign against ill luck, sticking his thumb between his two forefingers. 'He disappeared. Some say he may have drowned or . . .'

'Or what?' Amerotke demanded.

'He was a bachelor, a womaniser . . .'

'Did you know him well?'

Mareb shook his head.

'And how well did you know Weni?'

'He was a colleague, a companion. He was married to a Mitanni woman: totally besotted with her he was. According to the accepted story – well, at least before I met the Crocodile Man – she suffered a boating accident and drowned. Weni was never the same. I thought it was grief but it was murder. He killed her and invited Hordeth to this place, eh?'

'Correct,' Amerotke replied. 'He struck him on the back of the head and buried him beneath the flagstone. To make sure his soul would not progress through the Underworld, Weni also buried a curse with him.'

'Hordeth deserved it,' Mareb declared. 'I liked Weni. To discover his beloved wife had been unfaithful must have driven him mad. But,' he blew his cheeks out, 'I suppose Hordeth deserved a better death: no tomb, no mortuary priest.' Mareb's dark eyes creased in a smile. 'You are discovering a great deal, my lord Amerotke. Nothing is what it appears, eh?' He stared up at the sky. 'The Divine Hatusu will be impatient.'

A short discussion followed about what to do with Hordeth's

remains. Mareb agreed that it was a matter for the House of Envoys to decide. He would tell them what he knew and the remains would be taken across to the Necropolis. He helped Amerotke and Shufoy place the flagstone back.

'So, you are to accompany me to the Oasis of Palms?' Amerotke asked.

'I'd prefer not to,' Mareb replied over his shoulder as he led them towards the chariot. 'I have no love for the Mitanni. My father and brother were killed in the Divine One's great victory in the north.'

They walked out to the chariot. Shufoy gazed back. The derelict temple was bathed in shadows, no longer a shrine to Bes but the home of Seth, the red-haired killer.

Amerotke was ushered into the private bathing room of the Divine Hatusu. Outside, the sun was slipping fast into the west, bathing the luxurious marble room in red-gold rays. An exquisite place, open windows high in the walls which gleamed like ivory and were decorated with symbols and pictures of the gods. Most of them were female deities. Amerotke wryly noted how many of them looked like Divine Hatusu. Bowls of frankincense and sandalwood perfumed the air. The tiled floor gleamed in the light of the pure oil lamps in their alabaster jars. A statue of Horus, as a gold-winged falcon, stood on a plinth overlooking the indoor pool. The water was a dark blue; it rippled gently and the lotus blossoms on the surface swayed and bobbed. Hatusu, who so loved the glory, pomp and power, was seated on a quilted chair in the far corner. An oil-drenched black wig bound by a silver filet covered her head; a necklace of cornelian, carved into little flowers, hung round her throat. The linen robe she wore, tied round her waist by a golden sash, was diaphanous, billowing out around her feet, which rested on a footstool. Senenmut sat in a chair next to her, a scroll across his knee. Hatusu was studying her nails, head to one side. She looked up as the Nubian captain ushered Amerotke in, closing the door silently behind him.

'Look, Senenmut.' Her voice was hard and strident. 'Here comes our lord Amerotke, Chief Judge in the Hall of Two

Truths! He doesn't do what we ask him but wanders quayside taverns and ignores his Pharaoh's commands. He even forgets to kneel in her presence!'

Amerotke, who felt even more tired and dishevelled in such luxurious surroundings, remembered himself. He approached, knelt on a cushion dangerously near the side of the pool and pressed his forehead against the wet tiled floor. He expected a quick demand to rise but this didn't come. He sighed and kept his position.

'My heart is glad.' He intoned the official rite. 'And my soul delights in the light of your face, oh Divine One.'

He heard a sound and glimpsed Hatusu's sandalled feet: the nails were painted a dark green, small gold rings on her toes.

'I am your Pharaoh.' Hatusu's voice sounded hollow. 'Kiss my feet, Amerotke!'

He did so.

'Now, you may kneel back.'

Amerotke went back on his heels and stared up. Hatusu's face was now hidden behind a gold and silver mask: her eyes, peering through the slits, flashed angrily.

'You presume too much, my lord.'

'I presume nothing,' Amerotke retorted.

Senenmut breathed in a loud hiss. Hatusu's hand fell to her side. Amerotke wondered if she was going to slap him; instead her fingers came up and stroked his cheek. Taking the mask away, she crouched down beside him. You are truly beautiful, Amerotke thought, those lustrous eyes, light copper skin, perfectly shaped face, sensuous lower lip; her languorous perfume seemed to swim all about him. She allowed her robe to slip open. Amerotke noticed one nipple had been painted green-gold. She followed his glance and grinned.

'I inspected the palace guard this morning. I wore my crown and this robe.' The grin widened. 'The men loved it. A couple fainted! I won't do it again: I thought I'd die of heat stroke. Am I beautiful, Amerotke?'

'Yes, as the morning star, and as changeable as the moon.'

Her smile faded at the tinge of sarcasm.

'Do you lust after me, Amerotke?'

'No, my lady.'

'Why not?' The question was querulous.

'I lust after my wife, not a goddess.'

She touched him on the tip of his nose.

'Ever the clever one, Amerotke; even when you were a boy at Father's court, you always had the right answer.' She looked over her shoulder. 'He's a rare one, isn't he, Senenmut? Look at the pool, Amerotke, what do you see?'

He kept his gaze on her.

'Why, water, my lady.'

'And beneath?'

'More water.'

'Men are like that: Senenmut is. You are. But sometimes I wonder, Amerotke, all grave and solemn, so absorbed with your gorgeous wife. See.' She pointed a finger. 'I saw your eyes change. Is she all you lust after, Amerotke, the beautiful Norfret?' The tip of her tongue came out. 'And what else, Amerotke? Do you have fears?'

'Of course, my lady. I fear the dark, the unknown, failure.'

'And dogs?' she added. 'You do fear dogs?'

She got to her feet and helped him up. She kicked off her sandals, undid the bow at her throat and let the gauze robe fall about her feet. She turned, hands raised. Amerotke blushed. Senenmut was staring down at the piece of papyrus. Hatusu laughed and dived into the water. She twisted like a fish, her beautiful golden body skimming beneath the blue surface. She came up and her wig was askew. She laughed and put this in place.

'I always forget that.' She stood, treading water, arms out. 'Won't you come in, Amerotke? Try and catch me?'

'My lady.' Senenmut's voice was harsh. 'Lord Amerotke is tired and has not cleaned himself: the pool will be polluted.'

'You are just jealous.'

Hatusu grinned and swam to the side. She climbed up the steps and Senenmut hastened to put the robe around her. She went across to a small acacia-wood table laid with goblets of white wine. She returned to the chair and gestured for Amerotke to sit beside her. All flirtation and gaiety had now

161

disappeared. She sipped from her cup and leaned forward, one hand pulling the robe more tightly around her.

'The Mitanni leaders have left. You, Amerotke, will follow them. The herald Mareb will accompany you. You will give our greetings to King Tushratta. You will assure him that the deaths in the Temple of Anubis are not our doing. You will repeat our wishes for a peaceful settlement.' She paused. 'You will also carefully probe his mind, if that's possible.' She gestured at the leather satchel resting against the wall. 'Did he know anything about Sinuhe's death, the theft of his manuscript and the Glory of Anubis? Does Tushratta have a finger in all this dirt?' She waved a hand. 'I don't have to spell it out: learn what you can and return.'

'Tushratta's camp,' Senenmut spoke up, 'is at the Oasis of Palms. We have created an artificial border, a sort of no-man's-land between the oasis and our cavalry squadrons, no more than ten miles. The squadrons will take you to Makra, a lonely outcrop of rocks out in the Red Lands. After that you and Mareb will be on your own. The Mitanni will meet you and escort you into their camp.' Senenmut pursed his lips; his harsh face was lined, eyes heavy from lack of sleep. 'They will treat you honourably. Keep Mareb by your side. They don't like him, we'll come to that in a while. Stay there during the heat of the day, be careful what you eat and drink. At eventide return to Makra and the waiting squadron. They will bring you back to Thebes. Now, my lord, what have you discovered?'

'The Glory of Anubis?' Hatusu demanded.

'It remains a mystery, my lady.' Amerotke ignored her look of annoyance. 'The room was sealed and the door was locked. The pit of water was not disturbed. No sign of violence. Nemrath the guardian priest was found with a knife in his heart and the key to the door still on his belt.'

'I know all this!' Hatusu snapped. 'The assassin? The thief?'

'One, two or three people,' Amerotke replied. 'Khety, Ita and the captain of the guard.'

'I'll crucify them!'

'You can't do that, my lady,' Senenmut intervened. 'The priests of Anubis are powerful and we have no evidence. All three, however, are under strict surveillance and have been forbidden to leave the temple precincts.'

He looked expectantly at Amerotke; the judge shook his head.

'They may be guilty but I do not know how the theft, or murder, was committed. As for the other deaths . . .' Amerotke spread his hands, 'the dancing girl, Lord Snefru, Weni? The first two definitely died of some poison. How it was administered remains a mystery. On my return to the palace I reflected on Weni's death: there are many ways of killing a man. But why that?'

'Explain!' Hatusu demanded.

'Well, Weni could have been shot by an arrow, poisoned, garrotted, so why lure him out to be killed by a pack of wild dogs? A hideous death! It's as if the assassin wanted him destroyed both body and soul.'

'No corpse for the embalmers?'

'Precisely, my lord Senenmut. Whoever slew Weni had a personal grudge, a settling of scores. Who or why . . . ?'

Amerotke then described what he had learnt from the Crocodile Man. Hatusu's face went white with fury.

'I'll have *him* crucified!'

'I don't think so. He's already fled Thebes. I depend on Shufoy and Shufoy depends on the likes of the Crocodile Man for information, not only in this matter but others.'

'If I understand you correctly,' Senenmut spoke up briskly, 'Weni may have been a royal herald but he was also a killer, a professional assassin.'

'Apparently so, my lord. He killed his wife for her infidelity; and her lover, the herald Hordeth, and buried his corpse in a derelict temple. Encouraged by the Crocodile Man, Weni acquired a taste for bloodshed. He carried out murders in Thebes. He undoubtedly bought one of the knives used to slay Nemrath. So, he may also have had a hand in the theft of the Glory of Anubis. The derelict Temple of Bes was the scene of Hordeth's murder so Weni, according to custom, invited another victim, Sinuhe, there. He could have done this openly or disguised. What we do know is that someone wearing a jackal mask was seen down near the Temple of Bes. Weni killed Sinuhe, stole his manuscript and hid it in his tomb along with other treasures. Now,' Amerotke spread his hands, 'Weni may be the cause and origin of all that has happened. But why should he kill a dancing girl? The temple sheep or some of the fishes? Finally, who killed him? Who was responsible for the attack on the herald Mareb? Our only clue is that Sinuhe's neighbour mentioned a foreign woman being seen near his house.'

'The Mitanni?'

'I'd like to think so, my lady, though the evidence doesn't point that way. Weni was holding Sinuhe's manuscript but he was more interested in selling it to the Libyans. As for the sacred amethyst, only Anubis himself knows where that is now. Finally, how does Lord Snefru's death fit into all this?' Amerotke leaned back against the wall and sighed. 'My lady, Lord Senenmut, that is all I can say.'

'Well, we can add more. Show him!'

Senenmut handed across the piece of papyrus on the floor next to him. The manuscript was of good quality but the writing was scrawled, hasty hieroglyphics Amerotke couldn't understand.

'It's Mitanni script,' Senenmut explained. 'A communication between the King and his envoys. Naturally,' he added sardonically, 'the messengers carry two types of message, the public and the secret. Our House of Secrets discovered the Mitanni king was using a sand-wanderer to bring letters to Wanef and the others. We arranged a slight accident, some controversy over his right to enter the city and trade in the market. He was searched and his goods taken away: this was found hidden in a basket. Our scribes made a fair copy; the translation runs as follows.

'"Tushratta, King of the Mitanni,"' Senenmut began reading, '"to his well-beloved Wanef, half-sister and envoy to the Egyptian court. We have learnt about your stay in the Temple of Anubis. We give you fair warning that the negotiations must be completed whilst it would fill our hearts with joy if that which gleams and that which explains were delivered into our hands."'

Senenmut lifted his head.

'The Glory of Anubis and Sinuhe's manuscript?' Amerotke queried.

'It must be,' Senenmut agreed. 'So, we know Tushratta did have a hand in their theft.'

'Not necessarily,' Amerotke objected. 'What happens if the Mitanni king just learnt of their theft and, naturally, wants to get his hands on them?'

'Possible,' Senenmut conceded. 'But,' he returned to the papyrus, '"We have full confidence that you can use the Gardener."'

'Weni?' Hatusu spat the name out.

'"And deal with the jackals which snap at your heels."'

'Is that a reference to us?' Amerotke wondered.

'Strange,' he murmured. 'There's no mention of the Hyaena, the recognised name for the Mitanni spy.'

'"However, we must look to the safety of you and yours,"' Senenmut continued reading. '"If necessary return to the Oasis of Palms for fresh consultation. The peace treaty must not be threatened. Our interests and that of the Pharaoh-Queen agree on this. Be wary of the herald Mareb. He has good cause to hate us."'

'Yes, he does,' Hatusu declared. 'Mareb's father and brother were ambushed by the Mitanni. Both were killed, their corpses left out in the desert.'

'"Do not trust the Gardener,' Senenmut now returned to the papyrus, '"or the lord Senenmut. In these matters you know our mind." Well, that's the gist of it.' Senenmut put the papyrus back on the floor.

'So, it all revolves around Weni?' Amerotke mused. 'He's an Egyptian herald by day and an assassin by night. He offers to spy for Egypt but also works for the Mitanni. In truth, the evidence suggests he only worked for himself.'

'We believe,' Hatusu stamped her sandalled foot, 'that Weni was hired by the Mitanni, perhaps because of his marriage. They probably discovered the truth about him from the Crocodile Man or the Libyans, anyone prepared to sell information. The Mitanni wanted Sinuhe's manuscript because of the treasure house it contains, and the Glory of Anubis to shame us.

Weni, however, could not be trusted, so the Mitanni killed him.'

'It poses more questions than it answers.' Amerotke got to his feet. 'My lady, may I?' He pointed to the leather satchel. 'Examine Sinuhe's manuscript more closely?'

'Of course.' She smiled. 'Keep it safe. You must be gone by first light.'

Amerotke picked up the satchel. He turned to kneel but Hatusu rose and, standing on tiptoe, kissed him on each cheek.

'No need to kneel,' she whispered. 'Certainly not for Pharaoh's friend.' She pinched him playfully on the wrist.

Amerotke nodded at Senenmut and left.

Shufoy and Prenhoe, dancing from foot to foot, were waiting in the antechamber.

'A message from the lady Norfret!' the little man exclaimed. 'The key to her casket, it's . . .'

'Not now!' Amerotke snapped. He turned towards the window: darkness had fallen swiftly. 'Tomorrow's another day,' he whispered.

Grasping Sinuhe's manuscript firmly, Amerotke left the House of a Million Years and went back along the streets to the Temple of Anubis, unaware of the shadowy hooded figure following closely behind.

One of Anubis' principal titles was
'Lord of the Divine Pavilion'.

CHAPTER 10

The war chariot was of acacia, elm wood and birch. It was built for speed and attack, for smashing the lines of the enemy infantry. The chariot was reinforced with copper and electrum: it was the finest in Egypt's war squadron, with its red leather interior, bronze rail and high, six-spoked wheels protected by leather thongs. Amerotke clutched the rail. He turned to the north, caught the cool breath of Amun and murmured the dawn prayer. He glanced at the horses: two chestnut mares, the fleetest and the most beautiful from the royal stables, nicknamed 'the Pride of Hathor' and 'the Splendour of Isis'. They were yoked in an elegantly curved elmwood bar: the long reins were skilfully managed by Mareb, who snapped and pulled, guiding them expertly.

Amerotke and the herald had left the escorting squadron and sped like the wind across the dry yet magical landscape of the Red Lands east of Thebes. The sky was turning brilliant colours in the first rays of the rising sun. The light from the east rapidly changed the grey rocks, the dry rivulets and parched wadis into a landscape of various hues. Amerotke always marvelled at the beauty of dawn in the desert. The sand turned a purple shade, the rocks became rose-dappled, the harsh scrubs a sinister black. He glanced at his companion. Mareb was intent on managing the chariot, guiding the horses around rocks and across dips in the ground. Amerotke closed his eyes like he used to when, as a boy, his father would bring him out here so they could both worship the rising sun.

'I feel as if I am flying,' he murmured. 'I have become a hawk skimming over the desert.'

Mareb turned his head.

'An exhilarating feeling, my lord! Listen to the music of the charge. How it makes the blood sing!'

Amerotke opened his eyes and clutched the copper rail more tightly as Mareb urged both horses into a wild headlong gallop along the beaten trackway. An expert charioteer, the herald knew every twist and turn. Amerotke became aware of what the charioteers called the 'music', the rhythmic crash of the wheels, the swaying of the chariot in its own elegant war dance; the pounding hooves of Hathor and Isis, their heads bobbing, the black plumes fixed between their ears rising and falling as the horses revelled in their headlong charge. At last Mareb slowed down. The sun was rising, its rays so brilliant it now affected their sight.

'You wish to worship, my lord?'

Amerotke agreed. Mareb reined the horses in, talking to them softly, calling them 'beautiful girls', 'the pride of my heart'. The chariot stopped in the shadow of some rocks. Amerotke climbed down gingerly, as did Mareb. It was not unknown for riders to become dizzy, or even faint, after such an exuberant charge. Mareb quickly checked the horses, taking handfuls of feed from the small sack, wetting their nostrils and mouths from a waterskin. Amerotke checked the wheels, the lynch pins, the protective thongs, to make sure all was well. Mareb had drawn the best chariot possible from the royal stables, with its red and green ornamentation, the fighting warriors carved on the side. It also carried a great leather war sheath, stained a dark brown and stitched with gold thread, which held throwing spears, a sword, axe, bow and a quiver of finely plumed arrows. Amerotke laid his cloak on the ground. He and Mareb broke their fast with some dry meat and water. Afterwards they both knelt watching the Far Horizon and the glory of the rising sun.

'Your splendour fills the whole world.' Amerotke intoned the dawn prayer.

'You have gone down into the Underworld.
And successfully subdued all beneath your sceptre.
You have visited your mountains,
Your portals are of lapis lazuli,
Your walls of silver,
Your floor is of sycamore.
Your door is of copper,
Your throne is everlasting.
Your word goes out to the ends of the earth.
Oh, glorious Ra, all tremble before you!'

Amerotke bent, pressing his forehead against the ground; Mareb did likewise. Amerotke secretly wondered if the herald truly believed the words, or did he, like Amerotke himself have doubts? Amerotke murmured a silent prayer to the goddess Ma'at, imploring her wisdom and protection, both for him and for all he wished to pray for.

'We will be there within the hour!' Mareb exclaimed, getting to his feet.

Dressed in the dark green of a royal charioteer, the herald looked younger, face still slightly flushed after his exertion. His black hair was now held by a white braid, decorated with hieroglyphics which proclaimed him to be the mouthpiece of Pharaoh. The cord round his waist held the white staff of office decorated with a small gold eagle, wings extended.

'Do you fear treachery?' Amerotke asked.

Mareb grasped the rail of the chariot and stared out across the desert. The silence was broken by the screech of some bird. And, on the breeze, the muffled roar of a lion.

'If the truth be known, my lord, I am more concerned about this place than the Mitanni. It looks so empty but it's deceptive. You heard the lion?'

Amerotke nodded.

'Entire packs prowl here,' Mareb continued. 'The hyaenas, the jackals, the wild cats, not to mention the snakes and the scorpions. A terrible place to die, my lord. I have a nightmare,' he continued, 'of being alone in the desert at night and all around the killers gather.'

Amerotke repressed a shiver. 'And you don't like the Mitanni?'

'No, my lord, I don't, and they don't like me. My father and elder brother took part in Divine Hatusu's victory in the north. Both were killed. I couldn't even dress their corpses for burial.'

'And Weni?' Amerotke asked.

'I've told you.' Mareb got into the chariot and loosened the reins. 'A strange one.'

'How did the Mitanni regard him? Both of you served together as envoys?'

Amerotke climbed into the chariot beside the herald.

'At times Weni could be sullen, morose. He never talked about himself. Most of our conversation was about the House of Envoys: who was on the way up, who was on the way down. I knew about his Mitanni blood and that he had married a Mitanni woman so I kept my opinions to myself. Whenever we met Wanef, I always got the impression that there was something between them. The Princess is not the most beautiful of women, but,' he laughed, 'you know what I mean, my lord?'

'Do you think she controlled him?'

'In truth, all things are possible. Weni was no better than a whore. He'd go to the highest bidder: money was his god.'

'Whoever killed him must have hated him,' Amerotke declared. 'To have his body torn to pieces by wild dogs . . .'

'Perhaps the Mitanni did?'

Mareb gathered the reins, clicked his tongue and the chariot moved off slowly.

'We must be at the oasis within the hour,' Mareb declared. 'I would prefer the Mitanni to see me in my glory rather than sweaty and bedraggled.'

Amerotke clutched at the rail as Mareb urged the horses into a gallop. It had been years since he had visited the Oasis of Palms, but as they drew close, he recalled his memories of the place. The desert gave way to more scrubland: eventually the oasis, a sprawling green island in the eastern desert, came into view. Amerotke glimpsed the glitter of bronze, flashes of colour as the Mitanni dispatched war chariots to greet them. These were bigger, more cumbersome than the Egyptians':

172

four-wheeled, drawn by heavier horses. Each could carry three fighting men.

'Tushratta's showing off,' Mareb murmured.

Amerotke agreed. The Mitanni thundered towards them, the plumes of their war horses rising and falling. The soldiers within carried shields and wore cuirasses of copper, leather kilts and bronze helmets with ostentatious plumes. Mareb ignored them, keeping his horses at a gentle canter. The Mitanni war chariots circled before coming up on either side. Amerotke raised his hand in a gesture of peace. The commanding officer responded in kind, his face almost hidden by the helmet and a bushy black moustache and beard. He grinned in a flash of white teeth and shouted at Mareb to follow him. The Mitanni chariot careered in front of them, following the trackway into the oasis.

Amerotke was surprised at how busy it was. The oasis stretched for four miles on either side. The Mitanni court had taken it over with their brightly hued pavilions, tents, shops and horse lines. The air was thick with the pungent smell of wood smoke, cooking meats, perfumes and spices. The camp, however, despite its apparent chaos, was well ordered: artificial lanes and rows had been created. Its perimeter was protected by lines of soldiers and groups of war chariots. Some of these stood to arms, dressed like those Amerotke had already seen. Others were Canaanite mercenaries with their own exotic costumes, armour and headgear. A babble of voices, different nationalities; Kushites, Nubians, Libyans. Even mercenaries from the islands in the Great Green. Women clustered round campfires, naked children ran screaming and shouting, dogs barked and rushed out to meet them. Apart from a few surly glances from passing soldiers, Amerotke and Mareb's passage went unnoticed. At last they reached the centre of the oasis. The King had set his tents round the great pool, in the cool shade of sycamore and palm trees.

The royal pavilion was luxurious, coloured cloths stretched over poles. Caananite mercenaries, in white kirtles, bronze cuirasses and greaves, stood on guard with shield and lance. Amerotke and Mareb waited as the grooms unhitched the horses and led them away.

'My lord Amerotke, it is good to see you.'

Amerotke turned. Wanef, dressed in a dark green robe with a blue fringed shawl over her shoulders, stood smiling across at him. He sauntered over.

'Your journey was safe, I hope?'

Amerotke bowed.

'I hope it will be as safe when we return. My lady, why am I here?'

'Because of all that is happening! King Tushratta is very alarmed that one of his inner council has been found murdered. We need your assurances,' she chose her words carefully, 'that all is well.' She looked at Mareb, her smile fading. 'The King will see you now.'

She ushered them past the guards and into the royal tent. At first Amerotke was dazed. The interior was dark but very cool. He stood until his confusion cleared and stared round. Varicoloured cloths covered the ground. Cushions lay stacked around small tables, most of them covered with precious ornaments, statuettes, cups, jugs and bowls. Incense burners sent up plumes of perfumed smoke. Guards stood silent as statues, as did the fan-bearers with their coloured ostrich plumes which flooded the air with their heavy perfume.

The first part of the pavilion was an antechamber. Tushratta was waiting inside an inner, more opulent chamber. The King squatted on a pile of cushions, Hunro and Mensu on his left. Wanef went to sit on his right. Tushratta, dressed in a white robe with a purple sash running across his chest, raised his head. He was tall, muscular, with a harsh, cruel face fringed by oil-drenched hair which fell to his shoulders. His upper lip was shaven; his beard, carefully curled and oiled, fell to lie on his chest. He didn't look at Amerotke directly but, head down, stared from under bushy eyebrows, one finger scratching a fleshy nose. Mother-of-pearl dangled from his ear lobes, a jewelled gorget circled his throat, a prince's ransom in precious stones decorated his stubby fingers.

'I understand your tongue.'

Tushratta still didn't raise his head but gestured at them to sit on the cushions before him. Mareb and Amerotke obeyed. Servants served iced wine and sugared dates. Amerotke took the first but refused the latter. The King, however, grasped the plate and began popping them into his mouth, one after another, chewing noisily, a gesture of studied contempt. Tushratta belched and cleared his mouth.

'You have come to explain the doings in Anubis?'

'I've come to explain nothing, my lord,' Amerotke replied. 'Why should I explain what Egypt is not responsible for?'

'One of my envoys died.'

'So did one of our heralds.'

Tushratta picked at his teeth and smiled with his eyes.

'So why *are* you here, Lord Amerotke? Shouldn't you be in your court? True, we asked for your presence as a sign of reassurance, but what else have you brought?'

Amerotke, who'd been given urgent advice by Senenmut before he'd left Thebes, considered his reply.

'Egypt wants peace,' he answered, 'not war, but on the conditions of Divine Hatusu, the incarnation of the will of Ra.'

The smile faded from Tushratta's eyes.

'She has already decreed,' Amerotke continued, holding his gaze, 'what will bring a lasting peace. Egypt is not responsible for Lord Snefru's death: you asked for guarantees of that, which is why I am here.'

Amerotke ignored Hunro and Mensu's growls of protest. Wanef kept her face impassive.

'What are you implying?' Tushratta jibed. 'That Snefru's death was caused by someone else?'

'All things are possible, my lord.'

'Such as?'

'The Glory of Anubis, the death of Sinuhe, the theft of his manuscript?'

Tushratta's sallow, pitted face flushed with anger.

'We did not come to Egypt to steal.'

'So, you know nothing about these matters?'

Tushratta shook his head. Wanef coughed and cleared her throat. She picked up her cup in a clatter of bracelets. Amerotke was sure it was a sign for Tushratta to hold his peace.

'My lord Amerotke,' she murmured, 'we do know something; the death of your herald Weni . . .'

'He was a traitor,' Amerotke retorted. 'He was prepared to sell whatever he had to the highest bidder. Did that include you, my lady?'

'Weni was a spy.' Wanef smiled ruefully. 'He pretended to spy for us.' She made a mouth. 'But that's what traitors do, isn't it? I am sure somewhere in this camp my lord Senenmut has his spies. We have learnt,' she drew a breath, 'let us say from . . .'

'Your spies in Thebes?' Amerotke smiled.

'Most tactful, my lord. We have learnt that Weni killed Sinuhe. He took the manuscript and hid it in his tomb in the Necropolis. Oh yes, we know all about that. He also stole the Glory of Anubis and offered it for sale to others, but not to us.'

'How did he steal it?' Amerotke demanded. 'You have seen the Chapel of Anubis?' he added.

'According to our intelligence,' Wanef replied, 'Weni was in the chapel from the moment Nemrath entered. He killed the priest, concealed himself there, and left when the crime was discovered.'

Amerotke blinked in surprise. Mareb leaned forward as if to speak but Wanef, not even looking at him, held up her hand.

'Amerotke is Pharaoh's mouth!' she snapped. 'You are here as his guide and escort. We will have no more dealings with the heralds of Egypt.' She lowered her hand and stared at Amerotke. 'It is the wish of King Tushratta that we return to Thebes tomorrow morning to continue our discussions. We will seal the peace treaty. We will honour the marriage on two conditions: that Mareb here be removed from the Temple of Anubis, and the sarcophagus of King Tushratta's sister be taken from the Valley of the Kings and returned to us.'

Amerotke recalled Senenmut's advice.

'True, her corpse is embalmed,' he declared, impatient to return to Weni's crime, 'and it lies in the royal mausoleum. Cannot she continue to sleep in peace with Pharaoh her master?'

He paused, feeling Mareb stiffen beside him. 'And why should you object so much to Egypt's herald?'

'I think our requests are reasonable,' Tushratta responded

slowly. 'Benia was my beloved sister, a mere child when she married Pharaoh Tuthmosis.' His harsh face softened. 'When I sleep in my tomb, I wish my beloved sister to lie by me.'

Amerotke bowed. 'I will see to that personally, and our herald?'

Tushratta didn't even bother to glance at Mareb.

'Like many in Egypt, your herald lost kin at the great battle in the north. He should hide his feelings more carefully: the sly grin, the curl of the lip. We also think he's a spy as well as a herald.'

Amerotke gripped Mareb's wrist as a sign to remain silent and decided not to press the matter further. He didn't like the smirk on Wanef's face. Imperceptibly the atmosphere had changed. Hatusu held the reins of power and controlled the peace treaty: Tushratta would have to accept that, yet the Mitanni were laughing at her, Amerotke was certain of that.

'Why were we not told in Thebes,' Amerotke tried to assert himself, 'about Weni's doings?'

'We thought it safer to divulge such news here,' Wanef replied. 'It's only hearsay, and anyway, we only discovered it shortly before we left your city.'

Amerotke gazed at the insignia on the battle standard hanging behind Tushratta: a sickle moon, a burst of stars, the representation of a dog god. He was about to continue his questioning when the tent flap was pulled up. A chamberlain entered, resting on his staff of office; a curious line of servants followed bearing platters and dishes of roast quail, antelope, figs and other fruits. The air became savoury with cooking smells. Amerotke was more fascinated by the servants: their skins were black as night and they were no bigger than Shufoy. They moved with a remarkable grace; perfectly formed, they looked like children but they were men and women. They were naked except for leather decorated kilts; bangles circled their wrists, gold studs gleamed in their ears and the side of their noses. As one of the servants put a platter down, she caught Amerotke's eye and smiled dazzlingly.

'Exquisite,' Amerotke murmured.

He had heard stories of such people from the jungles far to

the south, but this was the first time he had ever encountered them.

'You like our little people, my lord Amerotke?' Tushratta demanded. 'There are twelve in all: the gift of their prince to me.'

Amerotke recognised the threat. Tushratta was reminding Egypt that he, too, had allies. Amerotke watched the line of servants leave. As courtesy dictated, he nibbled at the dishes offered. Mareb refused to touch anything but sat resolutely silent. Amerotke used the break to reflect on what Tushratta had told him about Weni. It would have been possible, when the priests were changed over, for someone to slip into the chapel and lurk in one of those recesses, kill Nemrath and escape in the subsequent confusion. Except, how did he get in so easily? Was it with the connivance of others?

'My lord Amerotke?'

He lifted his head.

'We accept Egypt's assurances that our envoys are safe,' Tushratta murmured. 'You shall leave this evening at dusk and formally advise the Divine Hatusu that the princess Wanef and my good councillors will return tomorrow morning: within five days the treaty will be signed.'

Tushratta turned to Wanef, a sign that the meeting was over. Amerotke sighed. The journey had been arduous but necessary. A Mitanni envoy had been killed. Egypt had offered its assurances of good will and these had been accepted.

Accompanied by Mareb, Amerotke got to his feet, bowed and left the pavilion. Outside, what Tushratta called his 'little people' were grouped round a chamberlain giving them honeyed dates from a dish. They turned their attention to Amerotke and Mareb, touching their arms, bracelets, the pectoral round Amerotke's neck displaying the goddess Ma'at. They chattered in high-pitched voices, the women being more friendly whilst the men stood a little way off. Amerotke noticed how some of these had little tubes pushed into the thongs round their waists, and small antelope-skin pouches about their necks. He wanted to draw them into conversation but the officious chamberlain intervened. He ushered Amerotke away to a small pavilion at the other end of the royal compound. This was well furnished with cushions and rugs: covered dishes of food and a cracked jug of chilled wine had been left on a table. The chamberlain gestured around and quickly left.

'That was insulting.' Mareb threw himself down on the cushions. 'They are barbarians.' His face was flushed with anger. 'Not even being allowed to clean ourselves before they offered food. They were mocking us.'

'Perhaps they were.' Amerotke sat opposite him. 'But let them have their hour in the sun. The Mitanni are defeated. Tushratta can swagger, boast, demand this and that, but he lost the battle and he lost the war. He has to come and accept Hatusu's terms. Oh, he may have had a hand in Sinuhe's death and the theft of the sacred amethyst. He may insist on the removal of Benia's sarcophagus, but all Hatusu is really concerned about is that Tushratta becomes a compliant king: that her troops, merchants and ships are allowed safe and free passage.'

'You could have objected,' Mareb retorted. 'I am the Divine One's herald.'

Amerotke leaned closer.

'Tell me, Mareb,' he demanded softly, 'speak the truth. Haven't you used your office to show disdain? A smirk, a narrowing of the eyes?'

Mareb bowed his head.

'It's hard,' he murmured. 'I loved my father and brother. Their killer squats feasting in a tent like the barbarian he is.' He raised his head, eyes gleaming. 'I wish the Divine One had marched on his capital, burnt it around his ears and crucified him as a warning.'

Amerotke heard a movement outside the tent and raised his hand for silence. A chamberlain lifted the tent flap and Wanef slipped in.

'Your quarters are comfortable?' she asked.

'They are but we will not be here long.'

'No, no, you won't be. Your horses have been fed, watered and gently exercised. I have asked our armourers to check your chariot to ensure all is safe.'

'They should not touch it,' Mareb interrupted.

Wanef glared at him.

'Your mission, my lord Amerotke,' she got to her feet, 'has been successful. You have smoothed matters over. I think it's best if we left it at that.'

She moved to the tent flap. The chamberlain lifted it and followed her out. Amerotke moved across to a small couch made out of cushions and sacks of flocked wool.

'We will rest, Mareb,' he declared. 'But once the sun begins to set, we will leave.' He glanced across and smiled. 'I advise you not to wander far from my side.'

Mareb just knocked a dish of food off the table and went across to his own couch. Amerotke settled himself. He murmured a prayer for Norfret and the boys as he tried to curb his own anxiety, a deep feeling of unease. Was this mission necessary? Why did the Mitanni find matters so amusing? Was Tushratta just enjoying the baiting? And why had they not asked for compensation for the death of Lord Snefru? But there again, if Egypt was not responsible for his death then why should such reparation be made? And the news about Weni's death? Had he acted alone or was there an accomplice? Amerotke, wishing Shufoy was with him, drifted into a deep sleep. When Mareb shook him awake, Amerotke realised the day had drawn on.

'The sun is slipping,' the herald said. 'I've been out, the horses are fine and the chariot is safe.'

Amerotke got up and washed his hands and face. They ate some of the food and had a sip of wine. Outside came the rattle of a chariot and the sound of horses. Mareb hurried out. Amerotke followed. The herald quickly checked the wheels, the yoke and the reins, totally ignoring the Mitanni officers who stood around.

'We will give you safe escort,' one of them declared, 'to the edge of the camp.'

Mareb ignored him. Amerotke agreed and climbed into the chariot beside the herald. The air was cooler, the sun had lost some of its brilliance, turning a blood-red as it slipped into the west and sent the shadows longer. The camp was all a-bustle, preparing for the night. Mareb snapped the reins, keeping the horses at a walk as, escorted by the Mitanni, they made their way to the edge of the camp. No words of farewell or greeting were exchanged, though Mareb turned, hawked and spat in the dust: a gesture of contempt. Flicking the reins, he urged the horses into a gallop, almost catching Amerotke by surprise.

'May the lord Amun be thanked!' Mareb shouted. 'To be free from their stench and out under the heavens!'

Amerotke agreed. It had been a long time since he had stood in a chariot racing across the evening desert, that magical time when the rocks, sand and scrub seemed to change both colour and appearance. Mareb was enjoying himself, shouting at the horses, getting rid of the fury boiling within him. They were now deep into the open desert. Amerotke glimpsed watching lions slinking behind a wall of gorse. Mareb urged the horses on, then muttered under his breath, pulling at the reins, staring along the outside of the chariot.

'What's the matter?' Amerotke asked.

'It's uneven.'

Amerotke steadied himself, holding the rail. Mareb was correct: he felt the slight judder.

'I am not sure,' Mareb reined in, 'whether it's the horses or the chariot.'

They climbed down. Mareb crouched by the right wheel, studying it carefully. The sun was now sinking beyond the horizon, a glowing ball of red fire. Amerotke shivered at the cold evening breeze. The desert was simply a place to pass through, but what happened if something went wrong? How far were they from the Egyptian chariot squadrons? He stared around and swallowed hard. On the hillock in the distance shapes were moving: the lions, their curiosity disturbed, were watching carefully. Mareb still crouched by the wheel.

'My lord, I can't see anything wrong. If you could check the horses?'

Amerotke went round, patting the horses on the withers. Mareb was now up, muttering about the other wheel. Amerotke lifted Hathor's foreleg and felt for any swelling or contusion: there was none. He moved to 'the Pride of Isis'. Again he could find nothing amiss. He was about to come round the chariot when Hathor reared in the traces, hooves lashing out. Amerotke backed away. Mareb hastened round, grasped the halter and quietened the animal.

'Possibly a snake,' he murmured. 'There's nothing wrong with the chariot.'

Mareb put away his herald's staff as if it was cumbersome and climbed in; Amerotke took his place. Mareb moved the chariot slowly off. He kept it at a walk, studying both horses carefully. Amerotke was about to declare it was nothing when Hathor reared up again, thrashing out, her hooves grazing Isis, who went down on her back legs. Something was very wrong with Hathor: the animal settled but began to tremble, moving from side to side.

'Jump!' Mareb urged and, pulling Amerotke with him, leapt from the chariot.

Hathor slumped, head going up, upper lip curling back. Mareb slipped in and cut the horse free of its traces: a simple task every charioteer was taught. Hathor fell on her side, legs thrashing. Mareb shouted at Amerotke to lead Isis away. It was a difficult feat, for the removal of the first horse had turned the chariot into a cumbersome load. By the time Amerotke had loosened and quietened Isis, Mareb had cut Hathor's throat, her blood spurting in a gushing red pool. The horse, all her splendour gone, lay eyes glazed on her left side. Mareb pointed to the distended belly.

'An accident?' Amerotke asked.

Mareb shook his head.

'Poison!' He stared past Amerotke. 'May the lord Amun help us!'

Amerotke whirled round. Isis, traces and reins dangling, was limping badly. Amerotke could see the bloody gash on her foreleg where Hathor, in her panic throes, had struck. Mareb grasped the horse, leading her up and down, talking to her softly. The magnificent animal was very badly injured, limping so badly Amerotke knew they had no choice.

'It's not just a bruise,' Mareb declared. 'Bones have been broken.'

Amerotke agreed. He turned away as Mareb cut the second

horse's throat. Amerotke looked up at the dusty dark sky and cursed. Despite the approaching night, the vultures had scented blood. Already three were circling above them. He glanced back towards the hillock: the dark shapes were now more pronounced. The entire pride had gathered. The lions, too, had noticed the horses in distress, the evening breeze wafting across the scent of blood.

'Before long,' Mareb declared, following Amerotke's gaze, 'we'll have every hunter in the desert here.'

Amerotke went and took the leather war sheath from the chariot.

'In which case,' he declared, 'let us put as much distance between us and them as possible!'

They started to walk. Amerotke glanced back. The lions, all fear of man forgotten, were bounding down the hill, sinister dark shapes, heading directly towards the widening circles of blood. Amerotke hurried after Mareb. The sun dipped quickly. Night fell like a black cloak. The cold night breeze strengthened. Amerotke tried to recall his training. The desert, a boiling cauldron during the day, would now become cold as ice.

'We can't keep walking,' he announced.

'Why not?'

'We have little food.' Amerotke gestured at the satchel Mareb carried. 'If the Mitanni poisoned our horses, I'd be careful of eating or drinking anything we took from their camp.'

'So, you agree Hathor was poisoned?' Mareb came back.

'I don't know.' Amerotke put the sheath of weapons on the ground between them. 'What accusations can we make? Hathor became troubled when she was on her way from the camp. She was highly strung. Horses become ill. By morning there will be very little evidence for anyone to examine.'

Amerotke paused. On the breeze came the muffled roar of a lion, a sinister coughing sound and, above that, the yip-yip of the great stripe-coated hyaenas, predators just as deadly, even more so, than the lions they followed.

'We can't walk on,' Amerotke continued. 'We have no food, whilst that blood will only whet the appetite for the hunt. Moreover, in the dark a man is just as vulnerable as an antelope.' He pointed to a hillock ringed with thick scrub and gorse. 'The only thing which will keep the predators away is fire. We have flint, bow strings . . . ?'

Mareb agreed and they hurried on. The darkness now enveloped them. Mareb tripped, the fall bringing him to his knees. He got up limping badly, cursing softly under his breath. Amerotke helped him up the hillock. The ground was well chosen. They pushed their way through the sharp shrubs which cut and scarred their legs, and prepared their defence against the prowlers of the night.

In early Egyptian history, the rites of
Anubis were reserved for Pharaoh alone.

CHAPTER 11

They collected kindling and dried scrubwood, and, using the flint and a bow string, managed to start a flame and build a fire. They cut more wood, using a war axe from the chariot. From the darkness of the desert echoed the cries of the night.

'Two beautiful horses,' Amerotke murmured, staring into the night.

'We had no choice, my lord.' Mareb stretched his hands out to the flames. 'Hathor was poisoned and Isis lame. Better for them to die quickly than be pulled down by the scavengers.'

'When do you think Hathor was poisoned?' Amerotke asked.

'Probably just before we left, but we have no proof. The Mitanni will dismiss it as an accident. They planned it well: a lonely chariot out in the desert.'

'But why?'

'My lord, they know you are investigating the deaths at the Temple of Anubis. You have a reputation for the ruthless pursuit of the truth.' In the firelight Mareb's face creased into a smile. 'They would also have destroyed one of Hatusu's closest advisers. They'd later explain how you left their camp alive and well and suffered some unfortunate accident.'

A lion coughed in the darkness. Amerotke got to his feet.

'And we still might.'

He glanced up at the stars which glinted like gems on a dark purple cushion: so close Amerotke felt he could pluck them out. The moon was full and strong. An icy wind ruffled his military cloak and made his sweaty skin shiver. Again the lion coughed.

Amerotke glimpsed dark shapes moving beyond the scrub and, in the fire glow, the occasional glare of amber eyes.

'Be careful, my lord,' Mareb warned.

He got up, notching an arrow to his bow. Amerotke felt uneasy.

'Give me that!'

Mareb handed it over. Amerotke ripped off a piece of his cloak, creating a makeshift bundle around the arrow head. He plunged this into the fire, waited for it to catch light and loosed the arrow into the darkness. It struck the pebbled ground some way off in a splutter of sparks and, for a while, created a small pool of light. Amerotke's unease deepened. More shapes than he thought. He recalled his training as a soldier, when he and other royal recruits were marched out by a drill-master to spend a night under the desert sky.

'Beware of the big cats and the hyaenas,' their drill-master had warned. 'Once they scent blood and their hunting instinct is aroused, they'll only be satisfied with a kill.'

Amerotke tensed. A shape was sloping through the darkness towards him. He pulled Mareb back, lit another fire arrow and loosed it. The huge lioness roared in frustration and slithered back down the narrow trackway between the gorse.

'They'll not be satisfied,' Amerotke declared. 'The two horses only whetted their appetites. They followed our trail here.'

Amerotke gazed desperately around. Mareb, his whole body covered in a sheen of sweat, grasped a spear. The herald jabbed the spear and screamed curses into the darkness. The situation was now truly desperate. All around them the night air was broken by the scream of hyaenas and the muffled roar of the lions. Amerotke hastily lit another fire. On one occasion the huge lioness, probably the leader of the pride, came creeping towards them and was only frightened away by Amerotke throwing a firebrand in its direction. A sound behind made him whirl round. In the firelight he made out the stubby jaw and long neck of a marauding hyaena. He drove the beast off. Mareb was beside himself with fear, cursing and screaming, mouthing obscenities about the Mitanni. Amerotke gazed up at the night sky. Once dawn came they might be safe, yet it would be hours before the first streaks of red lightened the sky. He was relieved at the gorse which ringed their camp site. The scrubs were harsh and grouped closely together, and these and the fire would keep the predators at bay, but for how long? Three small fires now glowed, but every time they needed fresh kindling, it meant they had to leave the circle of light: Amerotke did not know how close the marauders were. Sometimes, as the night breeze shifted, he caught a rotting stench, that strange feral smell of wild animals.

Mareb's increasing terror made him reluctant to leave the firelight, so Amerotke had to cut the kindling whilst keeping an eye on the moving shadows. On one of these occasions the lioness, accompanied by another, came crashing through the scrub. Amerotke had to shriek at Mareb to throw a firebrand and the attackers retreated.

'We must do something else,' Amerotke declared.

He glimpsed the leather satchel containing their food and a small jar of oil and snatched this up.

'We have no other choice,' he urged. 'We can't keep going out to collect kindling.'

'What then?' Mareb demanded.

At Amerotke's insistence, they fashioned proper fire arrows. Amerotke's cloak was cut into strips: these were soaked in oil and fastened to the ends of arrows. Amerotke loosed them into the dry gorse. At first he thought they had made no impact till he smelt the smoke and saw the flames coursing through the scrubland.

'We'll set the entire gorse on fire,' he declared. He grasped the herald's arm. 'It's our only chance. If we wait, the fires will go out whilst the prowlers beyond will become more bold.'

Mareb calmed down. Using both lance and arrows, they started fires in the ring of gorse around them. The season was dry and the vegetation soon caught alight. Fanned by the night breeze, the flames caught hold and roared up to the heavens. Sometimes the smoke came billowing in to sting their eyes; other times, it drifted out over the desert. The flames also illuminated the enemy beyond, and Amerotke's heart clenched with fear. It wasn't just one pride of lions: two or three had gathered, attracted by the smell of the blood. He also glimpsed the slinking outlines of the hyaenas. At first he couldn't understand such a gathering of killers.

'Of course!' he exclaimed. 'The Mitanni have been hunting, the antelope herds have been driven off. Most of the game in this area will have been trapped, hunted and killed for Tushratta's table.'

Mareb nodded in agreement. The herald had now recovered from his hysteria.

'That's why the beasts of the night are so intent.' Amerotke forced a smile. 'They must have regarded those horses as a gift from the gods.'

Amerotke sat in the centre of their camp and watched the fires burn. He was tempted to curse his own ill fortune. He calmed himself by thinking of Norfret's smiling face; Shufoy chasing his two sons; Prenhoe ever eager to tell about his dreams or Asural strutting about in his ceremonial war dress. He tried to sleep but found he couldn't. The ring of fire now sealed them in, the only irritation being the billowing smoke. Amerotke thanked Ma'at that the night was clear and for the flames which protected them. He silently vowed that, if he was safely returned to Thebes, he would make special sacrifice to the goddess. Mareb crouched beside him, teeth chattering with cold or fear, Amerotke didn't know which. They both stared towards the east, desperate to catch that first glimpse of the rising sun. The night drew on. The flames subsided, giving way to thicker, darker smoke.

'Couldn't they still charge us?' Mareb murmured.

'No animal likes fire,' Amerotke declared. 'Even the hungriest will not cross burning earth. Let's pray for dawn and that this smoke acts as a signal.'

At last it came. Amerotke rubbed his eyes and stared. Yes, the first glimpse of red-gold; the darkness was beginning to thin. Amerotke loved to kneel on the roof of his house and watch the sun rise; now he had never been so pleased to see a dawn. The sun rose quick and strong, that strange time when night and day met. The surrounding desert, the gorse, even the smoke changed in a bewildering variety of colours.

The cold disappeared, the breeze subsided. Amerotke knelt, forehead to the ground; Mareb did likewise, and they chanted a short hymn of praise and thanks. Then Amerotke got to his feet and went to the edge of the gorse. Picking his way carefully, he looked down the hill. His mouth went dry. The marauding packs had withdrawn but not disappeared. On a rocky outcrop, just before the ground dipped, he glimpsed the outline of a crouching lion.

'The hunters have not given up.'

Amerotke hid his despair. The fires still burnt but the dry gorse had been reduced to blackened ash. He leaned down and felt the ground, burning hot to the touch. He glanced over his shoulder. Mareb was looking to the west, eyes shaded.

'I think . . .' he exclaimed excitedly.

Amerotke hurried back and followed his direction. His eyesight wasn't as keen as Mareb's. The heat of the day now created a ripple effect. He was just wondering if the herald had seen a mirage when he caught the gleam of armour.

'It's a war squadron!' Mareb exclaimed. 'They saw the smoke.' He turned and grasped Amerotke by the arm. 'My lord, we are saved!'

Amerotke lounged in the cool of the evening in the gardens of the imperial palace, the Mansion of Silver, which lay on the west bank of the Nile just south of the Necropolis. The guest of the Divine Hatusu and Lord Senenmut, he sipped at his wine and gazed appreciatively around. The palace had been built by Hatusu's father, a veritable paradise with its landscapes and colonnades. The portico they were sitting in overlooked a terrace which fell away, stretching to the far walls. From where he sat, next to Hatusu, Amerotke could glimpse the doorposts of gold, mounted with copper and inlaid with costly figures of stone, which gave entrance to the various vineyards and orchards. Summer pavilions, fashioned out of papyrus and decorated with lotus blossoms, provided cool sanctuaries for Pharaoh's courtiers to drink, feast and even make love. The air was perfumed with the specially imported incense trees from Punt. The sea of greenery was occasionally

191

broken by gleaming lakes and ponds where rare fish and birds were bred; various statues peeped either above or between the trees. Antelope, oryx and ibex grazed serenely on the lawns next to exotic birds resplendent in their brilliant plumage.

'A different resting place from last night, eh, my lord?' Senenmut joked. He leaned over and refilled the judge's cup. Amerotke gazed quickly at Hatusu: this evening her mood had changed. She was at her most regal, a coloured shawl decorated with precious jewels about her shoulders. Her gown was of the finest linen with a girdle of gold; sandalled, jewelled slippers on her feet. Her hair was bound by a circlet, in the centre a spitting cobra; her face was specially painted, her fingers and wrists dripped with gold and silver.

The war squadron which had rescued him and Mareb had been dispatched by Hatusu. They had brought Amerotke here and taken Mareb across into the city. The palace servants had seen to his every need. He had been washed and bathed, his body pummelled and massaged. Fresh robes were laid out; Hatusu had sent him a small cartouche of gold studded with pearls as a personal gift. The servants had been clear about their instructions. The lord Amerotke was not to leave the Mansion of Silver but to wait until the Divine One 'manifested herself and allowed him to bathe in her smile'. She and Senenmut had been brought across by barge, accompanied into the palace by the clash of cymbals, the beat of war drums, the rattling of the sistra and hymns of praise. Hatusu had stepped down from her gold-encrusted palanquin. She had graciously thanked the chamberlain and captain of the guard. However, once the doors were closed and she, Senenmut and Amerotke were by themselves, she dropped the mask, her face contorted with fury. She had walked up and down, kicking away furniture, mouthing obscenities Amerotke had last heard in the barracks. She'd turned on Senenmut and punched him viciously in the shoulder.

'We should have sent out other chariots!' she shouted, her face only a few inches from his. 'It was a mistake.' She glared at Amerotke. 'You could have died. What use would you have been then?' She'd fought back the tears, walked over and nipped his arm, digging her nails in. 'You could have died, Amerotke, and whom would I have to tease? Who would speak the truth to me? Who would stare down at me and frown like an elder brother? Whom could I trust?'

She stamped her foot, viciously comparing Tushratta to the dung of a camel. She walked back to the door and turned, leaning against it.

'I know.' She shook her fist, making the bangles jingle. 'I'll send out war squadrons, thousands of chariots. I'll give him peace. I'll burn the Oasis of Palms. I'll make him pay, a thousand pounds of gold. Yes, I'll put that in the treaty. I'll make him come here, kiss my feet and kneel till his back breaks. I'll take that Wanef and impale her on a stake!'

Amerotke glanced at Senenmut, who, face impassive, just shook his head imperceptibly. Hatusu gave her rage full vent. The only thing Senenmut did was urge her away from the door so the servants couldn't hear. At last she calmed down and sat on the specially prepared throne, her breath coming in short gasps, spots of anger high in her cheeks.

'What can we really do?' she grated.

'What proof do we have?' Senenmut soothed.

He made Amerotke repeat the story the judge had told Hatusu's envoy. Both Pharaoh and her vizier heard him out. Hatusu sat forward, tapping her sandalled foot against the ground.

'You are right,' she confessed. 'If we accused Tushratta, what proof do we have? The horse could have died of natural causes. Something she ate, something in her nature: scorpion bite or snake venom.'

'It could have been a simple accident,' Senenmut added. 'Simple misfortune. How can we blame Tushratta? Or, there again, one of the Mitanni could have decided on an act of private revenge. Indeed, as we know, Amerotke, poisons and potions exist which can take hours, even days to work! Hathor could have been poisoned before she even left Thebes.'

'I'll never do it again,' Amerotke laughed. 'My lady, next time I go out into the desert . . .'

193

'We'll organise a royal hunt.' Hatusu smiled. 'I'll teach those lions a lesson. They, too, will feel Pharaoh's fury.'

She got to her feet, came over, put her arms round Amerotke's neck and kissed him full on the lips. She ignored his blushes.

'I know, I know.' She stepped away wagging a finger playfully. 'You'd love to see the Divine Norfret. But tomorrow, you, I and Senenmut, a select group of scribes from the House of Secrets and my bodyguard will enter the Valley of the Kings. We will visit my father's last resting place in the House of Eternal Years and remove the sarcophagus of Benia.'

Hatusu then turned playful. She clapped her hands and declared that Amerotke should enjoy an evening in stark contrast to the previous one. Servants were ordered out of the garden and she invited Amerotke into this shady portico. She listened intently to the rest of his account and was bemused by the Mitanni claim that Weni had stolen the Glory of Anubis.

'Do you think that's the truth?' she asked.

'I don't know,' Amerotke replied. 'I'll have to return to the temple.'

'But not now,' Hatusu announced. 'Tushratta wants the sarcophagus returned, then let it be so, as a token of our friendship. Our escort will leave in secret at dawn. My father's tomb is well hidden.'

Amerotke nodded. All of Thebes knew the story: how the war-like, repressive Tuthmosis I had decided on a magnificent burial place hidden in the Valley of the Kings. He had hired a master-builder, Ineni. Hundreds of prisoners of war, slaves and criminals had been marched into the valley, which had then been sealed off by crack infantry units. None of the workmen had returned. When Tuthmosis died only a group of 'secrets', mutes, scribes and priests, had escorted the corpse to the royal tomb for its journey to the Far Horizon. Master-Builder Ineni had been proud, boasting that 'Eye hadn't seen, nor ear heard, nor mind imagined' where the King could be buried.

'Why does Tushratta really want the sarcophagus?' Senenmut asked.

Hatusu replied in such a whisper, Amerotke did not hear her reply.

'My lady?'

Hatusu glanced round to make sure there was no one in earshot: the nearest guard was some distance away.

'There is a rumour in the Divine House, one I heard as a child, that my father was infatuated with Benia. In a fit of passionate love Tuthmosis strangled her after discovering her affair with a courtier. No one knew the real truth. Some people claim she was buried alive.' She paused. 'Tushratta may simply want to discover the truth. Tomorrow we shall see . . .'

Early next morning the royal party gathered at the mouth of the Valley of the Kings. They had been escorted from the Mansion of Silver by a chariot squadron, whilst archers marched by a large cart pulled by four oxen. The soldiers were now told to wait at the entrance to the valley, while the chariot carrying Senenmut, Hatusu and Amerotke led the rest of the party up the winding, narrow path which cut through the rocks into the Valley of the Kings. Hatusu was dressed for the part in a war kilt, her legs protected by bronze greaves, on her feet the marching sandals worn by infantry. A white robe covered her head and shoulders, bands of the same colour around her chest. She wore no jewellery or any ornamentation. She provoked laughter with the heavy gauntlets she had donned but she insisted Amerotke and Senenmut wear the same.

'You will see,' she warned enigmatically.

Tucked in her waistband was a copper cylinder: she grasped its top as if it was a dagger. She explained that it contained Ineni's plan describing the precise location of her father's tomb and the dangers within.

'Dangers?' Senenmut queried.

'My father was as sly as a hunting cheetah and, at times, as vicious as a cobra,' Hatusu retorted. 'He did not want his tomb to be disturbed. You will see.'

Now she clasped the chariot rail, staring up the valley. Amerotke always found this a lonely, haunting place. Cliffs rose on either side, light-coloured in the rising sun. The ground dipped and shifted; rock and scrubs stretched as far as the eye could see. The deeper they went, the more ominous the silence grew. The rising sun sent the shadows of the bushes racing across their path. Occasionally the silence was broken by the call of some bird stretching its wings in the warmth of the rising sun. Amerotke wondered if it was the shriek of a soul murdered in this desolate place. He looked behind. The secrets stayed well away from the dust thrown up by the chariot wheels. These were the mutes, the confidential servants of Pharaoh who saw and heard but could not speak. They had all signed a vow that if they betrayed what they learnt, their eyes would be gouged out and their bodies decapitated so their souls would be deprived of ever reaching the Fields of the Blessed. Some were old, some young: all had their heads shaved. They were dressed alike in white gauffered kilts, heavy-duty sandals and white shawls to protect their backs and necks from the sun. Some carried staves, others leather satchels with writing implements. The rest of the procession, about half a dozen walking at the far back, would remove the sarcophagus and bring it down to the entrance of the valley for transportation to the Oasis of Palms.

An unreal, ghostly experience, Amerotke reflected: the creak of the chariot wheels, Hatusu and Senenmut lost in their own thoughts, and these silent, trudging men. They passed the remains of the slave camps which Ineni had supervised when Tuthmosis' tomb was first built.

'Have you been here before?' Senenmut asked.

'Once,' Hatusu replied. 'My father brought me here to show me the entrance to the tomb. He thought I wished to be buried with him. But I will build my own tomb,' she added. Her hand rested on Senenmut's shoulder. 'We shall travel together in our journey to the Far Horizon.'

Senenmut gathered the reins in one hand and used the other to pat her arm: no longer Pharaoh and vizier but, in all things, man and wife.

They went deeper into the valley, following the pebble-strewn track. Amerotke studied the cliff face on either side. He could detect no sign of an entrance to some marvellous tomb. Abruptly Hatusu cried out for them to stop. She climbed down and, undoing the copper cylinder, drew out a piece of papyrus, which she studied carefully. She pointed to a small trackway no more than a goat path, which wound up behind a bastion of rocks.

'Is that it?' Amerotke exclaimed.

Hatusu, grasping the copper cylinder, strode off up the trackway, climbing expertly. Senenmut and Amerotke followed.

'I now realise why we are wearing the gauntlets!' Amerotke exclaimed.

The rocks were sharp and jagged, as if deliberately fashioned to cut and gash human flesh. They scrambled up, aware of the strengthening sun, the blast of heat from the rocks and the fine clouds of dust which rose to sting mouth and eyes. A snake, disturbed by the noise, darted out of a crevice. Amerotke froze; the snake disappeared. They reached the bastion of rock. Amerotke was surprised to see no sign of any entrance. Hatusu climbed on. Amerotke followed, the sweat now streaming down his back. He heard Senenmut exclaim and glanced up. Hatusu had disappeared, as if some giant invisible hand had plucked her away from the rock face. Senenmut and Amerotke hurried on.

'My lords!' a voice cooed.

They looked to their left. Hatusu was standing in a cleft of rock. This was cleverly concealed: even an expert mountaineer would have considered it a shadow, some trick of the light. They followed her in. The priests and scribes followed. Two had fallen and gingerly nursed bruised shins and knees. The cave entrance was cool and dark. Senenmut clicked his fingers. Pitch torches were quickly lit and a small fire started in the entrance to the cavern. Amerotke whistled with surprise. The cave was really a man-made chamber hewn out of the rock. The roof soared above them. Its walls were of dressed stone; a narrow path stretched deeper into the darkness. Hatusu grasped a staff from a scribe. Two of the torch-bearers were ordered to go before her.

'Walk slowly,' she declared. 'Do not leave me. When I tell you to, stop immediately. You understand?'

Both men nodded, their eyes fearful.

'If you obey my orders we shall all be safe.'

The procession moved off. Amerotke felt as if he was travelling through the halls of the Duat. They left the entrance cavern and moved along a narrow corridor. The walls on either side had paintings of dreadful beasts, the devourers and prowlers of the

197

dark underworld: exotic creatures with the heads of crocodiles and the bodies of hippopotamuses, baboons and monkeys with the faces of panthers and leopards. At last they reached the doorway at the far end. One of the servants hurried ahead. Hatusu screamed at him to stop but it was too late. The man was in the gallery, almost touching the door, when the ground gave way beneath him and he disappeared in a rumble of earth and rocks. Amerotke grasped the torch and edged forward. One of the scribes came up with a pole but Amerotke told him to stay away. He peered over the trap, throwing down a torch: the pit simply fell away into the blackness. Of the servant there was no sign.

'He can't have survived such a fall,' Hatusu murmured. 'There is a pit on either side of a narrow bridge to the doorway,'

Amerotke, using the staff, probed the ground carefully. Hatusu was right: a similar trap lay to the right of the door, but in the centre was hard rock. He went across: sacred seals displaying the heads of jackals had been placed round the rim of the door. Amerotke removed these and, with the help of a scribe, pushed the door: it was based on some system of poles and levers and swung smoothly back.

'Go no further!' Hatusu shouted.

A scribe brought a torch. Amerotke had expected the floor to be even, but the torchlight illuminated a narrow ledge which fell away abruptly. Any thief who survived the pit would stumble through the door and fall to his death. Amerotke glimpsed a narrow staircase and carefully went down. The others followed. They gathered at the foot of the steps, torches were brought and Amerotke gazed fearfully around. Skeletons lay heaped on either side of the pathway.

'The workmen,' Senenmut whispered. 'Those who finished the cavern must have been executed here.'

Amerotke walked through this place of the dead, watching the narrow path before him. He tried to ignore the skeletons heaped in a haphazard fashion on either side. He calculated that hundreds must have been killed here: a true place of terror.

'They must have been locked in,' he exclaimed. He paused to examine one body but could see no mark or injury. 'They were starved to death,' he declared. 'Afterwards, a path was cleared between them just before the tomb was finally sealed.'

At the end of the cavern Hatusu told them to stop. Two of the scribes went forward, knocking at the ceiling with their staffs; they fled backwards at a loud crack, followed by tumbling earth and rocks.

'Ineni was efficient,' Hatusu explained, coughing at the dust. 'But that is the last.'

They went through another door into a long gallery with beautiful decorations and paintings on either wall. They reached the royal antechamber, a stark contrast to the horrors they had passed. A treasure house, its walls were covered in eye-catching paintings depicting Tuthmosis' victories. All around were stacked exquisitely painted and bejewelled caskets, beautifully carved alabaster vases, black and gold shrines with statues of the gods, silver vases full of bouquets of dried flowers and leaves, beds and chairs with sculpted footstools, a silver and gold throne, cups and goblets shaped in the form of lotuses, overturned chariots, statues of the King in various poses and dress, couches, their corners carved in the shape of lions' heads and coated in gold and silver. Two huge statues of Tuthmosis, dressed like a soldier in full war regalia, stood on either side of the entrance to the burial chamber. Senenmut broke the seals to this and they went in. Here the walls were also lavishly decorated, depicting scenes from Pharaoh's life with a mass of hieroglyphics describing each incident. The chamber was dominated by a huge sarcophagus of gold and silver. Other funeral caskets lay on either side, along with the canopic jars and chests. If Hatusu and Senenmut had any fear of disturbing the dead, especially the Ka of Pharaoh, they hid it well. Hatusu became businesslike: a priest brought forward a bag of great keys to open the caskets and coffers.

'Disturb nothing! Touch nothing! Find the sarcophagus of Benia!'

This was soon found: a gold-inlaid casket, smaller and narrower than the huge one which dominated the chamber. Using a special T-shaped key, Hatusu undid the clasps and swung the lid back. She sighed in satisfaction: perfume billowed out from the mummy which lay beneath, swathed in its bands.

'At least it proves Benia wasn't buried alive,' she whispered.

She ordered a physician from the House of Life to carefully peel back the bandages. This took some time, the scribes moving the embalmed corpse carefully, fearful of causing any damage or injury.

'It will decay!' Senenmut exclaimed.

'Perhaps not,' Hatusu replied. 'It has been preserved well.'

They waited patiently. At last the face bands were removed: the features beneath had decayed and changed over the passage of years. Hatusu immediately ordered it to be rewrapped.

'The legends were false.'

She took a fan from the girdle around her waist and used this to cool her cheeks.

'Tushratta cannot accuse my father of any violence. So,' she ordered, 'the mummy is to be taken to the House of Life, swathed tightly in fresh bands and the sarcophagus resealed. If Tushratta wishes to disturb the dead, let's make it difficult for him.'

Amerotke relaxed and walked away. Hatusu declared they wouldn't stay long. The torch light and Hatusu's calm attitude dispelled any atmosphere of menace or violation. Throughout the examination, one of the accompanying priests had squatted and, opening the Book of the Dead, softly invoked the protection of the gods, a clear demonstration that Hatusu meant no sacrilege.

Amerotke was distracted by the paintings on the wall and went over to examine them. He exclaimed in surprise on realising that, whilst the rest of the tomb was being prepared, Ineni had used the painters to decorate the chamber with a myriad of scenes from the Pharaoh's life: his victories and royal triumphs, but also family scenes. Hatusu came across and showed him a painting of herself as a girl kneeling before her father, a hieroglyphic signifying her name carved beneath the small figure. She seemed, however, unwilling to indulge in memories or nostalgia from the past and walked away. Amerotke knew her attitude to her fearsome father: deep respect but very little else. He found a similar painting of himself as a boy. He smiled at how small the figure was: the shaven head, the sidelock, the jewelled collar and white robe of a member of the royal kindergarten. Other scenes were there: Tuthmosis decorating soldiers with badges of honour and collars of bravery. A whole series of paintings depicted Tuthmosis' generosity to scribes, teachers and physicians. When Amerotke noticed a scene showing Tuthmosis blessing the royal pages, he stopped in astonishment, biting back his exclamation of surprise. A long line of small figures, each with their names beneath: two of these were holding hands. Amerotke studied it again to make sure he had not misread it and then moved on to the wall on the far side of the tomb. This was dominated by Tuthmosis wearing the double crown of Egypt with the royal Nenes draped about his shoulders, accepting the submission of vassals and allies. Amerotke glimpsed a small group of the dwarfed Nubians, the little people he had met in Tushratta's camp. They too knelt before Pharaoh, hands extended, begging for his blessing. They were naked except for headbands of feathers and leather kilts. Amerotke studied these carefully, particularly the weapons they carried. He became so engrossed he forgot where he was. Images came and went: the dancing girl dying in the pavilion; Snefru on his bed; Weni being pursued by a pack of wild dogs.

'My lord? My lord? Is there anything wrong?'

Amerotke shook free from his reverie, smiled and bowed.

'No, my lady, only the past.'

He decided to conceal, for a while, what he had just learnt about the murders in the Temple of Anubis.

Anubis: 'He-who-is-set-upon-his-mountains'.

CHAPTER 12

The group of attackers were ready. They'd gathered in a lonely palm grove some time after dark, all swathed in cloaks, turbans on their heads, faces covered by cloths. They were armed with daggers and swords; some carried bows and quivers of arrows. The large cart had been inspected, its wheels checked, the axle greased with animal fat. The two bullocks had been selected for their strength and fitness, not only for carrying away the captives but for the other crime they'd planned. Their leader gathered them together. A small fire of dried camel dung had been made but now this was doused. All warmth had gone and the men shivered in the cold night wind: their leader was anxious that nothing went wrong.

'Remember,' he whispered hoarsely, 'your masks must not slip. Some of you bear telltale mutilation marks. The two captives must not be harmed.' He smiled behind his face mask. 'At least not now.' He turned to his lieutenant. 'You stay with the cart: when we return, have everything ready!'

Once again the leader checked each man, his weapons, the tightness of sandal thongs and face masks.

'Will there be servants?' one of the group asked.

'I don't know,' the leader replied. 'If there are, they too come under the knife.' He breathed in. 'All must go according to plan,' he urged. 'If it does, this time tomorrow we will be as wealthy as princes.'

'Why all this?' Another spoke up. 'Why can't you tell us now?'

'I've told you enough!' the leader snapped. 'Follow my orders and all will be well!'

The speaker leaned forward about to protest but the leader raised his hand.

'I have said enough. I still have business to do.'

He beckoned to his lieutenant and walked to the far side of the grove. The sand-wanderer, kneeling, his back to a palm tree, got up as they approached. He was small and wizened, reeking of sweat and leather.

'You did what we asked?' the leader demanded.

'Yes, Master.'

'And you memorised the way and have the map?'

'Like the palm of my hand. The signs were easy to follow.'

He handed across the makeshift map, scrawled on a piece of papyrus.

'You are sure?' the leader insisted as he pushed the map into the wallet on his belt.

'Master, if a fly lands in the dust I can tell you where and when. All will be ready but it will be dangerous.'

'Why?' the leader asked curiously. 'The place is deserted.' He laughed. 'There are no guards.' He clapped the sand-wanderer on the shoulder. 'You'll be with us, my friend, to ensure your map is correct. You wait and see, you'll be a rich man!'

'Where shall I meet you?' the sand-wanderer demanded.

'Out in the Red Lands,' the leader replied. 'Near the Oasis of Riyah. You know where that is? You'll be paid, like the rest, after it is finished.'

The sand-wanderer nodded. The leader was about to turn away.

'And if you do not come,' the sand-wanderer whispered, 'I can go myself or, better still, seek audience with the priests.'

The leader paused, closed his eyes and turned back.

'What did you say?'

'I was only joking,' the sand-wanderer stammered. 'I will be there.'

'Good!' the leader murmured. He walked away, then grasped his lieutenant by the elbow. 'When this business is done,' he whispered, 'cut that man's throat!' He pulled out the makeshift map and studied it carefully. 'It makes sense,' he breathed, studying the careful scrawl which delineated the path and the entrance to so much treasure. 'I'd kill him now, but we have to make sure.'

They rejoined the rest of the group. The leader whispered instructions. They filed out of the grove, slipping like shadows across the waste ground and up the narrow streets, hugging the blind walls, half crouching, pausing at prearranged signals. A dog barked and a scavenging cat, high on a pile of ordure, arched its back and spat. The group moved on. They reached the crossroads. One by one they slipped over. At the other side they regrouped and continued their journey. At last the leader reached the garden gate to his victim's house.

'We are at the back,' he whispered. 'A small garden!'

He cupped his hands, helped the first men over the wall then cursed as a dog came yelping up. He heard a muttered oath, the sound of a falling club. One by one the rest of the group clambered over the wall, not sparing a second glance at the dog which lay with its brains dashed out. The garden was well kept and tended. In the faint night light they made their way past the herb and garden patches, the small well and ornamental pool. The house itself was two-storeyed, a small colonnaded portico at the back. The leader tried the door but it was locked. He heard a sound, a muffled voice. He crept to the side: bolts were drawn, the door opened and an old woman, half bent, with greying hair, came out rubbing her eyes. She stood on the edge of the portico and called softly to the dog. The leader drew his dagger and stood behind her: one hand went under her chin and, in the blink of an eye, the old woman died, her throat slashed. He lowered her corpse to the ground and gestured at two of his followers.

'Clean the blood,' he urged. 'Bury her corpse and that of the dog in the garden. Quickly now!'

He and the rest stole into the house, past the earthenware stoves in the small kitchen and up the stairs. Three rooms stood on the polished passageway. One of them, its door open, was empty; another had a small grille. The leader whispered that it must be a storeroom and led his group to the main bedroom.

He lifted the wooden latch; the door swung softly back. The leader smiled. Of course, this was a locksmith's house: he would pay attention to a creaking door or a worn leather hinge. They tiptoed across, dividing to stand either side of the broad bed. The young woman was sleeping on her stomach, face turned to one side; the leader looked at the other and immediately recognised Belet.

'Even in sleep,' he whispered, 'he's ugly.'

He was about to crack a joke about how a man could snore without a nose, but remembered some of his companions were of similar ilk. The woman stirred, turning on her back. The leader admired the smooth curve of her neck, the rounded breasts and narrow waist. He pulled back the gauze veil. The woman opened her eyes. He clamped his hand across her mouth, flicking the corner of her eye with the tip of his dagger.

'Hush now, little one!' he murmured.

Belet woke up, lifting his head. He glimpsed the hand, opened his mouth to scream: this too was stifled. Both Belet and Seli were forced back on the bed.

'Now listen,' the leader urged. 'You can struggle or you can come quietly with us. If you scream or protest,' he threatened, 'or try to escape, I'll give your new bride to my men. They'll enjoy her and then cut her throat. Do you agree? You must agree before we take away our hands!'

Belet, eyes rounded in fear, nodded vigorously.

'Where is Aiya?' He sat up.

'She is your servant?'

'Yes, she sleeps downstairs. The watchdog is hers.'

'He's no more,' the leader replied. 'He has suffered an accident.'

'And Aiya?'

'The same accident happened to her.'

Seli opened her mouth to scream but the leader pricked her chin with his dagger, one hand slipping down to cup her breast. Belet went to knock his arm away but one of the group chuckled, seized him by the shoulder and dragged him back on the bed.

'She's as pretty as a plum.' The leader's eyes held Belet's. 'But enough of pleasantries. You are to come with us.'

Belet was now fully awake. 'I know you,' he said. 'I met you in the Place of Hyaenas.'

'That's right. I gave you an invitation; you refused. Now you have no choice.'

'Why?' Belet protested. 'What do you want with me, a poor locksmith?'

'Get dressed!' the leader urged. 'Come with us and you'll see.'

Both captives were dragged from the bed. There was muttered ribaldry about the young woman but the leader ordered them to be silent. The group watched as Belet and Seli hastily dressed, slipping sandals on to their feet. They were dragged down into the garden where they were given permission to relieve themselves, each guarded by two of the group. They were then hustled back into the house. The leader quickly checked the kitchen and storeroom. Bread, fruit and dried meat were hastily packed into a linen cloth. A waterskin was shared out and refilled at the well. The leader went out to inspect the handiwork of the two he had left in the garden. The blood had now been washed away; there was no sign of the old woman's corpse.

'We buried her,' one of them said. 'She can ripen, burst and fertilise the soil.'

The leader nodded and returned to the house to cover up any sign of forced entry. Once satisfied, he went back into the kitchen and studied the food piled high under linen cloths. Shaking his head, he went into Belet's workshop. He found his chest of tools, emptied these into a sack and returned to the garden.

'We have what we want,' he declared.

Belet was forced to open the garden gate. The group bundled their captives, faces shrouded, out into the alleyway. They returned to the palm grove. Belet and Seli's protests and questions were ignored as their hands were bound, mouths gagged. They were bundled into a cart and covered with a clean cloth. Staring in terror at each other, they had to endure the jolts and bumps as the cart wound its way along the rutted trackways. They stopped for a while, the leader telling them to be silent.

'We are now at the city gates,' he warned. 'We will soon be through. You must remain silent or both of you will die.'

Their nightmare journey continued, being jolted and thrown around the cart. At times Belet found it difficult to breathe; gazing across at his wife he noticed with relief that she must have fainted. As the night wore on, the cold seeped through, chilling their sweating bodies. Belet had almost forgotten about the Place of Hyaenas. He had received his pardon and married life had been so blissful. He thought of Aiya and cried for a while. He thought of that priest who'd also visited him. He shouldn't, perhaps, have agreed to his request. Was this the punishment of Anubis? Belet's sobs must have reached his captors for he received a blow on his shoulder. His wife stirred, moaning behind the gag.

At one point the cart stopped, the sheet was pulled back and the gags were removed. They were given stoups of water. Belet gazed around. The darkness was lifting. They were now out of Thebes. On either side the desert stretched under the moonlight, broken here and there by an outcrop of rocks or a clump of palms. Belet was forced to lie back and the journey continued. They had to endure another hour of torture before the cart stopped. They were dragged out, their bodies cut, their lips bruised. Seli immediately sank to her knees, her long black hair falling like a veil on either side of her head. She just crouched, whispering to herself. Belet knelt beside her, putting his arm round her shoulders, and glanced up at his captors. He tried to shade the rising sun with his hand but all he could see was a tall, thick-set man, head and face still covered, except for those mocking, cruel eyes.

Belet murmured endearments to his wife and stared around. The oasis was small but fertile: not only palm trees but shrubs and grass. The rest of the group were at the pool, slaking their thirst. Belet noticed they kept their backs towards him. He heard them speak and was sure he recognised some of their voices: people he had known in the Rhinoceri village. He could expect little mercy from them. They were envious of his good fortune. Seli lifted her head. Her face was tear-streaked, dirty and bruised, her soft shoulders and arms cut and marked. The leader crouched down.

'Look at me!' he urged.

They obeyed.

'Where are we?' Belet asked.

The leader struck him on the cheek whilst the other hand snaked out to squeeze his wife's breast. Belet protested until he felt the tip of a sword prick the back of his neck.

'You are here to do our bidding.' The eyes crinkled in amusement. 'Do you know where you are, Belet? At the Oasis of Riyah.'

Belet closed his eyes and groaned. They were out in the Red Lands, well away from the travellers' tracks or caravan routes. All around them stretched the hot, inhospitable desert. A place of scavengers, both human and animal. A well-known haunt of brigands and outlaws, as well as roaming bands of mercenaries, desert dwellers and sand-wanderers.

'Good!' the leader murmured.

He lifted his head and spoke quickly to the man behind Belet. The fellow went away and returned, throwing a sack on the ground beside the locksmith.

'Open it!' the leader urged.

Belet did so and recognised his work tools, and those of his father: keys, pincers, intricate copper T-shaped levers and clasps.

'I took these from your workshop.'

'What do you need them for?'

Again the slap. Belet cradled his bruised cheek in his hand.

'We are at Riyah,' the leader continued conversationally. 'You can't escape. If you do, we'll hunt you down and bring you back. We would track you, but before we take you . . .' he shrugged one shoulder, 'others might have you: marauding packs of hyaenas or lions!'

He gazed up through the branches of the palm tree at the blue sky.

'Not to mention the snakes and scorpions. And, of course, you'll have no water. Instead,' he continued, 'you can stay here with us. We have dates, figs, bread and cheese from your kitchen, as much water as you can drink. You two love birds can sit and coo to each other until dusk.'

Belet was about to ask a question but bit his tongue. The

leader grinned and tapped him on the scar where his nose had been.

'You are a good pupil, Belet. You are learning quickly. You don't ask me, or any of my men, questions. Just give answers. Now, as I have said, you will stay here until just before dusk. Others will join us. They'll bring dromedaries and pack animals. We'll go back in the direction of Thebes. Darkness will shroud us. You will accompany us, both of you. When we reach our destination, Belet, you will do exactly what we say.' He drew his dagger in a swift arc of light and pressed the tip against Seli's breast. 'Otherwise, we will begin to peel your sweet one here. Some of my men find her very pretty. They say she would be good to ride and they'll have their enjoyment. You will do what we ask?'

Belet closed his eyes and nodded.

'I know what you are thinking,' the leader continued. 'Where are we going and what are we going to do? Well, curiosity will keep you alert. If you co-operate,' his voice turned mellow, 'after it's finished, you'll be given your reward and be allowed to go on your way.'

Belet hid his fear. He knew this man was planning something heinous. When it was finished, he and his wife would not survive a few breaths. The man seemed to read his thoughts.

'All of life is a gamble,' he murmured. 'You had your time in the sun, Belet, now it's the turn of others. You've got no choice but to co-operate. Now,' he said, 'as I left your house I checked the kitchens. Bread had been freshly baked, food bought: were you expecting guests?' He lifted the dagger again.

'Yes,' Belet replied. 'A friend, Shufoy: he and Prenhoe . . .'

The leader's eyes were no longer smiling.

'The mannikin?' The words were spat out. 'Amerotke's body servant?'

'Yes,' Belet stammered. 'His master's away on Pharaoh's business.'

'Aye, of course he is.' The leader stared across at the pool. 'I know that little dog's turd.' Annoyed, he sprang to his feet. He walked to the edge of the oasis. 'When was he to come?' he shouted over his shoulder.

212

'Late in the afternoon.'

The leader called two of his followers across. Belet watched the leader whispering to them, emphasising his words with jabbing motions of his hands. The two men scurried off. Belet closed his eyes. He knew where they were going. They were returning to Thebes and his deserted house; they'd be waiting for Shufoy and Prenhoe to arrive. The leader swaggered back.

'Please,' Belet blurted out. 'Shufoy has done no ill.'

This time the blow to his face was harder. Seli protested; the leader grabbed her by the throat, squeezing his fingers tightly till Belet begged him to stop. The leader thrust her away. He emptied the sack on to the ground. Belet recognised how efficient this group of outlaws had been. None of the tools that lay there were for joinery or woodwork, only for locks. He turned to comfort his wife. She looked terrified, a drool of saliva trickling out of the corner of her mouth. Belet wiped this away, stroking her shoulder gently. The leader tapped him on the head.

'Soon,' he said, 'you'll be left alone and then you can comfort her. I want to talk to you about keys and locks.'

'But I haven't fashioned many,' Belet declared. 'Not since my . . .'

'Not since you were mutilated.' The twinkle returned to the leader's eyes. 'I don't want to talk about your locks but those made by your late lamented father. Now, come, I'm all ears.'

'I tell you,' Prenhoe insisted, 'the dream I had last night was truly remarkable.'

He grasped Shufoy's elbow with one hand and shooed away a scorpion man with a tray of scarab beetles around his neck who'd accosted them. Prenhoe was trying to distract the manni-kin: Shufoy had been concerned that he had not seen his master whilst hearing the most frightful rumours from a charioteer about an incident out in the Red Lands. He had, at last, been satisfied that his master had returned safely to one of the royal mansions: Amerotke had been taken deep into the House of Adoration for secret talks with the Pharaoh-Queen.

Shufoy's tummy rumbled. He was looking forward to a good

meal at Belet's house. He was also regretting sharing the invitation with Prenhoe, who was gabbling like a goose beside him. The scorpion man wouldn't be put off so easily. He came darting in. Shufoy raised his parasol. The fellow thought again and scuttled away.

'I tell you this,' Prenhoe repeated as they stopped by a meat stall: its owner had grilled fatty pieces of gazelle meat over a moveable stove. Shufoy's mouth watered. He was so hungry! The crowds thronged about him. He glimpsed two Nubian archers from the palace, bows slung over their shoulders, making their way across the market, and wondered again what his master was doing. A large, fat fly settled on one of the pieces of meat: this curbed Shufoy's appetite.

'Very well, Prenhoe, tell me what you dreamt.'

'I was making love to a beautiful girl by the riverside. What she could do with her lips, Shufoy, was remarkable! The land went abruptly dark. The sun turned black and strange red lights appeared all around me.'

'And, I suppose, the girl had fled?'

'I was by myself. Huge, fierce creatures slunk out of the darkness. They had the heads of lizards and the bodies of men. I thought they were the devourers from the Underworld. I was all alone. I saw a chariot speeding towards me. You came through the night . . .'

'On the ground or through the air?' Shufoy queried.

'Through the air. I didn't hear the wheels. The horses were a liverish grey with eyes which glowed like charcoal, whilst the breath from their nostrils smelt of incense. You swept me up and carried me away to a place of light.'

'This girl?' Shufoy asked mischievously. 'Any chance she'll come into my dream?'

Prenhoe sniffed. They turned off the main concourse, the Avenue of the Sphinxes, and made their way through the narrow side streets.

'We are here at last!'

Shufoy stopped by the doorway of a small two-storeyed house which stood by itself on the corner of a shabby marketplace. He gazed wistfully round.

'They used to sell love amulets here before misfortune befell me. I knew a girl who lived over there: slippery as a snake she was.'

Shufoy knocked on the door but there was no answer. He banged with his parasol, the sound echoing through the house.

'Are you sure they are expecting us?' Prenhoe demanded.

'Belet keeps his word. He wants to thank me for all I have done.'

'Is this an auspicious time for visiting?' Prenhoe asked. 'Is it the day when the god Thoth replaced the majesty of Atum at the Pool of Two Truths at the temple? Sometimes I get confused. I know it's not the day which marks the anniversary of Seth's attack on Horus, whilst tomorrow is when Sekhmet the Destroyer unveiled her eyes and unleashed pestilence on mankind . . .'

'Is that your birthday?' Shufoy asked innocently.

He wandered across the square and glanced at a sundial on its stone plinth.

'The time is right,' he remarked. 'Four hours before sunset: Belet said if we drank too much we could stay the night.'

'This reminds me of the Day of the Sphinx!' Prenhoe declared mournfully. 'Isn't Belet supposed to welcome us at the door with a garland of flowers for our necks and a cake of perfume for our heads?'

Shufoy wasn't listening. He scratched his straggly beard and walked down the alleyway to the garden gate. He glanced up at the small stela of copper fixed into a wall on the side: it showed Horus as a falcon, perched on a golden disc. Shufoy felt uneasy. Belet and Seli were hospitable and kind: they should be here welcoming them.

'Where did you meet Belet?' Prenhoe asked.

'When he first arrived in the village of the Rhinoceri,' Shufoy replied. 'He comes from good family, you know? However, his father developed a taste for heavy wines. A very rich man, Belet said he had nightmares, hideous dreams. He gave up shaving his head and drank from morning to night. By the time Belet was a young man, the family wealth was dissipated.'

'I had a distant kinsman like that.'

Shufoy wasn't listening. He pushed the gate open and went up the garden path.

'He's been digging in his garden,' Prenhoe called out.

Shufoy looked across. His unease deepened. He had been here before and Belet had shown him that plot, a favourite place to grow vegetables. These now lay scattered around the newly turned soil. They entered the coolness of the colonnaded portico. Shufoy pushed open the rear door.

'Belet, Seli, Aiya!'

Shufoy froze. Something was very wrong.

'Prenhoe,' he whispered. 'Sniff!'

'I can't smell anything,' the scribe replied.

'That's worrying,' Shufoy declared darkly. 'Belet said they were preparing a feast. If they've gone out, where's Aiya and her vicious little dog?'

Shufoy went into the kitchen.

'Nothing's out of place,' he murmured.

He felt the earthenware stove. The black charcoal still lay heaped and unfired. He noticed how the linen cloths had been thrown back; bread and cheese had been taken. He drew his dagger. Prenhoe, alarmed, also drew his. Shufoy climbed the stairs leading to the upper storey. He pushed open the bedroom door. He glimpsed the bed, its gauze veils thrown back, the pillowed headrest carved at each end in the shape of a roaring lion. He looked at the floor. There was dirt. Belet was a very proud man. The floor usually gleamed with polish. Shufoy's heart skipped a beat, and his mouth went dry. He took Prenhoe into the bedroom. They checked caskets and coffers.

Shufoy opened the bedroom door to leave. He was halfway out when he glimpsed a movement to his right. He brought the parasol up, hitting his assailant in the stomach even as Prenhoe screamed. Behind him Shufoy heard a clash of knives. He glanced quickly over his shoulder. Prenhoe was now struggling with a man whose head and face were masked and covered. Shufoy heard a sound. His assailant was coming in, knife snaking out. Shufoy ducked, driving his shoulder into the man's stomach. The silence in the house was shattered. Prenhoe was yelling like a warrior: educated as a scribe and a fervent believer

216

of his own dreams and anyone else's, he had also been trained as a soldier. The scribe soon realised his opponent had not. Time and again the man came in, but his use of the knife was clumsy. Shufoy, meanwhile, using his parasol as a spear, was driving his assailant towards the top of the stairs. The man found it difficult to deal with this mannikin who jabbed the parasol like one of Pharaoh's veterans would use a spear. He increased the jabbing. The man panicked, retreating in shuffling steps. He didn't realise he'd reached the top of the stairs. Shufoy lunged with his dagger. The man sprang back, missed his footing and crashed down the stairs. He hit the wall at the bottom, his head snapping to the right. Even from where he stood Shufoy heard the crack as the assailant broke his neck. He turned with a roar and raced to assist Prenhoe. The second attacker panicked. He threw the dagger at Prenhoe and, spinning on his heel, raced towards the window at the far end of the gallery. He pulled the shutters back. Prenhoe was faster. The man tried to lift his foot on to the sill. The scribe, full of the rage of battle, caught up with him.

'Don't!' Shufoy shouted. 'Take him . . .'

Too late! Prenhoe, using both hands, drove his dagger deep into the man's exposed neck. Coughing and choking, the assailant lurched back. He dragged down the face mask as if he wished to breathe but he was already coughing blood. He staggered forward and crashed to the floor.

For a while Prenhoe and Shufoy just stood, gasping for breath.

'I told you my dream meant something,' Prenhoe stammered, leaning against the wall, clutching his stomach. 'Faces of lizards they had . . .'

'Oh shut up!' Shufoy bawled.

He went to the man at the window, sprawled in a widening pool of his own blood. He turned him over and pulled back the face cloth. The face beneath was lean and vicious, marred by a large scar across the right cheek. Shufoy searched the corpse carefully.

'Nothing,' he murmured. 'A professional assassin.'

He hurried down the stairs to the second corpse. The man's

face was dirty and unshaven: his one good eye was half closed in death; the other was simply an empty black hole.

'A pretty pair of turtle doves!' Shufoy shouted.

He searched the corpse.

'Nothing,' he sighed. He called Prenhoe down to the kitchen. 'You did well,' he praised the scribe. 'My assailant had an eye missing. I wondered why he couldn't follow my parasol.'

The scribe had now recovered and was more concerned with proving his dream was correct. Shufoy held up a hand.

'I am thirsty and I am hungry.'

They found some beer, bread and cheese in the kitchen.

'Put that on the table,' Shufoy told Prenhoe. 'I just want to make sure this house is empty.'

He went back and searched, but apart from the two stiffening corpses and the signs of their struggle on the gallery outside the bedroom, Shufoy could see little amiss. He went out to the workshop: again nothing looked disturbed. He glimpsed the sandalwood tool-chest, Belet's prized possession. Shufoy had been with him when he had brought it back to his new house. The mannikin turned back the lid.

'Empty!' he murmured.

Scratching his head, Shufoy rejoined Prenhoe in the kitchen. They ate and drank in silence.

'What do we have here?' Shufoy exclaimed. 'Belet and Seli have gone. Some food has been taken and so have Belet's tools.' He cleaned his mouth with his tongue. 'Belet wouldn't return to his old ways: Seli would see to that. He was approached by someone at the Place of Hyaenas near the village of the Rhinoceri. My only conclusion is that whoever that was came back for him. Belet and Seli have been kidnapped, his tools have been taken and the robbery is going to take place soon.'

'They could have just come to silence him,' Prenhoe declared, 'then stolen his tools.'

'In which case, where are their corpses?'

Shufoy went cold. He put down the beer jug and, followed by Prenhoe, hurried into the garden. They knelt in the vegetable patch and scraped back the dirt. They soon uncovered the shallow grave. Aiya's corpse, soaked in blood; the dog, its skull shattered, thrown in on top. Prenhoe turned away to be sick. Shufoy, shivering, got to his feet. He stared towards the house. He had the most terrifying premonition that he would never see Belet and Seli alive again. He went over, patted Prenhoe on the shoulder and took him back to the house.

'Why?' Prenhoe gasped. He crossed to a water vase to clean his lips and chin.

'It's a pity we killed those two turtle doves.' Shufoy sat on the stool. 'I think it is the gang from the village of the Rhinoceri. They came here, killed the servant and took Belet and Seli captive. They also took his tools for key-making: that's because they intend to break into some House of Silver or treasure chest. The stoves are cold,' Shufoy continued. 'The house is untouched. I therefore suspect they were taken during the night.'

'But why were these two killers left behind?'

'Somehow or other their leader must have discovered that Belet was expecting guests. The two assassins were left to take care of us. Now that's interesting; why?'

Prenhoe just shook his head.

'It means,' Shufoy continued, 'that whatever they've planned is going to take place soon. Probably today or later tonight. Once the robbery has occurred, they couldn't really care who finds that Belet and Seli are missing. In fact, my friends could be blamed for the crime.' He picked up his beer jug and slurped from it.

'But why leave only two of the gang?'

Shufoy touched the scar on his nose and smiled.

'What do you find amusing?' Prenhoe asked.

'The fact that I have no nose,' Shufoy retorted. 'I suspect that most of the gang is made up of Rhinoceri. If the attack failed, the disfigured corpses might point to where the abductors of Belet and Seli came from.'

'Shouldn't Asural and some of his police go out to the village?'

Shufoy shook his head. 'That's a waste of time. They'll find some inhabitants missing but no one will know where they've gone or what they're doing. It also means,' Shufoy continued, 'that the gang is not a large one. They could only afford to leave

219

two men.' He smiled across at Prenhoe. 'They thought a dwarf and a soft-handed scribe would pose no real danger.'

'Well, they were mistaken, weren't they?' Prenhoe shouted.

'Yes, yes, they were. Look, Prenhoe, fetch Asural. Tell him to bring the police here. Aiya's corpse should have proper burial.'

'And you?'

'I am going to stay here for a while.'

Prenhoe needed no second bidding. He wanted to get away from this house of violent attack and horrid corpses. Shufoy waited until he had gone and then searched the place from top to bottom. He discovered nothing except a small coffer beneath the bed. He pulled this out. Inside he found papyri, nothing remarkable: some letters written by Belet to Seli. One yellowing, dingy scroll caught his attention. He unrolled this on the floor and studied it carefully. It had been written by Belet's father, Lakhet. The first part was in a scribe's hand but this broke off halfway through, to be continued in an almost illegible hand. It was a draft of a prayer, one of those paeans of praise much loved by courtiers and officials:

> 'I give you thanks, oh Osiris:
> Lord of two horns,
> Wearer of the Great Crown:
> I give you thanks for choosing me,
> Lakhet, your humble servant.
> I have been touched by Pharaoh's glory.
> I have worked for the great builder.
> I have fashioned doorways to the gods.
> And my work has been blessed . . .'

The hymn went on and on praising Osiris; it was also a clever boast on what Lakhet had achieved in his life. Shufoy sighed, dropped it in the chest and pushed this back under the bed. He gazed around. In a corner, on a beautiful carved acacia table, stood a statue of the jackal god Anubis. Shufoy felt a chill of fear. Crawling on his hands and knees, he went and knelt in front of the statue. He closed his eyes and extended his hands in silent prayer. In his soul Shufoy knew hideous deeds had taken place in this house. Belet and Seli had been abducted and marked for death. He went back on his heels and opened his eyes. But for what? What robbery was planned?

In the Hall of Judgement Anubis weighed the deceased heart/soul against the feather of truth.

CHAPTER 13

Amerotke sat on the roof of his house. Hatusu and Senenmut had supervised the removal of the sarcophagus and returned to Thebes early in the afternoon. He had promptly excused himself, insisting that he must see his family. The Mitanni delegation had just returned, so matters could wait for a while. He was also engrossed by what he had seen in the royal tomb: those telltale pictures on the wall. He wanted to gather all the information, everything he had learnt, and argue with himself about the different possibilities. Hatusu, relieved at what they had found in the sarcophagus, absent-mindedly agreed, though Senenmut insisted that he return to the Temple of Anubis the following day.

He'd found Shufoy waiting for him on the highway outside the gate to the house. At first glance he knew something was wrong.

'I don't want the lady Norfret to know,' Shufoy murmured, 'but Belet and Seli have been abducted. Their servant was murdered and buried in the garden. Prenhoe and I were attacked . . .'

Amerotke took him by the arm and led him back along the road to sit under a tamarind tree. He made him calm down and tell him exactly what had happened at Belet's house.

'You were right to wait for me,' Amerotke declared once Shufoy had finished the story. 'The only thing that agitates the lady Norfret is the prospect of us being attacked in our home. If she gets to know that a friend or acquaintance has suffered such a fate . . .' He patted Shufoy's hand. 'I apologise.

I still don't know what is planned, but I agree, whatever it is, it will happen soon. Belet has been abducted because of his skill as a locksmith; Seli was taken so as to ensure silence. But where?' Amerotke rubbed the side of his face. 'I could list a thousand and one places which brigands would love to rob: mansions with their treasure rooms, merchants and their warehouses, shrines, money-changers' shops, places I don't even know about.'

'Are Belet and Seli in danger?' Shufoy closed his eyes in desperation. His master's face told him everything.

'Brigands are not judges,' Amerotke replied. 'Once they have their hearts set on thievery, what does a human life mean?'

'What can we do?' Shufoy wailed, springing to his feet. 'I have Asural and Prenhoe combing the city.'

'I doubt if they'll find much,' Amerotke retorted. He got to his feet. 'But I thank you for waiting for me here. Once we are in the house, no mention must be made of this.'

Shufoy studied him closely.

'And you.' The mannikin pointed to the cuts on Amerotke's arms and legs. 'What has happened? I heard . . .'

'Oh, that's another thing we don't mention.' Amerotke smiled. 'We have problems enough, Shufoy. Let time pass before the lady Norfret gets to know. Now, come on. We must not be seen dallying here.'

Norfret and his sons were delighted to see him and asked question after question. Amerotke immediately dispatched Shufoy back to the temple to make certain enquiries whilst he and Norfret retired to their bedchamber, where, as Norfret put it, they could discuss matters more 'intimately'. After their lovemaking she questioned him closely. Amerotke grew evasive but he knew Norfret: she would return to the matter. She'd noticed the cuts on his body and referred to certain gossip Shufoy had picked up in the temple. Nevertheless, she had not insisted. She was now below stairs, arguing with the steward over what should be collected from the orchards. The boys were busy in the courtyard, where the carpenter was helping them build a toy chariot.

Amerotke, bathed and changed, sat enjoying the evening breeze whilst writing down all he had learnt. The elmwood table was now littered with inkpots and styli. He'd been so busy, his wrists and fingers ached. He put the stylus down and took Sinuhe's manuscript out of its leather case. He'd read some of it and was particularly interested in the traveller's tales of the different tribes which lived in the jungles hundreds of miles south of the third cataract.

'I can see why people wanted to buy this,' Amerotke murmured to himself.

Sinuhe was a born story-teller with a wealth of knowledge. He described paths and routes in great detail: how different villages and tribes should be approached; sources of water and food; the dangers posed by marauders or prowlers; and how directions were to be taken. Amerotke had read similar accounts and listened to the tales of self-styled travellers. Most of these were fantasy rather than fact, with their stories about frozen lakes which housed ravenous beasts. Sinuhe's account, however, rang true. He detailed everything, even drawing crude but very clear maps. Once again Amerotke turned to the section on the dwarf Nubians, their customs and, above all, their style of hunting and warfare.

Amerotke read this again, put the manuscript back and returned to his writing. His sons were now shrieking, echoing Shufoy's deep voice as he pretended to be a marauding baboon. The little man came up the stairs. His eyes had that aggrieved look. He had not relished the errand: he was more intent on finding out exactly what had happened to his master and his friend Belet, and how he could win the heart of that dancing girl.

'Well?'

Amerotke pulled across a stool and poured him a jug of beer.

'My love poems have not been successful, Master,' Shufoy declared mournfully. 'Listen to this.' He put the jug down and spread his hands.

'The voice of the wild goose calls me!
It calls and calls,
But I am entangled in the drawnet of your love . . .'

'Very good, Shufoy,' Amerotke interrupted. 'But that's enough of that.'

'I didn't find Prenhoe,' Shufoy whispered, 'or Asural. Master, what could have happened to Belet? Why did the thieves take all his work tools?'

'I don't know,' Amerotke retorted. 'Shufoy, all we know is that a robbery is planned. Asural has been alerted, yes? At this moment in time I can do no more.'

'You are no longer interested in me,' Shufoy declared petulantly. 'You won't tell me what happened to you.' His eyes became bright with excitement. 'I have heard rumours, Master.' He looked over his shoulder. 'If the lady Norfret knew . . .'

'If the lady Norfret knows,' Amerotke interrupted, 'you'll have more than the wild geese after you. I'll tell you later.'

'You were in danger, weren't you?' Shufoy asked plaintively. 'Prenhoe had a dream last night. He was down near the Nile with a beautiful woman . . .'

'The same woman from his former dreams?' Amerotke asked. Shufoy stamped his foot.

'The Temple of Anubis,' Amerotke insisted. 'What did you find?'

Shufoy sighed mournfully, and his master grasped him by the wrist.

'Shufoy, what did you discover?'

'I questioned people carefully, especially the priest Nemrath relieved after the day watch. He says it's possible, but not probable, that someone could have slipped into the chapel, but he doesn't think so.'

'And?'

'The same goes for Weni hiding in one of those recesses. He would have had to be very silent. If Nemrath had seen him, a stranger holding a dagger, he would have raised the alarm.'

Amerotke released his wrist.

'True, true. I'd thought of that myself. So, Wanef was lying.'

'I saw her and the other two in the temple,' Shufoy declared. 'Hunro and Mensu were as surly as usual but she looked like a cat who had caught a mouse. She asked after you. She said that as they had returned to Thebes they had passed the remains of a chariot and talked of gorse bushes being set alight.'

'Never mind.' Amerotke pressed his fingers against Shufoy's lips as they heard Norfret on the stairs.

'More secrets?'

Norfret stood, slightly provocatively, smiling at her husband.

'I've just remembered the message I sent to you.'

'What message?' Amerotke demanded.

'About the chest and the key.'

'I tried to tell him.' Shufoy spoke up. 'But as usual, the great judge was too busy to listen.'

'Tell me again.'

'The murder in the Temple of Anubis.' Norfret came and sat down next to Shufoy. 'You told me that the door was locked and the key still held by the victim, Nemrath, yes?'

Amerotke nodded.

'Well.' Norfret tapped the blue cord around her neck. 'I took a key from downstairs. I went into our bedchamber.' She grinned. 'I think you know where that is. I was sure I brought the correct key to the coffer. Now, I have used that key on countless occasions. However, this time, I brought the wrong one. I was really annoyed. I had to go downstairs and find the true one.'

Amerotke sat puzzled.

'I am sorry, I don't understand?'

'I do, I do.' Shufoy jumped to his feet, leaping about.

'How do we know,' Norfret continued, 'that the key on Nemrath's girdle was the one which truly fitted the door?'

'Because the key is specially made. Anyone who tried to replicate it, well, they couldn't. It would provoke suspicion.'

'No, no.' Norfret was beside herself with excitement. 'What's important about a key, my lord judge? It's not the rod, nor the handle, but the teeth at the end: that's what requires the skill of a locksmith. A key must fit into a lock and turn it, yes?'

Amerotke gasped.

'What happens,' Norfret insisted, 'if someone got into the chapel, killed Nemrath, took the sacred amethyst, put a replica key on his belt and left, locking the door behind him?'

'It's possible,' Amerotke conceded. 'But that makes Nemrath both victim and accomplice to the crime. Nemrath must have opened the door for his killer.'

'Agreed, Master, agreed!' Shufoy exclaimed. 'Remember what the Crocodile Man said about Nemrath: fat and lecherous! How he loved soft flesh.'

'Ita?' Amerotke exclaimed. He shook his head. 'The physician told me there was no sign of Nemrath having a sexual encounter before he died.'

'How do you know she even let him touch her?'

'True, true, Shufoy.' Amerotke now caught their excitement. 'But the replica key?'

'It's easily done,' Shufoy declared. He pointed to a key in a coffer near the table. 'You go down to a coppersmith or a bronze worker, you show him a drawing . . .'

'Of course!' Amerotke got to his feet; he grasped Norfret by the shoulder and kissed her full on the lips. 'If they ever need another judge in Thebes . . .'

'No thank you.' Norfret looked up, her eyes unsmiling. 'I do not wish to travel in a chariot across a lonely desert. I will have the truth, my lord judge.'

'Yes, yes, you will.' Amerotke sat down and tightened his sandals. 'And so will I.'

'You are going now?'

'Of course I am. Thanks to you, I know how Nemrath was killed and the Glory of Anubis stolen. Time is pressing on. The Mitanni will seal the treaty and be gone. I suspect the Glory of Anubis will go with them. Shufoy will accompany me. There are guards enough at Anubis so we needn't disturb Asural.'

Amerotke refused to be distracted or delayed. He reassured Norfret that they would return later that night. He kissed the boys and told them to be good, then he and Shufoy hastened out along the road back into Thebes.

The city gates had been closed but the night watch let them through a postern door. They soon reached the Temple of Anubis. The divine precincts were empty. Amerotke, exercising his authority, demanded to see the high priest. When he arrived,

Amerotke demanded to interview Khety and Ita in the chapel where the sacred amethyst had been kept.

'You have news of this?' the high priest queried, head going back, his sharp eyes bright with excitement.

'I know how it was stolen,' Amerotke confessed. 'But as to its whereabouts, that's another matter. Oh, the captain of the guard, Tetiky, can also join us.'

An acolyte priest took Amerotke along to the chapel. The place looked shabby, not swept or washed. The priest explained that it would only be reconsecrated once the sacred amethyst was found. He lit lamps and left. Amerotke re-examined the pool and recesses. He realised it would have been very difficult for Weni to hide there, kill Nemrath and escape. Footfalls sounded in the corridor outside. He and Shufoy organised three stools; Amerotke sat in the priest's chair, Shufoy standing beside him. Khety, Ita and Tetiky looked nervous as the acolyte priest ushered them in. Amerotke glimpsed the temple police behind: he ordered these to close the door and stay on guard.

'What is this?' Tetiky protested. 'I am brought here, by my own men, like a criminal!'

'I don't know if you are guilty or not,' Amerotke agreed. He pointed a finger at Khety and Ita. 'You two certainly are!'

'This is untrue!' Khety cried.

Ita sat, shoulders hunched, hands in her lap.

'I am tired of these allegations,' the priest wailed. 'Just because I was outside the door doesn't mean I am guilty.'

'I thought you'd say that,' Amerotke replied. 'It's a perfect defence, isn't it? You were near where the crime was committed but no proof links you to the sacrilege. In fact the reverse. So, provided you stay quiet and act the innocent, eventually you would be allowed to walk free.'

'Where is the evidence?' Ita spoke up.

'First things first; who was Weni?'

'I don't know.' Khety shook his head. 'He was a herald, wasn't he? Killed when the sacred pack broke free?'

'He approached you,' Amerotke continued remorselessly. 'Weni offered you a fortune to steal the Glory of Anubis.'

231

'A fortune?' Khety protested. 'Where would Weni get a fortune?'

'The Mitanni: they would love the sacred amethyst and be delighted to insult the Divine Hatusu. Weni was an Egyptian herald; he was also a spy and traitor. He came to you with a plan, didn't he? Let me put it this way: I know about the key!'

Khety paled; Ita swallowed hard and looked anxiously away.

'You put your heads together: all you had to do was steal the Glory of Anubis. You wouldn't have to sell it but hand it to Weni and receive a lavish reward. You'd then wait two or three months until the dust had settled. Khety wouldn't be the first priest to leave a temple and go elsewhere.'

'You are forgetting about Nemrath, aren't you?'

'No, I'm not forgetting Nemrath. I saw his corpse being prepared for burial. Has his Ka gone over the Far Horizon? Or has he stayed, Khety, to see justice done? Look around this chamber, how the shadows dance.'

Amerotke grasped the priest's shoulder and made him look around. 'Do you see the statue of Anubis, Khety? One day, perhaps sooner than you think, you'll travel the halls of the Underworld. You'll stand before the gods to confess your crime.'

Khety broke free.

'What crime?' he protested. 'What proof do you have?'

'Do you know the punishment for murder, sacrilege and theft?' Amerotke warned. 'You'll both be arraigned before me in the Hall of Two Truths. You will be sentenced to death and taken out to the Red Lands. Pharaoh's soldiers will torture you. Perhaps they'll enjoy young Ita. After all, once sentence is passed, you are no longer persons but Pharaoh's property. They'll maltreat you before digging deep pits in the sands and burying you alive.'

Sweat broke out on Ita's face. You are the softest, Amerotke thought: you never thought about discovery and punishment. He recalled Nemrath's corpse, the hideous sacrilege committed here, and kept his composure.

'They'll bury you deep and place rocks on the top. You will

try to dig yourself out but you'll find it hard even to move. The sand will clog your nose, mouth and eyes. You'll feel the searing heat and the cold of the encroaching night. Perhaps you might break free but you will be weakened.' He glanced at the woman. 'Have you ever been out in the Red Lands, Ita? I have. The lions are hungry because the Mitanni have slaughtered all the game. They'll smell your fear. Perhaps they'll come and try to dig you out.'

He paused. Ita was rubbing her arms as if freezing cold.

'Have you ever seen a pack of lions dig out a warthog? They stay at the hole for days.'

'Stop it,' Khety interrupted. 'You have no right . . .' He got to his feet.

'I have every right,' Amerotke replied. 'And where are you going, Khety?'

He glanced at the captain of the guard, sitting as immobile as a statue. The man looked fearful but Amerotke sensed he was innocent.

'Khety, sit down! Tetiky,' he murmured, 'you may stand outside. But don't go far. If Khety or Ita here leave without my permission,' Amerotke extended his fingers, displaying the ring of office, 'they are to be executed immediately.'

Tetiky got to his feet.

'Before you leave,' Amerotke demanded, 'tell me one thing. You were on duty the night Nemrath was killed and the sacred amethyst was stolen?'

'Yes, my lord.'

'You patrolled the corridors and galleries? Khety never left his post?'

'No!'

'And Ita here brought down refreshments?'

'I saw her come and I saw her go.'

'But when you saw her return to the kitchens, you said she was carrying a jug?'

'Yes, that's right!' the captain of the guard exclaimed.

Amerotke smiled. 'Now you are thinking as I do. Wasn't she supposed to leave the jug with Khety?'

Tetiky nodded.

233

'Oh, by the way,' Amerotke added, 'you mentioned stories about the god Anubis being seen round this temple. Do you believe them?'

The soldier smiled thinly and shook his head.

'Probably a priest,' he replied, 'wearing one of the sacred masks. It sometimes happens.'

'And who glimpsed him?'

'Some of the guards.'

'Ask them again,' Amerotke commanded. 'Say I want a close description of what they actually saw, particularly his hands.'

Tetiky agreed.

Amerotke waited until the captain had closed the door behind him before turning back to the other two.

'I am going to prove,' he continued evenly, 'that both of you are killers. You are quite the sugared almond, aren't you, Ita? Sweet and coy, a happy handful in bed, yes?'

'I am a priestess. You insult me!'

'You could be Pharaoh's daughter for all I care,' Amerotke retorted. 'You're still a murderess. Let me tell you what happened: Weni was a traitor and a spy. He was under orders to steal the Glory of Anubis. Any of Egypt's enemies would have paid dearly to hold the sacred amethyst and quietly mock the Divine Hatusu. Weni brought you a knife, one that could not be traced, and concocted a devious plot. Nemrath was lecherous. He lusted after you, didn't he, Ita? You would blink your pretty eyes and say your heart belonged to Khety. Only the gods know the tangled skein of your plot. Nemrath's appetite was whetted but Khety was the obstacle. Eventually Nemrath was presented with a solution.'

Amerotke paused. He just hoped he could break the stubbornness of these two killers.

'It is fashionable in the temples of Thebes for priests to share the charms and affections of a handmaid. Khety eventually proved no different; except that he told Nemrath that he didn't want anyone else to learn about this sharing.' Amerotke tapped his knee. 'Yes, that's it. Khety didn't want anyone to see or hear Nemrath enjoying the pretty Ita, nor did he want Nemrath boasting about his new-found conquest. Did Nemrath pay you,

Khety? I have yet to see the high priest. But don't the servants of the god keep their wealth and precious possessions in the House of Silver? Don't the scribes of the treasury make careful note of how much is withdrawn? I'll tell you what . . .' Amerotke paused. 'I have yet to check those records. I made a mistake, I should have done it earlier. However, I'll soon prove Nemrath made such a withdrawal, a considerable portion of his private wealth. No one will know where it's gone but I'll find out. Some merchant or banker in Thebes will have it under Khety or Ita's name.'

Both the accused grew agitated, moving restlessly.

'Good,' Amerotke murmured. 'I believe we are making progress! Khety and Ita received treasure, Nemrath would now enjoy Ita, but how and where? So Khety comes up with an ingenious plan. Nemrath is the vigil priest before the Shrine of Anubis. Khety is on guard outside. Night falls, Ita comes tiptoeing along, ostensibly bringing refreshments for Khety. He, of course, taps the door: he would do it when neither Tetiky nor any of the guards were around, a prearranged signal. Nemrath is beside himself with lust. He cannot believe his good fortune. He will lie with Ita. She will spend the night in his arms: who cares about sacrilege or desecration? He tiptoes across the chamber and unlocks the door. A makeshift bridge is laid across the sacred pool. Ita slips in. The bridge is withdrawn, and Nemrath locks the door. What Nemrath doesn't know is that Ita is carrying Weni's dagger. She has no intention of allowing the fat priest to enjoy her.'

Ita's face was now a sheen of sweat. She kept dabbing at her neck. Khety was glaring murderously at him.

'Please,' Amerotke warned, 'do not do anything stupid or you will die on the spot.'

'I don't think he will.' Shufoy spoke up.

He'd stood, fascinated, listening to his master, torn between admiration and incredulity at the soft, doe-like looks of Ita. He drew his dagger.

'My master is safe, isn't he, Khety?'

'I am still waiting for the proof!' the priest spat out.

'Oh, we'll come to that by and by,' Amerotke retorted. 'We

have plenty of proof.' He steeled himself for the lie. 'You see, Nemrath told someone about what was to happen.'

'He couldn't have done! He swore . . . !' Ita closed her eyes.

'You stupid bitch!' Khety hissed.

'As I was saying,' Amerotke continued, 'Nemrath was in here with Ita, beside himself with excitement. He rearranges the cushions for his bed of love. Ita approaches and strikes, driving the dagger deep into Nemrath's heart, a sudden killing blow. Nemrath would only have a few heartbeats before he dies. Ita then takes the Glory of Anubis from its repository and goes and taps on the door, a sign that all is ready.'

'But the key?' Khety exclaimed. 'The bridge wasn't disturbed.'

'Oh, there are some details I have not discovered: suffice to say that Ita uses the pool ledge to unlock the door. She then leaves the chamber. You, Khety, have the makeshift bridge, a plank of wood, ready. No one is around: you enter the chamber with the replica key which, in all aspects, looks like the one to the Divine Chapel. You put this on Nemrath's girdle, cross the wooden plank, withdraw that, swing the door closed and lock it. You hide the key on your person; as for the plank of wood? Well, there are windows and doorways in the gallery outside and you quickly get rid of it. Ita is standing on guard whilst you do all this. You now have the key, Ita has the sacred amethyst. The jug she has brought only contains a little wine or beer; that's emptied into your cup and the amethyst is put inside. Ita takes it off to the kitchen and you resume your vigil.' Amerotke pointed to the door. 'Now we come to the last and most dangerous part of your crime. The next morning the chapel has to be forced. All is confusion, Nemrath's dead, the sacred amethyst is missing. Who cares now about the key? Especially as it's still hanging on Nemrath's girdle. No one, in all that panic, bothers about a key for a lock that is broken. In the initial confusion Khety replaces the replica key with the genuine one and the mystery is complete.'

'But I was on guard,' Khety stammered. 'I knew I'd be suspected.'

'Really?' Amerotke retorted. 'That was your defence. How

could you get in and out? Tetiky did not notice anything untoward. So, why should you be accused? You weren't carrying the
sacred amethyst, and even if you had stolen it, how could you
sell it to anyone? True, the finger of suspicion might be pointed,
but as you keep saying, where is the proof? Now all has changed.
You'll go on trial for your lives. Shufoy here will search around.'
Amerotke used his hands to imitate the weighing of scales.
'We'll find more evidence. In the end, the only conclusion will
be that Khety and Ita are guilty of murder, sacrilege and theft.'
Amerotke got up and stared down at them. 'I will give you a
short while, only a very short while, to talk to each other.'

'What is there to talk about?' Ita protested, peering around.
'You've found us guilty, we are going to die.'

'Ah!' Amerotke smiled and sat down. 'You are most fortunate.
You see, what the Divine Hatusu wants is the return of the
Glory of Anubis. Nemrath, to a certain extent, brought about
his own death. If you confess and tell me all, if I can return
the Glory of Anubis to its shrine, then this is what will happen.
You will both be allowed to leave Thebes, dressed in the clothes
you are wearing. You will be permitted to carry one weapon, a
satchel of food and drink. Where you go and what you do is a
matter for you, provided you never return to Thebes. You are
banished for life, as you are from service in any temple in the
Upper or Lower Kingdom of Egypt!' Amerotke leaned forward.
'Think about it,' he said carefully. 'It's better than choking to
death out in the Red Lands.'

He got up and indicated that Shufoy follow him. They left the
chapel. Tetiky and his guards stood outside in the passageway.
Amerotke dismissed these but told the captain to stay. He then
looked along the passageway and glimpsed the window high in
the wall, noticing small recesses and corners, an ideal place to
hide the plank used to cross the sacred pool.

Tetiky was obviously still nervous.

'I am innocent, my lord.'

Amerotke clapped him on the shoulder.

'Of course you are, but those two aren't.'

The man's eyes rounded in amazement.

'They are guilty, my lord?'

'As the god Seth is of murder. You will be informed later.'

'And the sacred amethyst?'

'I hope, for their sakes, they return it. Now listen, Tetiky.' He grasped the man by the arm. 'These rumours of the god Anubis being seen walking through the temple?'

'I never saw it,' the captain replied.

'Then who did?'

Tetiky called one of the guards over, a small, soft-faced recruit who came hurrying up.

'Tell my lord Amerotke what you say about the god Anubis.'

'I didn't see anything,' the man stammered. 'It was probably a dream or a trick of the light.'

He glanced quickly over his shoulder at his companions at the end of the passageway. Amerotke smiled down at him.

'Captain Tetiky, this soldier is to be rewarded for his sharp sight and his vigilance. You did see something, didn't you?' he insisted. 'But now you want to dismiss it because others are teasing you? Yet, I am sure, if I went round this temple, some other servant or guard may have glimpsed the same.'

The recruit glanced nervously at Tetiky.

'Tell me the truth.'

Amerotke turned and peered through the half-open door: Khety and Ita were sitting close, heads together.

'Two nights before the dancing girl was killed,' the man replied slowly, 'I was on guard, or rather patrolling the area between the Gates of Pearl and the garden. I heard a sound and turned quickly. I only saw it for a few seconds: someone dressed like the god Anubis. Whoever it was had a black and gold jackal mask over their head, war sandals, a black leather kilt. A cloak hung down from the shoulders.'

'Was it man or woman?'

'I don't know, I couldn't tell, it looked like a woman. Something elegant.' He shook his head. 'I don't know.'

'Now.' Amerotke leaned closer. 'I want you to recall exactly what this figure was carrying. It was carrying something?'

The recruit closed his eyes.

'Yes, it looked like a short spear, I don't really know.'

'Thank you.'

Amerotke dismissed both him and Tetiky and walked back into the chapel.

'Well?' he asked, resuming his seat.

'Do we have your solemn oath?' Khety demanded.

'You do, but I need the Glory of Anubis and a full confession.'

Khety nodded at Ita.

'I need to collect something,' she said.

Amerotke allowed her to go and sat waiting for her to return. She came back carrying a small leather sack covered in dirt and mud.

'You buried it in the garden?' Amerotke demanded.

She nodded, undid the cord and drew out the beautiful amethyst in the shape of a large egg. Shufoy whistled at the brilliant beauty of the stone. Amerotke held it up against the torchlight: turning and twisting it, he noticed how, in the centre of the stone, the grains formed the head of a dog or a jackal. He examined the amethyst carefully: it was unmarked. Amerotke placed it by his chair.

'And your confession?'

'We were happy enough here,' Khety began. 'I earned considerable money from mortuary fees. I met Ita. Nemrath was always pestering her.' He rubbed his eyes and stared wearily. 'A humdrum life, my lord, until one day I was in my bedchamber.'

'When was this?'

'Oh, some days ago. Perhaps ten, fourteen, just after the Mitanni arrived. I don't know who the person was. Sometimes he called himself Weni, sometimes Mensu . . .'

'Mensu!' Amerotke exclaimed. 'But that's one of the Mitanni envoys.'

'I know, I know. I don't know whether my visitor was male or female. Sometimes the voice was muffled, sometimes clear, sometimes high, sometimes low.'

Khety scratched his brow.

'At one time I thought it really was Weni, then he was killed and somone else came who seemed to know everything, so I wondered, was it Weni in the first place? Anyway, my first mysterious visitor claimed I could become rich beyond my wildest dreams if I stole the Glory of Anubis. Of course, I replied that was foolish, no one could do it. A huge sum was mentioned, so much gold and silver.' Khety shook his head. 'I've never heard the likes of it. I replied that I needed to discuss it with Ita. My visitor was reluctant but agreed. On a return visit, I told this mysterious messenger that we would do it but we'd have to bring Tetiky or Nemrath into the conspiracy. I was told not to be a fool.'

'I came up with a plan.' Ita spoke up defiantly. 'Now, we have your word, my lord?' She paused. 'Nemrath was as lecherous as a goat. He'd always be whispering bawdy things to me but he was frightened of Khety. I told him Khety didn't mind. How he enjoyed the idea of sharing me with Nemrath. The fat fool believed this. Never once did we mention the Glory of Anubis. Nemrath paid and the rest is as you said.'

'Weren't you frightened of the guard?'

'Tetiky is like any soldier, no break to a set routine. The night we stole the amethyst, everything went according to plan. The only thing I was frightened of was this apparition, rumours about Anubis being seen walking the temple.'

'Did you believe them?' Amerotke asked.

'I don't believe gods walk.' She smirked. 'I don't believe in anything, my lord Amerotke.' Her eyes were hard. 'When you work in a temple with priests . . .' Her voice trailed off. 'I killed Nemrath. He deserved to die, he pestered me. I took the amethyst.'

'Why didn't you hand it over immediately?'

'Our visitor returned.' Khety explained. 'He told us to hold it. He would come back. We were visited again after Weni had been killed. By then I was totally confused. I suspected it was going to be handed over to the Mitanni: we were to hold it in case something went wrong.'

'So, your visitor could not have been Weni?'

'It could have been anyone. Man or woman, I don't know.'

'And there's nothing more you can tell me?'

'My lord?'

Amerotke glanced at Ita.

240

'We are to be turned out like criminals in our robes and sandals?'

'Well, that's what you are,' Shufoy declared.

'You have your life and your health, not to mention your freedom.'

'We can take some silver with us?' She held her hand up, bowing her head. 'My lord, I have information which may interest you: the dancing girl, the heset who was murdered in the garden pavilion?'

'You may take a little silver with you,' Amerotke replied.

'I knew her vaguely. On the afternoon before she died, she told me the Mitanni, I am sure she said that, had hired her to dance.'

'The Mitanni?'

'My lord, that's all she said . . .'

Amerotke picked up the sacred amethyst and weighed it carefully in his hands.

'You must be out of Thebes by noon tomorrow. What you take with you is a matter for you. If you return, you will be executed. Now be gone!'

They both fled the room. Shufoy went across and closed the door behind them.

'You pounce like a mongoose, my lord.'

'No, I don't.' Amerotke glanced down at the amethyst. 'But I tell you this, Shufoy, tomorrow morning I am going to trap a murderer. I have no more proof than I had with Khety and Ita. May the goddess Ma'at help me!'

Anubis carried out his judgement in the presence
of Horus, Osiris, Isis and Nephthys.

CHAPTER 14

Toreb, bodyservant to the Mitanni envoy, Lord Hunro, was deeply anxious. He had seen Amerotke, the Pharaoh's chief judge, arrive in the temple. Like all servants who acted as spies, Toreb wished to inform his master as soon as possible. Toreb had crept along and watched Amerotke being taken to the chapel where the sacred amethyst had been stolen. He'd tried to listen, to learn what had happened, but this time the guards would not be bribed. He was ordered away with surly looks and muttered curses. Nevertheless, Toreb was pleased.

'My master will pay me well,' he muttered.

Lord Hunro did not like the lady Wanef and was eager to collect information for himself. He and Mensu were always in close consultation, heads together. Now and again his master would betray his true feelings.

'I don't like being here,' Hunro moaned, cradling a goblet of wine. 'I'd prefer my lips to blister and my knees to swell rather than kiss the feet of the stonemason's bitch!'

Toreb sighed as he padded along the empty corridor: that was the way of the world! The great Mitanni chieftains wanted war but King Tushratta was intent on peace. There was no going back now. The Mitanni party had returned to Thebes with strict instructions: the treaty would be sealed. Hadn't Benia's sarcophagus arrived at the temple ready for transport out to the Oasis of Palms? Yet there were other matters. Had his master, the lady Wanef and others been involved in the theft of the sacred amethyst? Toreb couldn't say yea or nay, though when they were alone, the Mitanni envoys did chuckle at Pharaoh's discomfiture. However, these smiles soon disappeared. On one matter they were all agreed: Chief Judge Amerotke was a dangerous man and had to be watched. There had been fierce discussion about what they had passed in the desert. The lady Wanef had certainly been disappointed to learn that Amerotke had suffered an accident but survived to continue his snooping.

Toreb stopped at the corner and stared up at the great statue of the jackal god. Darkness had fallen and the torches in their niches along the walls made the place more ghostly, more threatening with flickering shadows, those paintings of war springing vividly to life. Toreb looked over his shoulder. The temple passageway was dappled in a strange light from both the torches and the silver-grey glow of a full moon. He didn't like it here. He left by a side door and crossed the gardens. On one thing Toreb was certain: the Egyptians knew how to create a paradise. The gardens were fragrant with their shady cypress trees, lofty sycamores and sweet-smelling vineyards. The breeze carried the sound of the yapping of the sacred pack, now much depleted. Toreb shivered. Surely the dogs would not be allowed to escape again? And Lord Hunro and Lord Mensu did like these gardens. Now, where was their favourite spot? Ah yes, an exquisite ornamental pool where bullrushes grew and lotus floated on the surface. Toreb recalled directions and trotted through the darkness. He reached the pool lit by three braziers along the edge. Someone had definitely been there: a tray of jugs and cups lay on the ground.

'My lord Hunro!' he called.

He stared round. Something was wrong. He glanced down at the water and stood rigid with shock. No illusion, no mistake! Two corpses floated, faces down amongst the lotus pads. Lord Hunro and Lord Mensu, their robes billowing about them. A night jar screeched, shattering the deathly silence. Toreb took one more look and ran screaming into the darkness.

Amerotke and Shufoy were on the point of leaving the temple

when the alarm was raised. A sleepy-eyed servant stopped them at the gate.

'The high priest,' he demanded, 'needs your presence. I also have to warn Lord Senenmut.'

Shufoy was amazed at his master's reaction.

'I thought as much,' the judge murmured. He sighed. 'But that's the way things must be.'

'Master?'

'Nothing, Shufoy. Let's see this bloody mayhem for ourselves.'

By the time they reached the pool, a crowd of servants, soldiers and priests carrying torches and lamps had gathered round it. The two corpses had been pulled out and laid sprawling on the side like dead fish. The physician from the House of Life was already examining them. Amerotke searched out the lady Wanef. She stood, surrounded by servants, staring down at the corpses. She glanced up as Amerotke approached.

'Is this how Egypt treats the envoys of the King?'

Amerotke stared back.

'Well?' Wanef insisted.

Amerotke tapped the pectoral on his chest.

'This is our symbol of truth, Lady Wanef.'

He lifted the leather satchel he carried and, opening it, allowed her to glimpse the sacred amethyst glowing there. The judge enjoyed Wanef's discomfiture: her jaw dropped.

'Aren't you pleased, my lady,' Amerotke whispered, covering the sacred amethyst, 'that the truth is out?'

'What is this? What is this?' The high priest, a sleeping robe round his shoulders, hurried over. 'Lord Amerotke? Is it true?'

'It is true.' Amerotke cut him off. 'The Glory of Anubis has been found, the perpetrators unmasked. No.' He lifted a hand. 'My task is to inform the Divine Hatusu and Lord Senenmut. The chapel will be reconsecrated.' He glanced slyly at Wanef. 'Divine Pharaoh must show all how she enjoys the pleasure of the gods: her wisdom, her devotion have led to the discovery of this sacred stone. She herself will place it back in the care of the god Anubis.'

The high priest couldn't argue with that. Torn between pleasure and desire to hold the sacred amethyst, he drew a deep breath and nodded.

'Of course, of course,' he murmured. 'But now these deaths?'

Wanef was about to launch into another tirade. Amerotke turned his back on her and went to kneel beside the physician.

'As before?' Amerotke asked.

'As before, my lord: no marks on the corpses. No obvious cause of death.' He pointed to the tray of cups and jugs. 'My servants have already examined those: there is no poison.'

Amerotke stared up at the starlit sky. Time was passing. He told Shufoy to send a servant to Lady Norfret.

'We will not be returning home tonight,' he declared. He drew the physician close. 'I want you to search the corpses carefully. Look for a small puncture mark, anything. You might find it in the same place on each corpse.'

Amerotke gestured towards the seat.

'I suspect they were sitting close.' He pointed to the bushes behind. 'The killer probably struck from there, so the puncture mark should be high, in the back of the neck, certainly no lower than their shoulder blades. They were probably killed whilst sitting and fell forward.' He pointed to the light bruising on the faces of both men. 'Their killer then tossed both into the water.'

'Why would he do that?'

'To cover what he used to kill them. Undress the corpses carefully,' Amerotke continued in a whisper. 'Hang their robes up and you will also discover a small puncture mark, like that caused by a needle, high in each garment.'

'You know how these men were killed, don't you?'

'Yes, I think so. Now I must trap their killer.'

Amerotke, accompanied by a mystified Shufoy, went over and demanded lodgings from the high priest. This was readily agreed. Once they were in the chamber provided, Amerotke shuttered the windows, bolted the door and piled up the furniture against it.

'Master, what is the matter?'

'We are in danger, Shufoy, from a hideous killer. One who would like to make a clean sweep, finish the task in hand.'

248

'Won't you tell me?' Shufoy glanced at his master, who now lay on the narrow bed.

'No, I am too tired and I might be wrong. Tomorrow morning, Shufoy, wake me before dawn. I want to be out of this temple and down to the House of a Million Years.'

And rolling over on his side, Amerotke went to sleep.

The night passed without incident. Just before daylight Amerotke and Shufoy washed, cleaned themselves and hastily left the temple. Shufoy had never seen his master leave any place so quietly, as if fearful of being trapped. On the road outside, they met a squadron of soldiers marching up to the city gates. Amerotke, using all the authority he could muster, demanded their protection as an escort down to the royal palace near the great mooring place on the Nile. Once they were through the soaring pylons and into the royal gardens, Amerotke relaxed. The soldiers were dismissed and he gave Shufoy an errand to do in the city. The little man protested.

'I am hungry, Master, and I didn't sleep very well. I am very worried about Belet.'

'You can feed your face in the marketplace.' Amerotke smiled, crouching down. 'Perhaps you can make enquiries for your friend. You know what to do. Speak to your acquaintances, the herbalists and scorpion men, then come back here. I'll be waiting in one of the antechambers or out in the chariot park. If you meet Prenhoe, don't tell him what's happening. Or when I return home I'll be presented with his list of dreams.'

Shufoy waddled off. Amerotke asked a servant to take him to the chariot park. The stables were a hive of activity: horses being led in and out, groomed and fed, ready for pasture or being hitched between shafts. Soldiers and their drivers sat around breaking their fast. A Master of Horse approached.

'My lord?'

'Do you miss Hathor and Isis?'

'Beautiful horses, my lord.'

'Tell me.' Amerotke pointed to a squadron of the chariots. 'They are hitched and ready to leave?'

'Of course, my lord, they are going out to patrol the Red

249

Lands. Some merchants have complained about marauding Libyan bandits.'

Amerotke walked over and, whilst the mystified Master of Horse watched, climbed in and out of a chariot. He then asked a charioteer to check the horses' forelegs and reins, absent-mindedly thanked him and wandered into the palace.

Chamberlains and servants, the Keeper of the Royal Diadem, the Custodian of the Royal Fan, the Holder of Pharaoh's Perfume, were all hurrying down the galleries and corridors towards the House of Adoration, Hatusu's personal quarters. A chamberlain promised that the Divine Hatusu and Lord Senenmut would be told of his arrival and solemnly agreed to convey the lord Amerotke's message to them. Amerotke had to sit and kick his heels for about an hour, fascinated by the stream of servants who processed solemnly in and out of the House of Adoration. Servants carrying robes over their arms and trays of jewels, amulets, earrings and bracelets. The Keeper of the Royal Slippers, barbers, masseurs, perfume-holders. Amerotke hid his smile. Hatusu, if she wished, could act the coy, simple girl or the foul-mouthed virago, and, in the twinkling of an eye, assume all the greatness and majesty of Pharaoh. Sometimes she dressed like a girl hurrying out to the market; other times the true incarnation of the Divine One. On occasions she loved the fuss and protocol of court; on others, she openly mocked it.

'Ever-changing,' Amerotke murmured. 'Like the moon.'

At last the antechamber fell silent. A unit of soldiers from the crack Vulture squadron took up position outside the doors under the command of an officer in full ceremonial uniform. These were the Nakhtu-aa, 'the strong-arm boys', the 'Maryannou' or braves of the king. They lived and died for Pharaoh and worshipped the ground Hatusu trod on. Amerotke was beginning to doze when the doors were thrown open and Senenmut came striding out.

'The Divine Hatusu is in a divine sulk!'

Amerotke grasped the leather bag more carefully.

'But I think,' Senenmut smiled, 'you are going to coax her out of it?'

Hatusu was indulging in the most imperial of sulks. She

was in the small throne room, seated in the lion chair, hands grasping its arms, her feet resting on a footstool.

'My lord Amerotke. More deaths at Anubis!'

Amerotke knelt, forehead touching the ground. As he did so, he let the leather satchel open and the sacred amethyst rolled out. He heard a sharp intake of breath, a patter of sandals. Hatusu pinched him playfully on the arm.

'Enough of that, up you get!'

When he did, Hatusu had the Glory of Anubis in her hands, lifting it up like some champion would a prize.

'I am the first you've told?'

Amerotke quickly described what had happened. Hatusu kept walking up and down, her face wreathed in smiles. She didn't even bother to curse the two perpetrators.

'I am going to love it!' she exclaimed. 'I want to process through the Temple of Anubis holding this, to show those priests, everyone in Thebes, how the gods love and favour me!'

She sat down on her throne, still nursing the sacred amethyst.

'We are pleased with you, Amerotke. Sinuhe's manuscript? You have that safe?'

'In my house, my lady.'

'And the killer?'

'I think I know.'

'Sit down! Sit down!' Hatusu fluttered her fingers towards a stool. 'Sit on this.'

When Amerotke did so, Hatusu rose and squatted at his feet, ordering Senenmut to do likewise.

'There we are,' she teased. 'The teacher and his two pupils.'

Senenmut was also pleased. Amerotke could tell that by the way he kept tapping his hand against his knees. Amerotke sighed and, getting up, pushed away the stool and sat on the floor with them.

'You received my message?' he asked.

'Yes, yes, we did. And the answer is Tushratta wants peace but many of his council don't.'

'And the other matter?'

'I can't tell. But I've sent a chamberlain to find out.'

251

'We'll have the confrontation here,' Amerotke murmured. 'When Mareb arrives, let him sit with us. My lord Senenmut, I would like you to make sure that he is not armed.'

Senenmut raised his eyebrows, got to his feet and walked to the door. Hatusu's mood had changed. Her face had grown severe. She was biting her lower lip, a constant mannerism when annoyed. Senenmut had hardly returned when they heard the knock on the door. A chamberlain stepped through and announced that Mareb was waiting. He looked rather surprised at the way Pharaoh, her vizier and chief judge were sitting, but Hatusu made an imperious movement with her hand.

'Our herald is to present himself. Tell the captain of the guard to ensure that he is searched from neck to crotch.'

The chamberlain withdrew. A short while later Mareb slipped through the door, his hair freshly oiled, face clean-shaven. Amerotke recalled the herald out in the Red Lands and steeled himself against any compassion. Mareb was an assassin, a man responsible for many deaths. The herald didn't know what to do but stood moving from foot to foot.

'Sit down, man!' Hatusu ordered. 'Here, complete the circle.'

Mareb, caught between protocol and the desire to please, nervously obeyed.

'My lady?'

'My lady nothing!' she snapped. 'My lord Amerotke has summoned you here!'

'You know,' Amerotke began, 'I have Sinuhe's maps.'

He gestured towards the throne where Hatusu had left the Glory of Anubis. The herald glanced at this. For a brief moment Amerotke glimpsed his surprise and consternation.

'Khety and Ita are in disgrace,' Amerotke murmured. 'They have been exiled from Thebes.'

'I am glad, my lord.'

'No you're not. You are worried, you are fearful and you have good reason to be. You are the Anubis killer. Mareb, you own a pair of war sandals, a black leather kilt, a cloak, a jackal-headed mask. You are responsible for the murders of Weni, Sinuhe, the three Mitanni envoys, the dancing girl. You also tried to kill me out in the Red Lands but it went hideously wrong.'

252

Mareb would have jumped to his feet but Amerotke grasped his wrist and squeezed hard.

'You are here in the presence of a god, Mareb. Divine Pharaoh will carry out justice.'

Mareb opened and closed his mouth.

'Let's begin with the office you hold,' Amerotke continued. 'You and Weni were pages, as was Hordeth, your good friend. You trained at the court of Tuthmosis, Divine Pharaoh's father. Afterwards, all three of you entered the House of Envoys. You were proud of your position, as probably were your father and elder brother. You did well in the academy, particularly in the study of tongues and the customs of those who live beyond Egypt's borders. You became a herald. First with Hordeth and then with Weni. It is a custom of the Egyptian court always to send two heralds to a foreign prince.'

'Hordeth? I told you, I hardly knew him.'

'No, that's the lie that trapped you. Let me tell you the story,' Amerotke continued. 'Years ago, during the reign of Divine Tuthmosis, Weni, Hordeth and Mareb were pages in the royal household. They later entered the House of Envoys. In Tuthmosis I's tomb there is a wall painting of the royal pages. It shows them kneeling before Pharaoh. I noticed two, beside each other, hand in hand: Hordeth and Mareb.' Amerotke paused. 'I am sure if I asked the House of Records to be searched, they would discover that you and Hordeth were very close friends. Time passed. Weni married a Mitanni woman. Hordeth lusted after her and she responded. Weni became mad with anger. He suffocated his wife during a boating trip, then invited Hordeth to the ruined Temple of Bes, where he killed him.'

Mareb's eyes grew more anxious.

'He killed your best friend,' Amerotke said softly. 'Hordeth was your best friend?'

'Yes, he was, but I . . .'

Amerotke raised a hand for silence.

'Now, Weni, his wits turned, found the disposal of his adulterous wife and her lover quite pleasurable and easy. However, the murders were also witnessed by the Crocodile Man, one of those flotsam and jetsam who live along the Nile. To cut a long story

253

short, Weni became known as the "Gardener", a professional assassin. Why? Possibly because he was being blackmailed by the Crocodile Man, but, overcome with grief and remorse at the loss of his wife, he was also intent on building a lavish tomb for her and himself out in the Necropolis.'

'Did you suspect Weni had killed your friend?' Senenmut asked.

'I think he may have done,' Amerotke intervened. 'But Mareb kept his suspicions to himself. Weni was also active as a herald. He became your companion, envoys to the Mitanni. Tushratta and Wanef soon recognised his venality. Weni was supposed to offer to spy for the Mitanni in Egypt. He probably did but they didn't truly trust him. They looked around for someone else.' Amerotke paused. 'I suppose Wanef and others carefully scrutinised Weni's life and found out about his hidden career. Other matters took over: last year Divine Pharaoh marched north. The Mitanni suffered a catastrophic defeat. Your brother and father were in her army. They weren't killed, were they, Mareb? They were taken captive and the Mitanni turned on you.'

Mareb's lower lip was trembling.

'What did they offer you, Mareb? Your father and brother's lives. Did they threaten to crucify them if you didn't co-operate? Did they offer you gold and silver? They also told you about Weni. How he was responsible for the death of your good friend Hordeth.' Amerotke spread his hands. 'Weni was a traitor. He'd sell to anyone. You were different.'

'Is it true?' Senenmut asked. 'Are your father and brother alive?'

'To me they are dead.' Mareb's voice was no more than a whisper. He suddenly looked haggard, losing the arrogance of his office and status.

'The Mitanni,' Amerotke continued, 'were forced to sign a peace treaty. They were compelled to come to Egypt. Tushratta may stay out at the Oasis of Palms but he is, in fact, begging for peace. To hide his shame, he wants to embarrass the Divine Hatusu as much as possible. He demands the return of his kinswoman's corpse. He's heard the rumours, which are not true, that Divine Hatusu's father killed her. The Mitanni are also great merchants. They've learnt about Sinuhe's manuscript and his maps. They want that. Above all, they want the Glory of Anubis. When did they approach you?' Amerotke asked. 'When you arrived at their court?'

Mareb stared back.

'Weni was to be their cat's-paw whilst you really managed affairs. First, the Glory of Anubis. Weni is approached by you. He doesn't know who you are: all he must accept is that you speak on behalf of the Mitanni king. You coax him with a mixture of bribery and threats; more gold and silver and, if he doesn't agree, then public exposure, trial and execution. He's to buy knives from the Theban marketplace and be told exactly how the sacred amethyst will be stolen. Weni, in turn, passes this on to Khety and Ita. He is your link with that villainous pair: greedy as hungry fish, they rise to the bait. Nemrath is killed and the Glory of Anubis stolen. Weni is also murdered, so you now take over his visits to Khety and Ita, who are told to keep the amethyst. The Mitanni will not collect their prized possession until just before they leave the temple. As you can see, I now have it back.'

Mareb blinked. He'd recovered some of his composure.

'My lord Amerotke, I am pleased . . .'

'Sinuhe you treated differently,' the judge continued. 'You are a master of disguise, Mareb, with your long, slim legs and girlish face. You can pass for a woman or pretend to be a Mitanni. Was that your idea or Wanef's? I suspect it was yours, a little protection for yourself, muddying the waters still further. You approach Sinuhe as a Mitanni woman, displaying Tushratta's seal as proof of your credibility. You offer Sinuhe treasure beyond his wildest dreams. Nevertheless, frightened of prying eyes, you invite him to meet you at the Temple of Bes. Ironic, isn't it, that that's where Weni killed your friend?'

'I was pleased when you discovered his remains.' Mareb smiled. 'I did not know what to say that day.'

'No, you didn't, and, I suspect, you said little to Sinuhe. You met him in disguise, similar to that used round the Temple of Anubis: the black and gold jackal mask, the war kilt, the soldier's sandals. Anyway, Sinuhe is murdered, his manuscript is stolen and you again meet Weni. You gave him the manuscript for safe-keeping. Our greedy herald was only too willing to take it. You ordered him to hide it in a safe and secure place: what better than his gorgeous tomb out in the Necropolis? You must have been very pleased with yourself. You had the Glory of Anubis and you had Sinuhe's map. The Divine Hatusu might suspect the Mitanni had another spy in Thebes, one they called the Hyaena, but there was no real proof. You used Weni to protect yourself. If Khety and Ita broke down and confessed, if they were tortured, the only name they could give was Weni's, not yours.'

'My lord, I have listened to you.' Mareb spoke up. 'And what you are saying,' he pulled a face, 'is logical enough. But if what you allege is true, why should I kill Weni if I was using him? And how am I responsible for the deaths at the Temple of Anubis?'

'Oh, you hated Weni,' Amerotke replied. 'He deprived your friend of life and proper burial. You watched him like a hunting snake does a rat. You may have suspected Weni of murdering Hordeth: the Mitanni probably supplied the proof but ordered you to wait. You did. Weni was greedy, the key to his soul was gold and silver. He was under strict orders, but of course, he would do what he wanted. The Glory of Anubis and Sinuhe's maps were meant for the Mitanni court but Weni opened private negotiations with Libyans, Nubians and, for all I know, Kushites and others. He was going to sell the Glory of Anubis and Sinuhe's maps to the highest bidder, so it was time for him to pay for his treachery and his greed. No swift death followed by honourable burial. No, Weni would die like Hordeth, and, like Hordeth, his corpse would be polluted and abused. You invited him down to the gardens.'

'I was asleep that night. I can produce witnesses . . . !'

Amerotke shook his head.

'You are an energetic young man, Mareb. I saw that out in the Red Lands. You were lying on your bed, cloaked and ready. Weni left through the door, you left through your window. You lured him towards the dog pit. The guard was killed, the gate opened and a trail of blood left to whet the pack's appetite. In any temple, after the sacrifices, blood is more plentiful than wine. Weni was killed barbarously, fitting revenge for Hordeth, and an end to his greed, treachery and venality. Weni's removal caused you no problems. The sacred amethyst was taken and Sinuhe's manuscript was safe in Weni's tomb. You could always go across there, under the pretence of paying your last respects, and remove the manuscript.'

Amerotke leaned forward and tapped the herald on the knee.

'What were you going to do, Mareb? Stay in Egypt or flee to the Mitanni? Ah, well!'

Ignoring protocol, Amerotke got to his feet and walked to a window overlooking the royal gardens.

'If you had your way, Mareb, I wouldn't be staying here, would I? My bones would litter the Red Lands: that's the other proof I have.'

'You can't say that.'

Mareb would have jumped to his feet but Senenmut had risen. He crossed to the herald and pressed him back down. Hatusu, as if aware of the danger, went across to her throne. She did not sit like a Pharaoh-Queen, just an ordinary young woman listening to a story which shocked and intrigued her. Amerotke, however, knew her mood. Once she was certain of Mareb's guilt, she would show her fury, that passionate hot temper which even the lord Senenmut was wary of.

'You'd been watching me,' Amerotke continued. 'Was it Wanef's idea or yours for the Mitanni envoys to go back to the Oasis of Palms? They didn't really have to consult! Whatever happened at the Temple of Anubis, they still had to sign that treaty. It was a pretext to lure me out as well as an opportunity to give you fresh instructions and encouragement.'

'But how did they know you'd go?' Mareb pleaded.

'Silence!' Hatusu straightened up. 'Silence your lying tongue!'

She sat back on the throne, elbows resting on its arms.

'They asked for you, my lord Amerotke, and they specifically asked for Mareb. They said it would flatter Tushratta, whilst that letter . . .'

'Oh yes, the famous letter.' Amerotke walked forward. 'They'd planned for that to be intercepted. They wanted to bait the Divine Hatusu, push all the blame on to Weni and depict

Mareb as someone they didn't like. When we reached the Oasis of Palms they continued the pretence. Our visit had one main purpose: to kill me.' Amerotke straightened his wrist guard. 'All pretence,' he whispered. 'Like the attack on you in my chamber. Wanef arranged that to deflect suspicion. I suspect she didn't even tell you: it was all preparation for what would happen out in the Red Lands.'

'That's ridiculous!' Mareb exclaimed, now visibly agitated.

'No, it's not. When I visited the oasis I met the dwarf Nubians; Tushratta calls them his "little people". I found reference to them in two other places: first, the tomb of the Divine Tuthmosis I. He, too, had met these people: his funeral artist depicted them as carrying small blow-pipes which shot poisonous darts. Sinuhe also repeated the description. Shufoy is now out in the marketplace seeking confirmation. The Mitanni gave you a blow-pipe and poisoned darts, didn't they? According to Sinuhe, the wound these inflict is no bigger than a pinprick, yet the poison they carry is deadly. It can paralyse and kill in a very short time.'

He watched the colour drain from Mareb's face. You are trapped, Amerotke thought. Despite what he knew, the judge felt a pang of compassion at the stricken look in the herald's eyes.

'I was to die out in the Red Lands,' Amerotke continued. 'There was nothing wrong with those two splendid horses or the chariot, but a skilled driver like you can make it look as if there was. I got down, at your request, and went round to check the horses. You carried that blow-pipe in your white wand of office. In reality it is a hollow tube. When the two ends are taken off . . .' Amerotke spread his hands. 'I don't really know whether it's the actual blow-pipe or just contains it. Sinuhe writes how a trained warrior can loose a dart in a few heartbeats. I was kneeling down, distracted. Do you remember? Examining the Pride of Hathor's hooves? Perhaps you were hasty or nervous. But you missed. The dart hit Hathor on the left side. In her death throes, Isis, too, was injured.'

Amerotke returned and sat down.

'Two beautiful horses, the pride of the gods, killed because of you!'

'I couldn't have done that,' Mareb murmured. 'You would have seen me.'

Amerotke brought his hand to his mouth and blew, imitating the action of a soldier shooting a blow-pipe.

'Sinuhe claims it takes a matter of heartbeats and, close up, is very accurate. I was to die. You'd remove the dart and struggle back to Thebes with whatever story you'd concoct.'

'But you would have seen the mark on the horse.'

'No, no, I wouldn't. I understand the darts are half the size of my little finger. Hathor fell on her left side.' Amerotke glared at the herald. 'You know what happened next?'

'You have no proof.'

'That's where you are wrong.' Amerotke kept his eyes and voice steady. 'My lord Senenmut,' he lied, 'sent out a chariot squadron to thoroughly search the area. One lion died of the poison, and searching amongst the bones and debris, the captain found a poisoned dart. He had seen them before.'

'That's a lie!' Mareb snarled. 'I was . . . !'

'You were told what?' Amerotke finished the sentence. 'Are you going to say that the lady Wanef secretly assured you there was no sign of your murderous assault? After all, she would have taken the same route into Thebes as we did.'

Mareb just bit his lip.

'Only the lady Ma'at,' Amerotke continued, 'knows the truth, but that was one attack which went terribly wrong. You might have been tempted to finish your bloody work, but out in the Red Lands, with snarling lions and hyaenas around, two is better than one. You probably burnt your deadly weapon in that ring of fire. We survived and returned to Thebes.'

'Are you going to allege I also murdered the Mitanni envoys?' Mareb demanded.

'Of course you did! Tushratta called them "jackals"!'

'But what am I then?' Mareb retorted. 'Friend or foe?'

Amerotke was about to answer but a knock on the door silenced him. A chamberlain came in and announced that messengers had arrived for Lord Amerotke. The judge asked the chamberlain to bring in the captain of the guard. When Amerotke went out, both the physician and Shufoy were waiting.

'As you say, my lord,' the physician declared, 'the Mitanni envoys were dead before they were ever placed in the sacred pool. I found small pinpricks high in their backs, and when I examined their clothes, small holes tinged with blood. The same cause of death as the others, some kind of potion which stiffens the muscles and stops the heart. Both of them died quickly. It was a poisoned dart, wasn't it?'

Amerotke agreed. 'And you, Shufoy?'

The little man opened his hand to display a small feathered dart, no bigger than an inch long. The feathers were minute, probably goose-quill; the stem was of fine wood and its point sharp as a needle.

'Would a dart like this inflict such wounds?'

'Yes, my lord.'

'And the poison?'

The physician pointed to the tip.

'I have heard of these darts. They are soaked in poison more deadly than any cobra or viper bite. A mere drop can kill a man.'

'That's what the merchant who sold them told me,' Shufoy declared.

He handed across a small black tube, hollowed out at both ends. Amerotke held this up and squinted down: the wood inside was carefully carved and fluted.

'I will show you,' Shufoy offered.

At first he fumbled, but at last all was ready. The small dart was placed in the mouthpiece, Shufoy aimed this at a statue of a charging lion on the table. He blew, a mere sigh, and the dart left the pipe as swiftly as an arrow would a bow, narrowly missing the lion.

'A little more practice,' Shufoy declared mournfully. 'Master,' he added, 'I have made careful enquiries throughout Thebes. No one knows anything about Belet and Seli but an acquaintance of mine, a scorpion man, talks of dromedaries and pack animals being bought.'

'I cannot deal with this,' Amerotke replied tersely. 'Shufoy, I'm sorry, but it must wait.'

And turning on his heel, the judge returned to Pharaoh's throne-room.

Anubis gave entrance to the afterlife to the souls
of the deceased who passed the test.

CHAPTER 15

Amerotke dismissed the captain of the guard. Mareb was clearly nervous. Hatusu sat like some graven image whilst Senenmut leaned against the window.

'Continue, my lord Amerotke,' Hatusu's voice hissed.

'Of all the deaths,' Amerotke began, sitting opposite Mareb, 'the most needless and cruel was that of the poor dancing girl. You took the blow-pipe and darts and tested the poison on sheep and fish, seeing how quickly it worked. Of course you always removed the dart, but a human being? Once again you pretended to be a member of the Mitanni cortège. Wearing that hideous mask, you invited the girl into a garden pavilion. She thought she was earning a few coins, the favour of a powerful man. You killed her to see how quickly the poison would work.'

'For that alone you will die,' Hatusu broke in harshly.

'Did you watch her die?' Amerotke murmured. 'Did you count the heartbeats, collect the barb and disappear? You moved round that temple like a ghost, you were glimpsed both in Anubis and down near the river. You killed Sinuhe the same way, the guard of the sacred pack and, of course, the Mitanni.'

'If I was their friend,' Mareb blurted out, 'their paid assassin, why should I kill them?'

'First, I think you enjoy killing. There is not much difference between you and Weni. But to answer your question: we group the Mitanni together. However, you know, I know, Tushratta knows, as does the lord Senenmut, that Tushratta's council is divided. Wanef, the favourite, leads the peace party. She is as cunning as a fox. She realises the Mitanni desperately need peace but not everyone agrees with her. Tushratta's kingdom is made up of powerful clans: Snefru, Mensu and Hunro were warmongers, yes, my lord Senenmut?'

The vizier nodded in agreement.

'Now these warriors demanded to be part of the peace delegation, ever looking for a chance to cause chaos and confusion. The theft of the Glory of Anubis, the appropriation of Sinuhe's manuscript would please them, but Tushratta had secret designs against them. You were ordered to kill them. He would be rid of three powerful troublemakers and be able to blame Egypt for the deaths of men he secretly regarded as jackals!'

'But that would be an act of war!' Mareb shouted.

'Would it?' Amerotke asked. 'The Divine Hatusu would be suspected but nothing proved. Lord Senenmut might be depicted as the murderer, or someone in Pharaoh's court who is out of control. Tushratta could act the angry prince and, I am sure, when Lord Senenmut fixes the seals to the treaty, Wanef will be strident in her demands for the most generous compensation for the deaths of these three lords.'

'I should have crushed that fox,' Hatusu murmured.

'Tushratta intends to journey back to his kingdom a happy man,' Amerotke continued. 'He might have to bend the knee, kiss Pharaoh's feet, sign a humiliating treaty, but he'd be laughing behind his hand. He'd achieved a great deal: the Glory of Anubis; Sinuhe's manuscript; the summary dispatch of three troublemakers, as well as a generous hoard of treasure from Egypt's House of Silver in compensation.'

'But Lord Snefru?' Senenmut spoke up. 'His chamber door was locked and bolted, the windows closed and barred.'

'Stay where you are, my lord Senenmut.' Amerotke made a pushing movement with his hand. 'Stay near the window. Do you remember when we found Snefru's corpse? The door was forced. I was there, so was our herald. Mareb went to the window.'

'I remember,' Senenmut interrupted. 'He claimed the shutters were barred.'

'Nothing of the sort,' Amerotke retorted. 'They were simply closed over. Mareb lied. He said they were barred and, of course, he opened them to allow in light and air.' Amerotke snapped his fingers. 'In a mere breath any evidence to the contrary was quickly hidden. Moreover, do you remember how Mareb stood leaning against the windowsill? He was brushing away from both the sill and the floor any marks of hands or feet. You climbed down from the roof, didn't you?' Amerotke demanded. 'The window shutters were open: you simply went through, killed Snefru and left, closing the shutters behind you. When the door was forced, you made it look as if the shutters had been clasped shut, then you leaned against the sill to brush away any signs of entry. I have examined Snefru's room: it would be easy for an athletic man to climb down from the flat roof, slip in and out and inflict the same death as you did the others. You also removed the barb, thus deepening the mystery. Hunro and Mensu's deaths were just as simple. They didn't like the Princess Wanef and went to confide. They thought, being together, that they were protected. They went to the sacred pool and sat on that bench. You followed them: both died fairly instantly. You removed the barbs and tossed both corpses into the water.'

Amerotke got to his feet.

'What do you say, Mareb?' he demanded. 'We can take you to the House of Death and torture you. We can even negotiate with Wanef. She won't protect you. We can search your possessions, your room for the same items you hid in Weni's.'

Mareb had stopped his shaking. He sat, hands on his knees, staring at the floor.

'I was happy once.' He raised his head. 'There was my mother, my father, my brother and myself. They were very proud of me being in the House of Envoys. I was happy.' He stared, white-faced. 'You are right about Weni! I always suspected he had a hand in Hordeth's death and I began to follow him. Do you know, he used to go back to the Temple of Bes and gloat over the corpse? Eventually I found the truth but I decided to bide my time. It was something which would wait, like you do a good vine to come to full flower, before you crush

267

the grapes. I travelled with Weni along the Horus road to the Mitanni kingdom. A blind man would have realised Weni was as treacherous as a snake. He was taking bribes. I thought that was the best way of destroying him: the execution of a traitor is particularly grisly.' He smirked. 'Then Divine Pharaoh died. Chaos and confusion here in Thebes whilst the Mitanni launched their attack across Sinai. My father and brother were officers in the Osiris regiment. They marched north with the rest. Most of them came swaggering back covered in medals and glory, bringing the loot from Tushratta's camp. My father and brother didn't. At first we were told they had been killed.' He glared at Lord Senenmut. 'The war ended and Tushratta demanded peace. I was sent out to meet the Mitanni envoys. Weni, well, as I've said, it was obvious Weni was up for sale, like the whore he'd become. He and I met the Mitanni envoys at the first oasis along the Horus road. We stayed two nights. Wanef arrived. One evening she demanded to see me. When I entered her tent, my father and brother were also there, gagged and bound. I was given a choice. I must work for the princess Wanef or my father and brother would spend the rest of their lives in the slave mines. It was dreadful. All around me was treachery. Weni, the murderer of my friends, buying and selling himself. Egypt not caring whether my father and brother were alive or dead.'

'You should have asked,' Senenmut intervened.

'Should I, my lord, and what would you have done? Would Wanef have confessed?' Mareb sneered. 'When they came to the Oasis of Palms, Wanef brought the little finger cut from my father's hand. She said I hadn't responded quickly enough. I agreed to do what they asked.' He raised his head and breathed in deeply. 'My mother had died, Weni was busy counting his silver. I became Wanef's mouthpiece. They wanted the Glory of Anubis and Sinuhe's manuscript, especially the latter for the routes across the desert. As a herald I was ordered to prepare the Temple of Anubis for the Mitanni arrival. I visited every nook and cranny: the chapel containing the sacred amethyst, the sacred pack of dogs, the garden pavilions. I also listened to the chatter of the temple servants. How Nemrath was lecherous and hot for Ita. The rest was simple. I used to meet Weni secretly. I gave him the knives and told him what was to happen. Princess Wanef provided me with a cartouche, the personal seal of Tushratta. I lured Sinuhe to his death: he was a garrulous, greedy old man. I am sorry about the dancing girl. The Mitanni had given me the blow-pipe and a casket of poisoned darts. I had to discover how quickly death came. The rest is as you've said. I did enjoy killing Weni.' He paused. 'How he must have screamed. I appeased Hordeth's spirit. The Mitanni?' Again the smile. 'I would have killed them all.'

'And me?' Amerotke asked.

'Mensu and Hunro demanded your death.'

'Did they know you were the assassin?' Amerotke asked.

'No, no, Princess Wanef instructed me. My lord, you should give thanks. You were the only one I missed. A mere fraction: you were very brave. You saved my life out in the Red Lands. I told Princess Wanef I would not try again.'

'Why are you confessing?' Amerotke asked. 'Did you really believe the Mitanni would hand your brother and father over?'

'Yes, yes, I did. Either that or I'd flee to Tushratta's court. It's all wickedness,' he added in a whisper. 'The song-writer is correct: men's mouths are stuffed with lies.'

'Death!' Hatusu's voice broke the silence.

She joined her hands over her breasts, adopting the pose of Pharaoh delivering judgement. As she did so, Senenmut and Amerotke fell to their knees. Mareb continued to sit, staring at the wall, lost in his own thoughts.

'I want you dead!' Hatusu declared. 'You took my lord judge out to the Red Lands and would have left him there. This is my sentence. You will be taken there yourself. You shall be buried alive at the very spot you tried to kill my judge. Lord Amerotke, you will personally ensure sentence is carried out!'

Mareb stretched out his hands, a strange choking sound at the back of his throat. Amerotke glanced quickly at him: had the herald taken some poison? Mareb fell to his knees, hands extended in a gesture of mercy.

'Divine One.' Amerotke kept his head down.

'Yes, my lord judge.'

269

'Mareb is a royal herald. In a sense he was forced. He was not like Weni, he did not sell Egypt for gold and silver but for his own kin's flesh and blood.'

'What are you saying, my lord Amerotke? That we should show him mercy?'

'Only in the manner of his death.'

Amerotke glanced sideways at Senenmut. He hoped that the chief vizier would support him.

'Agreed!' The word cracked like the snap of a whip. 'Let Pharaoh's will be done! He is to die now!'

Amerotke bowed out of the room. He was aware of Senenmut shouting. The doors to the antechamber closed behind him. Mareb was surrounded by royal bodyguards. His hands were quickly bound. Senenmut came out and, ignoring Amerotke, had a few whispered words with the captain, who nodded and ordered the captive to be taken away. Amerotke thought Senenmut would invite him back but the chief vizier held up his hand.

'You have heard the Divine One's judgement. You are to ensure that sentence is carried out.'

The guards were already marching away. Amerotke half suspected what would happen next. Mareb was taken through corridors, down steps into a dusty courtyard. One side consisted of military barracks, the other three of a soaring curtain wall. In the far corner stood a post driven deep into the ground. Amerotke heard a sound and looked over his shoulder. Shufoy had joined him. The little man stared, mouth open.

'Mareb!' he exclaimed. 'The news is already sweeping the palace!'

The herald was now being lashed to the pole. A group of mercenary archers came tumbling out of the barrack doors. For a while confusion reigned as men were sent back for armour, quivers and bows.

'He is to be shot to death?' Shufoy asked, coming up and slipping his hand into Amerotke's.

'It's better that way,' Amerotke replied. 'If Divine Hatusu had her way, he would be crucified on the walls of Thebes or buried out in the Red Lands.'

The archers were now preparing. There was little question or protest. Under the Divine Hatusu's father, such executions had been quite common. Mareb called Amerotke's name.

'You may ignore him,' the captain of the guard declared. 'My lord Senenmut's orders were quite precise: he is to be dead within the hour.'

Amerotke walked across. He was aware of the heat, the growing stillness, the puffs of dust, hanging in the heat. Mareb's hands were lashed behind the pole, feet likewise. The guards had ripped his robe, baring his chest. Someone had already helped themselves to the pendant round his neck. A bruise had appeared on the corner of the herald's mouth.

'What do you want?' Amerotke asked. 'No more mercy will be shown.'

'No more mercy?' Mareb licked dry lips. 'Couldn't I, just once more, taste wine in my mouth?'

Amerotke lifted his hand and shouted. A soldier brought over an earthenware pitcher and a shallow cracked cup. Amerotke filled this and allowed the herald to sip. Mareb did so hungrily: he breathed out, staring up at the sky.

'Each day,' he murmured, as if he was unaware of Amerotke, 'brings its own terrors.' He coughed and glanced at the judge. 'Will you say a prayer for me, my lord? I mean, once the archers have done their work?' His eyes took on a pleading look. 'For some of the things I have done, I am truly sorry. I ask for one last act of mercy.'

'Your body will receive honourable burial,' Amerotke replied. 'The Divine Hatusu's vengeance does not stretch across the grave.'

'I thank you.' Mareb laughed abruptly. 'You are a strange one, Chief Judge in the Hall of Two Truths. You show mercy for a man who would have killed you.'

Amerotke stared back.

'For that I thank you.' Mareb grinned. 'Now I shall tell you something else. You know the Street of Lamps near the great mooring place on the Nile? Before dusk, go down to a shop owned by a seller of bottles. I have a chamber above it. The seller of bottles is paid very well. In my room, beneath a small cot bed, you will find a hole in the wall. The darts and blow-pipes are hidden within. There is also a roll of papyrus. The lord Senenmut might find that most interesting.'

'Why?' Amerotke asked sharply.

'Just go, my lord. There's something else.'

Mareb cleared his throat and looked hungrily at the cup. Amerotke refilled it: he held it to Mareb's lips, ignoring the shouts of the captain of the guard.

'What else is there?' Amerotke asked.

'The Mitanni, they demand the return of Benia's sarcophagus, yes? The Divine Hatusu,' he smiled wryly at the royal term, 'was concerned that her father might have punished the Mitanni princess before she died. You now know, my lord, how that is untrue. The Divine Tuthmosis was a stern man but he did not make war on women and children.'

The captain of the guard came striding over. Amerotke ordered him back.

'If you go into Thebes,' Mareb continued in a whisper, 'and go round the temples, the Divine Hatusu has made great play about her divine origins. Yes?'

Amerotke nodded. Hatusu laid great emphasis on the now accepted story that she had been conceived in her mother's womb by divine intervention.

'Tell the Divine Hatusu,' Mareb continued with a smile, 'that Benia kept a chronicle of Pharaoh's court. Oh yes.' He caught the warning look in Amerotke's eyes. 'All the tittle-tattle and gossip. Hatusu is seen as either Divine Tuthmosis' daughter or that of a god. According to Benia, the Divine Tuthmosis was impotent.' He laughed and leaned his head back, staring up at the sky. 'Tell the Divine Hatusu to have the sarcophagus carefully examined, particularly the inside walls, for hidden drawers or places. Benia had the chronicle buried with her: that's why the Mitanni want it back.'

Amerotke stared in disbelief. If Mareb was correct, the Mitanni would seize and spread such scurrilous stories gleefully.

'But that is not all,' Mareb added. 'Weni and I were not the only villains in Thebes. Think, Amerotke, reflect on what you have learnt! Other mischief was planned.' He shook his head. 'Though I have little knowledge of it. Go to the Street of Lamps and find my list.' He smiled. 'For the rest, I have nothing to say. Now, I have a long journey to make.'

Amerotke stepped back. The archers advanced in a line. The officer imposed order: the realisation of what was about to happen quietened even those hardened mercenaries. An order was rapped out. The archers strung arrows to the bows. These came up, a range of gleaming white arcs. The officer waited for a while. The courtyard fell silent. Nothing but fierce sunlight, the white dust and the buzz of flies round the cooking pots in front of the barrack doors. Amerotke closed his eyes.

'Loose!'

The order shattered the oppressive atmosphere. A twang of bow strings, like some harpist getting ready to play, then the ominous thud as each arrow hit its target. Amerotke opened his eyes. At least a dozen shafts now pierced Mareb's body, still jerking in its death throes, before sliding down. The officer walked across; his dagger glittered as Mareb's throat was cut.

'We have witnessed the execution,' Amerotke murmured. 'Make sure the corpse is treated properly,' he called over to the captain of the guard. 'Have it embalmed. It is to be taken across to the Necropolis to the Tomb of Strangers.'

'And the bill?' the officer asked cheekily.

'Send it to me at the Temple of Ma'at.'

'Pharaoh's justice has been done!' the officer declared loudly.

'Yes, yes, I think it has,' Amerotke replied, and spinning on his heel, he left the sun-washed courtyard.

Shufoy was also affected by what he had seen. For most of their journey through the busy streets and markets, the dwarf held his peace. Only when they had reached the Street of Lamps did he begin to chant a death poem.

> 'Death is to me today,
> Like a sick man's recovery,
> Like going outside the confinement,
> Death, to me today,

Is like the scent of frankincense,
Or sitting under a sail
When the Nile flows free!'

'I much prefer your love poetry,' Amerotke declared.

'I am glad you mentioned that.' Shufoy smiled, grasping his master's hand. 'And what do you think of this?

'What heaven it would be
If my own heart's desire came true.
To love you and set you up
As mistress of my heart and hearth.'

'Very good!' Amerotke squeezed Shufoy's hand. 'But now we must look for another manuscript.'

They found the seller of bottles' shop: a dark, musty place. The stall outside was covered in different-coloured vases, cups, bowls: some of clay, others of expensive alabaster. The owner came shuffling out. Amerotke bought two vases and handed them to Shufoy.

'Anything else?'

The man screwed up his eyes against the sunlight.

'You want something else, don't you?'

'Yes, I do.' Amerotke stared round the shop. 'Mareb the herald hired a chamber here.'

'I have never heard of him.'

Shufoy dropped both vases on the floor with a smash.

'Why did you do that?' the man wailed.

'You are well paid,' Shufoy retorted. 'This is Lord Amerotke, Chief Judge in the Hall of Two Truths.'

'The chamber's upstairs,' the man gabbled. 'I'll show you there myself. Mareb hired it from me but told me to keep it a secret. He said if he was ever absent for five days in succession, I could help myself.'

'So you can,' Amerotke retorted. 'Mareb won't be coming back, but I have something to collect.'

The upstairs chamber was small and beautifully kept. A cloak and a gown hung on a peg against the wall. A table bore writing instruments but nothing suspicious. Amerotke told the bottle-seller to stay below and moved the bed. He found Mareb's hiding-place and pulled out various items. In the light of what had happened they looked pathetic: a scarab beetle, a bracelet, a throat gorget, some wooden toys.

'Keepsakes of his brother,' Amerotke murmured. 'Ah well, but here we have it.' He drew out the small, dirty papyrus roll and unfolded it. 'It's nothing but a list, done in strange hieroglyphics . . .'

Amerotke realised what it was.

'There's going to be some heartache in Thebes,' he murmured, 'when the Divine Hatusu sees this.'

'What?' Shufoy demanded.

Amerotke got to his feet and sat on the edge of the bed.

'Do you remember, when Divine Hatusu first seized power, opposition was rife amongst the priests and other officials? Her great victory in the north put an end to all that, but both she and Lord Senenmut were convinced that the Mitanni had agents in Thebes. Most of these have gone into the dark.' He held up the papyrus roll. 'This is a list of those who remain. Mareb had a copy so as to give him help and assistance here in Thebes. For example, the Divine Hatusu intercepted a letter from Wanef . . .'

'But that was arranged?'

'Yes, but some of the guardians of the gate are in the pay of the Mitanni. No important names, but the lord Senenmut will be pleased to catch them once and for all. It's Mareb's final gift to us.'

Amerotke clapped Shufoy on the shoulder and, making himself comfortable, undid the piece of papyrus and studied it again. The list was long, the writing almost illegible.

'By the serpent's eyes!' Amerotke muttered as one name caught his attention. He glanced up. 'Did you know Belet's name was on this?'

'Impossible!' Shufoy crouched by his master, peering at the list.

'There,' Amerotke pointed out. 'Belet, son of Ineni: that's been crossed out and replaced with Lakhet.' Amerotke leaned his head back against the wall. 'Belet, son of Lakhet,' he repeated. 'But they wrote Ineni.' Amerotke's fingers went to his mouth. 'Mareb said there was other mischief. So, we return to the question you've often asked, Shufoy. Why should Belet be abducted? The answer is because he's a locksmith. True, there are other such craftsmen in Thebes, but Belet is special. He's very good, isn't he? And above all, he's the son of Lakhet.'

'Oh, the turd of a dog!' Shufoy gasped. 'I found a poem in Belet's house: it referred to Ineni, the Great Builder. Lakhet must have worked for him.'

Amerotke clambered to his feet.

'I have never gambled at dice, Shufoy, but I'd do so now. Lakhet fell on hard times. You said Belet came from a good family. If the records are checked, I am sure we'll discover that Lakhet fashioned the keys and locks for the chests and coffers of Tuthmosis' tomb. Ineni the architect would especially have commissioned them. When I was in the Valley of the Kings, Hatusu used a special T-shaped key to unlock Benia's sarcophagus.'

'But Belet doesn't know where the tomb is!' Shufoy declared.

Amerotke closed his eyes. He recalled Hatusu and Senenmut leaving the tomb. How the Pharaoh-Queen had declared that she would return to the Valley of the Kings and put everything back in order.

'We left the valley,' he murmured. 'Hatusu took careful precautions to disguise our journey in and out, but signs would be left.'

'True,' Shufoy agreed. 'I know imperial scouts who can follow the trail of a beetle, but the elements would soon cover such signs up.'

Amerotke felt the nape of his neck prickle with cold.

'What happens, Shufoy, if someone was watching the valley? Someone who had been told that Hatusu would have to go there to remove Benia's sarcophagus?' He rubbed the side of his face.

'But the valley was sealed whilst you were in?'

'Yes, but once we had left, the troops were withdrawn. The watcher would have to wait for no more than an hour. If he entered straight away, I think he'd be cunning enough to pick up the track and even find the entrance.'

Shufoy's mouth gaped. 'That's why they took Belet in a hurry,' he exclaimed. 'He knows those locks. They seized him yesterday so their robbery must be planned for tonight.'

Amerotke's mind raced.

'Who are they?' Shufoy demanded.

'Why, the Mitanni: that's the real reason they demanded Benia's sarcophagus.'

'But they wouldn't soil their hands,' Shufoy scoffed. 'They wouldn't be so stupid!'

'No, they're not,' Amerotke replied. 'But they'd use others for such a crime. That's what Belet's mysterious visitor at the Place of the Hyaenas was talking about: a dangerous place to rob but with no guards. Now, tell me, Shufoy,' Amerotke declared, 'who could organise a group of brigands for such a daring venture? Whom have you recently met who seemed so helpful in telling us about Weni? Who also gave you the most solemn assurances that he was going to leave Thebes as quickly as possible?'

'The Crocodile Man!'

Amerotke grabbed Shufoy's arm.

'He's well named! He hasn't left the river, he's just hunting beneath its surface!'

Anubis: 'Chief of the Divine Pavilion'.

CHAPTER 16

Six chariot squadrons from the crack Osiris regiment fanned out in battle line and thundered across the desert. Darkness had fallen but scouts had been dispatched and the route had been plotted with fiery pitch torches fixed on poles driven into the ground. These now danced in the cold night air. The war chariots, too, had torches lashed to their fronts. The horses selected were the swiftest and most war-like in Pharaoh's stables. A magnificent sight, Amerotke thought: the night air was filled with the rumble of hooves and the crash of wheels. Every chariot bore a driver and a warrior, all of them hand-picked from the Nakhtu-aa, the Braves of the King. Each wore a golden bee on his armour, a sign that he'd encountered an enemy in hand-to-hand combat and emerged victorious. Behind the chariots marched troop after troop of Nubian mercenaries. They would reinforce the chariot line as well as protect their sacred Pharaoh-Queen.

Amerotke glanced to his right. Hatusu, armoured like a warrior, stood in the adjoining chariot clutching the rail, head slightly forward, staring into the darkness. To his left Senenmut was similarly armed. Somewhere behind was little Shufoy: Amerotke prayed he'd be safe. The mannikin would be clutching the rail, thrown backwards and forwards by the pace of this wild gallop under the starlit desert sky. The journey was short. They had taken a circuitous route around the Necropolis towards the Valley of the Kings. Eventually the chariot squadrons reined in. Senenmut and the captains clambered down. Maps were produced and, under the light of torches, Senenmut showed how the force would be deployed.

'They'll form a perfect horseshoe,' he ordered. 'Each end resting on the valley entrance.'

Hatusu, who wore the War Crown of Egypt, took this off and gave it to one of her bodyguard. Her face seemed thinner, harder in the light of the torch. So great was her fury that she had bitten her lower lip: a trickle of blood dried on her chin. Dust and dirt marked her paint-free face. She would have urged action but Senenmut held up his hand.

'We must wait, my lady,' he advised. 'Amerotke may be correct, but we could be chasing shadows.'

As if in answer a whistle came out of the darkness. An officer shouted. Amerotke looked up. Dark figures, 'Pharaoh's greyhounds', were making their way through the battle line. They were desert dwellers who now served as scouts for the Egyptian army. Small, lithe and silent, they carried small horn bows and quivers of arrows. They knelt before Senenmut, touching their foreheads against the ground. Amerotke held his breath.

'Well?' Senenmut demanded.

The leading scout lifted his head. 'We cannot be sure . . .'

'What!' Hatusu shouted.

Down went the scout's head.

'You cannot be sure?' Senenmut said gently. 'But your orders were quite precise.'

'We followed the Divine One's orders.' The scout was now trembling.

'I know my orders,' Hatusu intervened.

Senenmut took her by the arm and escorted her gently away, whispering fiercely to her. Amerotke suspected what he was saying. Pharaoh did not show her face. Her very presence, each word she uttered, would terrify the likes of these scouts, who would regard it as sacrilegious even to gaze on her face. Senenmut had his way. Hatusu strode off into the darkness surrounded by her bodyguards. Senenmut returned to the scouts.

'The Divine One says this,' he began. 'You will eat for the rest of your lives on the softest bread, chew the tenderest meat, drink the sweetest wine. Your children will bless your memory. Pharaoh has turned her face to you and smiled. You will know her pleasure all the days of your life.'

The scouts lifted their heads, eyes gleaming at the prospect of such lavish rewards.

'My lord, we did not penetrate deep into the valley,' their leader replied.

Senenmut nodded. Hatusu had specifically ordered them to find a trail but not alarm any intruders.

'I do not want all of Egypt,' she'd remarked, 'to know where my father is buried.'

'And?' Senenmut asked.

'Undoubtedly,' the leader continued, 'a troop has entered the valley just before dusk. We found dung from a dromedary still warm to the touch.'

Amerotke held his breath for the next question.

'And have they left?'

'No, my lord, all the signs are that they are still there!'

'Where is your fourth?' Senenmut demanded.

The man's face broke into a grin. 'They left a sentry.'

'So they must be there,' Amerotke declared.

The man shrugged. 'We did not know who it was in the dark. We were on him before he even knew.'

'How was he dressed?' Amerotke demanded. 'Head and face covered like a sand-wanderer?'

The scout spread his hands. 'Yes. We had no choice. I cut his throat. I left his body beneath some rocks. Our companion took his place.'

'Good! Good!' Senenmut declared. 'And how many would you say?'

The man gestured with his hands. 'On foot, maybe twenty or thirty, but there were pack animals as well: some could be mounted.'

Senenmut thanked them, slipping a small cube of gold into each of their hands. He beckoned Amerotke and they walked off into the darkness. The royal bodyguard had already set up a pavilion, a small tabernacle for Hatusu and her advisers. She was inside, pacing up and down. She gestured for them to sit on camp stools.

'Well, my lord Amerotke.' Her lips smiled but her eyes didn't. 'You were correct. So, whilst we wait, let me hear your story in full.'

'I was wrong,' Amerotke confessed. 'Tushratta's ambitions were more cunning and vicious than I ever suspected. He declared once, did he not, my lady, that he would burn Thebes and seize the heart of your father?'

'Tushratta boasts a lot,' Hatusu riposted.

'He's a boaster,' Amerotke agreed. 'But, influenced by Wanef, he can be subtle in his plans. He had no choice but to bend the knee before Egypt. He hated that but Wanef offered him a cup of comfort: to steal the Glory of Anubis, seize Sinuhe's map, rid himself of three of his most powerful war leaders, plunder your father's tomb and commit hideous sacrilege. Such a prospect would sweeten the cup of defeat. He could return to his capital and quietly gloat. Every time he handled the Glory of Anubis he would mock Egypt. Sinuhe's maps would be used by his merchants to forge new trade routes and amass more wealth. One day, my lady, Tushratta will go to war against you.'

Hatusu stared coldly back.

'In one respect,' Amerotke continued, 'Tushratta has been successful. I doubt if he will now ask for compensation for the deaths of his war leaders, Lord Snefru and the rest, but he has rid himself of three troublemakers without having their blood on his hands. We will be blamed for that.'

'And my father's tomb?' Hatusu asked.

'Tushratta demanded Benia's sarcophagus back,' Amerotke explained. 'He knew that would vex you, particularly if there were rumours that your father had treated her cruelly.'

'We now know that's not true.'

'But there were other reasons. Benia's sarcophagus contains papyrus manuscripts which include all the scurrilous details of your father's court.' Amerotke smiled grimly. 'On reflection, why should Tushratta desperately seek that? After all, he can make up lie after lie about you. No, his plan went deeper.'

'He must have known,' Senenmut intervened, 'that Tuthmosis'

tomb was cloaked in secrecy. My lady, you could wander the valley for years and never find that entrance.'

Hatusu looked at Amerotke, who took up the story.

'Tushratta and Wanef would realise that the only people who could approach that tomb were yourself and your closest advisers, men you could trust. Of course, the Mitanni could have tried bribery but that's too dangerous. They wouldn't know who to approach, and if that person refused . . .'

'I would know,' Hatusu declared flatly.

'Yes, my lady. So instead they hired a watcher. Someone who kept the Valley of the Kings under close scrutiny. During the day it's a place of scorching heat. In any other circumstances such a watcher would have to endure years of that before you ever approached the tomb.'

Hatusu closed her eyes at the mistake she had made.

'Tushratta and Wanef demanded to take Benia's sarcophagus back with them. Egypt,' Amerotke chose his words carefully, 'fell into the trap.'

'Of course!' Senenmut groaned, head in hands. 'The sarcophagus could have been sent back later.'

'Yes, that's why Tushratta demanded to escort it himself. By doing that, he created an opportunity for his spy: within a short space of time, you, Divine One, would have to enter the Valley of the Kings!'

'But we were careful,' Hatusu declared. 'On our approach and departure, scouts patrolled our flanks and sealed the valley entrance.'

'Tushratta didn't need that.' Amerotke shook his head.

'But we removed all signs,' Hatusu insisted. 'When we left the valley, slaves used dry brushes to wipe away tracks.' She sighed. 'I know what you are going to say: Tushratta didn't need that.'

'The Mitanni king,' Amerotke agreed, 'simply wanted to know that we had entered the valley and left with the sarcophagus. Once you had, the place becomes deserted. No guards patrol there because Egypt does not want to draw attention, and in the end, soldiers, like anyone, can be bribed. Tushratta's spies simply waited until all was quiet. We have scouts, they have scouts. They can hire men who can tell you if a pebble has been overturned. They moved quickly. Once the royal cortège was back in Thebes, they would examine the valley floor very carefully. Some signs would be left: traces of animal dung, the mark of a wheel . . .'

'And, of course,' Senenmut interrupted, 'the rock face!'

Amerotke stared out into the darkness.

'Given time, a few days,' he continued, 'such signs would disappear, but we left yesterday morning. Later that day Tushratta's scout entered the valley. He would look for signs and, I wager, find the entrance. He would report back to Tushratta's agent in Thebes and they would strike. Last night Belet and Seli were abducted and taken out to a meeting place in the Red Lands. Belet's father, Lakhet, was keysmith to Ineni, architect of your father's tomb. Lakhet was trusted, a powerful court official. He would have fashioned the locks for the tombs and caskets.'

'But he wouldn't know where the tomb was,' Hatusu declared.

'No, my lady, he wouldn't, but his tools, his keys, his knowledge of locks was inherited by his son Belet. In the intervening years Lakhet, remembering the bloodshed which marked the building of your father's tomb, brooded and drank himself to death. He dissipated his wealth. Belet, his son, turned to thievery in an attempt to furnish his parents with a proper tomb. He was caught, disfigured and banished to the village of the Rhinoceri. He'd probably forgotten about his father's achievements, more concerned with his own situation. Belet became law-abiding; he sued for pardon and was granted it.'

'But why was he approached?' Senenmut asked. 'Why couldn't the thieves just break into the tomb, ravage it and leave with their plunder?'

'The Mitanni hoped the Divine One would take them to the tomb, and we did. They also knew that any traps left by Ineni would be sprung by Pharaoh's servants as they entered the tomb and removed Benia's sarcophagus. It would be safer for them. We left in haste,' Amerotke explained. 'In a few days' time I am sure, my lady, you intended to send trusted masons and servants back into the valley.'

'Yes, I did,' Hatusu declared harshly. 'They would ensure all was well and replace the traps Ineni left.'

'Now,' Amerotke continued smoothly. He had considered his theory time and again since leaving the Street of Lamps. 'Tushratta knew that your masons would detect any violent robbery in the tomb. Chests and coffers can be ripped open. However, the thieves have a trained locksmith, someone who has inherited Lakhet's skills: everything can be opened quietly, pillaged and relocked. They will only take small objects, and there are enough of them . . .'

Senenmut whistled under his breath. Hatusu got to her feet and turned her back. The servants had poured her a goblet of wine. She picked this up. Amerotke saw her hand tremble.

'They will pillage my father's tomb of small precious objects, won't they? They'll violate the caskets. Take out his heart! Tushratta wanted to fulfil his boast, to burn the heart of the great Tuthmosis!'

'We should have trapped them before they reached it,' Senenmut declared.

'There wasn't time,' Amerotke retorted. 'More importantly, they'd have been warned off but would still possess knowledge of the secret entrance. They must all be killed tonight.'

Hatusu stood, shoulders shaking, sipping at the wine. She put it down quietly and returned to her cushion. She was more composed, but tear stains marked her face.

'I have failed,' she confessed. 'I believed Tushratta's request was reasonable. Egypt had often returned the corpses of foreign princesses. I entered the Valley of the Kings, removed the sarcophagus and believed I'd left no sign of my visit. Once matters were settled, I would have returned to ensure all was well.' She chewed her lip. 'And, of course,' she added bitterly, 'Tushratta would realise how Sinuhe's death and the theft of the Glory of Anubis would agitate the court of Egypt.' She pressed her fingers against her forehead. 'I did not think clearly.'

'No one did,' Senenmut reassured her. 'We believed Tushratta was coming to beg for peace. In my pride, I thought he'd wish to fix a seal, humble himself in the dust and leave Egypt as quickly as he could: the only demand he could make was for Benia's corpse.'

'For this I could declare war!' Hatusu whispered. 'I could march on the Oasis of Palms. I'd crucify Tushratta and the rest to the trees and leave their cadavers to the hyaenas!'

Senenmut, alarmed, grasped her hand. 'But listen to Amerotke,' he urged. 'What proof do we have? What real evidence? Mareb is dead. Weni is dead. Any confession forced from our herald would be dismissed as a lie. Tushratta would turn this to mock our promises. The Mitanni would proclaim how we enticed their king to Egypt, broke our oath and slaughtered him.'

'He has not been successful,' Amerotke said. 'And nor will he be tonight. Moreover,' he added, 'we must not betray our belief, even to the robbers, that the Mitanni are behind this. If we do that, our own troops might get to know: it would become public knowledge.'

Amerotke glanced at Senenmut, who nodded in agreement.

'We have our own war party: they, and the army, would demand vengeance.'

'The robbers might escape,' Hatusu retorted.

'With dromedaries and pack animals?' Amerotke declared. 'Their panniers full of treasures? Although they'd only take,' he conceded, 'that which is small, items from the coffers which, you'd think, have remained locked. Only a very careful scrutiny of the seals would reveal sacrilege had taken place.'

Hatusu was looking at Amerotke from under her eyebrows. The judge hid his own feelings. He knew that glance. Was Hatusu blaming him?

'Perhaps I should have known,' he confessed.

He paused at a sound and, looking over his shoulder, saw a guard blocking Shufoy's entrance: the little man was driven away.

'Perhaps,' he repeated, 'I should have known. I failed to realise who Lakhet was. Now it makes sense. The man who approached Belet at the Place of Hyaenas talked of a robbery which would lead to great wealth, dangerous but there'd be no guards. Even when Belet disappeared, I still thought it might be some temple or mansion, or bullion being taken from the mines.

When I found Mareb's list mentioning Belet son of Lakhet and the reference to Ineni . . .' he wiped the sweat from his brow, 'the solution became clearer.' He paused, choosing his words carefully. 'Lakhet fashioned the locks of the coffers and chests of your father's tomb. Belet was abducted to commit great sacrilege. The Mitanni are responsible but the Crocodile Man's the perpetrator. First, we have Weni buying those knives: they were jackal-headed and came from the Canaan.'

'Tushratta was taunting us?'

'In a way, yes. The Crocodile Man said he had stolen them from someone else: in truth, they were given to him by the Princess Wanef. It was no coincidence that the Crocodile Man and Weni met: it was planned. Weni was given those daggers by the Crocodile Man on the orders of Princess Wanef.'

'But your servant Shufoy discovered their origin?'

'People like the Crocodile Man,' Amerotke replied, 'have one great weakness: they are greedy. No.' He lifted his hand. 'No, that's wrong. The Crocodile Man wanted to sell those daggers to as many people as possible to create confusion. After all, someone else could have bought one of those knives and killed Nemrath. Shufoy discovered their origin and the Crocodile Man could scarcely deny it, could he? That would create suspicion. So he played Shufoy along. And why not?' Amerotke paused. 'If the Crocodile Man had been uncooperative Shufoy would have suspected complicity. So what does the Crocodile Man do? He tells Shufoy all he knows about Weni. Yes.' Amerotke tapped his fingers. 'Just like the Crocodile Man sold the same information about the herald to the Mitanni in the first place: that is how Wanef drew Weni into her net.' He smiled bleakly. 'I wondered how that had happened. The Crocodile Man was sly. He deflected suspicion from himself by sacrificing Weni. What did it matter? Weni had finished his task, been killed and revealed as a Mitanni spy. The Crocodile Man posed as a rogue trying to be helpful to Egypt, so why should he be linked to the Mitanni? Discovering that list in the Street of Lamps, together with Belet's disappearance, clarified something else.'

Amerotke wiped the dust from his mouth on the back of his

hand. Hatusu turned, took a cup from the table and pressed it into his hands.

'On reflection,' Amerotke continued, 'I realised that Princess Wanef dealt with Mareb, who in turn managed Weni.' Amerotke sipped from the cup. 'But there was a link missing. Tushratta sent messages to his kinswoman in Thebes. He must have known these would be intercepted; in fact, he planned that they would.'

'But Tushratta's real messenger to Princess Wanef,' Hatusu declared, 'was the Crocodile Man?'

'Yes, and what a perfect choice. A man who owes no allegiance to Egypt or its laws. A rogue who can wander up and down the Nile without provoking suspicion: after all, I accepted his story about the knives. A man who can hire brigands and thieves, go out to the village of the Rhinoceri and seek out Belet. In the end,' Amerotke concluded, 'a man who has nothing to do with Pharaoh's court or the Temple of Anubis. He made one mistake, a small one: he sold more knives than he should have done and so attracted Shufoy's attention.' Amerotke drank, staring over the brim of the cup at Hatusu. She sat, eyes half closed, lips moving soundlessly.

An officer came to the entrance of the pavilion and knelt, touching the ground with his forehead.

'My lord Senenmut, we have news. Our scouts from the valley report movement.'

Senenmut sprang to his feet; Hatusu and Amerotke followed.

'Tell the chariots to remain where they are!' the vizier ordered. 'Bring the Nubians up, they are to advance quietly and quickly in horseshoe fashion. None must escape!'

'Take prisoners!' Hatusu shouted. 'I want prisoners taken!'

Senenmut's officers quietly deployed their troops: Hatusu would stay behind in the royal pavilion. She wanted to go with them but Senenmut advised against it.

'These are desperate men,' he warned. 'And in the darkness . . .'

She reluctantly agreed, but made it very clear that prisoners must be taken and only she was to judge them.

The Nubians advanced in battle line: stretching out across

the desert floor, they advanced silently under the moon, shields up, long spears level. The chariot squadron was deployed on the flanks to cut off any fugitives. Senenmut was assured that the brigands could only leave by one entrance.

'They could try and scale the valley walls,' he remarked drily. 'But it's nigh impossible.'

Amerotke marched beside him in the third line of men. He wore a bronze helmet and had taken a shield and sword. He wanted to see what would happen and was particularly concerned that the Crocodile Man did not escape. Shufoy also demanded to come but Amerotke disagreed: the mannikin was very agitated about his friends.

'It's not your bravery or skill I doubt.' Amerotke smiled down at his manservant. 'I know you, Shufoy, you'll try and break through. You'll be more concerned for Belet than your own safety, so stay behind.'

Amerotke stared up at the starlit sky. Many years earlier, during military service in the Red Lands, he'd fought a group of brigands who had plundered a tomb in the Necropolis and escaped across the Nile. A bloody battle, Amerotke remembered, fought in the chilly darkness of the night, with no quarter being given and none asked. This would be similar, even though this time the brigands were heavily outnumbered. All around him the marching men made their own ominous rhythm, sandals and booted feet slapping the desert sand. Somewhere in the darkness a lion coughed, followed by the shriek of hyaenas.

'Strange, isn't it,' a soldier muttered, 'how the scavengers smell a feast before it even begins.'

Amerotke tightened the grip on his shield. The full moon slipped out from the clouds and bathed the approach to the valley in silvery light. The rocky outcrops which framed its entrance became clear and distinct. On the left and right flanks, both wings of the Egyptian force moved faster to close the trap. The chariots stayed at the rear. They would only advance once the conflict had begun. A scout came racing back. Orders were passed and the troops stopped: silent, ominous lines of armed men, forming a semicircle, sealing the entrance to the Valley of the Kings. All clatter and talk was forbidden. A chilling sensation. Troops always marched to the clash of armour, the bray of horns and trumpets, the shouts of officers, even battle hymns or regimental songs. This was different: the brigands would not know about the waiting troops until they had left the valley.

A dromedary, its rider whipping the animal's flanks, came out of the valley. Dark shapes slipped from behind the rocks. A net was thrown. The dromedary was trapped and pulled down on to its side. Even from where he stood, Amerotke knew what would happen: the animal's mouth would be tightly bound, the rider pulled off and quickly dealt with. He heard a faint cry and the scrambling figures disappeared. One of the scouts now mounted the dromedary; garbed similarly to the man just killed, he moved back into the mouth of the valley and made a gesture with his hands that nothing was wrong. Amerotke breathed in. The Crocodile Man and his thieves could not be too far behind. Again the whispered orders for silence, though the roars of the lions drew closer. All eyes were on the valley mouth.

At last the band of brigands emerged: dromedaries first, followed by carts, those on foot scrambling behind. They carried no torches, moving silently: the hooves of their animals and the wheels of the carts must be covered in sacking or straw. They seemed totally unaware of the waiting force, more concerned to put as much distance between themselves and the Valley of the Kings as possible. A trumpet blared through the night, followed by the rumble of wheels: a chariot, the soldier within carrying a torch, thundered through the waiting ranks of Nubians and headed towards the brigands. Amerotke could hear their cries of alarm. Some broke to the left and right; only then did they become aware of the trap which ensnared them. The chariot stopped a short way before them, and on the night breeze came the voice of the officer shouting at the brigands to lay down their arms and surrender. An arrow zipped through the air, narrowly missing one of the horses. The brigands had given their answer.

'I expected that,' the loquacious soldier murmured. 'What mercy can *they* expect?'

Orders were issued and the Nubians advanced at a trot.

Amerotke found it difficult at first. He stumbled and slipped; the lines broke into a full charge. The first rank of veterans circled the brigands and by the time the second and third lines came into action, the struggle was over. Riders were pulled down from the dromedaries; carts were seized. Some brigands had resisted, but the rest now realised that they'd encountered not just a desert patrol but a full corps of the imperial army, and they threw down their weapons. A few fought on and had to be forcibly disarmed. Amerotke pushed his way through into the fighting circle. Two dromedaries lay on their sides, legs kicking, until they were put out of their agony. The corpses of robbers littered the desert floor; piercing the darkness came the screams of fugitives as they were trapped and cut down. He moved amongst the prisoners. They were being forced to their knees, hands tied above their heads in a gesture of submission. Select officers of the bodyguard were going through the treasures loaded on to carts or in the panniers of dromedaries. These were all carefully removed, packed around the carts and covered with sacred cloths bearing the emblems of Anubis and Osiris, specially brought from the temples of Thebes. Senenmut was striding about, helmet off, issuing orders. Slowly but surely the scene was transformed. The Nubian troops now formed a huge circle lit by dozens of cresset torches, their poles driven into the ground. Night was transformed into an eerie, fiery day. The dead brigands were piled in a heap. Amerotke glimpsed one dead face: he was sure it was the story-teller he'd seen in the cookshop when he'd met Belet. The Nubians had only suffered minor casualties, and these were now being tended by the accompanying physician. Senenmut was more concerned with the captives. There were at least thirty of them. He went down the line ripping off turbans and face masks. Amerotke followed.

'You are right,' Senenmut murmured. He pointed to one prisoner, an ugly scar where his nose had been. 'Recruits from the Rhinoceri. The rest look like professional brigands, probably from the same gang.'

Some were begging for mercy, others just knelt, heads down. Amerotke studied each prisoner carefully. He stopped by one:

the man's face was lean, with a slightly hooked nose and arrogant eyes. Amerotke grasped the man's robe by the neck and ripped it: beneath he felt the inner coat of scaly crocodile skin.

'Do you know me?' Amerotke crouched down. 'You are the Crocodile Man, aren't you?'

The only answer was a sneer.

'Belet and Seli?' Amerotke demanded.

The man brought his head back, hawked and spat into Amerotke's face. The judge wiped the phlegm from his cheek.

'I have my answer.'

He paused by the next man, struck by his strange feminine looks, the woman's jewellery in his ears and around his neck.

'And you must be Shadow?'

The man's gaze fell away.

'Belet and Seli?' Amerotke demanded. 'The ones you took captive?'

Shadow's shoulders began to shake. The Crocodile Man mockingly whispered something about the man's tongue. Amerotke was about to continue his questioning when the night air was broken by the shrill rasp of trumpets. Hatusu, accompanied by a chariot squadron, swept towards them. She had prepared herself for this engagement. She had washed her face and hands. She'd donned the battle crown of Egypt and draped across her shoulders the gold-jewelled nenes or sacred coat of Pharaoh. She wore a leather corselet over her white tunic, bronze greaves on her legs; her feet were shod in fighting boots. In one hand she carried a whip, in the other the curved sword of Pharaoh. Senenmut and Amerotke hastened to greet her and were obliged to kneel on the ground before her chariot. She asked a few questions, her voice clipped and harsh. Senenmut replied that the brigands and all their loot had been seized, a few had been killed, the rest awaited her judgement.

'We have no knowledge of Belet and Seli.' Amerotke spoke up.

'Get one of them to speak,' Hatusu ordered.

Amerotke returned to the line of prisoners. At his orders, two Nubians dragged forward a sand-wanderer gibbering with fright. At first he claimed he had no knowledge of the locksmith and his wife. The Nubians beat him: he broke down and confessed he had last seen them alive near a rocky outcrop just before they'd left the valley.

'They were taken away,' he wailed. 'Not far!'

Three chariots carrying Shufoy, the prisoner and two of the scouts were immediately dispatched into the Valley of the Kings.

'In the meantime,' Hatusu declared, 'I will view the prisoners.'

She climbed down from her chariot. Accompanied by Senenmut and Amerotke, she made her way through the ranks and entered that now silent bloodstained circle. Amerotke had seen judgement carried out in many a court but nothing like this. There was something eerie, barbaric about that waiting circle of men, the plunder hidden under the sacred cloths, the long line of prisoners kneeling, hands bound up above their heads, the bloodstained ground and, now and again, the roars and cries of the waiting scavengers. The night sky had paled, the stars disappearing. Dawn was approaching but the cold wind chilled the body sweat. Hatusu seemed unaware of anything except the prisoners. She walked up and down, staring at each of them. Now and again she used her sword to force back a man's head.

'The Crocodile Man?' she demanded.

The judge pointed out the leader. Hatusu put the tip of the sword beneath his chin and forced him to lift his head. He was not so arrogant but gazed fearfully back.

'Cursed be you!' Hatusu shouted. 'Cursed be you in your living and in your dying! Cursed be you in this life! Cursed be you for ever in the darkness beyond!'

A low moan broke out from the prisoners around the Crocodile Man. The curse of Pharaoh was solemn and binding. The Crocodile Man swallowed hard, and his eyes took on a beseeching look. Hatusu moved the sword and, using its tip, forced his head down. The man whined and groaned but Hatusu dug deeper, not giving up until the Crocodile Man's forehead touched the ground. Unable to keep his balance, he fell with a groan on to one side. Hatusu passed on as officers dragged the prisoner back on to his knees.

Time and again Hatusu went up and down the line. Amerotke wondered if she had lost her senses. Her face was rigid, set like a mask. She seemed unaware of those following her. Eventually she left the prisoners and moved across to the plunder. The sacred cloths were removed and an accompanying priest pointed out what had been taken. Small statues, figurines, bracelets, rings and, above all, caskets from the canopic jars which bore some of her father's remains.

'They can be purified,' the priest whispered.

'Oh, they'll be purified!' Hatusu snapped. 'My lord Senenmut, you will personally supervise the removal of all this to the House of Adoration in the royal palace. They are to be guarded night and day.' Hatusu lifted the sword and pointed in the direction of the city. 'When this business is over,' she continued softly, 'you and I,' her gaze shifted to Amerotke, 'and you, my lord judge, will go out and do vigil in the Valley of the Kings. My father's tomb will be purified and reconsecrated. The traps cunningly relaid, locks and clasps renewed. For the next three years, in the Temple of Anubis, chapel priests will make special sacrifice and reparation.'

She had turned away as if to continue her study of the prisoners when the silence was broken by the rumble of chariot wheels. Murmuring started amongst the Egyptian ranks. Officers shouted for silence. Hatusu, Amerotke and Senenmut strode towards the chariots. The drivers were already down, laying two bundles on the ground. These were expertly tied. The cords were cut and the flaps of the military cloaks, used to cover the corpses, were pulled back. Belet and Seli lay side by side. Hatusu stood and stared at them.

'It's a pity,' she murmured. 'Yet perhaps . . .'

She did not finish her sentence, but Amerotke knew what she was hinting. Both the locksmith and his wife had discovered where the royal tomb was, and even though forced, they had taken part in its pillaging. Both looked as if they were asleep. An officer moved the heads; Amerotke saw the blows which had reduced the backs of both skulls to a bloody pulp.

'They must have died immediately,' the officer declared. 'The sand-wanderer we took broke down and confessed they had been hidden in a shallow grave beneath a rocky outcrop just within the valley.'

'Where is the prisoner?' Senenmut demanded.

'He tried to escape.' The officer got to his feet. 'I crushed him under the wheels of my chariot.'

Shufoy slipped into the circle around the corpses. The little man's face was pallid in the flickering torchlight. His grief was silent, tears running down his lined, worn face. He stood like a child, sobbing to himself. Amerotke went over and grasped his hand.

'Do not grieve, Shufoy,' Hatusu declared. 'I will have their bodies taken back to Thebes. The priests will observe the rites. They will have proper and dignified burial. Together their souls will go to the Far Horizon. I will pray that my father welcomes them into the Fields of the Blessed. Whilst you, Shufoy,' Hatusu's voice turned gentler, 'look on your Pharaoh's face.' Hatusu smiled at him. 'You will come to the House of a Million Years. I have heard of your love poems.' Her harsh face broke into a quick smile. 'We will put them to music and, perhaps, you can sing them to my maidens.' Her smile faded and she turned to the officer. 'Have these two corpses removed. Let the priests of Anubis bear the costs. Now, let me show these rebels Pharaoh's justice!'

She returned to her chariot. With Senenmut and Amerotke walking on either side, she passed through the ranks of Nubians and stopped in front of the line of prisoners.

'Listen now!' Hatusu's voice carried clear and strong. 'Listen to Pharaoh's justice! You have plundered and ravished my father's tomb, the god's own son. You have committed heinous sacrilege. I call on the gods and power of Egypt to be my witness. I curse your lives! I curse your descendants! I curse you in death! I will pray that your souls know nothing but eternal night and everlasting torment!'

Moans and groans rose from the prisoners. Officers moved down the line beating with whips for silence.

'Let earth and sky witness my justice and the vengeance of Pharaoh! You are to die now. Your bones will litter the desert floor. Sentence is to be carried out immediately!'

Amerotke watched as two Nubians strode forward, one armed with a bow string. They stopped by the first prisoner; the string was wrapped round his throat and he was slowly garrotted, his awful groans and gasps breaking the brooding silence. Amerotke felt himself tense, and the sweat broke out over his body. All executions were gruesome but none more than this: under the desert night sky and the gaze of the silent watching troops, those two black figures of death moved down the line. Each execution was accompanied by heart-clutching gasps and strangulated cries. Amerotke glimpsed faces twisted in agony, mouths open, tongues lolling, eyes popping. He glanced away. Hatusu, however, watched the detail of every death. When the executioners came to the Crocodile Man, she intervened.

'Not that one!' she cried.

The executioners moved on. At last they were finished and went back to stand on either side of the brigand leader. Hatusu grasped the reins of her horses, flicked them gently and moved forward. The chariot wheels creaked, its trappings clattered and rattled. She paused just before the Crocodile Man.

'For you,' she cried, her voice loud and threatening, 'death will not be quick! Cursed you are!' she shouted. 'And cursed you remain! Let his ears and nose be shorn! Let his eyes be gouged out! Let him be castrated!' She pointed back towards the valley. 'Dig his grave deep, there at the entrance. Bury him alive so his body can be left to the scavengers and his soul to the devourers!'

The Crocodile Man opened his mouth to protest but the executioners seized him and forced his head down to the ground. Hatusu gestured at Senenmut to come and take the reins. She turned to Amerotke, eyes blazing with fury.

'We shall return to Thebes, my lord judge. I shall bathe, I shall eat and I shall sleep. I shall also think about Tushratta and the lady Wanef. May the gods be my witness and give me strength! My life may be long, but before I travel to the Far Horizon, I shall make that precious pair feel the full fury and vengeance of Pharaoh's power!' She turned away.

The imperial chariot moved off into the darkness, accompanied by its bodyguards, leaving Amerotke in that place of death, with the cold desert air chilling his skin and the terror of that night darkening his soul.

'My lord!'

Amerotke looked round. An officer brought forward a leather bag which clinked as it moved.

'This was the locksmith's.'

Amerotke took it and, more to distract himself, knelt, opened it and sifted through the contents. He was about to close it when one item caught his eye: something which must have been thrown in when Belet's tool-box was raided. It was a rough cast of a key-head, shaped in the form of a jackal's head. Amerotke weighed it in his hand and sighed at the pity of it all. Of course! Khety and Ita would never have approached a reputable locksmith in Thebes. They, too, had gone out to Belet in the village of the Rhinoceri and sought his help. Amerotke closed his eyes: he thought of Belet sitting in the gardens of that cookshop.

'You were not so pure of heart,' he murmured.

'Master?'

Shufoy came out of the darkness.

Amerotke got to his feet, hiding what he'd found.

'Come on, little man!' he urged. 'Let's go home, drink some wine and sing a love song against all this darkness!'

Anubis: Protector of Isis.

EPILOGUE

Life, prosperity and health!' The crowd roared as Hatusu, garbed in the gorgeous robes of Pharaoh, was borne along the Avenue of Rams up towards the soaring pylons which guarded the entrance to the Temple of Anubis. Seated on a gold and silver palanquin, she sat as immobile as the statue she pretended to be. The sun caught the jewels and precious threads in both her crown and cloak, dazzling in the crook and flail held against her breast. Pharaoh was manifesting her divine presence to her people.

'She has bared her arm!' the priests chanted.

'She has shown her strength!

She has shattered her enemies!'

The refrain was taken up by the choirs behind the priests. The verses had been specially written to mark Hatusu's great victory over Tushratta.

'Our Pharaoh does the will of Ra!
She has protected the god's people.
Her words go forth to the ends of the earth,
Kings and princes tremble before her.
They go down into the dust
And humble themselves before her footstool.
The nation stands in awe at her glory and power.
She keeps safe the borders of Egypt.
She is lord of the desert and soars above it like an eagle.

Great is our Pharaoh, Beloved of the gods!
She is Sekhmet the Destroyer, she deals out justice,
Her name will live for ever!'

Amerotke, walking beside the palanquin, hid a smile: Hatusu
herself had insisted on the hymn.

The singers continued:

'The earth in all its fullness
Is our god's.
All nations shall bow the neck to you.
You have trampled the scorpion and the asp.
Your heart is full of gladness.
Your hands dispense wheat and oil.'

The singing was now taken up by the choirs and heset girls as
the palanquin entered the temple precincts.

'The beauty of Amun is in your eyes,
The Glory of Horus your golden flesh.
Light of the Divine Fire.
King of Kings.
Glory of Amun-Ra.'

Hatusu stared implacably before her as auxiliaries, helped by
the royal bodyguard, kept back the crowds. Huge pink ostrich
plumes wafted exquisite perfume around the Divine Presence.
Amerotke stole a look at Hatusu's footrest: a carving of a fallen
warrior dressed in the armour of the Mitanni. The procession
coiled its way up the steps; behind came a long glittering
chariot line with burnished harness, their horses adorned with
gorgeous perfumes. The great cedarwood doors of the temple
swung open. Priestesses came down shaking the sacred sistra.
Incense billowed through the air. Holy water was splashed on
every step, garlands of beautiful flowers were strewn about.

The Mitanni delegation was waiting just inside the temple.

Hatusu had insisted that they kneel. Tushratta was not present, claiming he had been stricken by some secret illness. Chamberlains and court officials swarmed round the palanquin. Divine Pharaoh was escorted off to her waiting throne. Proclamations were made and the huge cedarwood table bearing the peace treaty was solemnly carried in.

Hatusu sat on her throne, Amerotke stood on her right, whilst Senenmut sealed the treaty for Egypt and Wanef for Tushratta. Once this was finished, each of the Mitanni delegation came forward and, kneeling down, kissed Hatusu's sandalled foot. They were led forward by Lord Senenmut; Wanef came last. She kissed Hatusu's foot but, as an act of impudence, raised her head, eyes blazing with fury. Hatusu moved quickly. Breaking all protocol, she put down the crook and flail, leaned forward and seized Wanef's face between her hands. She kissed her gently on the brow as a sign of affection. Wanef's eyes became guarded, frightened.

'Divine Pharaoh,' she whispered.

'Princess Wanef,' Hatusu whispered coldly. 'Accept our pledge.'

'For what?'

'You are our sister.' Hatusu let her hands go but kept her face close to the Mitanni princess. 'There will be no talk of compensation for the deaths of Mensu and the others.'

'Of course not, Divine One! King Tushratta has already decreed this.'

'He can decree what he likes,' Hatusu retorted. 'I have asked him a great favour: to cement the bond between our two countries, he has agreed that you, Princess Wanef, are to stay in Thebes.'

The Mitanni's face paled beneath her paint.

'You are to be Lord Tushratta's envoy here. He has insisted, and we have demanded, that you be our guest in the Divine House. We shall keep you close, in the shadow of our hand.'

'But, but . . . !'

'Would you refuse?' Hatusu leaned back. 'It is Divine Pharaoh's will as well as that of your own king. Surely you will not refuse?'

305

Wanef remembered herself, though fear had replaced fury in her eyes. She bowed.

'If it is Pharaoh's will.'

'It is!' came the sharp retort, and Hatusu clicked her fingers as a sign for Wanef to withdraw. She turned to Amerotke.

'You did well, my lord. No, don't bow, just listen. Wanef will stay in Thebes.'

'For how long, Divine One?'

'She, not Mareb, is the real murderer,' came the whispered reply. 'She will never leave Thebes alive. Benia's corpse will not be the only Mitanni princess to be sent back to the court of Tushratta in a sarcophagus!'

And the Divine Hatusu picked up her flail and rod, a smile of contentment on her face.

AUTHOR'S NOTE

This novel reflects the political scene of 1479–78 BC after Hatusu swept to power. Her husband died in mysterious circumstances and she only emerged as ruler after a bitter power struggle. In this she was assisted by the wily Senenmut who had come from nothing to share power with her. His tomb is still extant, now known as Number 353, and it even contains a sketch portrait of Hatusu's favourite minister. There is no doubt that Hatusu and Senenmut were lovers. Indeed, we have ancient graffiti which describes, in a very graphic way, their intimate personal relationship.

Hatusu was a strong ruler. She is often depicted in wall paintings as a warrior and we know from inscriptions that she led troops into battle.

Egypt's rulers always had to keep a firm eye on opposition from abroad. In a sense Egypt had no real natural boundaries: it was only too aware of potent forces which could make their presence felt either from the Red Lands, beyond the cataracts or from across Sinai. Hatusu, like other great Pharaohs, was determined to keep Egypt's enemies at a far distance and under firm control. A glance at the map at the front of this book illustrates the constant dangers Egypt had to face. Whoever controlled the Nile would eventually control Egypt. This novel accurately describes the byzantine and complex schemes of Egypt's Pharaoh-Queen to be seen and accepted as the Divine One, the King of Kings.

The subtlety and complexity of the Mitanni plot against Egypt also reflects the attitude of the times. Kings were renowned for their cunning and trickery. The most important aspect of diplomacy in the Ancient Middle East was not just defeat of your enemy but his total humiliation. Peace treaties were signed and very rarely adhered to. Time and again, in the Old Testament for example, there are constant references to kings of Israel being provoked into war as well as the humiliation the ancient kingdoms loved to inflict on each other; be it the taking of hostages, the removal of sacred objects, such as the Ark of the Covenant, the desecration of shrines or the physical and mental degradation of a defeated ruler. Such a policy was not merely a cruel whim. Victory not only had to be assured, but widely publicised for all to see.

In most matters I have tried to be faithful to this exciting, brilliant and intriguing civilisation. The fascination of Ancient Egypt is understandable; it is exotic and mysterious. This civilisation existed over three and a half thousand years ago, yet there are times, as you read their letters and poems, when you feel a deep kinship with them as they speak to you across the centuries.

Paul Doherty